For Keiko Nishisato, leaving Tokyo is a rare adventure, but it's living in the quiet little town of Painchton, Scotland, that shows her how far she is from home.

Keiko has never met friendlier people than the Painchton Traders. Only the Pooles, the butchers below her second-floor apartment, want to keep their distance. Murray Poole attracts her right away. Mrs. Poole puzzles her—is there more than recent widowhood behind all that sadness? And then there's Malcolm. Massive and brooding, he hints at something dark behind the bustle and banter of this strange little town.

For such a settled place, a lot of young women seem to leave. But the more Keiko discovers the less she believes, until she can't tell where her fears end and the real nightmares begin.

ALSO BY CATRIONA MCPHERSON

As She Left It
The Day She Died

Dandy Gilver Mystery Series
After the Armistice Ball
The Burry Man's Day
Bury Her Deep
The Winter Ground
Dandy Gilver and the Proper Treatment of Bloodstains
Dandy Gilver and an Unsuitable Day for a Murder
Dandy Gilver and a Bothersome Number of Corpses
Dandy Gilver and a Deadly Measure of Brimstone
Dandy Gilver and the Reek of Red Herrings

come to harm

A NOVEL

CATRIONA McPHERSON

MIDNIGHT INK
WOODBURY, MINNESOTA

FIRST EDITION
First Printing, 2015

Book format by Donna Burch-Brown
Cover design by Kevin R. Brown
Cover illustration by Dominick Finelle/The July Group,
Cover images by iStockphoto.com/38126032/©Andrii_Oliinyk,
    iStockphoto.com/38126524/©Andrii_Oliinyk,
    iStockphoto.com/20477058/©KeithBishop,
    iStockphoto.com/34465526/©Dmitry Idanov
Editing by Nicole Nugent
Map by the Llewellyn Art Department

Midnight Ink, an imprint of Llewellyn Worldwide Ltd.

Library of Congress Cataloging-in-Publication Data
McPherson, Catriona, 1965–
  Come to harm : a novel / Catriona Mcpherson. — First edition.
    pages ; cm
  ISBN 978-0-7387-4387-5 (softcover)
1. Young women—Fiction. 2. Graduate students—Scotland—Fiction. 3.
Scotland—Fiction. I. Title.
  PR6113.C586C66 2015
  823'.92—dc23

                                                                          2014033921

Midnight Ink
Llewellyn Worldwide Ltd.
2143 Wooddale Drive
Woodbury, MN 55125-2989
www.midnightinkbooks.com

Printed in the United States of America

With love forever to Sheila,
who read it first.

ACKNOWLEDGMENTS

Thanks as ever to Terri Bischoff, Nicole Nugent, Beth Hanson, Kevin Brown, Bill Krause, and everyone at Midnight Ink; Lisa Moylett, wonder agent; my family and friends, once again.

Thanks this time to Mariko Kondo and Etsuko Oishi for all matters Japanese; Jake McGaw of the New Galloway Volunteer Fire Service; and Frances at Corson's the Bakers for the lowdown on cakes and pastries.

Special thanks are due to the fabulous Grierson Brothers (Butchers) of King Street in Castle Douglas, for advice, steak, inspiration, sausages, friendship, and knap bones.

And a lifetime of thanks to my sister Sheila, who read the first draft and encouraged me.

PAINCHTON TRADERS
IN ORDER OF APPEARANCE

John & Anne Sangster, chemists

James McKendrick,* ironmonger (chairman)

Mabel Watson, greengrocer

Kenny* & Rosa Imperiolo, restaurateurs

Petula McMaster, florist

Andrew & Etta* McLuskie, bakers (provost of Painchton)

Pamela Shand, gift-shop owner

Eric & Moira Glendinning, newsagents

Iain* & Margaret Ballantyne, publicans from the Bridge

Alec & Sandra* Dessing, publicans from the Covenanters

Estelle Morrison, charity shop volunteer

Lorna Anderson, retired (secretary)

*members of the committee

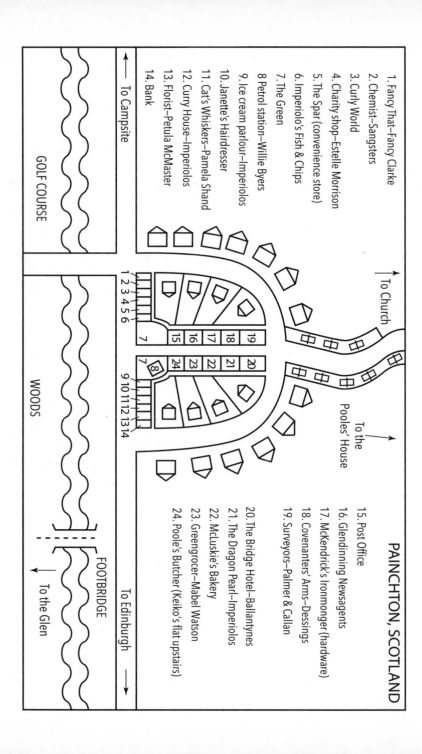

PAINCHTON, SCOTLAND

1. Fancy That–Fancy Clarke
2. Chemist–Sangsters
3. Curly World
4. Charity shop–Estelle Morrison
5. The Spar (convenience store)
6. Imperiolo's Fish & Chips
7. The Green
8 Petrol station–Willie Byers
9. Ice cream parlour–Imperiolos
10. Janette's Hairdresser
11. Cat's Whiskers–Pamela Shand
12. Curry House–Imperiolos
13. Florist–Petula McMaster
14. Bank

15. Post Office
16. Glendinning Newsagents
17. McKendrick's Ironmonger (hardware)
18. Covenanters' Arms–Dessings
19. Surveyors–Palmer & Callan
20. The Bridge Hotel–Ballantynes
21. The Dragon Pearl–Imperiolos
22. McLuskie's Bakery
23. Greengrocer–Mabel Watson
24. Poole's Butcher (Keiko's flat upstairs)

To Campsite

GOLF COURSE

To Church

To the Pooles' House

WOODS

FOOTBRIDGE

To the Glen

To Edinburgh

PROLOGUE

No one believes, not these days, that evil stays in the places that saw it fresh and heard it breathing. Pain casts no shadow and death leaves no echo. Blood spills, it is true, but spilled blood can be swilled away, smears wiped up, stains scrubbed out, until the last taint and tang are gone, until pine and lemon fill the air. And whatever has seeped in too deep to clean can be painted over, bright and fresh, to let life begin again with a new chapter. That's the modern way—no lasting marks. Nothing happened here.

ONE

Monday, 7 October

Keiko Nishisato was crying in her bathroom, six thousand miles from home. Crying as carefully as ever, with her head tipped back to keep her lenses in and her fingers pressed under her lashes.

It was the bath that had done it. That bath was the last straw. She'd heard about British plumbing but told herself it was a cliché for tourists, like the paper houses in Japan. Told herself she'd be fine. She'd have to be, after all those months spent reassuring.

"What will our friends say?" her mother had asked her. "When they hear that my daughter is…"

"They'll say, 'What a fine girl. Who needs a son when you have such a girl?'" Keiko had replied.

"Only afterwards," said her mother. "When you come home again. If all goes well."

"It will," said Keiko.

"But if something were to happen to you so far away. With no one watching over you."

"It won't," said Keiko, smiling. "And many people will be watching me."

This last was true. She had a scholarship from her new university in Edinburgh and would have to report to a committee; an award from her old one in Tokyo and another committee there; her savings from her grandmother, who would expect results; and, of course, the Painchton Traders, the last and most mysterious of her fairy godmothers, the ones who had made it possible for her to be here, in this bathroom, crying.

They had given her the flat, rent-free, for three years; this flat that seemed so empty and echoing above her head, the air shifting as she moved through the rooms, that seemed so quiet and solid under her feet, the floors silent as she padded around. It was very clean; wiped and scrubbed and smelling of pine soap and lemon polish. Which was good, surely. And it was so bright and fresh, everything newly decorated and gleaming. *It's lovely*, she told herself. *I'm such a lucky girl.*

There were four square rooms, tall windows, high ceilings. A living room in brown and orange, brown furniture with lanky wooden arms. Two bedrooms, although Keiko would live here alone. A kitchen, glossy white walls and new blue linoleum on the floor, with old wooden cupboards made by a carpenter, painted over so many times in their long life that their corners were blunted and their drawers snug, opening with a sticky sound as the newest paint, fresh enough to catch her throat, let go.

Also this bathroom, with its long white bath and no shower at all, just two knobbly taps sticking out at one end for the hot and cold water. She would have to sit in her dirt like a dumpling in broth, or crouch like an animal and pour cups of water over herself.

She gulped and pressed her fingers in harder, feeling her lenses begin to swim.

Why would anyone live this way? How could they?

"Who are these people?" her mother had said, peering at the letter and running her thumb over the logo. "Read it to me again, Keko-chan."

"Traders, Mother," Keiko said. "Good, kind, respectable people."

"But what do they want with you?" said her mother. "You cannot help their *trade*."

"They don't want anything from me," Keiko said. "They are benefactors. Philanthropists."

But even while she reassured, she wondered. Wall Street Traders she knew. *Trappers and Traders in Early America* had been the subject of a high school dissertation. And when she added what she knew of Edinburgh—a castle, a volcano, a city of dark alleys where body snatchers waited in the shadows and where Dr. Jekyll had, each night, become Mr. Hyde—the picture that emerged was ...

And then she would shake herself and imagine instead Painchton. A student neighbourhood near the university, surely, with bookshops and coffee shops and free concerts in the middle of the day. And the Traders were ... The Traders were ...

The Traders who came to the airport were Mr. and Mrs. Sangster. Mr. Sangster had a sign—*Welcome to Scotland, Miss K Nishisato*. Mrs. Sangster held onto his blazer sleeve, squeezing his arm, making the sign sway.

Keiko trudged towards them, willing herself not to bow, but when she was still paces away they both bowed deeply, Mr. Sangster showing the raked lines where his hair was combed across his scalp and Mrs. Sangster showing the furrows between each row of her new perm. They straightened up and Mrs. Sangster (unable to stop herself despite all her reading) surged forward and clasped Keiko to her bosom.

They propelled her through the airport and out into a car so quickly that she couldn't take in the strangeness she had been looking forward to throughout the flight. But she told herself that an airport was an airport anywhere in the world, and probably it was naïve to expect sights worth seeing. Mr. Sangster tucked a blanket of tartan wool over her legs as he settled her into the back seat.

"Catch your death," he said. "Wee sparrow that you are."

"Nothing of you," said his wife. "Not a picking."

"Thank you, thank you," said Keiko. "So kind."

"You'll need to come round to us for supper as soon as you're settled," said Mrs. Sangster. "You want a good feed, if you ask me."

Keiko had leaned her head against the car window, looking out at distant office blocks. When she opened them again, there were fields and hills going by and then, at a roundabout, they left the other lanes of traffic and were suddenly on a small road with hedges to either side. *A clever shortcut that only the locals know*, Keiko told herself, and sat up a little. She was waiting for the suburbs, watching for the glow of the city, but Mr. Sangster swung off the road and stopped. Keiko turned in her seat. Behind them was nothing at all, except some railings just visible in the dusk—a suggestion, no more, of distant trees and after the trees, blackness. Keiko opened the car door and stepped out, looking up and down the street at the row of small shop fronts, at the one they had parked beside, its plate-glass windows with their blinds drawn down.

"This ..." she said. "Where ..."

"Welcome to Painchton!" Mrs. Sangster said.

"This is Painchton?" She hadn't Googled it a single time, not wanting to spoil the surprise, to fritter away the newness on a screen instead of hearing the buses and taxis, smelling the food stands and coffee stalls, feeling the jostle of the city all around. She looked across the street at the opposite row of shut shops and above them at the single storey of windows, all in darkness.

Then, seeing movement, she brought her gaze down again. People were gathering, hordes of them, coming down the street towards her and crossing the road from the other side.

"I don't und—"

"Here she is, here she is," said a loud voice. Keiko swung towards it. A short man in a dark suit was striding up to her with his arms stretched wide. He engulfed her before she could stop him and then, grasping her by her upper arms, he stood back and beamed, looking proud enough to polish her. Keiko smiled at him and bobbed her head, taking in the grey hair, glittering with brilliantine, the dazzling white shirt collar and striped tie, the black shoes as hard and bright as beetles, then she looked up into his face again.

"Jimmy McKendrick," he said.

"Oh!" said Keiko. "Mr. McKendrick." It was the head of the Traders, the organiser, who'd sent the forms and signed the letters.

"Away!" he shouted, shaking her a little. "Jimmy, James, Hamish! Take your pick. We're all friends here. Welcome to Painchton. Here you are! Now," he went on, taking charge. All the others stood in a ring, silent and watching. "You've your own key and your entry"— he gestured to a black-painted door beside the shaded shop windows—"but you're right above the Pooles if you need anything. They must be away home, now, mind you." He peered at the edge of the paper blind, as though trying to see around it.

"You think she might have—" said one of the onlookers.

Mr. McKendrick turned sharply and the voice stopped.

He and the Sangsters between them bore Keiko and her luggage through the black door into a passageway. It reached clear through to the back of the building, deeper than she had imagined, but she was ushered up the stairs. Stairs that rose, solid stone with iron railings, turned on a landing and rose again, and at the top just one apartment door. Behind it, once they had left her, she crept around these four rooms, sniffing the fresh paint and the pine and lemon, bleach and wax, until she came to a standstill in the bathroom and gave way to weeping.

Briefly. Soon, she sniffed hard and smiled at herself in the mirror. *In some countries,* she told herself, *they wash themselves with ash and clean their teeth with dried dung. I'm going to be fine.*

She ignored the voice, her mother's voice, saying, *This isn't right, Keko-chan, this isn't what they said.* She didn't even hear the other voice, whoever it was, saying, *This is a bad place, you don't belong here.*

She dabbed out her lenses, went into the big front bedroom, slipped out of her clothes, and inserted herself between the covers, falling asleep before the sheets had even warmed against her skin.

TWO

Tuesday, 8 October

KEIKO FLINCHED AND HER eyes snapped open onto brightness. Had there been a sound? She turned her head towards the window, where daylight was pouring in, and felt the air move against dampness on her neck. Why was it so hot in there? Then the radiator, a monstrous thing five feet long and made of thick iron loops, newly painted in the same cream as the window frame, clanked again—the sound that had woken her—and Keiko laughed as she swung herself out of bed and went over to it. It was pulsing with heat, making the air above it shimmer.

"Good morning to you too," she said. "I'll ask the people downstairs how to tame you." Then she stepped to the window to take a look out at this most auspicious day.

Directly under her, a striped cotton awning hid the street from view, but across the road, below the grey slate roofs and grey stone chimneys, below the apartment windows, also grey from the net curtains that covered them, the shops had come alive.

There was an official-looking place on the corner that might be a bank or post office. Next door, a banner between the shop windows and the apartment above said, *Scotsman D.W. Glendinning, Newsagents and Tobacconists Evening News*—Keiko rolled the words around, savouring them. And then was a shop whose sign was written in such looped and elaborate gold script that she couldn't read it at all beyond a name that started with *Mc.*

"Newsagents and Tobacconists," she said to herself as she padded through to the kitchen. It was even hotter, with its own hulking radiator clanking away under the window and the fridge humming desperately back at it.

Looking inside the fridge, Keiko could not help her mouth dropping open. It was packed, every shelf stacked high, dark from the way the food was piled up in front of the little light in there. There were boxes of juice and smoothies, cartons of milk, trays of eggs, blocks of butter and cheese, packets of cured meats whose names Keiko had never heard, mounds of grapes and paper bags of mushrooms (four kinds), little plastic baskets of tomatoes and plums, tubes of meat spread and tubs of cottage cheese, pots of yoghurt and pudding and cream, and balanced on top of it all, two stuffed-crust, deep-pan, four-cheese pizzas.

She closed the fridge again, feeling a shudder pass through her, and opened a cabinet door. Cans of soup, bags of pasta, glass jars of jam and jelly and Frank Cooper's Vintage Oxford Marmalade. Plastic jars of salted almonds and cellophane packets of flavoured corn snacks, spicy salsa no artificial colourings or preservatives, boxes of double chocolate dipped choc chip chocolate shorties may contain nuts.

Jet lag, Keiko told herself, swallowing hard. And it was so hot. And the smell of all the new paint and something else, very faint, coming from the sink drain. She poured herself a glass of water and went over to the back window, determined to undo the unfamiliar catches and get some air in there.

Outside was a concrete yard, with green plastic dumpsters and grey metal garbage cans ranged up and down it on both sides, a small brick building at the far end. Someone had just been cleaning down there—there were still wet brush marks on the concrete and traces of soap suds around the wheels of the dumpsters.

Keiko jumped and almost dropped down out of sight when a door in the outbuilding opened and a woman appeared. She was carrying two metal pails with a mop handle sticking up out of each but she managed to keep the door half-closed as she came around it and nudged it shut again, manoeuvring herself with the ease of long habit. Her head was down, showing pale, pearly-grey hair that would have looked white except that she was dressed in such stark white clothes: an overall and apron and short rubber boots. Keiko, determined to be as outgoing as all the books had advised, knocked on the glass and waved.

The woman looked up so quickly, at just the right window in the row, that she must surely have known Keiko was standing there. She gave a single nod, then put her head down again and started walking, disappearing out of view under the windowsill, leaving Keiko with her hand raised and the smile fading on her face.

What a peculiar person, she thought, putting her chin in the air. She wouldn't mention this woman when she wrote to her mother and described the friendliness of everyone she was meeting, but even as she thought that, she could hear her mother's voice: *First impressions are thinner than new frost on a lake. Do not step there.* Her mother, who had never stepped on a frozen lake in her life. But she was right. Perhaps that woman—she must be the cleaner—was having a bad day.

———

Even still, when Keiko went out an hour later, she turned to the right, away from the shop windows beneath her own, not wanting to meet the woman again.

She had planned to use her first morning in Edinburgh learning the neighbourhood, its bus routes and backways, its budget supermarkets and student haunts. Here she was, however, in Painchton, which didn't have neighbourhoods, as far as she could see; which had—as far as she could see—one street with five shops on each side. *Don't be ridiculous,* she told herself. *The rest of the town must be ...* She looked downwards towards a field, which might be a park, a road, a grass bank with railings along the top and some distant trees. *So the rest of the town must be ...* She turned and looked up the street, then set off at a stride.

She didn't get very far. As she passed the shop next door, a small woman with sandy white hair shot out and stood in front of her, clapping her hands and making a series of little curtseys that were almost a dance.

"Keiko, my darling," she said. "Welcome, welcome. Oh, I'm that glad to see you, you've no idea! I was vexed to have missed you yesterday. I'm Mrs. Watson, darling. Mabel Watson, call me Mabel."

"I am very pleased to meet you," Keiko said.

"Oh, listen to you!" said Mrs. Watson. "What a beautiful speaker you are. And how long have you been learning English? Because I got a CD of Japanese from the library two months ago. *Two months.* And played it every night without fail while I was getting off to sleep and it's still double Dutch. Now." She gave Keiko a piercing look from out of her small, rather watery, blue eyes. "Have you got everything you need? Did you find your pak choi? Did you find your shiitake mushrooms? Am I saying that right?"

"Did you fill up my refrigerator?" said Keiko. "Was it you? You are very kind."

Mrs. Watson laid a firm old hand, like a claw, on Keiko's arm and spoke urgently to her.

"I can get anything at all at the market," she said, gesturing towards her shop window, where trays of fruit and vegetables were propped up to show their contents to the passersby. "Anything," she said again. "You've no need to go anywhere else. Kumquats, mooli, you name it. I could even have got seaweed—no word of a lie—but I thought you'd be glad of a break from that. And I told them it was a nice lot of fruit and veg you'd be after, not all them sausages and nasty packets of God knows what, but they'd never listen to me."

"They?" said Keiko, struggling to follow.

Mrs. Watson clapped a hand over her mouth and opened her eyes very wide.

"See now, that's me," she said. "But I know you're all watching your figures. My niece Dina used to eat like a pig in a pie contest until snap!" The little woman clicked her fingers in Keiko's face. "One day she was eating my profits, sitting there in her wee frilly dress, and the next she was dressed in black and couldn't manage a grape."

"I see," Keiko said, lying.

"Mind you ..." Mrs. Watson had been squeezing Keiko's arm as she spoke and now she pinched her cheek between two cold, dry fingers. "Maybe a sausage or two wouldn't go wrong. You're no size at all, are you? You'll need a wee bit round your ribs to do well here.

Come away in now and I'll give you a banana, keep you going. It's a cold day."

Keiko managed to stop her peeling one and standing over her while she ate it up, got away with taking it to go and promising if it wasn't finished by the end of her walk, she would mash it onto a sandwich with brown sugar and do herself a power of good.

At the shop next door—*A&H McLuskie, Master Baker*—the windows were steamed up but, where the condensation had begun to run, there were clear ribbons of glass and Keiko could see two girls in caps and aprons waving at her. One of them held up a pastry and raised her eyebrows. Keiko waved back, lifted her banana, and kept walking, past a closed restaurant called *The Dragon Pearl*, past a hotel called *The Bridge*, with baskets of flowers hanging between the downstairs and upstairs windows, and then stopped dead at the end of the row.

Streets led off in three directions, it was true, but the one ahead of her threaded between a meandering string of small houses, in blocks of two together, cars parked outside the garden fences turning the road into a slalom course; there could not be anything very much down there. And the cross street curved back on itself and must lead down to meet the road along the bottom again. She turned left and kept walking.

The houses were larger here, set well back in gardens with trees and lawns. The gates were open onto their drives and the outer doors of the houses themselves were open onto ... not porches exactly, but proper little rooms with wallpaper and lampshades and narrow tables with vases on them. Keiko was enchanted and hurried on to look at the next one and the next, and then she was at the end and was, as she had guessed, looking across the broad main road, at the grassy bank and the railings and the trees.

What were those railings fencing off? She crossed the road and began to pick her way up the bank. Halfway she thought she could hear water and when she got to the top, sure enough, she was looking down at a river, slow and brownish, small shrubs on the far side clinging to the dirt slope with their knuckles exposed and wisps of plastic caught around them. Beyond was the startling green of a golf course, a pair of bright figures marching up an artificial hill. Keiko watched them until they disappeared over the brow and then she leaned against the railings, looking down into the water.

Off to her right, a vehicle stopped and sat with its motor running for a moment or two before moving off again, but Keiko ignored it and went on gazing down at the loops and ripples in the brown water, enjoying the breeze, letting the slow drift of the river mesmerise her.

Then something caught her eye. Something was floating downstream towards her, a kind of raft, thick in the middle and sloughing off at the edges. She squinted, trying to make sense of it. Lily pads? It couldn't be. Was it a coat of some kind? A bundle of clothing? She blinked and then there were eyes, dozens of them, and teeth too and scraps of fur, all held together with a scum of blood, and Keiko spun away, gasping, and someone was running towards her across the road, dressed in white, hands stained red and dripping, reaching out for her.

THREE

"No!" she shouted, backing away and feeling her legs buckle.

"I'll kill him," said the girl, still running. "I'll kill him with my own two hands for that."

"No!" said Keiko again, pressed against the railings now.

"What?" said the girl. She was climbing the bank. "What's …" She followed Keiko's horrified gaze to her own hands. "Oh, Christ! Keiko, no!" She put her hands behind her back. "Oh, God, no, you poor thing. Jesus."

"What?" said Keiko.

"This is *food colouring*," said the girl, bringing her hands in front of her again and waving them, shaking a few drops of red off onto the grass. "That," she pointed to the empty road, "was the effing gamekeeper. I saw him stop, but I couldn't believe he would really … and he's been told a million times." She put her hands on her hips and blew out hard.

She was perhaps sixteen, very thin, wearing fluffy slippers not made for running in, and she hopped about a little to shuffle them back onto her feet.

Keiko let go of the railing. "What?" she said again.

"Benny McLucas," the girl said, "has the contract to keep the rabbits off the golf course. He sells to the Pooles like, but he dumps the skins in the river when he thinks no one's watching. It's totally disgusting and it drives me nuts. *Kids paddle in that river, Benny, you moron!*" She bellowed the last part of this over her shoulder to the empty road, and Keiko could not help smiling.

"Ah, rabbits," she said. "And food colouring."

"Definitely no connection." The girl looked down at her hands again and swallowed. "God, I never saw it like that before. That's disgusting. Sorry."

"It is all right," said Keiko. "Ummm…"

"What?" said the girl.

"You know who I am," said Keiko. "And I am very pleased to meet you…"

"Blimey O'Reilly," said the girl. "Fancy Clarke. Social graces, eh?" She smiled suddenly, dipping her head down between her shoulders as if someone had tickled her neck. She was older than sixteen, Keiko realised now, but not much.

"*Blimey*?" said Keiko.

"Fancy Clarke," said Fancy, poking herself in the chest with a forefinger and leaving a smudge of red on her white apron. "Very pleased to meet you too. Now, listen. You want to come over to mine and have a cup of tea and some chocolate. Seriously. You went pure white then."

Keiko hesitated.

"I don't want to breenge in," said Fancy. "I'm sure that lot"—she flicked her head back—"have nearly chewed you up and spat you out already."

"*Breenge?*" said Keiko.

Fancy tutted. "Wade in and take over," she said. "I've been here too long." She guided Keiko—one arm behind her but not touching—across the road and through a shop door, through a room with a counter and a photocopier, sequins and feathers, cardboard cutouts of cats and rabbits, a wall of hats, and out to a back kitchen. A cake was cooling on a wire rack and beside it sat a mixing bowl splattered red up the sides. In it was a lump of some white substance beginning to turn pink along the cracks on its surface.

Keiko and Fancy both stopped and stared.

"I know it's icing," said Fancy. "I made it myself. But my God it looks…" She shuddered.

"I'll finish mixing it," said Keiko, "if you make the tea."

———

She invited Fancy to her own flat, to repay the kindness. She was happy to. But as she left, with another swift look at the shop—stacks of coloured paper, hangers of sober coats and trousers in plastic covers, racks of pink fur body suits with tails—she couldn't help smiling. She would send an entertaining letter to her mother, all about Mrs. Watson and her mooli, the view of the golf course just like home, the Pooles (who she was sure were going to be delightful even if their cleaner was rather sour). But she was looking forward to the university in the middle of the city far away from cakes and rabbit catchers.

She reached the corner, the bottom of her own street, and stood hesitating at the edge of the open space where the grass began. Was it a park or a field? If it was a park, was it permitted to walk across it? Was it a "village green" of the type she had read about? It had no flowerbeds or pathways, just an absence of buildings, except for what looked like an abandoned gas station and body shop, painted a very peculiar colour. But that was on the other segment of the park, beyond the road that cut up through the middle. On this side there was nothing. She should walk around the long way, she supposed, until she knew.

While she was deciding, a young woman came out from under the Pooles' awning, tucked a package into the tray of a stroller, kicked the brake, and set off up the street. A package of what, Keiko wondered, quickening her step with a little skip. Fancy had said something about the Pooles. What was it? What would be behind those paper blinds now that they were opened for the day? As she drew close, she arranged a smile on her face and peeped around the edge of the window.

The blank square from last night had burst into shrieking colour. So many colours, from the sleek liver that was nearly black to the crumbling white fat tucked over rolled roasts like blankets of snow, pork winking and opaline with its oily hints of rainbows, sausage slices in flat, pink tiles on their tray. But most of all, and louder than everything, there was a throaty red bellow of blood. It coated a jagged mountain made from cubes of stewing steak, gluing them together, oozed from a coiled pile of ground beef, pooled under racks of ribs, beading the rough-sawn edges of the bones.

Keiko felt her stomach clench and rise but could not drag her eyes away. Then a hand—a paw!—pale and bristled, reached into the window and twisted up a clod of ground beef, leaving the heap seething. Keiko looked upwards and saw, behind the haunches of ham and festoons of sausages hanging on hooks in the window, the snout and jowls of a pig—its mouth wet, its skin in pale folds, its eyes swivelling to hold hers even as its face turned slowly away. She saw the dozens of rabbit eyes floating in scraps on the brown river, and the ground came up under her back with a thump.

She didn't faint. Of course not—she was on her feet again, scrabbling at her door before the first of them had time to reach her. It was the pig! Huge out here on the street, towering over her and broader than tall, leaning forward, reaching out with its greasy hands. She stepped back, pressing herself against the door. When he saw this, he shuffled backwards too, bowing his head, his jowls bulging out around his chin. She turned away, got her stairway door opened and closed again at her back before anyone could stop her. She ran up the stone steps two at a time, clawing for her key, and let herself in.

She was leaning against the hall radiator, feeling the warmth of its awkward bulk against her legs, when she heard the soft knock on the door beside her. She opened it. It was the woman in the white overalls, the cleaner, and the fat man (a man! not a pig) was behind her, halfway up the stairs, shifting from one foot to the other.

"Miss Nishisato," said the woman. "Keiko. Did you hurt yourself? Are you all right?"

"I'm fine," Keiko said. "It's just … jet lag and I tripped on the … I'm fine, really."

The man turned slowly and began to lumber back down into the dark.

"I'm Mrs. Poole, dear," said the woman. "From downstairs, and this is my …" She turned, but seeing that the man had gone, faced Keiko again. "I'm sorry we missed you last night."

Keiko heard the street door open. There was an instant babble of voices and above the rest of them, Mr. McKendrick. "What's going on? Look, I'll just go up, eh?" Then the sound of his metalled heels taking the stairs at a smart pace and the sight of his bright, black eyes, through the banisters and then at the doorway, looking from Mrs. Poole to Keiko and back again.

"It's all this air travel," he said. "How many times zones between Tokyo and Edinburgh? What you need"—he took Keiko's hands between his own and rubbed them—"is your feet up a while and then a right good feed of hot dinner."

"Is that on then, right enough?" said Mrs. Poole.

"Seven thirty tonight," said Mr. McKendrick. "Traders' welcome banquet, Keiko. I'll come and collect you."

"How kind," Keiko said. "Everyone is so very good. I should come downstairs and thank your husband for rushing out to help me."

Mrs. Poole looked down quickly and then said, "My son, dear. Malcolm is my son."

"Oh!" said Keiko, reddening. "Of course, yes. Well, he was very kind. And," she went on, rather frantically, "someone is coming for tea. So kind, everyone."

"Flattering for me," said Mrs. Poole, with an awkward little laugh. "Not so much for him, eh?"

"Who's this coming for tea?" said Mr. McKendrick, frowning. "There's no one scheduled."

"Miss Clarke," said Keiko. "From the . . . Fancy."

"Fancy *Clarke*?" said Mr. McKendrick. "How did that happen?"

"She helped me," Keiko said. "Benny McLucas was—"

"The rabbit man?" said Mr. McKendrick. "What have you got into, Keiko, on your very first day?"

"I—" Keiko began.

"We're the ones who're to help you," Mr. McKendrick said. "Mrs. Poole and the Traders and me. We'll keep you right and out of trouble. You're not needing Fancy Clarke."

She stared at him. Nothing in her guides to etiquette abroad had covered this. "Am I forbidden from entertaining her here?" she said. "In your apartment?"

Mr. McKendrick started, raised a hand to his head, and smoothed his hair. "*Forbidden*?" he said, with a laugh. "That's not a word you hear much. It's Mrs. Poole's flat anyway."

Keiko turned her eyes to the woman who was standing silently by.

"It's nothing to do with me," she said and turned to walk away.

FOUR

"Listen," said Fancy, hesitating in the doorway, "here's what: will I take off my shoes?"

Keiko shook her head, laughing.

"Yeah, nice try," Fancy said, pointing down at Keiko's slippers. "And your face says different too." She kicked off her sneakers without undoing the laces and left them out in the hallway.

"I'm sorry," said Keiko. "I was determined to be … but it's just … I know your feet are not dirty."

"I know," Fancy said. "Your hair looks dead clean too, but I wouldn't stir my tea with your comb." She was drifting about the hallway looking here and there with little quick darting glances, nudging open the living room door, poking her head into the bathroom.

"And it makes it nice and quiet for the people underneath," said Keiko.

"Nah, that's the stone floors," Fancy said.

"Upstairs?"

"Oh, yeah." Fancy jumped up and down three times, stamping her feet as hard as she could when she landed. The petals on a vase of chrysanthemums did not even shiver. "Stone floors, stone walls. Never hear your neighbours here, girl. You might as well be bricked up in a dungeon. And Mrs. Watson from the fruit shop only uses her upstairs for storage now since that weirdo niece stopped coming, so you haven't really got neighbours. Not at night, anyway."

"The peace will be very welcome," Keiko said.

"And what do you think?" Fancy asked. "Of the flat. Of the ..." She waved her hand around.

"It's very spacious," said Keiko. "Well equipped."

"You hate it," Fancy said. "I don't blame you. I said we should go to Ikea and get everything new but they were all, 'Oh, no, my granny left me that sideboard,' and 'we started out our married life with this bedroom suite. There's nothing wrong with it.' So tough luck and brown carpets."

"*They*?" Keiko asked, leading Fancy into the kitchen. She wondered if it was the same *they* who wouldn't listen to Mrs. Watson.

Fancy lifted the edge of the blue oilcloth to inspect the tabletop. "The Traders," she said. "Or—you know, the other Traders. Because I am one. I've got the shop and Pet proposed me and Craig seconded me, and it's his name on the lease over there so there was nothing any of them could do about it. Ha!"

"I wanted to ask about your shop," Keiko said. She had opened a box of biscuits and got a plate out of a cabinet.

"Yeah, see, what that was, was I had to find a niche, right? And fill it. But there wasn't one—just loads of bits of niches, so I'm filling them all." Fancy plucked three grapes from the bunch that Keiko had set on the table and threw them up in the air one at a time, ducking her head to catch them. "I've got a dry cleaning franchise and a pet food franchise and—this is a bit cheeky, but Viola's dad was married, see, and he was a rep for Canon and I managed to get a great deal on an old photocopier and a printer and a fax and all that. Well, they were free actually, but that's all I've ever seen from the bugger, so I'm not beating myself up about it."

"Who is Viola?" said Keiko.

"Oh yeah right, my kid," said Fancy. "My daughter, you know."

"I see," said Keiko, then frowned. "But all those feathers and pink fur …"

"Yeah, see no, that was the nuns. The nuns were mad keen on sewing. We kept telling them that word-processing or spreadsheets or that would be tons more handy, but basically they had loads of sewing machines and they didn't have no computers, so there it was. Anyway, it all started from people maybe bringing in stuff for dry-cleaning with like a button off or something. Or they might be getting stuff cleaned to pack it away because it didn't fit anymore. And I would go, 'Well, I could alter it instead.' And so I was slogging away one night and it hit me! Fancy dress costumes!"

"Of course!"

"Because you don't need expensive fabrics—you don't really want them to last, because of getting beer and that all over. You just knock them together and then chuck them when they get disgusting. So, six months and a few gorilla suits later and I'd paid back the startup loan. And then the novelty cakes thing grew out of the party costumes, really. And because Pet's a florist so she can always steer them my way."

"That sounds very sensible," said Keiko. "Who is Pet?"

"Petula McMaster," said Fancy. "My foster mum. So all I want now is a name that says cake, cleaning, and fancy dress. Everybody's got their own printer-scanners now so I'm only keeping that going till these machines peg out. And I've stopped the pet food, because pet food and cakes together was never going to be big. Craig McKendrick came up with 'Fancy That,' which is okay, but I don't know."

"McKendrick!" said Keiko, latching on to a familiar name like a drowning man to a buoy. "And Fancy is a nickname?"

"No, it's short for Frances, but yeah, kind of. And anyway I should wait till I see what ends up being the main thing, because the aromatherapy might take over completely. So long as I can ..."

"What is it?" said Keiko. Fancy had taken a deep breath and was letting it go slowly. "Are you all right?"

"God, I hope so," said Fancy. "I've spent a fortune on it, so I'd better be." She selected another grape, put it between pursed her lips and held it there for a second before sucking it in with a pop. "Anyway, didn't mean to go on. Only I don't often get the chance for a good old goss."

"You are surely very busy with your business and your daughter," said Keiko.

"Well yeah, there's that, but I'm not exactly in demand for tea and cakes. But I'm not saying anything. You'll make up your own mind."

Keiko thought of Mr. McKendrick and wondered if that was all that lay behind it: a single parent, a fostered child. "It was lovely to listen to you," she said. "You have a most easy to understand voice."

"That's cos I'm English, instead of Scottish," said Fancy. "From Bedfordshire. Near London, you know? I came when I was nine."

"To your foster mother," said Keiko.

"That's it," said Fancy, giving Keiko a square look.

"Who must be wonderful if you stayed here, so far from home."

"Well, I came back is more like it," said Fancy. "Landed on her doorstep with a baby and all my stuff in black bin bags." Fancy bit her lip. "I talk too much," she said. "Talked your bloody ear off, haven't I?"

"No," Keiko said. "You are very kind."

"Yeah, I'm some kind of angel, me," Fancy said.

"I mean it," said Keiko wondering what was wrong suddenly. "I need one person in this town I can understand."

Fancy smiled again at that. "I'm here for keeps this time," she said. "No matter what, I couldn't take Vi away from her granny. And speaking of Vi, it's chucking out time. Can I watch for her out the front?"

"Of course," said Keiko. "But... *no matter what?*"

"Ha!" Fancy said. "I thought you understood me."

———

They stood side by side in the bay window and looked down at the street.

"That's Janice Kelly. I was at school with her. I bet she looks up. Yep, there you go. Hi, Janice." Fancy waved to the young woman. and Keiko raised her hand shyly too. Janice Kelly gave Keiko a tight smile. In the distance a shrill bell sounded and almost immediately a faint bubbling chirp began, like far-off geese.

"She's a friend of yours?" Keiko said.

"School's out," said Fancy, and pressed her cheek against the glass, craning up the street. Keiko pressed her face to the other pane. "Janice? She's all right. They all are really, I suppose. Now, that—look quick—that's Craig McKendrick, in the ironmongers." A boy in a grey overall came out of the shop across the road, looked into the window for a moment, shook his head, and went back in.

"Mr. McKendrick's grandson?" said Keiko.

26

"His nephew!" Fancy wagged her finger, laughing.

"Just like this morning," Keiko said. "I thought the man called Malcolm was Mrs. Poole's husband."

"No!" Fancy turned towards her, eyes like eggs. "You didn't say that, did you?" she asked, but then seeing Keiko's brow crumple, she hurried on. "It doesn't matter really. It's just that Mr. Poole died not long ago."

Keiko put her head in her hands, but Fancy spoke fiercely.

"No! It's not your fault. Somebody should have told you."

Down on the street, gaggles of little children were beginning to tumble past, weighed down by the enormous satchels sliding down their backs.

"Poor Malcolm, though," said Fancy.

"He didn't hear me," said Keiko. "He wasn't there."

"Oh, so you haven't met him? Maybe I should tell you …"

"I've *seen* him," Keiko said. "He seems … very nice." They glanced at one another, not smiling.

"Have you seen his brother?"

"Is he … like Malcolm?"

"God no, not hardly," said Fancy. "Poor Malcolm." She sighed and then pulled away from the window slightly. "Here she comes. Check the state of her hair."

A thin girl, one of smallest ones, with hair the same bright brown as Fancy's but springing out behind an elaborate hair band, was hopping down the street, the middle one of three, all hopping and holding hands tightly as they bunched and surged.

"They're coming back to my place," said Fancy. "I said they could do face-painting if they were good." She let herself out of Keiko's flat, bounded down the stairs to the street, and stood hopping in front of the three little girls, making them laugh.

Across the street, behind the net curtain in the flat above the hardware shop, Mr. McKendrick stood looking over towards the Pooles, watching.

FIVE

Keiko, walking back through to the kitchen to wash the cups, threw a grape up in the air and ducked with her mouth open. It bounced off the bridge of her nose and fell back onto the table. She put it in between her lips and sucked it in, then coughed it back out of her windpipe and bit it in two before it could damage her any more.

"*Chucking out time,*" she said out loud. "*Check the state of her hair. Since that weirdo niece stopped coming.*" That was what she had been pining for: good, natural, idiomatic English that would stop her sounding like a schoolgirl.

"*I wouldn't stir my tea with your comb,*" she said and shuddering again decided her: she would indeed ask guests to remove their shoes. Which meant she needed a genkan.

In her bedroom, she tipped clothes out of the big case onto the floor, pulled out the thick plastic sheet that her mother had insisted she use to line it—*I'm going on a plane, Mother, not a sailing ship*—and carried it back to the front door. She would go to the hardware store later, the ironmongers as Fancy had called it, and see if there was something more sturdy, but for now she shook out the plastic and laid it flat, tucking it under the edge of the doorframe, trying to thread it along under the bottom of the radiator. But no matter how she worked away at it, pulling and coaxing, something was stopping it from going all the way.

Holding her hair back, Keiko bent her face down close to the carpet and peered under the radiator. What she saw there made her smile: the Pooles, the Traders, whoever it was who had painted the flat, had done it the easy way, just reaching in around the radiator with a brush. Here, right underneath it, the top half of the baseboard was a dark glossy green, and Keiko could see the faded stripes of old wallpaper too.

Now if she could just work the edge of the plastic past that little valve … But that was not what was blocking the way. Something else was in there. She stood up, but there was a shelf above the radiator and she couldn't see down behind it. She knelt again. She didn't want to put her hand under there without knowing what she was touching. But it couldn't be anything *too* bad, surely not anything *organic* because, trapped behind the hot coils of the radiator like that, it would have smelled and someone would have noticed. Keiko wondered for the first time who had lived here before and how long the place had been empty.

She was beginning to get a crick in her neck from crouching. And anyway, there were no snakes in Scotland, and there surely could not be mice in a flat with a stone floor. Very tentatively, she curled her fingers up between the pipe work and the wall, then she let her breath go in a rush. It was only a piece of paper. She gripped it between two fingers and drew it out. An envelope. It must have fallen down the back of the shelf above and been forgotten there. Then she looked at the direction on the front and frowned.

FOR YOU, it said.

For me? thought Keiko.

She sat back on her heels and stared at the thing. It was yellowed and brittle, dusty from its time in there. *So, not me*, Keiko told herself. But who then? And what was it? Was it a love letter? FOR YOU seemed very intimate, somehow.

She knew all about invitations and thank you notes and letters of application and complaint, but her English teacher had never covered love letters.

Whatever it was, she decided, it was the business of the flat's owner not its tenant. Slipping on her shoes, she trotted downstairs to hand it over to the Pooles.

She hesitated in the shop doorway for a moment, expecting smells to match the exuberant sights in the window, but it was mostly cold and soap with just the faintest metallic base note.

"Hello?" she said. The shop was empty—her voice rang back at her off the tiled walls and the glass counter—but there was a light on in a cubicle at the back, behind a frosted window. She craned around the counter to where a tiled passage with a red painted floor disappeared into darkness. "Mrs. Poole?" she called out. She stepped behind the counter and tapped on the door of the cubicle. There was a slow, shifting noise inside and the door opened. Malcolm Poole was standing there.

"Sorry," said Keiko and stepped lightly back so that she was standing on the customer side of the counter again. Malcolm, turning sideways through the door, came towards her.

"I'm sorry I frightened you. Before, I mean," he said. His voice was low and muffled, and Keiko had to lean in to catch his words.

31

"Not at all," she said. "You were very kind." And she held out her hand to shake his. Malcolm's hand did not reach far beyond his body and he leaned forward, apparently from the ankles, his white rubber boots squeaking. His hand was hot, as if he had just washed it in scalding water.

"And what can I do for you now?" he asked her.

"It's about … mail," Keiko said. "What to do with mail that's not for me. If any arrives." For some reason, she didn't want to give this man what might be a love letter. She had, without thinking, put the envelope behind her back.

"It shouldn't," Malcolm said. "Wee place like this. The postie knows where everyone is and when they move and where they move to. It's not like Tokyo." Then he moved forward again, just a pace. "You're … you're okay up there, are you? Finding everything? Don't need anything? Groceries or what have you?"

"*Need*?" said Keiko, stopping at the door. "I'll never use up what's there. I'd end up like an elephant."

Then feeling her face change colour, she bobbed a little bow and left him.

———

Mrs. Watson was in the window of her shop and rapped on the glass as she caught sight of Keiko. She held up a cauliflower and mouthed something.

"What?" said Keiko, putting just her head round the door.

"Just in," said Mrs. Watson. "Do you know how to make cheese sauce?"

"I'm going out tonight," said Keiko. "To a banquet."

Mrs. Watson hit herself gently on the head with the cauliflower, leaving a few sprinkles of its curds among her sandy hair.

"Of course you are," she said. "So am I too. Cheerio just now and I'll see you th—"

Keiko was halfway out the door and couldn't be sure, but she thought Mrs. Watson's voice had dried suddenly. She looked back in through the window. The little woman was standing quite still, staring at Keiko, at her hand, at the envelope she was holding, and her face had fallen out of its crinkled smile. She swallowed and, as if her strength had suddenly been sapped, the cauliflower dropped out of her hand and rolled away.

"What is wrong?" Keiko said, coming right inside. "Are you ill, Mrs. Watson? Do you need to sit down?"

"You've only just got here," Mrs. Watson whispered. She shook her head. "You've only been here a day." Then she hoisted a smile back onto her face and wiped her hands together. "Never mind me," she said. "I've not got the sense God gave geese."

"Geese?" asked Keiko.

Mrs. Watson laughed. "See? That's what I'm saying. Never mind me."

———

Keiko went slowly up to her flat again. She had put her hand against the glass door when she leaned in. How had she been holding the letter? Could Mrs. Watson have seen what it said on the front? Could she see FOR YOU?

Inside again, standing on the makeshift genkan, Keiko turned the envelope over and over in her hands. It was so dry from the heat the glue would give way if she flexed it, more than likely, and then . . .

Stop it, she told herself. She was here for one reason and one reason alone. Of course, she was very grateful to the people of Painchton, for the flat, and she would thank them tonight and acknowledge them in her thesis when it was done, but their feelings and their expressions—their leftover *mail,* for heaven's sake!—were nothing to her.

She laid the envelope down on the shelf and walked away.

SIX

THE DINING ROOM UPSTAIRS in the Covenanters' Arms was filled
with what looked to Keiko like people in uniform. Or at least the
men were in uniform—dark blazers with gold buttons and badges
on their lapels. The ladies were costumed like a chorus—pleats and
ruffles in just three colours: a muted pale purple, a soft turquoise,
and a very faint peach. They smelled sweet when they wrapped their
arms around her, their necks powdery and floral, their faces creamy
and rich as they transferred lipstick and foundation to hers. The
men did not kiss her but tucked her shoulders under one armpit
and shook her back and forward. Until Mr. McKendrick broke in.

"Now here's someone you need to meet," he said, taking her hand
in one of his and stroking it with his other. Keiko followed his eyes
and saw the young man from the ironmongers standing in the doorway, a glass of beer in one hand. He caught her eye and walked over.

"Craig McKendrick," Keiko said. "Fancy Clarke told me who you
were."

"That's the idea," said Craig McKendrick. "Get into the Painch-ton spirit from the off." He took a deep drink from his beer glass and looked around the room at the rest of the company.

"Where is Fancy?" said Keiko, looking around too. Apart from herself and Craig, no one else too young for turquoise ruffles was here.

Mr. McKendrick cleared his throat.

"I don't suppose evenings out are a regular feature, what with having to pay a babysitter," said a thin woman in pleated peach satin, walking up to join them. She wore a heavy chain over her shoulders, reaching to her waist where it met in a buckle the size of a tea plate. *It must be worth a fortune if it's real gold*, Keiko thought, but she could not translate this into anything sayable, so contented herself with trying to look impressed.

"Go and sit down, Mrs. Mac," said Craig, "Take the weight off your neck."

The woman narrowed her eyes at him then turned to Keiko. "I'm Mrs. Andrew McLuskie, my dear, the Provost, and on behalf of the whole of the burgh I'd like to—"

"Traders' Association," said Mr. McKendrick.

"I am the Provost of the—"

"A courtesy title, Etta."

"—ancient and royal Burgh of Painch—"

"Plenty time for all that later," said Mr. McKendrick. "We're here to eat."

The room was set up as if for a summit meeting: one large U-shaped table whose two arms ended about ten feet apart in front of the fireplace. Mr. McKendrick ushered Keiko into a seat at one of these ends, gestured to Craig to sit beside her, pushed her chair in, shook out her napkin, and then settled himself at the end of the other arm. Mrs. McLuskie and Mrs. Poole—Keiko hadn't noticed her before—faced each other at his left and right sides. The other place next to Keiko was empty, and she could see Mr. McKendrick twisting around, scanning the room, until the door opened again. He raised his arm to the figure in the doorway and motioned to the empty seat with a flick of his hand.

Keiko felt a tug of familiarity as he came towards her. He was a boy of Craig's age, she guessed—a young man really—slight and dark, dressed in a nylon sweater that zipped up under the chin and clung like a diving suit to his stringy figure. She heard her mother saying, *Tchah! Only good for the stock pot.* The young man inclined his head towards her as he sat, showing a widow's peak in his slicked-back hair.

"Go on then, pal," said Craig to the boy, pointing at Keiko. "Guess who this is."

The boy pretended to scrutinize her, looking first at the half-eaten pastry straw in her hand and then closely at her mouth. Keiko tried to brush her napkin over her lips without blotting off her lipstick.

"I give up," he said.

"Keiko, Murray. Murray, Keiko," said Craig.

"Ah, Murray Poole," said Keiko. "Now I've met the whole family!"

"You must be thrilled," Murray Poole said. His voice was as soft as his brother's, but sibilant rather than muffled. "So," he said, "how are you finding it?"

Keiko shook her head slightly and leaned towards him.

"What do you think of Painchton?" he said, very slowly and rather loud.

"Extremely friendly," said Keiko, just as loud and slow. Craig laughed and Murray smiled too after a moment, keeping his eyes on her as he leant back to let a waitress put a plate of soup in front of him.

"Not too far out?" he said.

Keiko thanked the waitress for her own plate and then turned back.

"*Far out?*" she said, thinking of California hippies and looking at Mr. and Mrs. Sangster seated directly behind Murray on the other wing of the table, waving their fingers at her as they caught her eye.

"Too far from the bright lights, big city," said Murray even slower than before.

Keiko wondered if he was speaking pidgin English, if he was mocking her. *Do not imagine trouble Keko-chan*, her mother would say. *Can't see it? Call it a flower.* She turned very deliberately to Craig.

"What is it you study?" she said.

"Business and economics," said Craig

"So then today, in the shop? You were practising?"

Murray snorted. "Tax dodge, isn't it?" he said.

Craig put his fingertips into his beer and pretended to flick it at Murray, who frowned and flinched away. Keiko though she understood then; this mocking was friendliness. She had heard it called *banter* although she had never fully grasped it.

"And you are a butcher?" she said, turning to Murray.

"So what's your PhD all about?" Craig said. "I must have read the sponsorship form when Uncle Jimmy had them, but ... which one was yours again?"

Keiko looked from one to the other. Murray was smoothing stripes into the condensation on his water glass with one careful finger. Craig was looking intently at her, forward in his seat as though desperate to hear her answer. No banter now.

She tried to remember the beginning of the speech she had practised for all those hours on the plane. It seemed like weeks ago.

"Actually," she said, "I've changed my proposal a little from the version I sent initially. I hope," she lowered her voice, "I hope Mr. McKendrick won't mind."

"Couldn't tell the difference if one was green and one was his granny," said Craig.

Keiko let out a sigh. "Well," she said, "I'm still interested in nutritionism as new folklore. *Feeding Belief* was the title I sent." Both boys looked back at her blankly. "But I'm less interested in the content than the movement of the knowledge itself now. In dense networks." More blank looks. "My new title is *Hot Gossip: the mechanics of construing common knowledge in social groups.*"

"Jesus Christ," said Murray. "You're kidding."

Craig swung back on his chair and let out a hoot of high-pitched laughter that made his uncle look over and subject them all to a stare. "You've come to the right place then," he said.

"I don't understand," said Keiko.

"I hope you two are being good hosts to our new arrival," said Mr. McKendrick, appearing suddenly at Keiko's shoulder and making her jump.

"She's told us about the new research topic," said Craig. "Hot gossip."

"Food," corrected Mr. McKendrick.

"Oh yes, health scares and food fads—excellent material," Keiko said.

"Scares and fads?" said Mr. McKendrick. "That's not what I understood. We take our heritage very seriously here in Painchton. And we're not the gossiping sort at all. A secret is safe in this town, that I assure you."

The waitress came to clear her plate and give her a new one, so Keiko had time to calm herself before she spoke again.

"Let *me* assure *you*," she said, "I'm an experimental psychologist. I work in lab conditions with controlled stimuli and cohorts of subjects all very carefully chosen. I'm not an anthropologist. I'm not interested in grubbing around in anyone's—" Except she had a flash of herself on her knees, in front of the radiator, trying to catch hold of the envelope with the tips of her fingers.

"I'm glad to hear it," Mr. McKendrick said and went back to his seat where his own new plate was waiting.

"Is that right then?" said Murray when he was gone. It seemed that he was looking at her properly for the first time. "I thought psychology was all about…"

"Lying on a couch crying about your mum," said Craig.

"No," said Keiko. Then she smiled. "Not absolutely all of it. My interest is in the hardwiring and the circuits. It's mostly quite dull."

Craig began to nod until he stopped himself, but Murray was gazing at her.

"It sounds pretty cool, if you ask me," he said. He bent his head close to hers, so close that she could smell the fruity shampoo he must have just used. "I'd still keep it quiet though. Not the food stuff—no worries there—but about the gossip anyway." He winked at her and sat up again.

———

Keiko ate steadily but without making much of a dent in her plate of dinner.

"What *is* Yorkshire pudding?" she asked after a while, starting to lift a corner of it out of the gravy to examine it more closely. But

40

Mrs. McLuskie was watching her, so instead she folded another pad of it onto her fork and ate it, smiling.

The waitress, when she returned, looked down at Keiko's plate in sorrow.

"You should have called me over, honey," she said, shaking her head and stroking Keiko's shoulder. "I could have got you an omelette."

"No, it was delicious," said Keiko, "but just so much." She looked up and down the table for corroboration, but saw an empty plate with a neatly meshed knife and fork at each place.

"It's a skill," said Craig. "Like sword swallowing. Takes years of practice."

"I'll make a doggy bag," said the waitress.

"Lovely," said Keiko, not sure what she was agreeing to. She lay back in her chair and sipped water but noticed the others beginning to stir.

"Ladies and Gentlemen, we will now adjourn to the Bridge for the remaining courses," said Mr. McKendrick. He wiped his mouth firmly with his napkin, folded it by his plate, then drew out a handkerchief and wiped the rest of his face and neck. Mrs. McLuskie picked up her chain from the back of her chair where she had laid it while she ate and draped it back over her shoulders.

Keiko lost Craig and Murray in the crowd and was swept up into a group of women, little Mrs. Watson among them, on the way down the stairs. She hesitated at the bottom, but the others carried on right out into the street.

"Well, I think it's a good idea," said an old lady to nobody in particular. "A breath of fresh air and a chance to stretch your legs. Well done, James."

"Fart break, in other words," said Mrs. Watson under her breath, making Keiko giggle.

"A piece of nonsense, if you ask me," said someone else. "It's not a competition."

They crossed the road in a straggling crocodile towards the Bridge. There were fairy lights in the flower baskets now, winking off and on. Mr. McKendrick sprang ahead and swept the door open.

"Where are we, James?" asked Mrs. McLuskie.

"In the Keeper's, Etta. Just go straight through."

Along a narrow corridor with double doors at the end, held open by two waiters in burgundy jackets, Keiko could see another room laid for dinner, another U-shaped table covered in glasses and candles, flowers and silver. She turned to Mrs. Watson in a panic.

"Dinner again?"

"Pudding, my darling," said Mrs. Watson.

Mr. McKendrick's seating plan didn't survive the change of scene. Although she could see his arm above the heads of the crowd and the flicking gesture as he tried to direct people to one place or another, everyone seemed ready just to drop down into the nearest space, Keiko still with her group of old ladies and Murray and Craig nowhere to be seen, until she caught sight of the side of Murray's head at the far end of the table, when he tilted back on his chair and tossed his hair out of his eyes.

So … more Yorkshire pudding, more plates of roasted meat. Some ancient barbaric feasting ritual, obviously. But how many times would they do it in one night? And what was the etiquette? Was it better to turn down their generosity or to crawl under the table to vomit? Keiko swallowed hard as the waiter approached, carrying a dish piled high with some kind of soft, pale substance dotted with dark buttons. Mashed potato? Olives? She looked closer: ice-cream and berries of some kind, pastry underneath.

"Dessert?" she said. "Just dessert?"

"Aye. Pudding," Mrs. Watson said.

Keiko, reckless with relief, didn't refuse when the waiter returned with a tall jug, but just watched him pour a coating of yellow cream over the tower on her plate until the berries were gone and the bowl was filled to the brim and close to overflowing. She picked up her spoon.

"Stop!" A woman was standing beside her chair with her hand up. She was wearing a dark purple garment with wide sleeves and made a dramatic figure. "Keiko, don't eat that."

The room had gone quiet.

"What the—" said Mr. McKendrick's voice.

"I can't believe you people," the woman said. Her face was flushed and her chest rose and fell rapidly. "This is criminal."

"What is it?" said Keiko, peering hard at the berries and then looking around the room.

"Cream," said the woman, her voice trembling. "And ice cream. And probably butter pastry too. *Dairy*."

"For the love of Mike," someone said.

"How many times did I tell you?" the woman shouted. "Japanese people can't eat dairy. What's wrong with you?"

"Oh," said Keiko, and she tried hard not to smile. "How thoughtful, but I'm one of the lucky ones. I'm fine."

"But I thought it was all Japanese people," said the woman, crestfallen now.

"Not all," said Keiko. "Not me. But thank you."

43

"I'm sorry about that, pet," said Mrs. Sangster, drilling a look at Keiko's saviour as she went back to her seat. "She doesn't come from Painchton."

"Pamela Shand."

"With the gift shop."

"Glasgow."

"We don't go in for all that here."

"All what?" Keiko said, looking up. She was spooning the pudding into her mouth as fast as she could, not even following the voices as they came at her.

"Intolerances and what have you."

"We're old-fashioned here."

"Eat what's put in front of you and be thankful."

"Never did me any harm."

Mrs. Sangster leaned forward and stroked Keiko's hair, smoothing it back from her face, cupping her cheek in one warm palm. "You must come to supper with us as soon as soon can be and let me show you," she said. The waiter whisked away her cleared plate and substituted another clean one. "Roast, glazed ham I'll make. I'm noted for my glazed ham."

Keiko nodded, swallowing.

"We were supposed to take turns," Mrs. McLuskie called over, hearing this. "Once we find out which evening Keiko prefers. And I've got a goose."

"Crying out loud, Etta," said Mrs. Watson. "She's not here on a catering course. She's a psychiatrist."

"Psychologist," said Keiko, but quietly, remembering what Craig had said to her.

"I thought it was physics," someone added, a large woman wearing the same dress as Mrs. McLuskie, but in a different colour and without the provost's chain.

"She needs building up, whatever she is," said Mrs. Sangster. "You'll be no good to anyone if you waste away, pet." She gave Keiko one last pinch and sat back, picking up her own spoon again.

Keiko looked down at her plate and then looked away. "Is Mrs. McMaster here?" she asked, thinking that conversation would give her a break from eating. "I would so like to meet her."

"Where *is* Pet tonight?" said Mrs. Watson, looking round.

"Off at one of her foster care meetings," said Mrs. McLuskie.

"No!" said Mrs. Watson. "She's not at *that* again. She swore she'd never let herself in for more of that heartbreak."

"Heartbreak?" said Keiko. "Fancy?"

"Aye, well her too at the time," said the woman who thought Keiko was in physics. "But at least she came back. Not like the other one."

"Tash," said another woman Keiko didn't know, very well-groomed and wearing a mask of make-up.

"Tash!" said the larger version of Mrs. McLuskie, as if the word was impolite in some way.

The well-groomed woman frowned.

"Now, how do they organise fostering in Japan?" said Mrs. Watson after a hurried look at both of them.

"Well," said Keiko, "families are more... Not so... I'm not sure." Then, to get a break from talking, she had to eat again. Cheese and crackers this time, with Pamela Shand glowering. When the cheese was cleared, she hid mint chocolates in her bag, passed on the coffee, choked on the whisky, and eventually climbed the stairs to her flat again, holding her stomach in both hands.

She had forgotten about FOR YOU as the evening wore on and seeing it again as she slipped off her shoes, she groaned. *Put it in the trash,* Malcolm had said, so she picked it up and folded it into a paper plane, looking around for a wastebasket to fire it into. Just as she had told herself it would, the glue on the flap cracked and gave way. She hesitated for a second, then flattened the envelope again and lifted the flap open. Inside, there was a sheet of paper folded in half. She could poke it apart with a finger and see what was written there without even taking it out. She snapped on the overhead light, held the envelope up to it and squinted inside.

I KNOW WHAT YOU DID. I SAW YOU. I WILL TELL THEM ALL

Keiko smacked her hands together to close it up again. For a moment she stood quite still, listening to the echo of the smack in the empty air. Then very slowly she turned to the shelf above the radiator and inserted one corner of the envelope behind it, wiggling it back and forward until it was almost all gone. She let go, heard it drop down, heard the tap of one edge hitting the plastic sheet, and leaned back against the front door again.

She was facing straight along the corridor into the living room and across to the dark windows on the other side of the street. She was standing here in bright electric light, against fresh white paint, with a big bay window and a wide open door between her and the outside. Anyone could have seen what she just did.

Then she shook herself and tutted, told herself not to be silly. No one was watching.

SEVEN

IT WAS IN THE basket on the back of the door, hand delivered, hours before the post was due, the direction—FOR YOU—clearly visible through the wire. The dog had grown out of letter-chewing now, but they kept the basket because it was easier on the lumbar discs not to bend down to the floor every morning, even if clumsy morning fingers sometimes fumbled at the catch trying to open it. It took several attempts that day, and then several more to get hold of the loose edge on the flap in shaking fingers and tear it open.

I SAW YOU AGAIN. YOU CAN'T HIDE FROM ME. I WILL TELL THEM ALL.

And just like the first one, this one was taken straight to the fireplace in the lounge, crumpled up—envelope and all—and had a match held to it until it caught, flared, and died down in sheets of ash to be stirred away to nothing with the poker.

Wednesday, 9 October

Later in the afternoon she had an appointment with Dr. Bryant, her supervisor, her mentor, Socrates to her Plato, Plato to her Aristotle…

Well, she had an appointment anyway. But she wouldn't waste the morning. She set up her PC on the big table in the bay window and started typing.

Facts, Scams and Scares: the production of consensus in dense social networks, she wrote, editing out the gossip right away. *Consensus as (arti)fact: scams and scares in the construction of knowledge.* A cup of coffee on her right and a cup of pens and pencils on her left made a neat arrangement. *Consensual knowledge in networks: scares, fads and density.* To be confirmed, she decided and typed: *Something with a colon: the title of a thesis in social psychology.* She put in a page break and started typing again.

The ~~aim intention~~ *objective of this* ~~thesis project research~~ *enquiry is to* ~~enquire discover explore develop~~ *provide an* ~~account mechanism model explanation theory~~ *hypothesis for the…*

I will listen to people talking to find out…

She shut her laptop and took a sheet of paper instead, uncapped a pen.

Title
Introduction
Literature Review
Find subjects
Develop psych-test materials
Dry run
Organize group
Develop main test materials
Experiments (test, feedback, retest)

Analysis
Write thesis
Graduate & accept job at Oxford/Cambridge/Harvard or similar

And wondering what sort of job openings there would be if she were looking for one today, she opened her laptop instead and waited. Then she remembered she didn't have an Internet account yet. No wonder she felt so marooned and peculiar. No phone yet, no WiFi. But as she was thinking it, a dialogue box popped up telling of a connection, asking for a password. She typed the password she used for everything—*phdgirl*—and, looking at the red X denying her access, she had never felt so far from home.

———

Murray was alone in the shop, standing not behind the counter but out in front, tidying the notices on a corkboard behind the door—*Brownies Barbie-Q night, firewood for sale, greenhouse wanted will collect*—lining them up and pushing pins into all four corners, stripping off the tattered ones as he went. His white coat and apron were freshly starched and dazzling, sticking out at the edges like the new blue oilcloth on the kitchen table upstairs.

"Day off already?" he said turning to her and smiling.

"Sorry?" said Keiko.

"I thought you'd be away into town."

"Later."

"I'm not complaining," said Murray, his smile even wider. "What can I do for you?"

"Ah, yes," said Keiko. "I seem to have Internet upstairs but no one told me how to get onto it. I wondered if you knew. Or your mother maybe?"

"Mum?" said Murray, laughing. "She doesn't even use a calculator, never mind computers. It'll be Jimmy McKendrick that's set that up for you. He'll know."

"I see," said Keiko. "I thought because it was your flat..."

"Who told you that?" Murray said, giving her an exaggerated frown but still smiling.

"Mr. McKendrick did," said Keiko, frowning herself, trying to remember. "I'm sure he said so. 'Above the Pooles and they own it,' he said. And I remember most particularly because I didn't know it was a name at the time and 'above the pools' sounded so refreshing."

Murray laughed again then. "Yeah," he said. "We own it."

"And I'm very grateful for it," Keiko said.

"You don't need to be *that* grateful," he said. "Better than having it sit there empty."

"But surely such a lovely flat can't have been empty for long?" said Keiko. "In Tokyo—" She bit this off. Her mother had told her to be careful not to say too much about Japan. *If they cared they could come and see for themselves, Keko-chan. Just as I could go to Sydney and take my own photographs of the opera house if I wanted them. My sister-in-law does not need to come home and share hers with me.*

"Well, it's a place to stay," said Murray. "But you don't have to let yourself get sucked in."

Keiko shook her head at him, but before she could ask what he meant, the bell dinged above the door.

"Afternoon, young man," said a woman, hefting a shopping basket onto the counter and leaning against it. Murray had flitted round to his station behind the register when he saw her coming.

50

"Mrs. Glendinning," he said.

"And how are you today, Keiko?" said the woman. Keiko bobbed her head and smiled. She couldn't remember ever seeing this woman before but supposed that she might have been at the feast in peach ruffles or turquoise satin. And her name did seem familiar.

"Right then," Mrs. Glendinning said, peering into the display. "I'll take a pound of your steak mince for tonight." She gave Murray a sharp look. "That's today's mince, eh?"

Murray nodded. He had pushed his hands into plastic gloves from the dispenser and had twitched a sheet of cellophane onto the bed of the scales.

"And a pound—no make it two pounds—of pork links and they'll do for his breakfasts too. Couple of gigot chops, maybe three, eh? They're no size. Another pound of mince—beef just, for meatballs—and, em, Friday, Friday, Friday... Well I'll take a good two pounds of Ayrshire back anyway and a wee tate of pudding slices for the weekend. Friday, Friday, Friday... Och, why not? That sirloin looks a bonny colour, two steaks'll do us fine."

"Malc?" shouted Murray into the back of the shop.

Keiko cocked her head. Almost immediately, along the corridor that led from the back, came the sound of Malcolm moving, a low pounding, rubber boots squeaking, the chafing of cloth and slow breaths, until he appeared in the mouth of the passage. He wore the same clothes as his brother, but his apron was dark from work, his coat sleeves pushed back as far as they would go up his wrists. But still they were edged with rust colour.

Murray was weighing and wrapping, turning the waxed sheets into bags and sealing them, deft and precise, never touching their contents. He spoke without looking up. "Couple of sirloin for Mrs.

51

Glendinning, pal." Then he snapped open a carrier bag and began to stack the packages inside.

Malcolm turned away to where a wedge of meat sat like a rock on a high cutting board and bent over it. Although his hands must be moving, all Keiko could see was his back, a wide block of white broken by apron strings. There were two muffled thumps that made Malcolm's back judder, and then he turned around to face them, slapping the bricks of cut meat from his bare palms onto the scales.

"I've left the fat on, Mrs. Glendinning," he said, his soft voice booming a little as he strained to be heard over the width of the counter and the sound of Murray rustling the carrier bag. "You don't have to eat it, but don't go trimming it before you fry them, because—"

"I'll manage from here, son," said the woman, winking at Keiko. "It's like taking a chick from under a hen getting a steak out of Malcolm sometimes."

Malcolm smiled but was already moving away again.

The shop bell sounded and a man strolled in. Fishing in his jacket pocket for his wallet, he joined the woman at the counter.

"Well, what's the damage, then?" he said. "What are you after from us today?" He looked at Keiko and chuckled. "Aye, they're doing all right are the Pooles."

"We're managing, Mr. Glendinning," said Murray, in a level voice. "The three of us."

"Och away, I'm just havin' a laugh with you," said the man. "Let's just hope this one lasts, eh?"

"Wheesht, Eric," said his wife. She smiled tightly at Keiko. "Just ignore him, lovey."

"Ignore what?" said her husband. "I'm saying I hope she stays. I'm hoping the luck's turned. Where the harm in that?" He grasped the bag that Murray held over the counter to him, groaned at the weight of it, and walked out. Mrs. Glendinning took the change with another tight smile and followed him.

"Tosser," Murray said when they had left.

"What did he mean?" said Keiko.

"Nothing, he's just a stirrer," Murray said.

"Did he mean me? *This one*? Is that me?"

"Now why would you think that?" Murray said, very still and staring at her.

"I—" She gulped. There was no reason, except jet lag and dreams she could not quite remember and just the strangeness of everything. Except...

"Girls leave," she blurted out. *The weird niece, Dina.*

Murray's eyes widened.

"Do you cook?" said Malcolm's voice suddenly, making her jump. He had reappeared at the back of the shop, holding a tray. She composed herself and answered him gently.

"A little. Easy things Soup, noodles."

"What about this?" Malcolm said, shuffling forward and showing her the tray. On it were three skewers threaded with pieces of chicken curved like little seashells, perfect white cubes of mushroom flesh, slices of garlic—sheer and glistening—and discs of baby sweet corn like the wheels of a toy car. The skewers were finished off at each end with tiny onions.

"Five ingredients," said Malcolm, "because four is unlucky."

"You made kebabs?" she said.

"They were supposed to be yakitori," said Malcolm, looking down at them. "Off the Internet."

"Well, you must come upstairs after work and help me eat them," Keiko said, looking at Murray. "Both of you."

"These were meant for you," said Malcolm. "But I could make some more, I suppose."

"Just a wee snack, eh?" said Murray. "From the king of portion control."

Mrs. Poole had appeared in the doorway to the back shop and looked intently at Keiko before she spoke. "There's no need for you to be laying on catering up in the flat," she said. Then with a visible effort she continued, "You should come to our house."

"Thank you," said Keiko. She had no phrases in her repertoire to help with such a reluctant invitation. She waited to see if Mrs. Poole would say any more, and it seemed to her that both sons were watching their mother too. The woman said nothing. *How*, thought Keiko, *do you leave in silence if you can't bow? I must ask or look it up.* Then with a flush of relief, she thought of something to say.

"The Internet!" She turned to Malcolm. "You have it here in the shop?" He nodded. "Ah! I think I'm picking up your connection in the flat then."

All three of the Pooles looked up at the ceiling.

"What?" said Mrs. Poole. "What are you picking up? What have you seen?"

"Nothing," said Keiko. "Goodness, no. Just a prompt. And I wouldn't— I don't know the password anyway. I'll get my own service, naturally."

"No need for that," Malcolm said. "Waste of money. I can set you up no problem with a password. It'll be nice. Sharing."

"But—" said his mother.

"It's two different computers, Mum," said Malcolm. "We'll all be safe as long as we wear our foil hats when we're emailing."

Keiko snorted with laughter and turned to Murray, but his face was without expression, and his mother's might as well have been carved from stone.

"Well, thank you, Malcolm—for the yakitori," she said, taking the tray.

She glanced at her watch as she left them. Almost time to go to the university, where she would be at home, among friends. Where she would know what people meant when they spoke. Where people would be like her. Her heart lifted and even returning to her flat up all those stone stairs couldn't lower it again.

EIGHT

DR. BRYANT READ WITH his chin sunk on his chest, his lips pushed forwards and pressed together, making his ginger moustache bristle. From time to time he crunched his mouth up even more, working his glasses up his nose and scraping the moustache hairs against the undersides of his nostrils with a rasping sound.

"That all seems in perfect order," he said at last, signing the last page. "Your customary efficiency in full swing."

Keiko stared at him. He had never met her before. *Japanese* efficiency, did he mean? He stared back. Was she only imagining a bloom of colour on his cheeks?

"Tell me a little about your proposal," he said.

Keiko nodded and cleared her throat. "The construction of knowledge in social groups," she said.

"A very well-researched area," said Dr. Bryant.

"In general," Keiko said. "But I've chosen a focus that's relatively—"

Dr. Bryant's eyes had strayed to his computer screen and he was reading something there.

"Food as modern folklore," said Keiko.

Dr. Bryant touched his mouse and his screen scrolled upwards. "Yes … yes …" he said. He clicked his mouse again.

"I'm thinking about q-methodology perhaps for the profiling, or a Likert line, created stimuli for the feedback into the networks."

"Good, good." *Click, click.*

"And there will be useful insights from anthropology and sociology. From the literature, I mean." She took a deep breath. She could always claim language problems. "And embroidery and some snowboarding."

"Yes, I see," said Dr. Bryant. "Well I'm very glad to hear someone giving proper consideration to a robust theoretical grounding right from the start."

"Yes, I see," echoed Keiko and, thanking him in such a soft voice that his attention was not hooked away from his screen by the smallest fraction, she let herself out.

———

Charismatic teachers are really for undergraduates, she told herself. *Or high school English teachers who lend their personal copies of Faulkner; even grade school teachers who take seven-year-olds to their first ballet.*

Her studies, her time here—the early blossoming of her career as she would no doubt call it in years to come—would be made up of her own careful probing scholarship, bounced off the other young minds, fresh bright minds, just beginning, like her own.

What she should be doing was meeting her office mates. She checked the floor plan on the wall of the entrance atrium and set off into the dark halls and stairways. Already she could see the three of them sitting in armchairs, or maybe the two of them sitting in armchairs, listening, while Keiko stood on the rug by the fireplace and read a draft of a paper to them, and how they would put down their sherry glasses and stare at her as she finished, how one would whistle and one would clap and they would toast her and tell her to send it straight to the journal. And she would say she couldn't have done it without their help, and someone would knock at the door and it would be Dr. Bryant, asking her if she wanted to see him and she would say, 'No, I don't think so,' and he would close the door again.

She was in the right corridor now and she shook her head, dispersing the daydreams and told herself to pay attention. She walked slowly, trying to fix the moment, so that later, in the years to come, when she ran along this corridor every day, she would still remember the first time.

And there it was. She paused outside to read the names on the door: *Grete Marr, A.L. Ebberwood, Keiko Nishisato*. She raised her hand to knock but then instead, tracing her fingers over her own name, she turned the handle and walked in.

It was a smallish room although high-ceilinged. Rather awkward actually, with once-white walls and once-blue carpet, worn dark and shiny over years. There were three desks. The one under the dusty window and the one on the long bare wall were occupied, two students hunched over laptops, both wearing ear buds and typing furiously. Neither of them looked up at her. The third desk, the smallest, was in the darkest corner by the door, half-covered in bales of yellowing paper and clusters of smoked-glass coffee mugs with cold, cloudy dregs in the bottom. On the bookshelf above, a spider plant had died, and dried-up nodules of it had fallen on the bales of paper and the coffee mugs, like little brown squid.

Before picture, Keiko told herself. She stepped into the room. One of the others—the female one (Grete?)—hit the save button twice, plucked out an ear bud and turned to Keiko.

"Okay," she said. "Here's the deal. I've been working on my thesis for five years"—she turned back to her keyboard and hit the save button again—"I'm nearly finished and I can't have any disruption. I asked Lynne—the secretary—not to put anyone in here, but there's no space anywhere else." She put her ear bud back in, hit the save button yet again, and started typing.

"You're talking," said the other student, without turning. His voice was a flat drone. "It's happening already. She's here and you're talking to her." He turned up the volume on his own ear buds and put his head down.

Keiko stood in the doorway for a moment listening to the midget *tsk-tsk* of the two iPods, then stepped back into the hallway and let the door close quietly behind her.

————

Those people with the sherry, she told herself, *are literature scholars, not psychologists. Work like mine demands solitude and sobriety.* She found the secretary's office, knocked, and went in. A woman was standing with her coat on reading pieces of paper and throwing them into her waste basket.

"Lynne?" she began. "I'm Keiko Nish—"

"I know who you are," said the woman.

"I have something to ask you. A big favour."

"I've been to the dentist today, and I'm leaving early," the secretary replied.

"I hope you'll say no if it's too much to ask," said Keiko. Lynne raised her eyebrows and waited. "I wondered if I might have a change of office." The eyebrows moved even higher. "When one becomes available. I realise it may be some time." The woman's stare had become fixed. "But I would be most grateful if you would put me on the list."

"Well, we'll have to see, won't we?" the secretary said. "There isn't a list as such. I just allocate rooms first come, first serve. They're pretty much all the same."

"Oh yes, yes of course," said Keiko. "But perhaps there's a room where all the students are just starting?"

"Yes, well, the thing is that the *home* students"—she paused—"all arrived on time, last month, at the start of the semester. It's only ever *international* students"—careful articulation there—"who keep us waiting and then roll up with a list of demands."

Keiko took a moment to process this. "Ah yes, I see," she said. "We have to arrange our visas and funding."

"Precisely. You need *permission* to take up a place, and you cast about for *money* wherever you can."

"And the overseas fees are so very expensive."

"But still they keep coming. Floods of them, every year. A deluge."

———

She couldn't face the bus stop, so she hailed a taxi with a surly driver who asked to see cash before he'd start on so long a trip and kept an eye on the meter, ready to stop and pitch her out when it rolled round past twenty pounds, which was what she'd shown him. But he kept the other eye on her, in the rearview mirror, and saw her tip her head back and press her fingers along her lashes, heard her gulp and sniff but refuse to let go. So when the meter hit twenty, he just switched it off and kept driving, all way to the empty street with the shut shops and dark windows. And he waited until he saw a light come inside her flat before he drove away.

Strange place, he thought, looking all around him, up and down the streets, and a phrase of his mother's came back to him. *Not a soul astir,* she used to say. He looked at the closed-down petrol station sitting out on its own and shook a sudden knot out of his shoulders. He wasn't sorry to get to the open road and the sixty-mile limit to put his foot down.

NINE

KEIKO DIDN'T NOTICE THE quiet, except to be glad that she got inside without anyone seeing her.

Inside the old petrol station on the corner, Willie Byers was glad of it too. He was sick of them all, with their hints and their nagging. They didn't even have to open their mouths these days; he could see it in their eyes, could easily imagine what they said about him.

He had bought the garage as a going concern, right there by the main road and ten miles from the nearest chain with its discounts. And Painchton folk didn't hold with new cars every three years, so there was good trade in keeping their old ones going. And Mr. Byers could surely live cheap, with his quiet ways and no wife to his name. Could have taken on a lad right away—people made mental notes to mention that to him whenever he should come to his first Traders' meeting. He never did come though, just as he never bought so much as a newspaper or a packet of cigarettes at Glendinning's or in the Spar, although he stopped in at both of them to read the headlines.

At first, Iain and Margaret Ballantyne assumed he had plumped for the Bridge, and Alec and Sandra Dessing guessed he'd taken to the Covenanters' and it was six months before it dawned on the four of them that the new mechanic didn't drink anywhere. Not so much as a single glass of beer after bending over an engine all afternoon on the hottest day of summer.

And so with nothing to build fellow-feeling, the judgement began. It was a work of willpower, said Kenny Imperiolo, to make a garage fail. Even a handless mechanic could have lived off the passing trade from the petrol pumps if he'd only kept the place tidy and put in the hours. But Byers took half-days here and weekends there and shut for Easter, and when he was tinkering away with his body repairs, he rested doors and wings and bumpers up against the outside walls to spray them and left stencil-ghosts all around so that tourists would slow down, but then shake their heads and look on the map for the next place to fill up.

Eventually, judgements made, the Traders turned on him in a pack with the full might of the town behind them. He complied with the order that his "premises should be predominantly uniform in colour." Technically. He spent one Sunday slathering on pink industrial paint with a nine-inch brush, all over the walls, right over the doors and window frames, up over the roof, unprimed and on top of the dirt. He worked on until his paint ran out and then burnt the tins on a bonfire the next morning, the women right up that side of the main street whipping in their Monday wash to get it away from the smoke and fumes.

And still none of them had seen it coming.

They were looking right at it now, though. As Keiko dried her tears and Byers enjoyed the quiet, up in the Covenanters' sat the same people around the same horseshoe-shaped table, which looked shabbier in the daylight, clothless, covered in folders and coffee cups, phones and elbows. Byers was the business of the day

Mr. McKendrick ran his hands through his hair.

"I'll talk to him," he said. "Again. There's no reason whatsoever for him to be hanging on to that site." Fancy was waving at him. She had arrived late and unexpected. "Miss Clarke?"

"Don't we already own the site?" she said. "Aren't we only trying to buy the buildings?"

"Is that a point of information or a question to the chair?" asked a sharp little woman sitting to Mr. McKendrick's left, scribbling minutes.

Fancy sighed. "Sorry, Miss Anderson, it's a point of information. Mr. Chairman, can I remind the meeting that the Traders own the land and only need to buy out the buildings and the business."

"Thank you, Miss Clarke," said Mr. McKendrick, blandly. "I stand corrected."

"Business!" said Mrs. McLuskie, jaunty today in a golfing sweater and check trousers and without her provost's chain. "What business? He's running it into the ground, the lazy beggar."

"Live and let live," said Miss Morrison from the charity shop.

(Mrs. McLuskie didn't think a charity shop selling old clothes and odd china was a business either and so Miss Morrison, in her opinion, didn't belong in the Traders.)

"I'd let him live if he wasn't killing it for the rest of us," Kenny Imperiolo said. "Of course, we've got our loyal regulars, but you need passing trade too. Fresh blood."

"Meat," said Mr. McKendrick. "Fresh blood would be a new business in competition with us. It's fresh meat we're after." No one answered. "To turn to happier news," he went on, "our international initiative has come to fruition."

"Ah, how is the wee lass?"

"How's she settling in?"

"I saw her sitting there working away at her books last night."

"She's loving it," said Fancy. "She's—"

"No report on Miss Nishisato's arrival is scheduled, Miss Clarke," said Miss Anderson, without raising her head.

"But I still don't see—if I'm honest, Jimmy," said Mr. Glendinning, "what she's doing here." There was a sound somewhere between a rumble and flutter, with some clear voices breaking through:

"You and me both, pal."

"Good question."

"No harm to the wee soul, but..."

Mr. McKendrick's voice rose above all of them.

"Several of our target funding sources look kindly on international reach," he said. "And cultural exchange."

"But why a Japanese?" said a voice. "Why not the likes of Canada or New Zealand or somewhere? My Auntie Margaret's boy Stewie would have—"

"Oh aye, some big cultural exchange that would be, your Auntie Margaret's boy Stewie!"

"*If* we can move on?" said Mr. McKendrick. He looked over the tops of his spectacles, sweeping a look around the room until it fell silent. "I'll speak to Byers again unless there are other volunteers."

"I wonder if maybe Mrs. Poole might have a word with him." People craned round to see who had spoken. Sandra Dessing, Mrs. McLuskie's buxom counterpart, sitting next to her and, like her, dressed for golf, stared defiantly back at them.

"Grace?" said Mr. McKendrick, and he leaned forward to look along the table at Mrs. Poole, who was sitting quietly next to Pet

McMaster from the florist, watching her knit. "I'm not with you, Sandra," he said.

"Since she's in an interested position," Sandra continued. There was a mild shifting in seats.

"You mean because Murray rents his workshop from Mr. Byers?" Mrs. McMaster asked loudly.

"I think Grace has done more than enough already," said Mr. McKendrick, "in offering the flat."

"Oh I see," breathed Sandra. "I hadn't heard that the terms had changed. That's most generous of you, Grace."

Mrs. Poole looked fixedly down at the knitting needles.

"It's well seen I'm not sitting beside her, Grace," whispered Mrs. McMaster, "or she'd have one of these pins in her fat behind."

"The cost of Keiko's accommodation is being borne out of Traders' funds as is only proper, Sandra," said Mr. McKendrick. "That's very clearly set out in the accounts appended to the minutes that we passed at the start of this meeting."

"And as I understand it, Sandra Dessing," said little Mrs. Watson, "Murray is giving up his tenancy, aren't you pet?" She looked at Murray for support, but he was watching his mother.

"Well, if Byers loses the income from renting out the workshop, that can only benefit us," said Sandra. "That's a piece of lucky timing."

A babble of voices broke out, and Mr. McKendrick banged lightly on the table. "Mrs. Dessing," he said in an unsteady voice. "Can I remind you that Murray is back in the butchers instead of in his own place, because of his father dying."

"Oh for heaven's sake!" said Sandra, with her chin up. "Grace knows I didn't mean anything to do with Duncan. Stop stirring it up."

"As the pot said to the kettle," said Mrs. McMaster.

Mrs. Watson said something too soft for Murray and Craig to catch.

"I think," said Mrs. Poole, and the room immediately quietened. "I think we should get back to the business at hand. I accept Mrs. Dessing's apology."

"I nev—" Mrs. Dessing began, but she stopped before she could say more. Instead she brushed imaginary specks from the front of her powder-pink golf jersey with three hard swipes.

"Don't minute that, Miss Anderson," said Mr. McKendrick. 'So, I'll speak to Willie Byers. And I'll get back to you at our next meeting, which is on the..."

"Twenty-third of October," said Miss Morrison.

"At the Bridge," said Mr. Dessing, of the Bridge Hotel. It was the first time he had spoken; his wife fought her own battles.

"Back here," said Mr. Ballantyne, of the Covenanters' Arms. "Mr. Chairman, we agreed that meetings would alternate. There's a meeting scheduled for next week. So that'll be across the way and then back here on the twenty-third again."

"No Iain, that's a committee meeting," said Mrs. Dessing. "It was my understanding, Mr. Chairman, that the full meetings were turnabout and the committee were suiting themselves."

"What committee?" said Fancy. "I thought we were the committee."

"The inner circle, Fance," said Craig. "The hard core."

"The grandmasters," said Murray. "The high priests."

"I'd rather not discuss the committee while we're in full session," said Mr. McKendrick, glowering now.

"Secret order," said Craig. "Like *Opus Dei*."

"Enough," said Mr. McKendrick, sending a black look down the table to Mr. Ballantyne for bringing it up, and the meeting was over.

The Traders straggled out to their cars in weary ones and twos except for Mr. McKendrick, Kenny Imperiolo, and Iain Ballantyne, who came downstairs together and, like a shoal of mackerel, executed a sharp right into the public bar. Mrs. Dessing and Mrs. McLuskie, ruffled and too late for golf, went off for a tetchy half-hour in the practice range. Craig, Murray, and Mrs. Watson came reeling out in fits of giggles and ran into Mrs. Poole and Mrs. McMaster standing at the kerb.

"Your mother and I are just going to take a walk up by," said Pet McMaster to Murray, nodding her head towards the top of the road.

"D'you want me to come with you?" asked Murray, moving away from Fancy and Craig. "Mum?" Mrs. Poole looked at him without expression, then turned to the beckoning arm of Mrs. McMaster, who bore her away.

"Okay, pal?" said Craig, as they began to head down the street towards home.

"We all know how it feels to lose a loved one, Murray," said Mrs. Watson. "No shame in sorrow."

"I'm fine," said Murray. "Bloody nuts, anyway." He spoke too softly for the others to catch his words, then he winked at Craig and went on, louder: "What did you call Sandra Dessing, Mrs. Watson?"

"What did you say, Mabel?" said Fancy.

"It sounded like 'Vinegar Tits' to me," Craig said.

"I did not say any such thing!" Mrs. Watson protested. "Murray, you're a disgrace to your poor mother and the memory of your father. And you, Craig McKendrick, your uncle would be ashamed of you."

"Ha! Lucky me then," said Fancy. "No good name to lose!"

"Och, you and your nonsense," said Mrs. Watson stepping into her shop doorway and picking over a bunch of keys. "I'm away in to give this place a good clean."

"Don't forget to wash your mouth out," said Fancy, but Mrs. Watson just tutted and went inside.

"Hey!" said Craig, looking up at the big bay window, where Keiko and Viola were watching them. "I thought she was away into the uni."

Fancy shrugged. "She came back. Offered to baby-sit."

"Offered?" said Craig.

"Well," said Fancy. "Didn't say no."

"She looks a bit fed up with it," said Murray, squinting up at Keiko.

"Nah, she was fed up already," Fancy said. "I think she'd been crying."

"What?" said Murray. "Bloody hell, Fancy. Why are we standing around down here staring at her then?"

———

"So how did you get on?" he said, upstairs in the kitchen, blowing on the top of his tea. "First day and all that."

"Fine," said Keiko. She smiled at him. "Thank you for asking." Her voice wobbled as she spoke. "Please eat. I have plenty." The bottom cupboard was stacked with cash and carry multi-packs of Kit-Kats and Bountys and Mars Bars, crackling heaps that threatened to slide out onto the lino whenever she disturbed them. Craig dipped his Twix in his tea and stirred it around before sucking off the chocolate.

"I can't believe you still do that," said Fancy, shaking her head at him.

69

"How come?" said Craig, taking the Twix out of his mouth with a long suck that put deep dimples in his cheeks and left a ring of chocolate on his lips afterwards. "Don't you still do anything you used to do at school?"

Fancy blinked and snapped her head around to stare—without seeing—at Murray instead.

"So, Murray," she said. "What's em … Where's—yeah!—Where's your mum off to with Pet, then?"

"Cemetery," Murray said.

"Who's dead?" Viola asked with her eyes wide.

Fancy shushed her. "Murray's daddy, sweetheart," she said. "You know that. And so his mummy's gone to visit him. Sorry. Really. Sorry." She glared at Craig.

"Bloody nuts," said Murray again. "Visiting his grave. As if he's in there waiting for company."

"Er, Murray," said Fancy nodding at Viola who was owl-eyed now.

"Viola, ask your mum what Mrs. Watson called Mrs. Dessing," said Craig. Fancy smiled at him, forgiving.

"Mrs. Dessing that hates you?" said Viola.

"Who hates you?" said Keiko. "Why?"

"I made posters advertising massage treatments," said Fancy. "And Sandra Dessing reckoned she'd cracked the code."

Craig shook his head and laughed. "But what old Vinegar"—he glanced at Viola—"Bits didn't get was how a letter in the local paper condemning Fancy's morals was gold dust. Like saying a book's full of filth. Instant bestseller! Nobody would have looked at the posters if she hadn't kicked up—no offence."

"None taken," Fancy said. "Like how nobody ever reads their junk mail."

"Ha!" said Keiko. And they all turned and stared at her. Even Viola, sitting on Keiko's lap, twisted round to look. "Junk mail!" she said. "It's getting cleverer and cleverer. And then we get more and more sophisticated. So it gets cleverer still. Until it looks like a cheque or a credit card or even something sent to frighten you."

There was a silence.

"Okay," said Fancy slowly. Craig frowned and Murray gave that look of his with one eyebrow hooked up under his hair. Then Keiko laughed and they joined her, still not understanding.

And suddenly, sitting there with her fingers laced across Viola's warm middle, listening to them all, she felt all the daydreams go: the circle of friends sipping sherry and savouring disagreement; the like-minded others somewhere else in the department, somewhere Lynne let only favoured, *home* students go; the mentor she had dreamed of, the sage at whose feet she would sit and from whose wisdom she would grow wise. She wouldn't want to be anywhere near Dr. Bryant's feet anyway.

Painchton, she thought. And really, how much more typical for it to be so unlikely. A better story in the end. Fancy and Murray and Craig. A living room covered with books and papers and pretty tea-cups. Wine glasses even. And a solitary scholar: Trollope in the post office, Einstein in the patent office, Nishisato above the butchers. She would *not* be like those other girls, who disappeared leaving tears and worry behind them. This one would last.

"Can I ask?" she said. "Who is Mrs. Dessing? I know Pet—your foster-parent, Fancy—and Mrs. Watson with the vegetables, of course. But Mrs. Dessing?"

"Where do you start?" said Craig, lacing his hands together and cracking his knuckles.

71

———

Downstairs, Malcolm could hear them laughing even over the noise of the suet grinder. She was settling in; she would stay.

He worked until there was no more work to do and even then waited until he had heard everyone leave and Keiko begin to run bath water before he let himself out of the shop and set off home.

TEN

Wednesday, 16 October

"THEY SWALLOWED IT WHOLE," said Kenny Imperiolo. All five of them were in the room above the ironmongers, glasses of good wine at their elbows, trays of nibbles in the middle. "International outreach to get lottery funding to do up the Green and plant some petunias. I thought they'd balk at some of it for sure."

"Well, to be fair, Ken," said Sandra Dessing, "Jimmy did have to field some awkward questions."

"Aye, especially when you let slip about special committee meetings," said Iain Ballantyne.

"Me?" Mrs. Dessing began, but Mr. McKendrick shushed them.

"Children, children," he said. "Why are you bickering? Everything's going to plan. We should be congratulating ourselves. Quietly, of course." He grinned around them all. "Softly, softly, cooky monkey."

"*Catchy*," said Iain Ballantyne. 'It's '*catchy* monkey.'"

Mr. McKendrick frowned then threw back his head and roared with laughter.

"Freudian slip!" he said, his eyes merry. "Oh, that's a good one." Then he sobered, seeing that no one was laughing along. "What's wrong?" he asked. "What's the matter with you?"

Kenny, Sandra, Iain, and Etta did not look at one another and slowly they dropped their eyes until they were not looking at Mr. McKendrick either.

"Nothing wrong with me," said Kenny at last. "I mean, except that it's a lot to take on—changing hearts and minds—and people are always looking to catch you out these days."

"Sandra?" said Mr. McKendrick. "Iain? Tell me you're not getting cold feet too."

"I don't like to think of my name and face splashed all over the papers if I'm honest," said Iain Ballantyne. Mrs. Dessing nodded.

"No such thing as bad publicity," said Mr. McKendrick. "And if Etta's all right then you should be, by Jove, for she's got more at stake here than us all."

Etta McLuskie took a sip from her glass to steady herself before answering.

"I can't say I don't have concerns, Jim," she said. "I mean, don't misunderstand me, I absolutely share your desire ... I'm just not sure it's right. Never mind legal."

"Oh-ho! It's not legal," said Mr. McKendrick. "That's for sure. But Painchton is a special place—a unique place—and this is a unique opportunity. The world's too bland these days and we're standing against that. Come on, people! We need to stick together."

"Aye, but we're not, are we?" said Mrs. McLuskie. "We're not even all here."

"Grace has a lot on her plate," said Mr. McKendrick.

"She surely doesn't look very happy," said Mrs. Dessing.

"Well, not when you had a go at her in front of the whole board," said Iain.

"I did no such thing," said Mrs. Dessing, hotly, suddenly upright in her armchair.

"Oh, leave it," said Iain. "Your tongue's that sharp sometimes, Sandra, you could floss your teeth from inside."

She turned and gaped at him, her eyes filling with tears. "I thought I could count on a bit of—" she said, then bit her lip and turned to Mr. McKendrick. "*Is* Grace okay, though, Jimmy? Speaking of counting on people."

Mr. McKendrick's face fell into sombre lines and all other questions, all the squabbles, faded away. *Was* Grace okay?

In the months after Duncan's death, of course, no one looked for her to be cheery. Grace had lost her man and it could be years before she was back on her feet and over it again. But she was surrounded by friends. He'd told her so and she'd laughed and said didn't she know it. Mrs. McLuskie always invited her, in a silky voice, to join in with whatever she and Mr. McLuskie had planned for the weekend. Mrs. Watson told Grace she knew how it felt and how, when she had lost Robert, talking was the only thing that did any good. Mrs. Mc-Master remembered as clear as this morning how, all those years ago when she was widowed, the last thing she wanted to hear about was how somebody else had fared and how they were now. *She* talked about Duncan the first time they met after the funeral, laughed about something he'd said—that was what *she* had wanted—but Grace bowed her head at the sound of his name, and Pet could have kicked herself. She made up a posy and brought it round, saying it was a cancelled order and just the colours of Grace's dining room.

Oh, Grace knew very well there was a net beneath her. She was the grieving widow of a well-loved man, a card that often turned up as small-town life shuffled itself, so she stood on her mark and played her part without faltering. And slowly the town forgot that the sadness had started before the dying.

Mr. McKendrick wasn't content to be a net in case she fell. A man of action, was Jimmy McKendrick. He wanted something to do. His fingers twitched whenever he looked at Grace, itching to make it better, which made her smile. *If he was a Labrador,* she would think, *I'd have every tea-towel in the house on my lap whenever I sat down.* She laughed.

"What? What is it?" he would ask, truffling after the laugh to plump it up and have done with the sadness.

"Oh, James," she'd say, her face resettling. "You're a good man. You've always been a good friend to me."

"Gracie," he said, plunging in as he knew he would no matter what he told himself sternly in the mirror each morning. "Gracie, I still am. I'm right here. You just say the word. I'm right here and I'm not going anywhere any time soon." She smiled and nodded—to stop him talking, though, not to agree with him. How could she *say the word*? If she said any of the words, how would she ever lift her head again?

Friday, 18 October

Why does that woman hang her head so?, Keiko wondered, standing at the kitchen window with her bowl of rice on Friday morning. She had stopped moving away when Mrs. Poole came out of the small building with her two buckets of water every day, never looking up, just walking to the drain in the middle of the yard with her gaze trained on the ground.

And what is she cleaning? Then sniffing and wrinkling her nose, she wondered if perhaps Mrs. Poole was right and she was wrong. The faint odour she had noticed when she first arrived was still there, no stronger but never going away completely.

Mrs. Poole tipped each pail carefully so that the grey water poured into the centre of the drain without touching the sides, then she swept the few splashes inwards with four or five swipes of her brush and stood for a second, facing away from the house, before turning and disappearing from Keiko's view, her opening and closing of the back door causing hardly a sound before the building settled back into complete silence.

Five hours of work, Keiko had told herself. Five solid hours, with some time off for lunch maybe, before the trip to town on the bus with Viola Clarke. But already the errand was distracting her; she imagined what the little girl and she would talk about on the journey, whether she should take a storybook to read, where she could get one, whether Viola was still young enough to be read to ... *Baby-sitting later*, she told herself. *Work first*. She nodded firmly. With a short walk in the fresh air to break it up in the middle.

When her coffee was brewed she padded through to the living room, to the big table in the bay window she was beginning to think of as her desk.

Find subjects. Undergraduates? Pay them? Continuity.

What she needed was a cohort of fifty individuals who would return at intervals over the next three years to be retested after the initial profiling. She thought of the herds of pierced and shambling students she had seen in the halls of the department and the task of catching them between hangovers and holidays and ... details, details.

Psych profile of subjects. What scale? What test?

Published source? Expense? Make up own? Time?

Details, details.

Run first questionnaire

Report to subjects and run second questionnaire

Repeat steps 2 and 3 twice more. Three times? Five in all for luck?

Write up.

Graduate.

Apply for, be offered and accept job, find beautiful house in vibrant city.

Fresh air *first* perhaps and then four and a half hours of solid work with her lunch at her desk? Keiko shook her head as she stood. This had never happened before. From the days when she was learning to read and add simple figures together, she had always been able to focus. She looked around the living room. And this was the quietest, largest, most comfortable study she had ever worked in. She stamped her feet, as she had taken to doing since Fancy had showed her the trick that first day. Solid. Freshly painted and comfortably furnished and, never forget, *free*. She picked up her new phone and clicked through the contacts, smiling at how many there were already. The friendliest place she had ever been, with the most time she had ever had—no classes to attend, no mother to placate— and the longest line of well-wishers ready to entertain her when she needed a break from it. So what was wrong?

"You think too much, Keko-chan," her mother would say. "And you drink too much coffee."

"I'm a psychology student, mother," Keiko would reply. "What do you recommend, instead of thinking?" At least, in her head she would reply that way. Under her breath, she would. Out loud she would say perhaps she needed some tea to clear her mind and would her mother like some?

"That's right. Forget your brain for once and listen to your tummy."

And actually, Keiko thought to herself closing her phone again, *that might be the trouble after all.* It had been years since she had made herself rice and miso for breakfast instead of toast and jam, but this morning, after last night, there had been no question.

Because last night she had been the guest of the Imperiolos. Or Rosa at least; Kenny had been at a meeting.

———

"He says he's asking after you," Mrs. Imperiolo had told her. "He's sorry he couldn't be here, but he's a busy man. Got a lot on his mind. Stressed to his oxters, actually." A frown passed over her face but only fleetingly, then she smiled again. "Now, Keiko," she said, "you're in for a treat today. I'll order for you this time, seeing you're new to it all. I hope you're hungry."

She was, but the air in here—hot, thick, and heavy in her mouth and spiked with vinegar scent in her nose—was filling her up quite nicely without the need actually to eat anything.

They were sitting in the window seat of Imperiolo's Fish Restaurant, looking out over the main road towards the river railings. "Two fish suppers with peas, bread and butter, and tea," said Rosa to the waitress. She turned back to Keiko. "I know how much Japanese people like fish," she said. "And Joe, our fish fryer, took us to the national finals last year."

She pointed to a man in a white hat behind the service counter. Keiko watched him through the shimmer for a moment. He was Italian, like Rosa and Kenny, and she could not drag her eyes from his black hair. When he was turned away she could almost believe he was someone from home with that hair, she thought, surprised that she cared, surprised how odd it was to be where no one looked like her. Even Rosa with her olive skin had springy black curls, and Kenny was bald.

"Of course, we're lucky in a way," Rosa was saying. "Cod was never a favourite here. It's more of a southern taste, really. And the haddock is fine, touch wood. So that's lucky."

"*Touch wood?*"

"Anyway," Rosa went on, quite loud, "it really doesn't matter. It could be anything. As long as it's fresh and handled properly. It's the batter that counts. And the fat. What's inside is neither here nor there."

At the next table, Mrs. Sangster—who had been unable to help overhearing—turned round and cleared her throat at Rosa.

"Anne," said Rosa. "I didn't see you there."

"Is this on the schedule?" said Mrs. Sangster quietly, and then in a louder voice, "Hello, Keiko pet."

Keiko nodded, smiled and tried not to listen.

"The schedule's the baseline," said Rosa. "The schedule's to make sure Keiko doesn't starve to death all on her own up there. It wasn't supposed to set a limit."

"I don't want to cause any—" Keiko said. "I've been taking care of myself for—"

"And don't you listen to Mrs. Imperiolo, getting carried away!" said Mrs. Sangster in the same bright, loud voice. "Batter and fat and who cares what's in it! What must you think of us, eh?" She dropped her voice again. "The Japanese are a very fastidious people. Very precise people. Easy scunnered, I'll wager."

"Not at all," said Keiko. "I know what *scunnered* means and I'm not. Extremely robust appetite, I assure you."

The waitress returned with two plates and put them down. Mrs. Sangster, after a hard look at Rosa, turned back to her own party.

"*Haddock* and chips and peas," Rosa said. "How good does that look, Keiko?"

Keiko stared at her plate. It was oval, like a serving platter, and almost half of it was taken up by a glistening golden object, sinuous and slightly twisted, still fizzing and popping with heat, both of its tapered ends flexed up in the air. A stack of thick yellow chips was heaped up against one of its sides and a mound of greenish sludge sat in a small dish balanced on the far edge of the plate along with a slice of lemon.

"How lovely," she said. She broke open the golden package with her knife and sat back as a wave of steam rolled up into her face. Rosa chuckled and blew on a forkful of chips.

"Joe's an artist," she said. "Famed far and wide. Tuck in and let's get some roses in those cheeks, eh?"

The roses reached from her scalp to her collar by the time they left; she was gasping, shiny-lipped and slack-eyed, her mouth pricking with salt and her teeth rough from the cups of tea, each one stronger than the last, that she'd used to wash the salt away.

"We own the ice cream parlour too," Rosa said. "Kenny's grandad opened it when he came from Naples. I bet you've never had a knickerbocker glory, eh?"

"Sounds big," said Keiko, feeling bubbles rise in her gullet and uneasy about saying more.

"You won't believe how big," Rosa said, chuckling.

———

So no wonder she needed miso and rice this morning. Keiko left the flat, walked down to the bottom road, and was standing on the corner of the Green looking both ways when she heard her name and felt a little swoop, up and down again, thinking she recognised the voice. She turned and sure enough it was Murray Poole, striding across the grass towards her with his coat flapping.

"Another day off?" he said, coming up beside her.

"Just getting some air before I start," she said.

"Me too," said Murray. "At least, Malc's busy and there ain't no fresh air in the shop, that's for sure. You been to the glen yet?"

"I don't think so," Keiko said. "I haven't been anywhere yet."

"Want to see it?"

"I want to see everything," Keiko said.

Murray smiled. "This way," he said, turning her with a hand on her shoulder and propelling her gently.

They passed the ice cream parlour, and Keiko waved in at the girls who had served her the evening before.

"Mrs. Imperiolo took me out for tea last night," she told Murray. "Moby Dick and chips."

Murray gave a shout of laughter that rang out in the air like a bell. "Brilliant," he said. "Still, could have been worse. They own the curry house and the Chinese too."

"I like curry," Keiko said. "And anyway, I didn't mean to imply … it was delicious."

"Yeah, but did she give you the bit about how it doesn't matter what's inside the batter as long there's enough grease?"

"Well," said Keiko. This wasn't strictly accurate but close enough.

"Yeah, you want to hear her on how it doesn't matter what's in the curry if the sauce is hot enough and how you whisk the sauce to suspend the fat and keep it thickened, and if you serve free chapatti people don't eat them, but if you charge through the nose for stuffed naan they want to get their money's worth and mop up the sauce with it."

"Stop!" said Keiko.

"And her home cooking's worse," Murray said. They had passed the last of the buildings now and he led them over the road and across a footbridge above the river.

"She's Italian, yes?" said Keiko. "Mediterranean?"

"See, the thing about battered haddock or curry—or sweet and sour pork—is that even Rosa Imperiolo wouldn't finish the whole thing off with a shovelful of grated Parmesan, but you show her a plate of pasta and all she can think of is cheese."

"Please, stop!"

He turned now and looked at her, pulling back to get a clear view. "You're not joking, are you?" he said. "You've gone green."

"Sorry," Keiko said, but he was smiling at her.

"Jesus Christ," he said. "Have you ever come to the wrong place!" Then he dipped his head very close to hers, as he had done before. "But I'll take care of you."

Keiko put her head down to hide her smile and noticed that the ground beneath her feet was not pavement now but chipped bark. She raised her head again and looked around. They had passed through a small opening and were on a path under a close canopy of trees.

"Where are we going?" she asked.

"Into the woods," said Murray. "To the glen, like I told you. Now here's something to take your mind off . . . all that. Tell me about the tea ceremony."

Keiko groaned. "I knew this would happen," she said. "My mother warned me. She told me to take some classes before I left so that I would be a better guest when I got here. I don't know anything about the tea ceremony."

"How can you not know about your own …?"

"Because I'm not a proper girl," she said. "I'm determined to grow hunched and grey sitting over a computer and I might as well be a brain in a jar."

"And there's your mum again!" This time they both laughed and when they stopped, Keiko could hear running water, just faintly, somewhere in front of them.

"A waterfall?" she said, looking up at Murray.

He waggled his eyebrows. "Come and see."

The ground had been falling away on one side and now the path rounded a corner to show a deep gully, thickly wooded, opening below them. There was a little bulge, a viewing place, built out over the drop with a wooden rail for safety. Keiko stepped forward and looked down. It *was* a waterfall, flashing thinly over the black rocks before dropping the last few metres into a pool.

"We used to swim here when we were wee," said Murray, pointing out a set of wooden steps, half hidden by ferns.

"Brrr," said Keiko, hugging herself. The waterfall kept the dark pool endlessly rolling and bulging, the surface of the water looking leathery in the gloom. It smelled of wet earth and old leaves.

"Yeah, you're not kidding," said Murray. "I wouldn't do it now. Not even to piss off Sandra Dessing, and you can guess what she thought of wee boys splashing around in the scuddy."

"Mrs. Dessing aside," said Keiko, "this must have been a lovely place to grow up. I'm not surprised you're so fond of it."

"Now, where did you get that idea?" said Murray, folding his arms and staring at her with one eyebrow peaked up under his hair and his smile more crooked than ever. "Me? 'Fond' of Painchton?"

"I mean, not just you," said Keiko, hoping the low light would hide her face changing colour. "Everyone. It's a very settled kind of place, isn't it? Everyone is so kind to everyone."

Murray said nothing but turned and looked down into the pool again.

Keiko watched his profile for a while and then joined him, gazing down. Briefly, she remembered the river and the rabbits' eyes and turned round, leaning against the rail and looking back into the woods the way they had come.

"Anyway," Murray said, turning round too and bumping his shoulder against hers, smiling again. "You picked Painchton out from all the places in the world you could have gone. I don't want to put you off it."

"I didn't pick it exactly," said Keiko. "I was looking for sponsorship. I was invited. Painchton picked me."

"Painchton picked you," Murray repeated. It was dark under the trees and the look on his face was hard to see clearly. She could tell he wasn't smiling. "Did you ever ask why? Did you wonder?"

She hesitated. "My mother did!" she said in the end.

"Look," said Murray. "Ignore me. You'll probably be fine. I'm just not Painchton's biggest fan. I don't ... I don't really belong here."

"Are you going to leave?" said Keiko. "Like the others?"

"What others?" Murray said.

"Like that man said—the tosser—I can't remember his name. I thought he meant me. Was it *you*?"

"I'm here—at the moment—because of Dad dying," Murray said, and his voice was colder and darker than all of the deep black water and the steep banks of wet earth. "I can't just walk away."

"I'm sorry," said Keiko.

"Nothing for you to be sorry for," said Murray, and just like that he sounded normal again. "Someone like you, doing what you do ... you could hardly help asking questions. That's why it's good to have you here."

"I'm not sure I follow you," Keiko said.

"You solve puzzles, don't you? You get to the bottom of things. You work stuff out."

"I can't work *this* out," said Keiko. "I don't know what you're talking about."

"And I can't tell you," Murray said. "Not in a million years. But it's still good to have you around."

And since it seemed to be that kind of conversation that they were having here in the dark of the woods, for some reason, Keiko found herself saying:

"It's good to have you around too, Murray."

He gave a laugh like a snapping twig. "You have no idea," he said. "Stick with me."

ELEVEN

At half-past three she was outside the flat, watching for Viola. Should she take the little girl's hand when they crossed the road? Would that be too intrusive, maybe? Too patronising?

But when they reached the crossing place, Viola slipped her hand into Keiko's as if out of habit and kept hold of it when they reached the other side. Keiko kept her fingers very still, as if trying not to scare away a small creature who was taking crumbs from her.

"Martha Anderson in my class thought you were called Cakehole," said Viola in a scornful voice, then she looked up to check that Keiko was laughing. "Why don't you wear a kimono?"

"I've got a kimono with me," said Keiko. "For a special occasion. Like a kilt."

"Kilts are scratchy," said Viola. "I had to wear one at Miss Munro's. I'm glad I'm going to proper dancing now, and not Miss Munro's stupid baby dancing. I'm glad you can take me." She squeezed Keiko's hand. Keiko relaxed her fingers. "I can do the money on the bus if you get stuck, you know. It's two pounds sixty-five for you and a pound for me. And I've got my own pound in my purse."

"Thank you," said Keiko. She squeezed Viola's hand back. "Let's get it ready before the bus comes. That's what I do."

At the bus stop were two young women Keiko had never seen before, who didn't speak to her although they both turned slightly as she joined them so that they could shoot glances at her shoes and clothes out of the sides of their eyes. Viola looked them up and down once and then turned away and began to practice tap steps, counting under her breath, her bag slapping against her back as she bounced from foot to foot. Under the spiked glances, Keiko checked through her own bag as though for something she thought she might have forgotten, then looked up at the sound of an engine slowing. A white van had drawn up and Malcolm Poole was leaning across the seats as the window slid down.

"Where you off to?" he asked. Viola stopped dancing and came and put her hand back into Keiko's.

"We're going into the city on the bus," said Keiko. "I'm going to the university and Viola is going to Tollcross to her dancing school."

"I'm going right past," said Malcolm and, shifting the van out of gear and unbuckling his seatbelt, he hauled himself across and opened the passenger door. Keiko looked down at Viola and hesitated. She glanced with silent appeal at the two young women, but they studied the ground, smirking. Then she looked back at Malcolm.

"Thank you so much, but..." She was groping for the turn of phrase she needed, knew it was one she had learned, but it was gone. "You're very kind," she said. "We're most grateful." Then, her mind still blank, she stepped forward and hoisted Viola up before climbing in behind her, hearing a cackle of laughter from the bus stop as they pulled away.

"Can I sit beside the window?" asked Viola, already squeezing past and settling down at the extreme edge of the seat. Keiko busied herself with the seatbelts, Viola's first, pulling it in as tight as it would go and buckling it across the little girl's chest, so that she was pinned back with her legs poking straight out, her feet wagging gently. Keiko's own seatbelt buckle was doubled up just under the outside edge of Malcolm's nearest thigh. She held the strap over her body with one hand and braced her feet against the floor.

"Here," said Malcolm, in his quiet honking voice. He bent his whole body towards her and she stiffened until she realised that he was reaching his arm around his leg and rummaging underneath himself. He held out the buckle to her and she fastened herself in with her head down.

"What kind of dancing school is it, Viola?" Malcolm asked.

"Everything except disco," said Viola. "Are there dead animals in the back?"

"No," he said. "I'm on my way to get some, though."

"Yuk," said Viola, "We're getting the bus home, Keiko, eh no?" Keiko laughed and gently pinched one of Viola's skinny knees.

Malcolm, she noticed, was slumped slightly to stop his head from brushing the roof. He really was very tall, a fact that should be plain but somehow got hidden in the overwhelming girth of him. And his girth combined with the slumping meant that his stomach jutted out around the steering wheel and he had to breathe in sharply when he needed to turn it so it seemed as though it was the sudden jerked breaths that were steering the van and not his hands at all.

When the silence had gone on beyond all normalcy, when Keiko thought that Malcolm must be able to hear her thinking about him, she looked up at him with a bright smile on her face, giving a little preparatory cough. His hair was as dark as Murray's but longer and swept to the side in wet-looking straps, like seaweed out of water. His face was still except that, although he breathed through his nose with his teeth shut, his bottom lip hung open under its weight and trembled at every bump in the road.

"Are you busy at the uni today or just killing time waiting for the wee one?" he asked suddenly, as they joined a main road and the van sped up.

"I have one or two little things I need to do. I…"

"I just wondered if you wanted to come with me?" He paused, but Keiko said nothing. "To the meat wholesalers. It's really interesting." He hefted himself round and looked at Keiko, who could feel her face draining and had to make herself blink her eyes before they dried.

"The slaughterhouse?"

"Just to the market, not to the processing end."

"I really have to get a few things done," she said. "And I wouldn't want to put you to any trouble, thanks all the same." This, she realised, was the phrase she had needed at the bus stop. Too late now.

"I hear you were out at Kenny's last night," Malcolm said, smiling as he checked in his rearview mirror and waved his thanks to the driver behind who had held back and let him in.

"I like their pickled onions," said Viola. "They're great big mambo ones, not like those wee white ones Granny gets that you couldn't choke on."

"You would make a good little Japanese girl, Viola," said Keiko. "Sour flavours are very dear to us."

"I do their dripping," Malcolm said.

"Eh?" said Viola.

"The Imperiolos. I render their dripping for them. My father used to do it and I took over. It's nice to be nice."

"What's 'render their dripping', Malcolm?" said Viola.

"You roast up all fatty scraps, in a hot oven and the pure fat drips out and then you can use it for frying in," Malcolm said.

"For frying *fish*?" Keiko asked him.

"Oh yes, best there is. It's clarified ghee in the curries so I can't help them with that, and they use veg oil in the Chinese, but it's best pure dripping in the chippy. Gorgeous stuff. My father taught me."

"Yuk, yuk, double yuk," said Viola. Keiko knew that she should scold the little girl for rudeness but could not bring herself to.

"And I tell you what else," said Malcolm. "The dried scraps at the end are absolutely braw. Bit of salt and pepper."

"Yuk, yuk, double yuk, and blergh," said Viola, making a very convincing vomiting noise.

"Yum, yum, double yum, and save me some for later," returned Malcolm. "There's nothing wrong with a bit of fat."

Viola's eyes lit up with devilment, but Keiko broke in before she could answer. "I went for a walk to the glen this morning," she said. "Murray told me you used to swim in the scuddy there."

The van lurched and Viola let out her held laughter with a fizzing sound, like a bottle opening.

"Right," said Malcolm. "Did he?"

"Yes, under the waterfall? In the pool? The *scuddy* pool, is it?"

"Ah, right," said Malcolm.

They dropped Viola off first, double-parked on a narrow, bustling street. Keiko fumbled the door open for her to jump down and they watched her slip into the surge of little girls going into the building. Malcolm waited until her bright ponytail had disappeared through the doors before he moved, ignoring the horn blasts and revving behind him, then he turned the van and set off through a warren of back roads.

"I should probably tell you," he said, without looking at her, "before you say it again to someone who matters. *Scuddy* isn't a kind of pool. Swimming in the scuddy means . . . no trunks."

"Oh," said Keiko, feeling the familiar wave of warmth flooding into her cheeks; she had never changed colour so much in her life as in the last week, between the gaffes and the Gaelic coffee.

"Don't worry," said Malcolm. "My father used to say, if you can't keep your foot out your mouth, you could always get work in a circus."

Keiko couldn't help laughing. "It's nice to hear you speak of him," she said.

"It's nice to get the chance to," said Malcolm. "Murray and my mother . . ."

"I know," said Keiko. "I made Murray sad this morning. No—not sad, but upset. Not thinking, I said how nice it was in Painchton, how close and settled everyone is!"

"That wasn't about Dad," said Malcolm after a long pause.

"I think it was," said Keiko. The next pause was even longer.

"No, see Murray broke up with his girlfriend. And he's not really got over it. He's been sick to the back teeth of Painchton ever since then."

Keiko groaned. "That *would* make more sense, actually."

"Oh?"

"Yes, he talked about a puzzle he had to solve and maybe I could help him—doing the kind of thing I do."

Malcolm, suddenly, was as still as a stone and the van slowed as though even his pedal foot had frozen. Keiko turned and looked up at him, at the Easter Island set of his face and the dark emptiness of his eyes. The van stopped completely.

"We're here," Malcolm said, his voice softer than ever. Keiko looked around and recognised the ornate lump of a building they were parked beside, just across the square from the psychology department. She must have imagined the freezing—she didn't know how to drive and couldn't tell what sudden bursts of concentration it might take to stop in the middle of a busy city. Thanking him, she jumped out and slammed the door, then stood and waved as he pulled away. She must *surely* be imagining what she was seeing now, the effort it was taking Malcolm to heave a smile onto his face and raise his arm to wave back to her.

She heard her mother's voice. *The great expert on the human mind, Keko-chan? You could be Sigmund Freud himself—but even monkeys fall out of trees.*

TWELVE

It was in their slot in Glendinning's one day, tucked inside the Radio Times. But the layout of the shop—paper rack out of sight of the counter, in between the dairy cabinet and the bakery trays, so that people could pick up their milk, rolls, and newspaper in a oney and not make a crowd by the till while they were at it—that meant anyone could have put it there safe and unseen.

When it was opened, the message was clear. I see what you are. I know what you do. I will tell them all.

They didn't have a fireplace in the new house, and even a match in a wastepaper basket was taking a risk, with all the smoke alarms ready to shriek out they way they did at the toaster set on frozen, the griddle pan on its fourth chop, the steam from the shower if the bathroom door was open onto the landing. So it was shredded, in the little hand-wound shredder they'd got for their statements and bills. And then went into the compost, mixed with the lawn clippings, potato peel on top and the last of the faded marigolds as well, until it was gone.

Monday, 21 October

Fancy was busy with the photocopier, so grimly bent on it that she could do no more than nod at Keiko and jerk her head towards a chair. She lifted a pile of red sheets from the out-tray, backed around to the in-tray and flipped them over.

"Same way up, turn them short side over short side, try one to start with ..." She punched a button on the copier and stepped round to the out-tray to wait. "Bugger it! Upside down again." Finally, she turned. "Hiya. Sorry, but I really thought I had it that time. So what, yeah? But this coloured paper's dead expensive and you have to use like ten times as much toner to make it show up. Check the state of it." She held out the printed page to Keiko, turning it this way and that.

"I'll do it," Keiko said, "if you have the manual. You're trying to make a leaflet with two folds, yes?"

Fancy fished inside the front door of the copier and held out a booklet, looking dubious. "I'll put the kettle on," she said. "I want fifty, by the way, if you work it out."

When Keiko took the fifty copies through to the kitchen, Fancy hugged her, squashing the sheets of warm paper between their bodies, then sat down at the table, divided the pile into two and started folding. Keiko sat down on the other side of the table and got to work too.

"Did you read it?" said Fancy. "What d'you think?"

"I didn't, in case it was confidential," Keiko said. She took a drink of her tea and read the front page of the leaflet she had just finished folding: *Do you spend your days at a desk, on your feet, up a ladder, or under a car? Use the voucher on the back of this brochure and spend a night in the hands of an expert.* Keiko turned the page. *Aromatherapeutic techniques to soothe and refresh the tired bodies of busy people—*

neck, shoulder, back, leg, and feet treatments available individually or in combination.

"It sounds lovely," she said. "I would like relaxing neck and shoulders, please, since I only sit at a desk typing."

"You can have a freebie when I'm finished with the course. And Sandra Dessing can stick it."

"Vinegar Tits?" said Keiko. "How is it her business?" She managed to get that much out before she gave up trying to keep her face straight and started laughing along with Fancy. "You know that's what Murray called her. I, of course," she clasped her hands under her chin and gazed upwards, "don't even know what that means."

Fancy finished folding and kissed the top of the bundle. "So," she said, "Murray Poole." She smirked at Keiko.

"So, Craig McKendrick," Keiko replied.

Fancy spluttered a mouthful of tea. "I thought Japanese people were meant to be dead polite."

"Can I ask a question then?" said Keiko. "Since I'm busted already." Fancy nodded. "What do you know about Murray's girlfriend?"

"Nothing," said Fancy, looking away. "I never met her."

"Oh! It wasn't a serious relationship then?"

"Can't have been," said Fancy.

"Only Malcolm said that Murray wasn't over her." Fancy was still staring at the cluttered sideboard. "Can I ask another question?"

"Absolutely," said Fancy, turning back to her.

"Why did Mrs. Watson's niece leave?"

"What? Dina?" said Fancy. "She didn't. Well, she stopped coming, I suppose. She never lived here."

"But the other girl lived here," said Keiko. "Tash. Did you live at Mrs. McMaster's house together?"

"Look," said Fancy. "What is this?"

"I don't know," Keiko said. "A puzzle. I'm trying to make sense of things Murray said to me."

"Ha!" said Fancy. "Good luck then."

"Can I ask one more question?" Fancy nodded. "What did Mr. Poole die of?"

Fancy blinked so slowly that it seemed she did not understand the words. "Nothing contagious," she said finally. "You're not worried about the flat, are you? He hadn't lived there since the boys were at primary school, anyway, when they all lived above the shop together. You're *not* worried, are you?"

"No, not about that," said Keiko. "Just ... there was no kind of mystery about him dying, was there? No kind of question or anything?"

Now Fancy turned her head slowly to one side while still staring hard, as though she would be able to get a clearer view of Keiko from the corner of her eye. It made Keiko think of dolls' eyes or a mannequins', and she shifted uneasily.

"What the hell has Murray been saying?" Fancy asked, but she went on before Keiko had a chance to answer. "No, of course not. I suppose it was a heart attack."

"You mean you don't actually know?"

"I'm trying to think if anyone said for deffo," said Fancy, screwing up her face in concentration. "I think we just assumed. He was that kind of age, you know, and ... Well, that kind of shape. I didn't get all the gory details," Fancy groaned. "God, speaking of which"—she fanned out the pile of red leaflets—"I really hope this works out, and I'm pretty sure it's not gonna."

"What's wrong?" said Keiko.

"It's costing a fortune, for a start," Fancy began. "And it's dead, dead hard, but mostly what's wrong is it's bloody traumatic and I'll be a basket case before I'm qualified." She shuddered. "It's the anatomy module."

"Cadavers?"

"God Almighty, no!" Fancy shrieked. "Practically, though. There's physiology and we had to watch these totally disgusting films all about the muscle groups and that." Her face was beginning to blanch, the skin around her eyes fading to pale yellow and her lips turning blue. She gulped and went on. "Then the practical work . . . we have to practice finding all the different muscles and tendons in each other, and you can really feel the gristle and stringy bits moving about." She stopped and bent suddenly at the waist as though hit in the back of the neck with a sandbag.

Keiko chewed her lip in silence. After a moment or two, with her head still between her knees, Fancy went on.

"And the worst of is that after I've been to the class all I can think about whenever I'm moving around is all these, all these . . . bits. It does my head in. I have to go and lie flat. Once I had to go to the sick room in the college, cos I could hear all the strings in my hips clicking when I was walking to the bus stop and I fainted."

"Isn't that going to be a problem when you're doing the treatments?" asked Keiko, struggling to keep the hoots of laughter tucked down inside.

"Just a bit," said Fancy, sitting up. She sighed. "As if Old Vinegar Tits Dessing isn't bad enough."

"You can practice on me," said Keiko. "I don't mind if you faint."

"You're a pal," said Fancy. She was fiddling with one of the leaflets. "Sorry I got weird about Tash. We *weren't* here at the same time, to answer your question. She came after me and she was gone before I got back. Usual story—hit sixteen and legged it."

"But she didn't return."

"Not so far," Fancy said, folding the leaflet into a fan. "She wasn't happy here. Didn't fit in."

"How do you know?" said Keiko. "If you and she didn't overlap. Oh! Of course, Mrs. McMaster."

"You're kidding," said Fancy. "Pet never speaks her name. Nah, just gossip. I know she had a fella," she paused, "a boyfriend, I mean, and a job—which was more than I ever got, but she didn't settle. Piled on a ton of weight before she left and that's usually misery, innit? Mind you, it was Etta McLuskie who said that and she's a total body fascist, so who knows?" Despite the price of the red paper and the extra toner, Fancy screwed the leaflet up into a ball, threw it up in the air, and flicked it into the wastebasket with a jerk of her head.

"No more questions," Keiko said. "I'm sorry I upset you."

"Me?" said Fancy, wide-eyed. "Why would any of that upset *me*?"

———

It was only three o'clock when she stepped out onto the street to go home, but the light, already milky, was about to begin its long fade and the town was hushed, balanced on the moment before the children were let out of school. They would be lining up right now waiting for the bell to release them like breath on a seed-head. Keiko smiled to herself and Murray, coming towards her, couldn't tell whether the soft light and quiet brought the smile or the smile softened the light and stilled the air around her. He was beckoning her across the road towards him when she noticed him at last.

"Do you still want to see my place?"

"Of course," said Keiko, asking herself when she had said so.

He led her over the corner of the Green to the pink building, fiddled with a padlock, and then hauled open a door, rattling it right to the end of its runners.

"This is your place?" said Keiko. She tried not to let her thoughts show on her face, but he guessed anyway.

"Nothing to do with me on the outside," he said, twinkling. "I just rent this one room from old man Byers. He owns it and the colour's his fault."

Inside, Murray punched numbers into the alarm panel and then flipped a row of switches.

Keiko stepped into the sudden dazzling light, taking in first size and emptiness, freshly whitewashed walls, enormous mirrors, and ranks of shelves. Then she noticed the canvas-covered hulks, six or eight of them, some on a soft green mat which covered half the floor, some resting on clean, grey-painted ground. She raised her eyes to question Murray's in the mirror opposite them.

He had taken off his coat and now he strode to the middle of the room, lifted one of the covers by two corners, and swept it up and off with one practised, billowing crack.

"Ta-da!" he said.

It was a motorcycle, black and silver, glittering under the lights. One of the old ones that looked more like a bee or a fly than something made by man. Before she could think of what to say, Murray had swept off another of the covers. This one was yellow with a duller gleam, just as old. The third—red, more paint and less chrome—shone as though water was flowing over it.

"They're beautiful," said Keiko. Murray was facing away from her, pulling the canvas from one too big for his matador flick. It was blue and very heavy. So heavy that the paint and chrome bulk of it

100

seemed almost to scrape the ground between its tyres, like an overladen hammock.

"Harley Davidson," said Keiko. Murray, rolling the canvas cover up in his arms, lifted his head to one-side with a slow wink and a click of his tongue. She looked towards the last of the shrouded shapes on this bare-floor half of the room, but he shook his head.

"It's not finished, not fit to be seen." He laughed. "Nobody's Bantam ever gets finished. It's traditional."

"Not finished?" Keiko echoed. "You mean you made these?"

"Kind of. Well, yeah, I suppose so."

"So *this* is what you do," she said. "You're really *not* a butcher."

"I'm really not," said Murray. "This is what I do. I strip them down and work out what's wrong, get new bits, and put them together again. Or hit things with hammers when I'm really stuck."

"No!" said Keiko. "How could you hit these beautiful things with hammers? "

"You like them, eh?"

"I love them. They're like sculptures." He frowned. "Don't you think so?"

"Oh, yeah, they're the best. Never thought of them as sculptures." His eyes met Keiko's in the mirror. "But I see what you mean."

Keiko walked over to him to look at the Harley close-up. She didn't have to be told not to touch it. "How old is it?" she asked.

"Knucklehead. Hard to say, really," said Murray. "How long is a piece of string? I'm going for early forties. See this?" Keiko craned her head to look down at it from the same angle as Murray. "That's a cat's-eye dash. See? The way the lights look? That puts it between 1936 and '46, but this tank had a two-light dash when it came, '47 to '54, so who knows? It's about two and a half years old, is the short answer."

He walked over to the black bike like a fly, Keiko following him.

"This one," he stopped, and arched an eyebrow at her. "Sure you want to hear any of this?" Keiko nodded. "Okay, this one's a Vincent Rapide, 1948."

"Really?" Keiko murmured, looking between the splendour of the Harley and this ungainly creature. "That's hard to believe. It's so much more primitive-looking."

Murray made a show of looking around to see if anyone had heard her. "Watch it! That's a British bike. Postwar austerity. They were short of tubing, so the thing about the Rapide is it's got no frame." He crouched down and started pointing. "The rear swinging arm pivots from the gearbox and rear suspension and the steering head for the front forks is attached to the oil tank." He looked up at her expression. "Not so keen on this one, eh?"

"No frame," she said. "Everything just bolted to everything else. Is it safe?"

"Completely," said Murray. "What's probably bothering you is the front forks." He pointed. "Brampton forks—pretty spindly compared to the rest of it."

Keiko nodded. "Yes, you're right. That *is* why it looks so peculiar—compared with the Harley."

Murray laughed at her again. "You'd get lynched if anyone heard you. Seriously, British bikes. I got into a bit of bother when some people heard I'd got a Hog. BSA parts guy in Liverpool assumed I would be selling up and came all the way up here to get first crack at the Gold Flash. Couldn't believe it when I said I was keeping both." Keiko shook her head along with him. "Speaking of the Gold Flash," Murray went on. "You haven't been introduced."

But Keiko held up her hands to stop him. His frown flashed down until she explained. "I'll forget if you tell me any more," she said. "A Harley Knucklehead and a Vincent Rapide. Cat's-eye dash, no frame, Brampton forks. We should stop there for today."

Murray relaxed completely into a smile again and began to replace the covers. Keiko wandered around the back of the room looking at the shelves of boxes and trays hoping that her *for today* hadn't been presumptuous.

"So many tools," she said. "And some of them seem to be exactly the same as the others."

"Well, you need different spanners for the American and the British bikes," Murray said. "Different everything."

Keiko looked at the five identical trays of wrenches and raised her eyebrows.

Murray laughed. "Yeah, okay," he said. "What's the diagnosis then?"

"Oh, you're a very sad case," said Keiko. "I diagnose … doing what you like with your own things in your own place and harming no one."

Murray laughed even louder. "You totally get it, don't you?"

"I can't work unless my printer tray is full and there's a block of extra paper still in its wrapper too."

"What could be more normal than that?"

Keiko waited for him to finish tucking the covers around the wheels and straightening the folds. "Murray," she said. "Can I ask a question?" She pointed to the canvases on the green mat. "Why do *these* bikes get to be on a rug?"

Murray laughed. "They're not bikes," he said. "Have a look."

Keiko didn't even try his flamboyant trick with the cover; she was too short and could never carry it off, might even fall over. She just bundled the sheet off the shape underneath, dumping it into Murray's arms as he came up to join her.

"Ah," she said looking at what she'd revealed. It was a weight lifting machine—multi-gym? Bench press? She knew the words but not the meanings. Next to that was something like the harness from a glider but without the wings. She frowned at them.

"Not sculptures? Not beautiful?" asked Murray. Keiko looked at him in the mirror. He was hugging the bundle of canvas and there were shadows on his arms showing the outline of the tendons between wrist and elbow. Under his rolled-up sleeves, his biceps and shoulders curved like sand dunes, separated by a dip that Keiko could have spanned with her hands. *Stock pot*, said her mother's voice in her head again. Keiko turned back to the equipment and bent her head letting her hair drop forward across her face.

"Have you ever done any weight resistance?" Murray asked.

"I'm a brain in a jar, remember?"

"I can't agree with you there," he said. "You're a fine feat of engineering. Well worth taking care of."

"That is the strangest compliment I've ever been paid," said Keiko.

"At least you're laughing," said Murray. "You didn't slap me."

"I'm catching it from you," she replied, thinking she had never known someone laugh at himself so much, thinking it was a very good thing in a man.

"Me?" said Murray. "I laugh so I don't scream." And, of course, saying this he laughed again. "You can use the gym equipment anytime you like."

"I wouldn't know where to begin," said Keiko.

"I can show you." He wasn't laughing at all now. "Then they can do their damnedest and it won't get them anywhere."

"Who?" Keiko said.

"All of them," he said. "They're no match for me."

THIRTEEN

Saturday, 26 October

FANCY DROPPED VIOLA OFF with Mrs. McMaster after breakfast and, leaving Keiko standing to attention behind the counter at Fancy That, walked to the top of the town. Pamela Shand in the Cat's Whiskers took a flyer, asked for a poster to put in her window, and made an appointment for a peppermint foot massage later that week. *All very well and good,* Fancy thought, *but you're an incomer and a bit of a flake, so that doesn't get me anywhere.* At the hairdressers, she went right inside (Janette Campbell had a tattoo and couldn't stand Mrs. Dessing) but she walked straight past Pet's flower shop, telling herself that she could give Pet a leaflet anytime and Vi wouldn't want her boring old mum cramping her style on her day at Granny's.

Meanwhile, Keiko took details over the telephone of two children's party cakes, booked out a Viking costume for the following weekend and, in the long pauses between calls on her attention, tried to work on her psychological profiles.

suggestibility/skepticism
suspicion/trust
innovation/conservatism
list making/actually doing something

She chewed her pen. You could buy profiling packages, but they were expensive. You could copy them, but everyone said the big professional profiling companies were crazy about protecting their copyright and always sued, every time. So she would make up her own.

If extraterrestrials contacted me, I would: see a doctor / call the police / find a priest / assume it was a hoax. She nodded. *If I read that tomatoes caused cancer, I would: stop eating them / stop eating them raw / eat only organic / keep eating them.* She tapped her pen on the paper. *If I found a letter not meant for me I would: tear it up / open it / put it back where I found it.* She crossed that out but immediately thought of another one. *If two young women had suddenly left my town, I would: wonder why / try to find them / watch my bac—*

She looked up as the shop door opened and Malcolm Poole sidled in.

"Malcolm, good morning," she called out, safe and powerful behind the counter. He looked up in surprise and then smiled, coming towards her in an awkward route around the obstacles of copy machines and racks of costumes.

"Malcolm, can I ask you a question, please?"

"Anything."

"What would you do if you read in the newspaper that tomatoes gave you cancer?"

"I'm not that keen on tomatoes," he said.

"Or how about this one?" said Keiko. "If extraterrestrials contacted you, would you call the police, a priest, or a doctor? Or the army?" she added.

"Is this a joke?" asked Malcolm. "Oh, okay." She watched him, her pen hovering ready to record his answer. "If extraterrestrials contacted me, I would … um … I would see what they wanted, I suppose. Get to know them." He stopped and dropped his head under Keiko's stare.

"Thank you," she said. "That was most helpful."

"Is that how you do it?" Malcolm said. "You ask a real-life question first and then you do your special ones?"

"N—" Keiko began, then checked herself. "I'm not supposed to reveal my methods," she said. "Now, what can I do for you?"

"Just some copies," he said slowly, bending one arm in towards his body and plucking some papers from inside his jacket. He laid them on the counter and smoothed across them twice with both hands. "I want these made into wee flyers. A5, I think it is." Keiko slid down off her stool and took them over to the machine, Malcolm drawing up beside her just as the first sheet curled out and she held it up to show him.

"That's perfect," he said, with such animation that she looked to see what was on the paper; she had thought at first glance it was just a list of products and prices. "You get it?" he asked, and she looked again as the next sheet glided out. "We do these freezer packs. A Lean Selection—loin chops, chicken breasts, and that; and a Busy Pick—stir-frying, minute steaks, all ready-marinated. But the budget packs have never sold well. And I think it's the name: Cheap

Cuts." He edged closer to Keiko to watch the flyers emerging. "So— here's the genius—I'm relaunching it, but I'm calling it the Hearty Appetite—good big rolled cuts for slow cooking, nothing expensive, sausages—nice big thick ones to go in a casserole. And I thought I'd put in one different thing each time, with a recipe. Oxtail maybe, or tripe. Try to get people interested again. You see, the way I'm thinking, if people think they're buying a budget pack it makes them feel poor and that makes them feel sad, but if they buy a Hearty Pack with my old-time recipe revivals they'll still be saving the money but they'll feel happy about it. It's all about getting people over the door, really. Youngsters, I mean. Kids that weren't brought up to go to the butchers. Once they're in the shop I can talk them round to anything—even tripe!—but it's getting them started. If I can just get them started, I'm laughing. And they'll be the better for it, get them off all those pizzas and God knows what."

He bent over slightly to look up into Keiko's face as she rolled the sheets up and snapped a rubber band around them.

"That's very kind," she said. "What's tripe?"

"Sheep's stomach lining," said Malcolm, "Delicious, really tender. You cook it slowly in milk and onions and it comes out like a kind of rich, creamy soup you eat with buttered bread." Keiko felt her face twist and she swallowed hard. "It's lovely," he said. "The butcher does all the cleaning and the first cooking in the shop, so all the stomach contents and juices are gone by the time you…" He stopped.

"I don't have a freezer," offered Keiko.

"Don't forget we're having you for lunch tomorrow," Malcolm said.

———

She hadn't forgotten. Of course, she hadn't. She had already bought a box of mint chocolates and a potted chrysanthemum to take with her. Fancy's advice.

"A bottle of spirits would be a scandal, see? Might as well take a five-quid baggie. Wine is like saying their own might not be worth drinking. Flowers are a bit too swanky, but a plant—better value and more boring—is fine. Chocolates are a tough call. Anything in a flat box with a ribbon is showing off, anything in a stand-up box, likes of Celebrations or that, is thumbing your nose at them. Safest bet is something minty—not nice enough to be a proper treat, but kind of saying it's a posh meal like you'd have mints after."

"Are you joking?" said Keiko. "Thank God Rosa took me out to the chippy."

"Yeah, just as well you've got me as a Sherpa."

"Eh?"

"Don't say *eh*. And don't say *God*. Or *chippy*. What's happened to you? If your English goes up the spout, who d'you think's gonna get the blame? Muggins here."

"*Muggins*?"

"Don't say that either."

"So many rules," said Keiko, rolling her eyes. "No one told me hostess gifts in Britain were such a minefield." She threw teabags into two mugs and poured over water from the kettle.

"This ain't Britain," Fancy said. "This is small-town east-coast Scotland. Cue the banjo music. You're in lonely country now."

"You are joking, aren't you?" Keiko said. "This is a safe place really?"

"What you on about?" Fancy said, rummaging in Keiko's cupboard for a packet of biscuits. "You're not making much of dent in this lot, are you?"

"They brought more," Keiko said. "I'm on about…" She didn't want to mention Tash again after the atmosphere last time. Fancy had denied it, but Keiko knew better. But she didn't have to mention Tash because that's not all it was. "Do you know Mr. and Mrs. Glendinning?"

"From the newsagents? Course I do. He's got a belly like a beach ball, she's got a face like a smacked arse. Why?"

"They said something I can't get out of my head."

"Oh?" said Fancy.

"They called me *this one*. But I thought the Traders had never sponsored a student before. So how can I be *this one*? It smells fishy."

Fancy sniffed. "Something does," she agreed. "No offence, Keeks, but you should get yourself over to McKendrick's and get a sink trap. Your drain's minging."

"It's been like that since I got here," Keiko said.

"Probably something in U-bend," Fancy said. "If you get something hard stuck, it clogs like nobody's business. You need to get Malcolm or Murray up and see."

"Murray," said Keiko, then flushed as Fancy arched an eyebrow. "Malcolm wouldn't fit under the sink."

"Good point," Fancy said. "You forget once you're used to him."

Sunday, 27 October

She made her way towards the Pooles' house at noon with the mints and chrysanthemum, passing the Bridge Hotel, crossing the street of big houses, through the street of small houses with chain-link fences and cars parked at the kerb, onto a quiet curving road where bungalows were set on green cushions of lawn that rose plumply from the pavement's edge. *Where is everyone?* she wondered. It was a pleasant autumn day, but the streets were deserted. Where were all the people?

A few at church; a few more at golf; many still in bed or at least in dressing gowns, with the Sunday papers almost read and the third pot of coffee brewing. And upstairs at the ironmongers five of them were sitting round a table, no armchairs and crystal glasses of wine this morning, big decisions to be made today.

"Is it my imagination," Mr. McKendrick was saying, "or am I still sensing cold feet here?"

Kenny Imperiolo, Etta McLuskie, Sandra Dessing, and Iain Ballantyne looked at one another, waiting for someone to speak first. At last, Sandra shook her head.

Mr. McKendrick saw the shake and pounced. "Good," he said. "Maybe you can talk round this lot, then."

"It's just…" Sandra began. "We do see, of course. And we do all feel the same way you do. We're Painchton folk. And we agreed we had to do something. To get fresh … whatever. It's just that…"

"Keeping up with the cover story isn't easy," said Iain Ballantyne. His hand shook a little as he fiddled with his pen.

Mr. McKendrick noticed but his expression showed nothing. "I wouldn't say *cover story*," he said. "I'd say what we told the open meeting was for general consumption in the meantime. But come the hour, come the day, they'll all be invited to the party. There's plenty for everyone."

The silence in the room lasted even longer this time and was only broken when Mr. McKendrick spoke again. "And as to confidentiality," he said, "it's Etta it's weighing on. The rest of us just need to hold firm."

Etta McLuskie turned and looked out through the net curtains to the bay window above the Pooles'.

"Is Grace coming?" she asked. "I'd be happier to hear from her own lips that she's still with us."

"She's busy today," said Mr. McKendrick. "Making Keiko Sunday lunch."

———

A figure, garbled by the frosted glass, came towards the door and opened it. Murray. He started to hold out both hands towards her but then stepped aside, smoothing his hair back, gesturing for her to come in. Mrs. Poole was standing at the back of the hall, silhouetted in a doorway by harsh kitchen light and looking strange without her overall. She said hello and then went back to her cooking with a distracted glance over her shoulder. Murray led the way into the living room, where Malcolm was halfway across the thick carpet towards the door.

He stopped as they entered and turned back. "You found us okay, then," he said, his voice seeming more muted than ever, as if soaked up by the room, by the plush upholstery, textured wallpaper and velvety rugs, thick drapes hanging snugly ceiling to floor, creamy net muffling the window.

Keiko sat down in one of the bulbous armchairs, sliding herself backwards until she rested against its cushions with her feet off the floor, and looked between the two brothers, smiling what she hoped was a friendly smile. Malcolm had settled into another chair and sat back, his head cradled, his feet firmly planted and a hand clasping each of the arms.

Murray perched on the sofa, making no impression on its muscular cushions, his head bowed under the lea of the headrest. "So," he said. "Wild weekend so far? Ready for more?"

"It's good to see you here at last," said Malcolm. "We've left it too long."

"Not at all, please don't mention it," said Keiko. "It hasn't been a time for visiting."

Malcolm glanced towards the fireplace, where framed photographs were arranged, and in the lull that followed, Keiko went to look at them. There were studio portraits of babies and little boys, a wedding photograph of a young Mrs. Poole in a bushy veil and tight dress, and a black-and-white picture of Mr. Poole, half-hidden by a spray of freesia. He was in a suit and tie, with Mrs. McLuskie's chain of office around his neck and he must have been a huge man, since the chain that reached to Etta McLuskie's waist was stretched wide across his suit shoulders and rested between his lapels.

He explained Malcolm, Keiko mused, but not Murray. Except that the face in the picture, when she looked closer, was an unsettling mixture; the peaked hair and lifted eyebrow of Murray along with the high plane of cheek and long stretch of jowl of Malcolm. It was as though the shadow of each of their faces lay in his wherever she was not looking, and when she shifted her gaze to catch it, it shied away again.

Beginning to wonder if she was being rude, she turned back to the room. Both boys were staring at her. Both looked away as Mrs. Poole come in with a tray of glasses. Keiko picked up the chrysanthemum and chocolates and went towards her.

"Just a ... a wee something," Keiko said.

"Have a cheesy biscuit," said Mrs. Poole over her shoulder, as she went back to the kitchen. "Have a Twiglet."

Keiko sat back down, alternately sipping and nibbling. Murray went back to his perch. Malcolm heaved himself up and came towards the table, bent over with a sigh, and swiped a glass up off the tray. He raised the glass to Keiko and emptied it into his mouth.

"Time to carve," he said, "and make the gravy," and started moving towards the kitchen.

Murray tucked his feet up and wrapped his arms around his legs. "Thanks for coming," he said.

"Of course," said Keiko. "Thanks for asking me."

"I didn't. I wouldn't," Murray said. "But I'll take care of you now you're here." She smiled uncertainly at him. He shuffled closer to her and set his chin on his knees. "So," he said. "What can you tell me about tea *now*? Have you been doing your homework?"

Keiko laughed and bent her head. She had indeed spent a good few hours scouring websites and explaining it to herself in the bathroom mirror.

"First of all," she told him, "you must appreciate that the tea ceremony is not really about drinking tea..."

She was still laying out specks of detail when Mrs. Poole put her head round the door to summon them to lunch.

Rich smells were wafting from the kitchen and Keiko stopped dead in the dining room doorway, making Murray walk into her back. He steadied himself with a hand on her shoulder then left it resting there.

"It's not..." she began, then swallowed and started again. "I mean—have you made milk and stomach soup?"

Malcolm looked back at her for a moment before understanding spread over him. "Oh, tripe!" he said. "No, tripe's not really a Sunday lunch kind of—"

"God almighty, Malcolm," said Murray, moving his hand down around Keiko's shoulder to hold the top of her arm. "Jesus Christ!"

Keiko went to her seat with her head bowed, but when Mrs. Poole set a wide plate of dough-coloured liquid down in front of her, she could not help herself turning to check.

"Cream of mushroom," Malcolm said, and she looked quickly down again, shaking out her napkin.

When Keiko and Murray were halfway through their soup, Malcolm placed his hands flat on the table and got to his feet, taking his empty plate away. After a moment the door swung wide and he came back in, carrying a dish at shoulder height, gazing at it as he paced towards the table and set it down. On it lay a squat roll of meat, bulging between laced strings, one end sliced thickly and fanned out in glistening slabs. Waves of steam curled off it, rising to settle on the glass droplets of the centre light, turning them misty. Murray left and came back with a tray of vegetable dishes and then slid into his seat to wait in silence with the women until Malcolm returned from a second trip. He put a long, shallow jug down at Keiko's side and waved his hand over it, scooping billows of steam towards her face.

"Gravy," he said and padded around the table to his chair. Keiko nodded towards the plate of meat.

"What is it?" she asked.

"Loin," said Malcolm. "I boned and rolled it myself. Listen to this." He picked up a spoon and tapped the meat three times. It made a spitting, rattling sound like a well-wrapped parcel. Malcolm beamed and tapped it again. "Crackling, see? Crisp as anything. Mind and don't pour your gravy on it." He slid a knife under one of the slices and lifted it towards to Keiko's plate, stretching right across the table, his face bunching between his shoulders, holding the slice of meat steady on the blade with one pudgy finger.

Keiko thanked him.

"*Crackling*'s another word for *skin*," Murray said. "You don't have to eat it. You don't have to eat any of it if you don't want to."

Keiko looked at Mrs. Poole and Malcolm, then back at Murray again. "It all looks lovely," she said.

Mrs. Poole served herself with meat and gravy, potatoes and vegetables, and began to eat staring straight ahead. Murray, working with the delicacy of a watchmaker, excised the rim of fat and crackling from his one thin slice of meat. Malcolm, just as intent, loaded potato onto the back of his full fork and ran it round the edge of plate like a shovel until it was soused in gravy, then he lifted it to his mouth with his eyes shining.

When lunch was over, Murray took Keiko out into the back garden. She picked her way around its edge and looked at the last of the flowers in the neat strips of earth, feeling one cheek almost tingle under his gaze. Mrs. Poole, standing at the sink in the kitchen, watched her until the window steamed over and then bent her head to the full basin and began to work at the dishes with firm scouring strokes.

"What are these called?" Keiko asked, pointing to a cluster of pale fleshy-leafed plants with seed heads floating above them. Murray shrugged.

Malcolm opened the back door and stepped down onto the path. Leaning against the wall, he bunched his arms up in front of his face with his hands cupped and a second later a puff of smoke flared.

"It's a sedum," he said, taking a skinny cigar from his mouth and nodding towards the plant. He must have been watching them, seen her pointing. The sweet smoke drifted just as far as Keiko before it dispersed, and she leaned forward slightly to catch more of it. "Butterflies love them," Malcolm added.

Keiko turned to share her smile with Murray, but he waved a hand in front of his face to blow the smoke away. Her smile faded.

"Dad used to be driven demented with the caterpillars in his lettuce," Malcolm went on, "but he loved the butterflies so much he wouldn't rip out the sedum."

"He sounds like a lovely man when you speak about him," Keiko said.

Murray turned right round and looked over the fence into the garden next door.

"Of course, it's no problem now," said Malcolm. "We don't grow any veg now." He pointed towards a patch of grass that Keiko could see was greener than the rest.

"Your father was the gardener, then?" she said. "You're not? Even though you know the names?"

In the kitchen, Mrs. Poole had wiped a clear patch in the misted window and was watching the three of them, stuffing a cloth into a wineglass and screwing it round.

"Malcolm's a butcher," said Murray, turning back at last. "That just about sums it up as far as Malcolm goes. Not much of a one for lettuce, really."

Malcolm said nothing. His little cigar stuck out of his face like a teaspoon in a bowl of pudding.

What am I doing here, Keiko asked herself, *when none of them really wants me? Murray is not himself when he's with them. I cannot eat enough to please Malcolm. And as for her . . .*

"I'm a terrible guest," said Keiko, looking up at the kitchen window. "I should be helping your mother." She turned from both of them and walked away.

Mrs. Poole, grinding away at the glass, flinched and looked down as Keiko entered the kitchen. Then cradling the glass carefully in her hands, she turned away to let the broken pieces fall into the pedal bin, throwing the cloth and its danger of tiny shards in after it.

FOURTEEN

Tuesday, 29 October

DR. BRYANT PURSED HIS mouth in time with his breathing as he read, making his pale moustache bristle. Keiko looked away to his over-stuffed bookshelves, every volume well-worn and topped with a coxcomb of markers. At exactly head-height opposite the chair where she sat, where every visitor to the office must sit, was his own PhD thesis, *Undergraduate networks and their effect on employment choices*, and two editions of the book it eventually became: *In with the in-crowd: student networks and the workplace*. He cleared his throat and she turned in time to see him suck the ends of his moustache back down with a wetted bottom lip.

"Food," he said. "You're quite settled on that then? It's going to be rather a straitjacket down the line."

"I think passions run high around it," said Keiko. If he knew she was thinking of Pamela Shand and her dairy crusade he would swallow his moustache. "Investment. Engagement. And since I'm keen to have the subjects return several times, I need to interest them."

"The perennial problem," he said, lying back in his chair. "The undergraduates do get sick of spending lunchtime in the lab and—as I'm sure you'll appreciate—the staff projects come first." Keiko inclined her head. "Of course, there was a time the typical Japanese student would have funding to pay subjects as part of their award, and nothing says it like cash as far as the first years go. They would let you drill into their skulls for the price of a pint. Still, I'm sure you'll sort something out." He bared his teeth at her.

"Yes, indeed, I'm most hopeful," Keiko replied.

———

"I hate him," she said to Fancy, kneeling in front of the washing machine to haul out wet clothes. "His moustache looks like biscuits."

"How?" Fancy asked. "Round and crumbly? Choc chips in it?"

But Keiko wouldn't smile. She peered inside the machine to check it was empty and slammed the door.

"Does he keep it in a packet in his desk drawer?" Fancy persisted.

"Bampot!" Keiko said. "No, just the colour. And his trousers are too loose and his shirts are too fitted."

"Oh yuk, yeah, I hate that," said Fancy. "So it looks like they're falling down?"

"And you can see the shape of his stomach between his hip-bones—" Fancy had paled. "Sorry, sorry!"

"No, it's okay, just that that's one of my worst bits, that pelvic girdle," Fancy said. "Pelvic! *Girdle!*" She shuddered. "Anyway, *bampot*? Where are you learning these words? Is it Murray?"

"Oh no," said Keiko. "Murray is even stricter than you. He's got big plans for me."

"What does that mean?"

"He wouldn't tell me. It's starting tomorrow night, but that's all I know."

"So who taught you *bampot* then?"

"Wee boys on the bus. But what am I going to do if I can't get any subjects?" she said, shoving the basket along the floor to the dryer. "My pilot's ready to run, but my whole idea needs me to have the same people over and over, and it won't work any other way."

"How come?" said Fancy.

"Oh, knowledge units as artifacts in the construction of blah, blah, blah," said Keiko, then seeing that Fancy was really listening, she tried again. "I test their judgements on a set of questions. I report the results of the test back to them—who believed what, how many people rejected what kind of thing—and then I run the test again to see if hearing the results of the first one changes what they think. Does that make sense?"

"Cool," said Fancy. "You're totally messing with their heads."

Keiko stopped stuffing clothes into the dryer. "*Do not tumble dry*," she read from a label. She scrabbled about inside the drum, pulled out another bundle and shook it. "I could get around having different people every time if I profiled every time before and after the test, but it's still not going to show the long-term changes and it would make the sessions twice as long, so I would need to pay them more and I don't have any money to pay them anyway." She found another label and read it. "*Do not wring. Do not tumble.* Well, how am I supposed to dry it then?" she shouted.

"That's nothing," said Fancy. "I had this black and white stripey dress once, that said *wash dark colours separately.* Do they have to know what it's about?"

"Sorry?" said Keiko.

121

"The people who do your experiments. Do they need to know what it's all about? Because if not…"

"No, they *mustn't* know what it's about. That's why researchers always use first-year students, before they learn anything." Keiko finished loading the dryer and stood up with her wet bundle of leftovers at arm's length.

"Well, what's the problem then?" said Fancy. Keiko shook her head and waited. "You're looking for a bunch of people who don't know anything?" said Fancy. "God's sake, Keeks, open your eyes! Look out the window. You're smack in the middle of Know-Nothing Central."

"Painchton people?" said Keiko. Her heart had leapt, but it just as quickly sank again. "I don't think so."

"Why not?"

Because they are secretive, she thought. *They hide things and don't answer questions.* But she couldn't say that to Fancy, whose face clouded more than anyone's when questions were asked and would never admit it.

"It's about food," she said, at last. "And the people here don't seem… normal about food."

"Normal? How?"

"Well, Malcolm and his crackling and Mrs. Sangster with her ham. Mrs. McLuskie said she'd give me a jar of goose fat."

"You noony!" said Fancy. "Course they're normal. They're just not Japanese."

Keiko considered being offended but the relief at the possibility of having subjects won in the end. She threw her armload of laundry up in the air and caught it again. "Do you really think they would do it?" she said. "I suppose some of them would, wouldn't they. I know *you* would."

"I don't want to," said Fancy.

"The experiments aren't physical," Keiko said.

"I know," said Fancy. "But I don't want to be one of your guinea pigs because I want to know what it's all about. That Dr. Biscuit-tash is no bloody use and you'll need *someone* to talk to." She dipped her head slightly. "I'll concentrate dead hard."

Keiko threw down her bundle onto the table and seized Fancy's arms in her damp hands, making her yelp at the cold. "You really want to help? You can proofread my stimuli, check my English. You can look over my experimental design."

"I wouldn't understand *that*," Fancy protested, but Keiko puffed in scorn.

"You understood it already. In two minutes," she said. "You, with your eagle eyes to find the logical flaws on laundry-care labels. It'll be a skoosh for you."

"Okay," said Fancy. "But *a skoosh*? First thing, if I'm in charge of your English, is you have to stop listening to little boys on buses, right?" Fancy walked over to the window and peered down. "And there's posts down there to put up a drying rope. Just ask Mrs. Poole for the key."

———

So when Keiko heard the shop awning being rolled up at the end of the afternoon, she trotted downstairs and popped her head out of the street door to see Murray in shirtsleeves unhooking the pole from the winding mechanism.

"Hi," she called. Murray turned suddenly and Keiko ducked away as the brass hook on the pole swung towards her.

"Christ, sorry!" Murray said leaning the pole against the window and reaching out to her. "Are you okay?"

"Don't kill me yet," said Keiko. "I haven't even asked my cheeky favour."

"Well, whatever it is, the answer's yes," Murray said.

Mrs. Poole came outside. "Murray? What are you doing leaving that up against the glass? Oh. Hello." She stopped with the pole in her hands and nodded towards Keiko. Murray let his hand drop from her shoulder.

"I have two favours to ask you, Mrs. Poole," said Keiko. Malcolm appeared in the doorway. "From all of you, one of them."

"Come away in, then," Mrs. Poole said, but she stayed where she was, with the pole held in both hands in front of her chest so that Murray and Keiko had to squeeze past her in the doorway.

"Two favours," said Keiko again. "The first is that you would all consent to act as subjects in my experiments." She waited. "Just answering questions for ten minutes."

Murray looked at his feet. Malcolm, who had moved back behind the counter, sprayed cleaning liquid onto its marble surface and, ripping a swathe from a roll of paper towel, began to wipe it in slow careful strokes.

"Psychological experiments?" asked Mrs. Poole.

"Well, yes, but nothing personal, you understand, the same questions for everyone." Malcolm sprayed the scales and wiped them, the numbers jumbling on the display as the weight of his hand crossed back and forth.

"What is it you're wanting to find out, then?" asked Mrs. Poole. Murray shifted.

"I'm testing your response to various scenarios," said Keiko, her happy mood dissolving.

"Like those inkblots," said Malcolm.

"Nothing so intrusive," Keiko said. "Nothing so revealing."

"I don't mind," said Malcolm, looking at his mother.

"No," said Mrs. Poole. "I'm sorry, dear, but I don't think it would be a very good idea."

"And besides," said Keiko. "It's anonymous. All the responses are logged with just a number. Complete anonymity guaranteed. No one would ever know—me included—what you'd written."

She had never thought of Mrs. Poole as wearing cosmetics, but now she saw the lipstick and rouge jump out as the colour behind them drained away from the woman's face.

"Mum?" said Malcolm.

Mrs. Poole attempted a smile. "You're a city person, Keiko," she said. "And it's different in a big city, but in a wee place like this, there's no such thing as anonymity."

"Mum, you've got totally the wrong end of the stick here," Malcolm said. "It's nothing to do with … anything. It's made-up things."

"It's very easy," said Mrs. Poole, "when you live so close, to … encroach."

"I wouldn't dream of encroaching," said Keiko, rising up a little. "Malcolm is right, Mrs. Poole. I have no interest in anything personal."

"Malcolm was telling me you'd been asking Murray who lived in the flat before you," said Mrs. Poole.

Keiko did not take her eyes away from the woman, but she got the impression that both boys had become very still.

"What's the other favour?" Malcolm asked.

Keiko smiled her relief. "Ah yes, I wanted to ask if I may hang my washing in the yard on a rope. Is there a key to the back door?"

Malcolm crumpled up his handful of blue paper towel and turned away, scraping it over his hands. Murray glanced at his mother.

"Something wrong with the tumbler?" asked Mrs. Poole.

"Oh no, no. Most generous and very handy. But for a few things, delicate things that can't be put in it?"

"But would you want your delicate things hanging out in the yard?" asked Mrs. Poole, flicking a look at Murray.

"Delicate fabric, I mean," said Keiko, blushing. "Rayon dresses, and woollen, not..."

"They should have thought to give you a rack," Malcolm said.

"Of course, these houses all had dollies," said Mrs. Poole in a louder voice. "In the kitchens. And I could never see the sense in it. Always taking things down and putting them up again if you were cooking. Malcolm's right, a handy wee rack over the bath is the easiest thing. I have a spare one, dear. I'll pop it up to you." And with this series of informative little remarks and jabs of kindness, she drove Keiko out of the shop and closed the door.

It wasn't until she was standing outside that she remembered the smell in the kitchen. She should have asked for the plumbing work to be done. That would have got Mrs. Poole down from her high horse. But she did not go back in.

———

The phone was ringing when she got back upstairs.

"Right," said Fancy over the line. "Pet wants to know whether it's one by one up at your place or if she can just take questionnaires to the Guild with her and dish them out and if so when. And Kenny said to her to say to me to say to you that he'll do the golf club and the bowling club, and I'll give Vi a note to ask if the teachers will do it, which is another nine, so that's nearly a hundred before you've put up a single poster. Ta-da!"

"Are you sure no one minds?" said Keiko. "Mrs. McMaster and Mr. Imperiolo?"

"They're gagging for it," said Fancy. "You have to make your own fun in Painchton, Keiko. Nothing ever happens here."

FIFTEEN

Wednesday, 30 October

IT WAS A DARK afternoon, the clouds looking as though only the chimney pots and old aerials were stopping them from settling down on top of the roofs like a shroud. Keiko stood looking out of the kitchen window at the dim outlines of the yard, her breath fogging the view even more, and her chest started to rise and fall again just from thinking about Mrs. Poole and the scene in the shop the previous day. *Encroaching!* Malcolm hadn't minded. She tried to remember if Murray had said anything or if his mother had silenced him completely.

And why shouldn't she wonder about her flat? Why shouldn't she think it was strange that such a comfortable place lay empty? Where was the harm? *A three-inch tongue can kill a six-foot man, Keko-chan,* said her mother's voice in her head. But how could a woman be so very concerned about her own privacy and then tell tales of her sons in front of a stranger? "Malcolm was telling me you asked Murray," said Keiko under her breath in a sly, mincing voice, nothing like Mrs. Poole's.

She picked up the bundle of slips she had printed out and put them on the shelf in the hall to remind her to take them to Fancy.

And anyway, she told herself, it couldn't be the thought of being talked about that was worrying Mrs. Poole, because even the assurances of anonymity did nothing to help. If anything, the idea of it being anonymous was what had—

Yes! It was when Keiko talked about writing anonymously that Mrs. Poole had gone grey behind her make-up and had started babbling about city-dwellers and washing lines. *No such thing as anonymity in a small town*, she'd said. But no one else in this small town was worried. They were delighted to be part of the fun, and Keiko looked forward to them all trooping upstairs to help her. She hoped Mrs. Poole saw every single one.

Then, thinking about the visitors she was expecting, Keiko sniffed the air, grabbed her wallet, and trotted across the road to the ironmonger.

It was just as old-fashioned as the butchers, and had probably been there just as long. But where Pooles' Butcher had white tiles and shining steel, McKendrick's Ironmonger had old wood and brass. The shelves and counters glowed, polished by hands and time, and the cupboard handles and label-holders on the shelf edges gleamed in the soft light from dusty bulbs.

She did not know where to begin to look for what she needed. Every shelf and stand was packed. Boxes of nails and screws and hooks, bottles of solvent and cleaner and oil, rolls of wire, binfuls of brooms, and stacks of charcoal in paper sacks with sewn ends. And hanging from the ceiling, mobiles and wind chimes and hammocks and even a small canoe, so high Keiko could not see how it could ever be brought down if someone should want to buy it. While she was gazing upwards, a voice startled her.

"Taking up kayaking, are you?"

"Craig!" she said. "Here again."

"It's Wednesday," Craig said. "Traders meeting and Uncle Jimmy needs my vote."

"I was planning to replace my genkan—uh, the doormat," Keiko said, but remembering the letter FOR YOU and loath to disturb it again, she hurried on, "but really what I want is a sink trap and some kind of unclogging solution."

"Ew," said Craig.

"Yes," said Keiko, blushing.

"End aisle," said Craig, coming out from behind the counter and leading the way. "Listen," he went on, when they were standing in front of an array of plungers and rods and bottles of terrifying acid with warnings in red. "Are you okay over there? Apart from the crappy old pipes? Okay with the neighbours?"

"I'm fine," said Keiko. "Why?"

"Oh, just, I know you've been round at Murray's and been to the house and …"

"They are very kind," said Keiko.

"Listen, you don't need to do the nice wee girlie bit with me," Craig said. "If you're not okay, just tell me."

"I have no idea what you mean," said Keiko. Then, seeing that he was about to give up, she gathered her courage and went on. "But I know that people—nice wee girlies—have gone away from here, suddenly."

"Exactly," said Craig. "My cousin Nicole used to live over the shop." He pointed upwards. "But not anymore. And she never really said why she was leaving except for this one time when I was joshing her about her deadbolt and chain, she mentioned 'that creep across the road.'"

Keiko felt her scalp prickle. "Your cousin went away?"she said.

"Forget it," said Craig. "I shouldn't be saying this at all. We've all been pals since we were wee."

"But your cousin," said Keiko. "Is she all right now?"

"Look," Craig said, "I didn't mean to frighten you."

Blindly, Keiko grabbed for one of the little mesh discs hanging from the display rack and picked up the bottle with the biggest, reddest warning. She carried them back towards the register and then stopped dead in her tracks.

Mrs. Poole was standing at the counter with a white plastic clothes drier in her arms, her face as stony as Keiko had ever seen it, her eyes flat and dead even as she met Keiko's gaze.

"I never heard you come in, Mrs. Poole," said Craig.

"I get that sick of my own shop bell dinging all day," said the woman, "I'm a dab hand at getting by them." She held the rack out to Keiko. "This is for you," she said. "You might as well take it with you."

"You told me you had one at home," said Keiko.

"I remembered wrong," said Mrs. Poole. "Here, take it."

Keiko took the rack and scuttled out, forgetting to pay for her trap and solvent. There were three of them now. Tash, Dina, and Nicole. Three girls gone, up and left. She closed her front door behind her and pushed the button to double-lock it. But as soon as she did, her heart started to pound. Instead of feeling safe from intruders behind her locked door, she felt ... trapped.

Perhaps she should go to the department every second day instead of once a week. Perhaps being in this little town was beginning to affect her reasoning. And perhaps she should try the first-year students after all.

But Fancy had said all those people were willing to help her. Settled, dependable people right here. She could rattle through her study at double-speed. If she could just forget Tash and Dina. And now Nicole. If she could just forget them, stop seeing trouble where there was none, and do what she had to do.

Dumplings over flowers, said her mother's voice. *Forget all this imagining and take what you need.*

———

Sometimes, all three Pooles left when the shop closed and the building was still, the stone walls and floors not even creaking around her. Other times just Malcolm and Murray set off, and then Keiko knew that Mrs. Poole was down there. She felt through the silence for some trace of another person under the same roof, but the only clue of Mrs. Poole's presence would come hours later, when the shop door opened and shut below the bay window and quiet heels moved away up the street.

Once before, *two* sets of steps had left. Leaning sideways from her chair, Keiko had seen Mr. McKendrick step neatly behind Mrs. Poole and guide her towards the inside of the pavement with one gentle arm. Today for some reason, through the quiet, Keiko thought he might be there again. *Intuition,* she wrote on her scribble pad. *Would you trust intuition,* she typed, *for personal matters only / for financial decisions / for questions of health?* Then she held a finger down on the arrow key until she had deleted it.

———

Downstairs, Jimmy McKendrick blew steam across the surface of his coffee and cocked his head up to one side. "Is she always this rowdy?"

Mrs. Poole smiled vaguely at him. She was sitting at the desk in the back office, both hands cradling a cup and saucer on the bare surface of the desk. "Aye, but she's up there," she said. "She studies at the table in the big room, keeps a good eye on things."

"And I hear she's quite taken with Fancy Clarke, despite our warnings," Mr. McKendrick went on. "You wouldn't think they'd have much in common. But then they're young, the pair of them. And Murray too, eh? And Malcolm," he added.

"And Craig when he's here," said Mrs. Poole. Mr. McKendrick looked sharply at her. "She's thick as thieves with Craig."

"A nice crowd of young ones," said Mr. McKendrick in his jovial voice. "Where would we be without them?"

Mrs. Poole lowered her eyes and kept them down. Mr. McKendrick, looking at his watch, gave an ostentatious start and swigged the rest of his coffee. "Are you coming along then?"

"I've got paperwork," said Mrs. Poole, glancing towards the filing cabinet, neatly locked.

Mr. Poole seemed to rouse himself at that and look around the office for the first time at the bare desk and shut drawers. "Gracie, Gracie, you didn't need to be sitting here like a tea-party at the manse. You should have just cracked on with it all, I'd have been just as happy sitting quiet and watching you. More than happy." He leaned towards Mrs. Poole, considering saying more, but he caught the slight droop of her shoulders and sat back. "Or I could help, even. Duncan always took care of the books, didn't he?"

"No, I'm fine," she said. "We did it together. I know what I'm doing." Then she rubbed her hands and spoke, suddenly rather brightly. "But it'll all be there in the morning. I think I'll come to the meeting and put in my tuppenceworth."

Mr. McKendrick groaned. "Take a ticket and get in the queue." And the awkward moment was gone.

———

An hour later in the function room of the Covenanters', Mr. McKendrick was in shirtsleeves with his tie loosened, wishing he'd never stopped smoking.

"Hanging baskets and benches," said Rosa Imperiolo, snorting. "We'll fair stand out in a crowd with that."

"A bandstand, a bandstand," said Mr. McLuskie. He had been saying just that for several minutes now.

"And where would we get a band, Andrew?" asked Mrs. McMaster. "How much does it cost to hire them and how many people actually want to listen to them?"

"A brass band in a bandstand is an *English* thing," said Mrs. Sangster, as though that should settle the matter.

"Good point, Anne," said Craig McKendrick, "Uncle J, how much would it cost to build ourselves a wee crag and have a bagpiper on top of it?"

"You'd be able to see up his kilt," Fancy said.

Mr. McKendrick frowned.

"There's a bandstand in St. Andrews, and that's Scotland right enough," said Mr. McLuskie.

"Hey," said Fancy. "Wouldn't a bandstand be the perfect place for kids to go and take drugs when it's raining?"

"Order, order," said Miss Anderson, but she stopped at a look from Mr. McKendrick.

"Yes, order," he said. "We've agreed on a roasting pit, a clay oven, and banqueting tables. That's the main thing."

"How come?" said Fancy. "Why is that the main thing?"

"Miss Clarke," said Etta McLuskie, "with all due respect, you are a newcomer to Painchton and you'd do better to listen and learn than question every last word."

"Yeah, Fancy," said Craig. "You can't learn by asking good questions, you know."

"Let's call it a night," said Mr. McKendrick. "The only other outstanding business is a name for our launch event."

"Why don't we just call it the Jimmy McKendrick Experience," said Mrs. Watson, downing the last of her martini. "Bring in the drug-shelter crowd."

"I was against holding these meetings in a bar, Mr. Chairman," said Miss Anderson, under the laughter. "But you know best."

While people were struggling into their coats, Fancy stood on her chair and addressed them, waving little slips of paper.

"The first dry run of Keiko's profiling questionnaire starts Monday at ten," she shouted. "Upstairs at the Pooles'. Come to me for the details." She hopped down again and—stepping out of the way of Miss Anderson, who had come to inspect the chair and was wiping its velour seat with a tissue and muttering—caught Mrs. Poole's eye for a moment. She was looking at Fancy without expression and although her jaw was clenched tight making little pouches at the sides of her mouth, the quick movement of her chest showed that she must be breathing hard though her nose. Suddenly she winced and stretched her mouth wide open for a second to release the pressure, giving Fancy the swift and unpleasant impression that she was screaming. Fancy looked away and immediately broke into a smile at the sight of Mabel Watson, who was clapping her hands together and bouncing up and down.

"I can't wait, Fancy," she said. "I love doing them, even if it's just for a catalogue, but this!" She sighed, clasped her hands to her heart in a gesture of bliss that was only half-joking.

"I would have thought I could count on you for a bit of loyalty," Andrew McLuskie muttered as he helped Etta on with her coat. She turned to him in surprise.

"Why?"

"What do you mean 'why'?" he said. "You're my wife."

Etta McLuskie stopped buttoning her coat and stood looking at him. This was a thought she rarely allowed to form while he stood in front of her. She was delighted to be Mrs. McLuskie, of course, wife of a prominent businessman, provost of the burgh, but when Andrew himself was right there...

"And," he went on, "because you certainly have mine. No matter what you're up to and even when you go ranting on at Fancy for no reason."

Although he had stepped back from her, Etta could still smell him—that warm sweet smell that hung around his clothes and his hair—and she thought she could see a faint powder dusting his hairline and caught in his brows. He would never open a second branch and start a chain, she knew that now, would never stop getting up at four in the morning and spending the day in the bake room, would always smell of flour and yeast and sugar and never see the need to wash it off himself.

"Have your what?" she snapped, brushing the shoulders of her coat as though he spread flour from his fingers like a human dredger.

"My loyalty, Henrietta," he said. "More than you know."

"What's that supposed to mean?" Etta said. She had a high colour and always wore green basecoat, so she was safe from untoward flushing, but she could not help her eyes growing round. How could he know anything? What made him think for a moment there was anything *to* know?

"Don't look so worried," he said, for he was fond of his wife, proud of her, and liked life easy. "Like I just told you, you can count on me."

"My God," said Craig quietly to Fancy. "It's supposed to be us young ones that fall out and have a go at each other in the pub. Look at Etta and Mr. Staypuff. If looks could kill!"

"Craig," said Fancy, catching another glimpse of Mrs. Poole, who hadn't moved although the room was emptying from around her like water draining from a bathtub and leaving her stranded. "Do you ever think there must be more going on round here than what your uncle tells you? The *state* everyone's in."

"Everyone who?" said Craig. "What do you mean?"

"Oh. Well, nobody," said Fancy, turning away from Mrs. Poole again. "Yeah, you're right. Nothing."

SIXTEEN

The security light clicked on most nights, flooding the back of the house and the patio with a white glare that banished sleep as instantly as snapped fingers. Roaming cats set it off, tree branches in high winds, even a hedgehog one time. They had learned to ignore it and so the delivery went unwitnessed. The letter didn't make itself known until the next morning. Then there it was, propped against the kitchen window, held in place with one of the large polished pebbles from the water feature, facing in, the front of it—FOR YOU—pressed against the glass, ink bleeding a little from the dew. And inside: THERE'S A NAME FOR PEOPLE LIKE YOU. THERE'S A WORD FOR IT. I WILL TELL THEM ALL.

As soon as the house was empty for the day, it was taken upstairs, up the Ramsey ladder, to the attic, into the eaves. It was filed between the pages of a weekly magazine, fifteen years old, one of hundreds, yellowing. It was put towards the back of the issue too, with the dress patterns and recipes, the black-and-white pages, where no one flipping through to see the articles and photographs would ever go looking.

Monday, 4 November

The first knock came half an hour early. Keiko was ready though, a pile of questionnaire papers and a mug of biros set out in the living room, the whole bottle of chemicals tipped down the kitchen sink and a vanilla candle lit, the door to her bedroom and bathroom safely closed.

She stepped back when she saw Malcolm Poole standing there but managed, moving sideways, to turn it into a gesture of welcome.

"I'm not coming in," he said, his voice booming around the high empty landing. *The creep across the road*, Craig's cousin had called him. "I just wanted to warn you to close your back windows. Mum said your bathroom window was open."

"Yes," said Keiko. "I open it every day. I didn't realise. Please make my apologies to your mother." Could a creep be female? She could ask Fancy.

"No," said Malcolm. "Just this morning, I mean. I'm doing kidneys."

"Oh yes?"

"Cleaning them. And they smell a bit."

Keiko took a little sniff, feeling her lip curl and Malcolm, looking up briefly, noticed and smiled.

"I haven't started yet," he said. "They're lovely, once you've soaked and blanched them. But they do smell at first, so I do a whole load of them together and freeze them down. I'll go up to McLuskie's after this and tell the girls to take their aprons in off the line." He seemed to be waiting for a response, looking from side to side at the edges of the doormat.

"You're very thoughtful," said Keiko. "So … you'll be busy in the little house in the yard this morning."

He looked at her properly then, closely into her face for the first time, then shook his head, and made a massive movement of relaxation, leaning against the doorframe and throwing one leg in front of the other. He almost filled the doorway, an iceberg in his white overall and white boots, leaving just a sliver of space that she would have to jump through if she decided, for some reason, that she needed to get past him.

"No," he said. "I do everything in the back of the shop. We don't really use the slaughterhouse anymore. Hey!" he said, suddenly loud, the sound echoing. Keiko could feel her heart banging. "Hey! I'll bet you've never had a steak and kidney pudding."

"You're right," said Keiko.

"I'm going to make you a steak and kidney pudding. I only make pies for the shop, of course. They keep better. A pudding has to be made and cooked in a oner, unless you're very careful, but there's nothing like it. I'll use ox kidneys. Beef suet. You know, suet is kidney fat. Makes sense, eh? All these old recipes."

"You're very kind," said Keiko again.

"You've no idea," said Malcolm. "Wait until you taste it. I'll need to come up here to boil it, though. Easiest all round and let's face it, the smell of it cooking is half the pleasure. You name the day and I'll be here."

Keiko's thoughts raced. Then she said, "Come and cook it for lunchtime while I'm running my dry run. And all the people will smell the lovely smell and come downstairs and buy a pudding to take home!"

"A pie," said Malcolm, slowly. "Puddings don't keep to sell in the shop." There was a pause. "So you're starting your work this morning?" he said. "I saw the sign downstairs."

Keiko made a gesture of mock panic, but her eyes were dancing. "You could come in and be the first person," she said. "Your mother seemed a little … but it's really nothing to be concerned over."

"I'm already the first person," said Malcolm, smiling down at his feet again. "Alien spaceships and killer tomatoes. Been there, seen it."

Keiko laughed in surprise. "I forgot!" she said. "Yes, of course. But Fancy's taken away my aliens. She said they were too distracting. She's very firm."

Malcolm uncrossed his legs and, bending one knee slightly, pushed himself up off the doorframe and stood straight. "Right. You go and push back the frontiers of knowledge, and I'll go and blanch my kidneys." He turned and moved away.

———

Mrs. Watson, it turned out, was the first person. She knocked on the door at quarter to ten, and then put her head round and called along the passageway.

"Shout at me, Keiko my darling, and tell me to get out and come back when you're ready, but you'll have to shout at me, for I'm that excited I can't wait."

"Mrs. Watson," said Keiko coming along to the door. "You're going to be so disappointed. It's so very dull." Mrs. Watson's head disappeared and when Keiko opened the door, she was standing half-turned away on the mat. "But how can I shout at you, when I am so excited myself?" She took Mrs. Watson's arm, walked her to the living room, and settled her down at the table.

"Now," she said in a high voice. "Please read the instruction page and then ask me if anything is unclear."

"Och, away," said Mrs. Watson. "You tell me about it yourself. You'll know it all back to front."

"No, I can't," said Keiko in her normal voice. "Everyone has to have exactly the same introduction so that I don't give more information to some and not others by accident and confound my methodology."

"'Confound your methodology,'" echoed Mrs. Watson. "Your mother must be so proud." She nodded conspiratorially and turned her eyes to the page while Keiko sat in an armchair and pretended to read. When Mrs. Watson looked up, she leapt to her feet.

"Is everything is clear? Good. If everything's clear, please go on to the sample question. We can talk through this one."

Mrs. Watson nodded with shrewdly narrowed eyes and read aloud: "*Mark the line to show how strongly you agree with the following statement: There's no smoke without fire.* You know what this is like? This is just like a séance. Make the mark wherever you feel drawn to make it. Let yourself be guided, empty your mind."

"Well," said Keiko, but bit her lip as Mrs. Watson marked the paper with a languid hand.

"What would you do if people started coming out with real messages," she said. "Could you use that?"

"Do you believe in the spirit world, Mrs. Watson?" Keiko said, sidestepping Mrs. Watson's question. She hadn't put anything in the profiler about such paranormal things, since most British people were supposed to be so rational that they would scoff. And she didn't want to offend the others.

"I'd like to," said Mrs. Watson. "I sometimes feel as though there's someone nearby. Don't you?"

"Not really," said Keiko, although she shivered as she spoke. "But I've never lost anyone close to me."

142

"And long may that last," said Mrs. Watson. "I don't recommend it."

Keiko hesitated. Was Mrs. Watson thinking of her niece Dina? If she was speaking Japanese she would have been able to tiptoe up to the questions, but in English the intrusion would be—

The doorbell rang.

"You run along," said Mrs. Watson. "I know exactly what to do. You concentrate on the newcomers."

It was Mr. McKendrick, dressed in a dark suit and black tie. He checked his step for a moment in the living room doorway when he saw Mrs. Watson bent over her paper, and looked rather ostentatiously at his watch.

Mrs. Watson raised her eyes without raising her chin, regarded him over the top of her spectacles. Then taking in his black tie she lifted her head. "Of course, it's Tam Cleland's funeral this morning," she said. "I couldn't believe it when I heard he was gone."

"Aye, he looked such a tough old goat," said Mr. McKendrick.

"But Mrs. Mackie was saying there's nothing at the church."

"No, it's the crematorium, just. And no do."

"Crematorium!" said Mrs. Watson. "He'll be turning in his grave." Then she put one hand over her mouth to smother the giggles.

Keiko got Mr. McKendrick settled and took him through the introduction, Mrs. Watson looking up at intervals and nodding. He viewed the mug of biros sternly and reached into his pocket for his fountain pen.

"*No smoke without fire,*" he said softly. "*No smoke without fire.* Would that be barbecue smoke? Because this was supposed to be about food, if you remember."

"The food questions will come later," Keiko said. "This is just smoke."

"You're not allowed extra instructions, Jimmy," said Mrs. Watson. "It wrecks the methodology."

Mr. McKendrick turned slightly away from her and addressed Keiko. "It's true, you know. I was a volunteer fireman in my younger days. Even when there's only smoke there's either just been a fire or there's going to be a fire. Or if there isn't, it's because someone sees to it that there isn't. So would that be a yes or a no?"

"It's not a clear yes or a clear no," said Keiko. "You need to mark the line to show what mixture of yes and no. More yes? More no? Can't say?"

"Just let your mind drift, Jimmy," said Mrs. Watson, without looking up.

"And if you don't know, if you can't say, you leave it blank?" said Mr. McKendrick.

"No," said Keiko. "If you can't say then it would be in the middle. Neither yes nor no. You see?"

Mr. McKendrick nodded, kindly. "Aye well, I suppose that's why you do a dry run, isn't it after all," he said. "To iron out these wee hitches. You'll need to ditch this one before you get going for real, eh?"

Keiko smiled tightly. "Mr. McKendrick," she said, "remember these answers are strictly anonymous. You should use one of my pens instead of yours, so that all the sheets are the same."

Mr. McKendrick moved as though to put the lid back on his pen, then catching sight of Mrs. Watson staring at him, he set the nib down on the paper.

"I've nothing to hide," he said, "and I trust you."

SEVENTEEN

By evening, she had twenty-five completed papers and was sitting at her desk rewriting the instructions—*Do not confer during the experiment* and *Please do not discuss your answers with anyone*—when Murray arrived, dressed in running clothes.

"How did it go?"

"Tremendously well," said Keiko, flopping back down onto the sofa. "But I'm exhausted. Twenty-five people and it might have been more, except there was a funeral."

"Tam Cleland, yeah," Murray said. "So now you know all there is to know about the people of Painchton?"

"More than I expected to," said Keiko with a laugh. "I know that Tam Cleland's daughter-in-law is to blame for such a small funeral and she's 'been through the house and stripped it bare.' Miss Morrison told me all about it."

"Miss Morrison." He nodded slowly. "Okay. You're fine with her."

"What do you mean?"

"You wouldn't understand," Murray said.

"Who am I *not* fine with?"

"Well, there's me," he said, grabbing hold of her hand and pulling her to her feet. "I didn't tell you in case you tried to get out of it, but I reckoned tonight would be the perfect time to get started on you." Keiko opened her eyes wide. "At the gym." He looked appraisingly at her and she felt her neck lengthening, her chin lifting. "I know you never came round like I said, but have you got any workout clothes?"

———

It was only a few yards round the corner to the workshop, but still Keiko let go a breath of relief when they arrived without being seen. She felt fluorescent in the unaccustomed pale clothes and her feet, darting in and out of view, drawing her eyes down towards the tennis shoes, were as white and bulky as puffballs. She had imagined the people in the flats above the shops leaving their armchairs and padding to their windows to see her, drawn from the television by something even brighter.

"New trainers, eh?" said Murray with a small smile as he stooped over the padlock at the workshop door. "What brought that on?"

"I'm going to be very fit and healthy despite the steak and kidney pudding and the apple pie and the cheese scones," Keiko said, stepping neatly around the question.

"You don't have to, you know," said Murray, clicking switches off and on until the right selection of spotlights left the motorbikes draped in darkness and picked out the exercise machines. "Just say you're not hungry."

"But they're all so kind," said Keiko. "Mr. McLuskie brought me a pie the size of a tyre when he came today." Murray said nothing. "And a big bowl full of extra … whatever it was that was in the pie."

What Mr. McLuskie had told her was in the pie was squashed flies.

"A fly pie, hen," he'd said. "Also known as a flies' graveyard. Fine old traditional names are dying out. Like blood oranges. Ruby red oranges they call them now, and these would be Abernethy slices, I suppose, but the Japanese are not a squeamish people, I know, so fly pie it is. And I've put a wee bowl of extra filling in your fridge for you to make toasties. I know you've a toastie-maker in that kitchen of yours because I gave it myself."

"Thank you," said Keiko, meaning it to encompass everything.

"Och," said Mr. McLuskie, flicking his hand that way that had seemed so rude to her at first, but which she was getting used to. "I promised Etta I'd do my bit, keeping you from fading away, wee thing that you are, so far from home and you must wonder what the he—eck you're doing here, eh?" He sat down heavily, one hand on each knee, dropping backwards into the seat with a sigh. As he did so a gust of warm sweetness rushed towards Keiko's nostrils and, as she bent over him to explain the questionnaire, was she only imagining that she could taste it, like a cloud of icing sugar hanging in the air around him?

"*No smoke without fire*," he said, stifling a yawn.

"Would you like a cup of coffee, Mr. McLuskie?"

"Och no, I wouldn't want to put you to it," he said. "But if the kettle's going on anyway, I'll keep you company. Tea, mind, not coffee. Nice change to be asked too. Etta's up to high doh this weather and I can raffle."

"I'm sorry?" said Keiko.

"My wife is not herself these days," said Mr. McLuskie. "Anybody's guess why not. So it'll be a wee treat to have somebody make me tea."

"And a slice of pie?" said Keiko, holding it up to him as though she had made it and was tempting him.

"I shouldn't really," he said. "I brought it for you."

"But I like that," said Keiko. "I mean, the way you appreciate your own ... Mrs. Imperiolo took me out for fish and chips, and Malcolm is doing something with suet and kidney for me."

"Fish, eh?" said Mr. McLuskie. "Well, at least she never had you at that so-called Indian or the so-called chink—uh, Chinese, I beg your pardon."

"I don't understand you, Mr. McLuskie," Keiko said. He had followed her through to the kitchen and was watching her setting out cups and plates, the questionnaire forgotten in the other room.

"See, me? I'm a traditionalist," he said.

"I am very glad to hear it," said Keiko. "You will be an important part of my study. I cannot tell you why, but I assure you."

"I make plain and pan, morning rolls, bridge rolls, cottage, farls and batch. Mince pies, steak pies, sausage rolls, bridies. All with Malcolm's special mixture. Honest food from right here."

"And you make the pastry to go around?" said Keiko.

"Aye, from the finest flour, butter, lard, and salt, with these two hands," he said. "And then there's fruit scones, drop scones, tattie scones, soda scones; never mind the teacakes. And speaking of cakes! Vanilla slices, cream horns, French fancies, coconut rocks, your fly pie there, fruit slab, Chelsea buns, yum-yums ... you name it. Of course I could fling together a hundred kinds of muffins, wee bits of dried blueberry and choc chips that might as well be rabbit pellets for all the taste of them. Of course I could be shovelling out croissants and cookies and rocky road—a child of five could. But I am a Scottish Master Baker, see? And there's nothing can go inside a panini that can't go in a good morning roll."

Keiko formed her lips to attempt a reply but could not think of anything. Mr. McLuskie sailed on.

"But the thing is, Imperiolo's café and chippy and Indian and chink—Chinese—you'll forgive me, hen—have got folk from all over the country, down south, *France* even, raving on about how marvellous it is, all over that Internet, and then there's McLuskie's Bakery and … not a sausage! Nothing! My customers just aren't the type to…"

"To post online reviews," said Keiko.

"Exactly! It doesn't mean I'm not as good a baker as Kenny is a whatever he calls himself these days. He hasn't shaken a basket of chips for twenty years. I'm still up at four every morning with my yeast. He just sits in his office at his computer."

"He's probably writing reviews," said Keiko. Mr. McLuskie crashed his cup down into its saucer. "I didn't mean that," she blurted. "I was only joking."

"Ho ho!" said Mr. McLuskie. "You've hit the nail on the head, hen."

"I was joking."

"Oh no, you've cracked it."

"Please!"

"I am going to make you a cake," said Mr. McLuskie, standing up. "Royal icing and sugar roses, because you are a wee sweetheart. You've made my day." And he left, the questionnaire forgotten.

———

"Keiko?" said Murray. "You're miles away."

Keiko blinked and smiled at him. "Sorry," she said. "I was thinking about Mr. McLuskie."

"I bet nobody's gone off in a dwam about him for a while," Murray said laughing.

"I told him something about someone and I shouldn't have."

"Who?" said Murray, staring hard at her.

"Kenny Imperiolo."

Murray considered this for a moment and then shook his head. "You're better off staying away from both of them," he said. "Best thing."

"I can never tell whether you're serious or joking," said Keiko staring at him.

"I'm never joking," Murray said. "Remember? I only laugh so I don't scream. Right then." He walked towards the gym machines, but Keiko put out a hand to stop him.

"I'd like to learn another bike first, please," she said.

"Gold Flash," he said, once again doing the trick with the tarpaulin that made him look like a children's conjuror and made Keiko want to giggle. "BSA Golden Flash. 1950 to 1961. So called because of the colour. Although they did do them in black and chrome too—pretty rare. I've had a set of black front forks and mudguards for years, probably never get a hold of the rest."

Keiko listened and nodded but could not see in this machine anything like the glamour of the Harley or the spidery elegance of the Vincent. This one seemed to be nothing but trouble. Murray told her about the innovative plunger suspension, which wore out too quickly, and the brakes not strong enough to allow a sidecar. She could feel a frown form on her brow, too tired to take a scholarly interest in such a catalogue of failures. She was glad when he stopped talking and threw the cover back over the bike again.

"Right. No more skiving," he said. "What do you weigh?"

"Ah, fifty kilos," said Keiko. "I don't know in stones."

"That's okay. Metric's best," Murray said. "Do you mind?" He walked towards her and put a hand around her upper arm, warm thin fingers reaching right around it. "Flex," he said. Keiko tensed the muscle with all her strength, one foot lifting slightly off the floor in its weightless trainer.

"Go on, flex your bicep," he said sternly.

"I am flex—" she started.

Murray smiled. He squatted down in front of her, cupped one hand around her right calf, lifted the leg from the floor and laid the other hand flat against the front of her thigh.

"Point your toe," he said, curving his palm around her thigh as it stiffened. Keiko wobbled and put one hand on his shoulder to steady herself. She stared down at the top of his head, at the glint of his eyes through his lashes.

"Flex your foot up?" he asked quietly, and she did, feeling his hand squeezing the small ball of her calf. She relaxed and Murray set her foot gently back down. She took her hand away from his shoulder and crossed her arms as he stood upright and looked down at her.

"It's a miracle," he said. "You have absolutely no muscles. How do you walk around?"

Keiko started laughing. "You're very rude to me," she said. "Maybe I'll go home and eat my pie."

"Multi-gym, leg press, incline bench, treadmill, cross-trainer," said Murray—cursory, so different from his caressing descriptions of the motorcycles—then started to work at the fastenings on one of them. The contraption, which looked to Keiko like the mechanism of an elevator, had no obvious place in it for a human body to be added.

"Weight-lifting?" she asked. He smiled at her over his shoulder but said nothing, spun the loosened weights free, and stacked them in their place in the pile. Then he straightened and held up his hands to Keiko, showing her two absurdly tiny weights like doughnuts in his palms.

"No," she shouted. "I am not as feeble as that."

"Nothing feeble about it," said Murray. "You have to start from where you are. This is where you are."

He settled Keiko into the contours of the machine, nudging her feet into place and pushing her head gently back into the rest, then swung the bar over her, talking her through the exercise in minute detail. When she tried it, just as he said, shoulders down, stomach tight, her eyes opened wide with surprise at the resistance of the silly little weights. She felt the tendons on her neck and heard her ears crackle.

"Won't this make me look like those orange ladies?" she asked, releasing the hold. "They're very ugly."

"How can you ask questions when you're breathing in?" said Murray watching her arms.

She stopped and replaced the weight. "But will it?"

"No," said Murray. "They increase the weight. You're going to up the repetitions. You'll look more like me than them. As long as you do what you're told. Do you trust me?" She nodded. "Will you do what you're told?" She nodded again.

"And if I eat the pies? Will it cancel out?"

"You can't eat the pies," said Murray. "You don't want to, do you?"

"Malcolm wants so much to show me the pudding."

"You don't need to worry about Malcolm," said Murray. "I'll tell him to leave you alone."

Keiko lay down and moved the weights again. "Have you always done this?" she asked him. "Have you always been …" She couldn't think of a way to say it that wouldn't make his eyebrow lift that way it did. "Only Malcolm and your father are so different."

"Dad?" He was surprised, she could tell, but not shocked, not horrified. Perhaps Malcolm was right and it wasn't Mr. Poole who had made Murray so sad after all.

"I saw his photograph," Keiko reminded him. "And I just wondered if his health, you know, was what made you decide to be the way you are and why Malcolm didn't … join you."

"His health?" said Murray.

"I assumed it was a heart attack," Keiko said.

"I think most people did," said Murray, nodding.

"But it wasn't?"

"Not so far as I know."

She sat up and hooked her arms over the bar, slouching. "Is that the puzzle you talked about?" she asked him.

"Not exactly," Murray said. She started to speak again, but he talked over her. "Like I said, you wouldn't understand. And even if you did, you wouldn't believe me. And even if you bel— Keiko, have you ever heard the expression 'What you don't know can't hurt you'?"

She blinked. That was more or less what she had decided. For almost a week she had refused to think of them. She had not said their names even to herself and had not used the phrase that scared her even when it was only inside her own head. But all the words came back to her now, as clear as ever. *Dina, Tash, Nicole. The missing girls.*

"I've heard that forewarned is forearmed too," she said to Murray.

"You don't need to be either. I won't let anything happen to you. And to get back to your question—yes, I've always been 'the way I am.' I've never been 'like Malcolm.'"

He watched over her through one complete set of exercises, moving her between machines, hardly looking at her, speaking a word or two at first and then less and then nothing, moving her feet and hands instead, pressing her into place.

And as she went through the movements in the lengthening silences, the clack of voices from the long day gradually left. She came back from the nest of words and paper around her head, back down into her body, the sound of her breaths, and the feel of her hot hair.

She blew upwards at a stray wisp, and Murray's hand came into view. He swept the strand off her face with his fingertips and tucked it behind her ear. Then with one finger he continued to trace around her jaw, wiping the trails of sweat gathered under her chin. She stopped moving.

"You're finished," he said. "Well done." He straddled her legs facing away from her and unbuckled her ankle straps. Keiko lay still, letting her blood stop pumping, looking up at the dark web of metal rafters above the lights and the odd shapes suspended there.

"What are those?" she said.

"What?" said Murray. She pointed, wincing a little as she stretched her arm. "Man, I forgot they were still up there," he said. "Nobody much ever comes in here but me."

Keiko screwed up her eyes, trying not to let the low-hanging lights dazzle her, and peered harder at the pale, delicate, structures, perfectly still, throwing a tracery of shadows onto the ceiling.

"But what are they?" she said. "Airplanes? Toys?"

"Birds," said Murray. "Models."

"Why put them up in the roof space?" Keiko said. "You can hardly see them."

"I used to be quite into them for a bit," said Murray. "I shoved them up there because they were taking up too much space. Couldn't store them any other way. They're kind of fragile." He held out his hands to her. "Come on, keep moving or you'll feel rough."

Keiko took his hands and sat up slowly, feeling the blood surge into her head, then swung her feet to the floor. He handed her sweat suit top to her, and she took it and held it under her chin, hoping that the pale colour would take some of the flood of heat out of her face.

"Put it on," said Murray. "Don't get cold."

"What now?" she asked.

"I'm going to start my workout," said Murray.

"What will I do?"

"You need to get home, straight into a warm bath." He turned away from her and starting to swing his arms around.

Keiko stood up quickly and pulled her top on. "Of course," she said. "I've been taking up all your time."

"I enjoyed it," he said. "But you mustn't get cold. You have to go."

———

She lay in the bath for a long time, gazing up through the steam at the patterns in the rough-textured paint on the ceiling, the getting-familiar faces and animals. The silence was heavier than ever after the flat being full of voices all day, and the smell of the new paint and new grout on the tiles was strong enough in the steamy air to drug her. She felt herself begin to drift.

So many things he had almost told her, so many things she didn't quite know. He had said she wouldn't believe him. *Why do you think you're here?* he had asked her. *Who are these people?* her mother had said. *How long will this one last?* said Mr. Glendinning. *Tash piled on the pounds,* said Mrs. McLuskie. *Dina couldn't manage a grape,* said Mrs. Watson. *I've never been like Malcolm,* Murray said. *Stick with me.*

She sat up with a jerk, making the water suck and slosh against the enamel sides of the bath, making it even harder to hear anything through the empty silence all around.

EIGHTEEN

Tuesday, 5 November

SHE WOKE AT THE first chirp of her alarm clock as usual, tried to reach out to stop the noise, and couldn't. It bleeped on at her—ten, twenty times—until she managed to swing her arm out of bed and clump it down on the snooze button. She stretched out her legs and both calf muscles snapped into cramps, skewers of pain shooting down to her feet and drawing her toes up like bird claws.

"He's killed me," she said, and even her jaw ached as she whispered.

After ten minutes, she rolled onto her side, pushed herself upright with both hands and stood up in five slow cranking movements. Ignoring the tightness across the base of her spine and the stabbing pains deep in her buttocks, she lumbered a stilted, Frankenstein walk towards the bathroom, her breasts crooked in her elbows to stop them moving.

"You're mad," she told her reflection in the mirror. "Steak and kidney pudding wouldn't have done this to you."

Once the shop was open but well before she expected her first subjects, she went downstairs, two steps to each stair all the way, alternating which of her trembling calves she trusted with her weight. Murray was waiting behind the counter, laughing.

"I heard you coming," he said. "How are you?"

"Greatly deceived in your character," said Keiko. "You are not a kind person."

Mrs. Poole emerged from the cold store, carrying a tray balanced on each hand. Murray stepped out of her way. "Son," she said, and held one tray out towards him. He took it in his fingertips, looked at it briefly, and put it down beside the rest of the bacon behind the glass, slotting it deftly into its space. Mrs. Poole hefted the other tray, piled high with chops, into both hands and jostled it into place with a rattle, then slapped the chops back into a neat heap and tucked in a few trailing edges.

"Can I help you with anything, dear?" she said.

"Ah no, thank you so much," said Keiko. "I just came to speak to Murray." She smiled towards Murray, who said nothing. Mrs. Poole went along the corridor out of sight.

"The thing now," Murray said, "is not to give in. Don't give up. If you do a short workout tonight, you'll be ten times better tomorrow. If you do nothing tonight, you'll be like this for days."

"Hmm," said Keiko. "A great deal of information, suddenly. There was no talk yesterday evening of this pain or what to do about it."

"Trust me," said Murray. "You trust me, don't you?"

"Of course I do," Keiko said. "You strap me to tables and hurt me. Why wouldn't I?" She heard the sound of Malcolm's breathing coming towards them and turned to greet him. Malcolm, like his mother, was carrying two gleaming trays, his piled with sausages. He didn't ask Murray to help but laid one tray down while he put the other into the window and turned back, puffing. There was a single space left in the display, right at the front of the case next to the glass, and Malcolm had to lean out over the counter to drop the tray into it. He seemed to roll slightly on his belly as he stretched, and Keiko, seeing Murray look down and raise his eyebrow, thought Malcolm's feet must have lifted off the floor. A pale high cleavage had formed at the open neck of his shirt as he squashed himself against the marble. Keiko looked away towards his hands, but the pile of thick sausages and Malcolm's greasy fingers clutching at either side of it seemed just as much something to avert her eyes from and so she looked back at Murray, who was studying the ceiling and moving his lower jaw from side to side with his lips slightly parted.

"What time tonight?" she asked him.

"About the same. Sevenish," said Murray.

Malcolm, the tray fitted in as well as he could get it, backed himself upright again and wiped his face with the back of his hand.

"Murray tells me you don't fancy steak and kidney after all," he said. "You should just have told me yourself." He swept his coils of fringe off his face and, although they fell back again, Keiko was startled to see a peak of hair just like Murray's, briefly revealed by that Murray-like gesture. "Although," he went on, "it seems a shame, when you haven't even tried it. Seems a shame to come all this way round the world and not try the things you find there."

"She didn't come halfway round the world for your steak pie, Malcolm," said Murray, rolling his eyes at Keiko.

"Pudding," said Keiko and Malcolm at the same time, and they both smiled.

"You know, you're right?" Keiko said. "You *are* right. I would scoff at someone who came to Tokyo and only wanted McDonald's. I'd love to try it."

"If you're going to eat stodge, you won't be able work out after," said Murray.

"Even if I have it at lunchtime?" said Keiko. "Surely it'll all be worn off?"

"You've obviously never had steak and kidney pudding," said Murray, half under his breath. He gestured at Malcolm. "And you can see for yourself, it doesn't 'wear off.'"

Keiko blinked, but Malcolm either hadn't heard or didn't mind. "Well, what's the first day there's no workout?" she asked.

"Sunday," Murray said, not meeting her eye.

"Sunday," said Malcolm, with a wide smile. "Traditional."

"And I'll ask Fancy and to come and join us." She glanced at her watch, wincing as she twisted her wrist—time to get to work.

The ache in her legs eased over the course of the morning as she trotted back and forth to the front door, but the less-used muscles sat bunched and stiff, ready to catch her out. A spasm at the side of her jaw when she reached across to fill the kettle, and when she started to squat to tie her shoelace before going out at lunchtime, the stab came back as fierce as ever to her buttock. She tried bending from the waist instead, but her stomach muscles sang as she crunched them. When she tried to stand straight and bring her foot up to her hands, a ripping sensation spread through her thigh, brought her foot down hard to the floor, and kept her crouched there for a moment until the shaking stopped. In the end she put first one foot then the other up against the radiator and hunched over them with her other leg half-bent beneath her. This gave her a feeling like twisted candy wrappers crinkling in the back of her neck, but no real pain.

As she straightened, slowly, carefully, both hands in the small of her back, she saw Janette Campbell, the hairdresser, who had just finished the last of the morning's questionnaires, staring at her from the living room doorway. Keiko smiled and gave the radiator an absent-minded polish with the palm of her hand.

"I did a new workout last night, Mrs. Campbell, and I feel as if I've been pressed under a road-roller."

"You want to be careful," Mrs. Campbell said. "Even at your age. Although, you could always get Fancy to fix you. D'you know, she did my scalp three days ago, and I can still feel the benefit."

"Did you enjoy it?" said Keiko.

Mrs. Campbell pursed her mouth slightly and leaned closer. "It was hardly decent, it felt so good," she whispered. "She's got a talent."

"And was she…" Keiko stopped. She wanted to ask if Fancy had been sickened. "Does she talk to you, or is it quiet?"

"She chatted away quite the thing before and after," said Mrs. Campbell. So maybe Fancy was getting better? Or perhaps there simply wasn't anything upsetting under a scalp? "But very professional during the actual *treatment*," Mrs. Campbell went on, with a kind of defiant emphasis on the last word. Keiko felt sure, although she couldn't see how, that it was Sandra Dessing who was being defied.

"I hope it's a great success. I hope nothing or nobody spoils it for her," Keiko said, her heart hammering as she dipped this first toe into unknown waters.

Mrs. Campbell nodded twice with mouth pursed and eyebrows raised. "I think we both know who we're talking about, don't we?" she said. "So we needn't say any more."

Keiko nodded back at her, pursing her own mouth just as tightly.

"So," said Mrs. Campbell in a leave-taking voice, "you be careful with these aerobics."

"Of course," Keiko said. "But it was weight machines, actually."

"Oh no!" said Mrs. Campbell. "No, I'm serious, Keiko. You shouldn't go near anything like that without supervision." She darted glances all around Keiko's body as if, now that she knew, she expected to notice broken bones poking against her skin.

"I have supervision," said Keiko and decided to repay Mrs. Campbell with a gift of new gossip. "Murray was showing me what to do. He's got a gym set up over in the building, at the back." She waved her hand as best she could towards it.

"Oh," said Mrs. Campbell, the single syllable dropping cold into the air between them, unmarked by any swoop of interest. "I see."

Keiko ran over her words again in her mind, wondering if she had made some mistake, if she had caused some offence with her bad English, like when she had said *I don't care* instead of *I don't mind* to a visitor in high school and made the teacher angry. She couldn't think of anything and smiled uncertainly at Mrs. Campbell.

The woman's face had turned blank. Like Mrs. Poole's face. Like Craig's face when he'd been overheard. Like Malcolm's face in the van that day and Mrs. Watson's face through the window. Keiko had never seen so many blank looks in her life before. *The inscrutable Scots,* she thought to herself. *Why did nobody warn me?*

"I'm sorry," she said.

"What for?"

"I've obviously said something—"

"Away," said Mrs. Campbell, but she still was not smiling. "I'd better be going, anyway. I only had twenty minutes between ladies."

What am I doing? Keiko longed to shout after her. *What is it that I keep doing? If I should stay away from all the friendly people, and I offend all the others without even trying, soon there won't be anyone left for me to talk to.*

And suddenly not having to talk to anyone seemed like a treat she could afford. There were forty completed papers now and, even with the confounding effects of Mr. McKendrick, that was surely enough. So she perched at her word processor and typed. *The pilot study is now complete, thanks to the most generous help of those who participated. The timing of the next exercise will be announced in due course.* She centred the text, clicked it to bold, set the font size to sixteen, and clicked the print icon. When the warm sheet had curled out of the printer, she signed her name at the bottom, took it downstairs, removed the old sign, and pressed the new one firmly to the blobs of Blu-Tack on the door. Only then did she see that she had written her name in a neat block of kanji characters and not the string of English letters they would be expecting.

Tough, she thought. *Hard cheese.*

———

But cancelling the afternoon's slots meant she didn't get the chance to trickle away any more of her bad mood on casual meetings before Murray arrived in the evening. She was still irritable when she saw him jogging towards her, his breath pluming. Not only was it a colder evening than the one before, but it seemed darker, as though the season had lurched forward in just a day.

"How cold does it get here?" she asked.

"Not much worse than this," said Murray, lifting his head and looking around himself. "It gets wetter, and the wind makes it seem colder than it is, but the dark's the thing that bothers people if they're the sort to get bothered."

She waited for him to undo the padlock, peering up past the yellow blear of the street lamps at what seemed to her like already perfected blackness.

"How dark does it get?" she asked.

Murray laughed. "It doesn't get *darker*," he said, shaking his head in small movements but keeping his eyes on her face. "It just gets darker earlier and earlier and stays dark later and later. In December it gets dark at four and isn't light again until eight."

"No worse than Tokyo."

"And people moan like you wouldn't believe."

"But we have lights," said Keiko, frowning. "What's their problem?"

"Exactly," said Murray, and he held the door open for her to pass into the workshop. Just like that her crossness was gone. Two peremptory questions about her precious host country, one gratuitous mention of Tokyo (*They don't care, Keko-chan*), some out-and-out criticism of the locals … and Murray didn't mind any of it.

"Can I ask you something?" she said.

"Depends what," said Murray.

"What do you think of Janette Campbell?"

Murray blinked, but he thought about it before he answered, took it seriously. "Don't know her all that well," he said in the end. "Don't have any plans to know her any better."

Keiko nodded. "That's an admirable attitude," she said. "I should be more like that. Not let people nibble at me."

"Yeah," said Murray. "The world would be a better place if everyone was a bit more like you and me." Keiko laughed. "Painchton would anyway." He stretched and turned, smiling, towards the machines and the mirrors. "So …"

"I can't remember much," she warned him, smiling back.

"You're not doing the same tonight anyway," he said. "Tonight you're just going to stretch your muscles to loosen them off."

"But that's exactly what you said last night," said Keiko. "You said I was going to stretch out my muscles because I had been sitting all day."

Murray ignored her, folding covers and stowing them away in a space on one of the metal shelves. "Come here," he said when he had finished. They stood side by side in front of the mirrored wall and Murray told her to watch while he rolled his head and shoulders, flexed his arms, rolled his back up and down, and squatted deeply on one leg and then the other.

"Now copy me," he said, and Keiko began, letting her head loll backwards.

"Oh," she said, looking up. "What happened to the mobiles?" The hanging shapes above the roof beams were gone, just an empty dim space above the lights now.

"I took them down," said Murray. "Chucked them out."

"No!" said Keiko. "You threw them away? But you must have worked so hard on them."

"They were falling to bits," Murray said, "when I got them down and had a good look."

Keiko shook her head and smiled at him. "If I could make anything so beautiful, I would keep them forever," she said.

Murray smiled back at her. "Speaking of making something beautiful," he said and rolled his shoulders again.

Keiko flushed and his eyes flashed wide.

"Sorry!" he said. "Christ, I didn't mean you're not. I didn't mean..."

She felt her flush deepen even further. "I'm not offended, " she said. "I'm flattered. I'm..."

"Right," he said. "Good, then. Let's crack on."

In the mirror, as he moved, it looked more like ink falling in water than a person's body. Keiko wanted to gaze but kept being distracted by her own little figure beside him as it jerked and wobbled, her hair falling forward in hanks and then back again to reveal the grimace of concentration on her face.

"Should I hear things crunching?" she panted, but Murray only frowned and kept his eyes shut, the flick of lashes on his cheek mirroring the arcs of his black brows. He dropped his head and started to roll down again, until the backs of his fingers rested against the mat. Keiko dropped forward too, catching her breath as her knuckles banged on the floor. He turned and squinted at her then, his head hard against his braced knees, smiling; a strange smile since his face was upside down, with an unfamiliar line underscoring each eye as some slight swell of flesh, usually invisible, moved out of place.

"You should be rolling forward trying to feel each vertebra moving separately," he said. "There shouldn't be any clunking." Keiko giggled. "Feel me," he said, and taking her hand as he straightened, he reached up and placed her fingertips against the nape of his neck. "Press harder," he said. "Feel the bones." He closed his eyes and bent his head forward again. Keiko rubbed her fingers over the bones in his neck. When his chin was completely tucked into his chest, he let his shoulders sag and more knots sprang up between his shoulder blades. She traced down each one as it rose out of the muscles around it, feeling the curve of his back rising and the bones of his spine pass one by one under her fingers until finally he was drooped right over and she stood with her palm on the highest point of his body, digging the heel of her hand in gently between pads of muscle to find the last one.

She hoped it didn't feel too different when he did the same with his hand on her, but she couldn't ignore her sudden lurches forward, and she knew when she stopped that she wouldn't look drooped like a lily on a broken stem; she was straining to keep the position, with juddering legs and a line of sweat forming between her buttocks. Murray pinched each vertebra hard between thumb and forefinger knuckle and tutted softly.

"Okay," he said and caught her under her arms as her legs gave way. "That's as good as it's going to get tonight. Let's get started."

———

Throughout the rest of the week, Keiko came to feel as though she were living two lives side by side.

Her silent life was all day up in her room, in the bay window. She read, wrote, checked and rechecked her writing, and might have been alone in a capsule on the moon. From time to time she would turn and look across the street at the clouded windows, showing her nothing. And every night when it was dark she stood beside Murray in even deeper silence, and his face—his dark eyes— showed even less.

Then there was her other life.

Wednesday evening tea at the Sangsters, slices of the noted roast glazed ham and a basin of potato salad as big as a washing-up bowl, the potatoes floury and still warm when they were dressed so that the mayonnaise clung to every fragment as they crumbled.

Friday was supper with Mr. McLuskie while Etta was at a meeting. A proper fry-up, he told her, a good old mixed grill. Bacon and chops and liver and sausage squares with eggs and bread fried off in the grease. She tried her best, even though Mr. McLuskie entertained her by telling her all the recipes he knew by heart: *hot water lard crust, rough puff, flaky, short* and *choux* until her head as well as her stomach was rolling.

He talked almost as much as Fancy. Fancy, endlessly inventive, tirelessly imaginative, popping round, emailing, texting, phoning, filling Keiko's head with characters, places, puzzles, jokes and punch-lines until, as well as twenty-five careful, probing stimuli there were twenty-five decoys straight from Planet Fancy. The study would be what it was, as thorough as she could make it, and perhaps she would graduate, but the filler questions—those would go down in history.

By Saturday the work was finished, and when she stood beside Murray she could see a difference, feel it too. She smiled at him, wondering if he was pleased with her.

"Rest tomorrow," he said.

"Are you sure you won't join us?" Murray said nothing. "Fancy and Craig are." Craig had not hesitated for a second when she had asked him. Creep across the road or no.

"News to me that there *is* a 'Fancy and Craig," he said. Already he had withdrawn his gaze from her shoulder angles and the set of her knees and begun to look at his own body in the mirror instead.

"Well, Fancy's coming and Craig's coming—I asked them separately—but who knows what might happen."

"Over a suet pudding," he said. "If I can't talk you out of it, at least I'll stop in later on, check that you're okay."

NINETEEN

Sunday, 10 November

SHE WAS SITTING AT the window with her legs tucked under, watching for Fancy but checking every few minutes that Malcolm's van (or even the slightly smaller bulk of Malcolm himself) wasn't approaching from the other end of the street.

They came together as it turned out, laughing at the door when Keiko opened it to them. Fancy hefted two plastic bags and waved them, and Malcolm looked at the box he was carrying with a sheepish, down-turning smile.

"Where's Vi?" asked Keiko as they negotiated passing bags and boxes, taking off coats and shoes, Malcolm turning slowly as the two girls darted around him.

"She's at Pet's," said Fancy, with the smallest flick of a glance towards Malcolm's back. Keiko nodded and followed him to the kitchen.

"That drain still bothering you?" he said.

Keiko blushed. It was not her fault, but still she blushed.

Malcolm wiped down the countertop nearest the cooker and began lifting things from his box: two cellophane bags, one lolling and dark with blood, one a pale block. Beside these he set out a bag of flour, a small dark bottle with an orange label, and an onion.

"And that's it," he said. "That's all that's in it. It's that simple. The best ingredients carefully chosen and combined."

"You don't agree with Mr. McLuskie, then?" Keiko said. "He told me about bridies and about how the meat doesn't matter as long as the pastry's right and you use enough pepper."

"What a bloody cheek," said Fancy. "Doesn't he get his meat from you?"

Malcolm nodded, looking unperturbed. "He didn't mean it that way," he said. "He means it doesn't matter what kind of meat it is—mutton, beef, pork, you name it—he didn't mean the quality. Besides, he's a baker: of course he's going to care most about the pastry. Each to his own."

"You're nicer than me, Malcolm," Fancy said.

"Suet," said Malcolm, tearing at the pale bag and lifting it, letting a white loaf of fat fall with a thud onto the plate. He moved a hand towards the dark bag but stopped before he picked it up, plunged one arm into the box, and shook out a clean apron. He pushed his head through the neck strap and poked the strings around his sides.

"Let me," said Keiko. She picked up the end of one apron string and held it while she walked around Malcolm for the other. Each string had an extra ten or twelve inches neatly stitched on to the end.

Malcolm made a single huge movement, brushing Keiko off him. She took a step backwards, but he was smiling down at her.

"Don't crowd me," he said. He tipped out a thick slice of beef and a cluster of dark kidney then wiped his bloody hands down his clean apron. Keiko squeaked.

"You use up paper, I use up aprons," Malcolm said, looking away and missing Keiko's quick smile, then he took out a flat wad of kitchen paper and unravelled it carefully to reveal a knife, ten inches long and four inches high, the blade glittering and the handle gleaming almost as much through use and care. "Which reminds me," he added, "how did the pilot pan out?"

"Are you going to do it, Malcolm?" asked Fancy. "Because if you are, we can't talk about it."

Malcolm shook his head. He had his eyes fixed on their faces as his hands worked away at the beef, the blade in his right *thunking* over and over again down into the meat and his left scraping the cubes away from it and flicking fatty scraps aside.

"Be careful," Keiko said.

"Good idea," said Malcolm, solemnly. "I'll do that." Keiko and Fancy laughed and he turned back to his work, nicking at the kidneys with the point of his knife now, stripping nameless strings away from them.

Fancy turned back to Keiko. "I've had a couple more ideas."

"Too late," said Keiko. "The new questionnaires are printed."

Malcolm was mixing the flour and suet, stirring his knife round in the bowl, adding water drop by patient drop.

"Listen," he said, and they both leaned forward. He added another drop and from the bowl came a sticky sound as though a small creature was chewing on something wet.

"Nearly there," he said and smacked his lips. Another drop and the sound changed again, slower and more muffled, then he put down the water jug and knife, lifted the tangle of dough out of the bowl in both hands, and began to work it around on the board, the blood between his fingers streaking and spreading through the ball as he kneaded.

"You never warned me you were printing them already," said Fancy, grimacing as she watched Malcolm working.

"*Already*?" Keiko cried. "It starts tomorrow. I've almost finished the stimuli for the first full run of the actual study—the questionnaire after next."

"The food ones?" said Fancy. "Get lost, you have not."

"Kale juice to lower blood pressure," Keiko said, "chocolate worse than cheese for cholesterol, toxins concentrated in the skin of apples but solved by peeling them, and fecal contamination in ready-to-use organic salad leaves."

"And you'll check back later to see if some idiot thinks there's shit in kale?" Fancy said.

"Uh, to see if the message stays attached to the context so … yes, roughly."

"What do you think, Malcolm?" said Fancy.

Malcolm shrugged, the movement making the cloth of his shirt creak. He had rolled the pastry out and now he took a bowl from the box and started to press the sheet of dough into it, working with deep concentration, his hair falling heavily over his face. Then he lifted the chopping board and Keiko was astonished to see the pile of meat and sliced onion disappear comfortably into the bowl that had seemed so small under his hands, hardly room for him to move his fingers around. He carried the filled bowl to the sink and held it under the cold tap.

"No!" said Fancy. "What are you doing?"

"Making gravy," he said, grinning.

"You can't pour water into pastry, Malcolm," insisted Fancy. "Even I know that."

"But suet pastry," said Keiko, "it is like dumpling dough, isn't it?"

"Hmm," said Fancy, "I've never really believed in dumplings. How can you boil flour?"

"How can you not believe in dumplings?" asked Keiko, laughing and trying to catch Malcolm's eye.

He waited until their attention was back on him and then walked carefully back and set the brimming bowl down again. He laid a blanket of dough over the top and tucked it in fussily, nipping at the edges with dampened fingers. When it was tamped down to his satisfaction, he took a piece of folded foil out of the box and fitted it over the top, then tied it tightly to the rim of the bowl with a length of string and fashioned a handle, his thick fingers working quickly over the knots.

"Now," he said, dangling the trussed bowl from one fingertip, "you steam it gently for five hours and it's ready." His smile widened as Keiko and Fancy's faces fell.

"Malcolm, this was meant to be lunch," Fancy began, but he held his free hand up towards her and inclined his head patiently with his eyes closed.

"This one goes home with me tonight," he said. "And this one"— he lifted an identical pudding basin out of the box—"which I prepared earlier and cooked for four hours this morning, goes back in for an hour and will be ready at one o'clock sharp." He began to tidy away his things, lodging his scissors safely in the middle of the ball of string and stacking the used plates.

"So that was all for show?" Fancy said.

"Keiko wanted to watch," Malcolm said.

"Right, my turn," said Fancy. "And if you think *that* was impressive…"

Craig arrived as she was sorting through a heap of packets tipped out on the table. He rapped on the door, shouted hello, and strolled along the corridor towards them, his shoes making the same metallic clunk as his uncle's on Keiko's thin strip of carpet.

"Where's Murray?" he asked as he entered the kitchen. Fancy rolled her eyes and Malcolm turned away towards the sink and started to run hot water.

"Would you like a drink?" said Keiko.

"Wait two minutes," said Fancy. "Watch this, Malc. Sherry, cream, choc chip cookies." She poured a pool of sherry onto a plate, took a biscuit daintily by its edge, dipped it briefly and laid it down. When there was a soaked biscuit on each of four plates, she plopped dollops of cream down on top of them. Then more biscuits, soaked and pressed down on top of the cream, and she carried on until there were four squat towers of biscuits, spreading slightly at the base as the sherry softened the bottom one. She spread the rest of the cream on top and shook a packet of chocolate buttons over them. Most of the buttons stuck, a few landed on the plates, and one rolled away under the fridge.

"Ta-dah! And the really neat part is …" Fancy poured sherry into four glasses, filling each one perfectly to the brim and ending with the bottle upside down and empty. Keiko clapped and Malcolm followed her, clumping his hands together three times then letting them drop to his sides again.

"Nothing like good home packet opening," said Craig. "Isn't Murray coming? Where is he?"

———

Murray was in the workshop. He sat on his heels by the Harley, at his side a blue four-bottle wine carrier holding chrome polish, wax, and leather food, the last compartment stuffed with a soft roll of chamois leathers and yellow dusters around a dry paintbrush that he used for the awkward corners. Beside the Vincent was a red wine carrier; there was a green one by the Squariel, and two yellow ones lay between the two BSAs, the finished Golden Flash and the poor deformed Bantam, which sat cocked onto their rests at just the same angle, their front wheels turned in to face each other, looking like two dancers frozen in the middle of their minuet.

Murray's small window looked out at the lane and the yard wall, taking in just a corner of the Pooles' slaughterhouse, and he knew that even if he moved right up and put his face against the glass, he couldn't see into Keiko's kitchen. Instead he had to content himself with looking out at the sliver of view they shared and straining his ear to catch some sound of the four of them, perhaps sitting there in the steamy warmth with the window thrown open, laughing and drinking.

In fact, Malcolm was in the kitchen alone. Keiko and Fancy were setting the big table in the bay window. Craig picked up a completed questionnaire and started leafing through before Keiko could stop him.

"Okay, okay," he said when he saw her face turn pale. "But what a temptation. Who all did it?"

Keiko ignored him.

"If you want a gossip," said Fancy, "how about why Janette Campbell would be so pissed off that Murray's showing Keiko how to lift weights."

Keiko stared at her. That had been a confidence shared between friends: two confidences, in fact. Fancy must know that.

"Search me," said Craig, throwing himself into an armchair and turning to face the doorway as they all heard the sound of Malcolm coming out of the kitchen. "*You* got any clue?"

175

Malcolm surveyed the narrow armchairs before moving towards the sofa and settling himself. Fancy took the other chair and Keiko perched up at the far end of the sofa from Malcolm, both heels hard on the carpet, bracing herself against the gradient that threatened to throw her down against him.

"Mrs. Campbell?" said Malcolm. "I can't think. Unless ... Did you mention Byers's place? This is going back years, mind, but she can be bit funny about Willie Byers."

"Who can blame her?" said Fancy. "'A bit funny' is the only way to be. Why, though?"

Malcolm rubbed his chin for a moment before he went on. "As far as I know, she took quite a fancy to him when he first came. It wasn't long after her divorce. And one Halloween everybody was out on the Green and Willie Byers was still at work—everybody could see him—and Janette Campbell decided she'd go and drag him out to join the party. She'd had a bit to drink, by this time." Malcolm laughed and shook his head.

———

Janette Campbell had had exactly four glasses of the gluey white wine that was laid out on a trestle table under the streetlamp. Four glasses on top of the large gin it had taken to get her out of her house for the first time since Mr. Campbell had left her. She wasn't drunk. And Mr. Byers, who was new in town, was sitting in his office with the desk lamp on, sideways to the bonfire, never so much as glancing up at it.

"He's a strange character, right enough," said Mr. McKendrick. "I mean, there's others haven't come tonight and that's fair enough, it's not everyone's cup of tea ..."

"But that's just thumbing your nose, isn't it," said Mr. Poole. "Sitting there like that."

"Maybe he's shy," said Janette Campbell. "Maybe he just needs a bit of encouragement." From someone who knows what it feels like to be alone, was what she meant. She set off across the dark green towards the desk light.

"Fiver says he won't come, Janette," shouted Kenny Imperiolo after her. She ignored him. She hadn't drunk enough to have to concentrate on walking, but she shouldn't risk trying to look over her shoulder with everyone watching. Outside the shop she arranged a smile on her face and knocked. Byers raised his head from his papers and squinted out into the dark. She waved. Away across the Green everyone could see her hand silhouetted against the brightness. And then the light clicked off and Janette stood facing the suddenly black glass and the reflection of her own startled face in it. She heard a cackle of laughter, swiftly smothered, from behind her, and her eyes filled with tears.

"Old misery guts," someone shouted.

"Come away and leave him to stew, Janette," called a woman's voice. Mrs. Campbell walked as quick as she could without breaking into a run, round the corner and towards home. She stumbled once and had to put out a hand to steady herself and, although she was out of view, still the shock and the shame of nearly falling started the tears for real and she blundered on faster, sobbing, until she heard a low voice calling her name. She thought perhaps it was him, come out the back way, but when she turned gulping, streaked with mascara, it was Mrs. Poole she saw hurrying towards her with her arms outstretched.

"Don't go!" Mrs. Poole called. "Oh, come on back and see the bonfire. Come on." She put her head on one side and beckoned.

"You go back if you want to, Grace," said Mrs. Campbell, shaky and louder than she meant to. "You go back to all your friends and your two lovely children and your husband and James McKendrick hanging around just in case. And I hope it chokes you."

———

"I don't know what she said to Mum or what Mum said to her," Malcolm finished, "but she's never been in our shop since and Mum gets her hair done at Curly World now."

Craig laughed unkindly, long hooting laughs, and looked at Fancy to share it, but Fancy winced and shook her head.

"Poor Mrs. Campbell," said Keiko. "It's no wonder then. If it were me I would still be blushing."

"Hey," said Craig, "I know what! What's the most embarrassing thing that's ever happened to you?" Everyone groaned. "Oh, come on. I'll start."

"Not now," said Fancy. "Not in the cold light of day on one sherry."

Keiko was jolted out of her musing. "Of course," she said. "Who would like another drink?"

"Oh, come on," said Craig again. "I'll start it. What's the most embarrassed you've ever been?"

"Malcolm, would you like a glass of wine?" asked Keiko. Malcolm turned to face her just as she began to rise, and the brief lifting of his bulk at one end of the sofa caused the springs under Keiko to drop away at the very moment she transferred her weight to her feet and she fell towards him. She put her hands out to stop herself then pulled back, scared of hurting him, and ended up rolling in his lap, helpless as an upturned beetle, while his arms flailed. Then, as she tried once more to gain purchase, one knee connected with some soft part of him around his middle and he gasped, making a sound like the first punch into a bowl of risen dough. Keiko caught her breath and stopped wriggling, letting Malcolm clamp one hand around each of her upper arms and lift her up and back, onto her feet. They looked into each other's faces for less than a second, then Keiko shot out of the room. She heard Craig trying to speak.

"So Malcolm, what's the most emba—" he managed to get out before he collapsed into silent, wheezing laughter.

Keiko was staggering around the kitchen, doubled up, trying to catch a breath, holding her lenses in with the sides of her fingers, when Fancy scurried in, hand clamped over her mouth, and slammed the door behind her. They gave way as quietly as they could—there was no use trying to fight it completely.

"Is he laughing?" asked Keiko finally, in a ragged whisper. Fancy shook her head and wiped her eyes. Keiko cleared her throat. "He smells like rosemary," she said, and they both straightened up with deep sighs.

"We have to go back in," Fancy said.

Keiko raked her hair back into place. "I'll take the glasses, you bring the wine." She picked up two glasses in each hand and marched towards the living room. Malcolm was halfway along the corridor towards her.

"Did I hurt you?" she asked. He shook his head. Behind him she could see Craig still sprawled in his chair with his slim legs stretched out in front of him.

"Funniest thing I've ever seen in my life," he called to them.

Keiko stepped out of his eye-line and fleetingly tried to hug Malcolm, stretching her arms across his front, the wine glasses clinking.

For just a second she laid the side of her face against his chest and breathed in the scent of rosemary again. Malcolm raised his hands, perhaps to hug her back, but she stepped away and was into the living room before he could stop her.

TWENTY

WHEN MURRAY HAD OILED and waxed all five of the motorbikes, he began on the chrome, starting as usual with the Harley, applying the polish with a duster wound round two fingers on the larger areas and a cotton bud in the awkward places. After an hour's work it looked perfect, from a distance, but if he squatted down close and looked properly, he could still see a sticky line of leftover polish where the chrome dash met the paint on the petrol tank. He threaded the edge of a duster in between the two halves of the tank and up under the dash, pulling it back and forward, feeling it slip easier over the drying surface. Then he rolled up the cloths and brushes and shoved them into the wine carrier. It looked even better now, but he knew the polish was there, sitting in the crevices, not just on the tank but between the taillight and the rear mudguard, around the badge and under every nut, where it would congeal, darken to yellow and dry to a crust. He turned to the rack of metal shelves for a set of sockets, softly whistling.

Outside was perfectly black now. Since the long row of buildings shielded the yards from any streetlamp glow, the only light would come from windows in the backs of the upstairs flats. So if Keiko was still in her kitchen, if everyone was still there, if lunch had turned into drinks and then supper and they were all still sitting there, full and hot, there would be a shaft of light across the yard. Even if the curtains were shut, there would be spikes of brightness falling somewhere.

Murray clicked off all the lights then returned to the window and stared out beyond the reflection of his own face, waiting for his eyes to adjust. After a moment the dark square resolved itself into shapes, but there was no gleam of light, just two shades of black and the soft line between them showing where the roof of the slaughter-house stopped and the sky began.

Murray turned back into the room. He knelt down beside the Harley again in the darkness and opened the case of sockets. They lay in rows like knuckles, like jewels against velvet. He closed his eyes and ran a hand over them, finding the size he needed, frowning at how this one, most often used, had a different rougher feel from the others; he would need to replace it. For now though, it would do.

It was after eleven when he padlocked the door behind him and walked round the corner. Outside the shop, he paused under Keiko's window. The curtains were closed, but one side sash was lifted an inch or two at the bottom. There was no sound of voices. Murray held his breath and listened, then smiled at the unmistakable soft groan and whirr of her printer.

———

Keiko wasn't really working. The sherry and wine from lunchtime had long since gone, leaving an ache in her temples as dull as the weight in her stomach, but she felt too restless to switch off the computer and call the day over.

She jumped at the knock on the door, hesitated, then went out into the hallway. Murray's workshop light had gone out hours ago. It couldn't be Fancy; it was long past Viola's bedtime. She crept along the passage, paused again, listening, on the spot where she had so briefly put her arms against Malcolm's body and felt him move in response. If she had some glass in the door or even a peephole, she would be able to tell at once if it was him and creep away again. Then she realised that if it was him, if he had just climbed the stairs from the street, she would surely be able to hear him breathing. She listened again and heard nothing.

"Hello?" she said.

"Keiko?" said Murray's voice. "I just wanted to check on you."

She opened the door wide, relief turning her smile of welcome into a laugh. "Come in, come in, come in," she said.

"Three times?"

"Mrs. Watson always says that and it makes me feel welcome," Keiko said, going to the living room. "Sit down, sit down, sit down," she said. "On the sofa, the sofa, the sofa."

"Are you drunk?" said Murray leaning away slightly.

"No," she said, thinking about it. "No." She was sure she wasn't, it just somehow seemed that tonight there was no need to pick her way so carefully towards him and no need for him to hint and hide. They could just talk to one another. Right now, they could just let go. "I'm just very pleased to see you. Why shouldn't I show it?"

Murray's eyebrows rose, his forehead nothing but ripples all the way to the peak of his hair as she moved towards him. She closed her eyes, thinking that they would eventually cross if she kept them open. She must look even sillier though, standing with her eyes shut and face turned up, waiting, but just as she began to wonder how to get out of it, Murray kissed her. His arms and chest were hard and she could still feel the cold coming off his clothes, but his lips were soft, dry as paper. She breathed in and opened her eyes.

"You smell of beeswax," she heard herself saying and wondered if she was as sober as she thought, after all.

"You taste like fat," said Murray. "How *was* lunch anyway? It still stinks in here, by the way." He flung himself down at one end of the sofa and stretched an arm along its back in invitation. Keiko groaned and sank down beside him, fitting herself under his arm, the muscles under his shoulder even harder than the thin padding on the back of the old couch.

"I'm never going to eat again," she said. Murray patted her stomach. "The reason it still smells is that while we ate one, another was cooking. Hours and hours. And I can't get the grease to come off the washing-up bowl. Also, Fancy made a dessert with cream and chocolate and sherry, and Craig made a pink drink with cream and sugar."

Murray was rubbing small circles on her stomach as if polishing her. "So you forgive me?" he said. "For not coming?"

"Of course," she told him. "But I'm glad you're here now."

"I'm glad you're here too," said Murray, not looking at her, still rubbing. "You're about the only thing that makes it okay." He stopped speaking and took his hand away. "Except I'm not really glad you're here. I'm not glad either of us is here. It's been killing me all day thinking of you up here with … It kills me thinking of you here at all. I wish I could just run away and take you with me."

"Why?" said Keiko, blinking at bit at the rush of words. She had wanted to make him talk more, but this was as if she'd turned a tap and watched a dam bursting.

"You wouldn't believe me if I tried to tell you," Murray said. "And anyway, while you're here it's better you don't know. But this is not the place for you. Or me."

"What? Painchton? Scotland? Europe?" She bit her lip to stop herself saying *the world, the galaxy, the universe*, like when she was a child.

"The shop," he said. "For starters."

"I know you're not happy there."

"Understatement of the century," said Murray. He put his head into his hands. "I've got to get away again."

"What's stopping you?" she said.

He ignored the question and kept talking. "You should definitely get away."

"Yes, but away from *what*?" Murray didn't answer. "Or *who*, even?" She thought for a moment, staring at the rings on the coffee table, shutting one eye and then the other, making them jump side to side. Then she shook herself. "And what *is* stopping you?" It came out more terse than she had intended, so she went on: "You've been kind, helping your mother, but she wouldn't want to hold you back." She shook her head again against the memory of Mrs. Poole's stony blank face, so different from her own mother's sharp looks and constant plucking.

"If Willie Byers sells his place to the Traders, I'm sunk," Murray said.

"Three things," said Keiko, thinking that this was how her mother would say it. "I don't think Mr. Byers is going to sell. From what Mrs. Aitken said to her son's wife—"

"Who?" said Murray.

"Mrs. Aitken. She doesn't live here any more and she's married again. You'll know her as Mrs. Mackie." Murray stared at her and shook his head. "Her daughter-in-law works in the Spar?"

"Oh, right. Gordon Mackie's mum, yeah," said Murray, then blinked. "You really are getting pulled right in, aren't you. You need to be careful, Keiko. Watch them. Please."

"The Mackies?" Keiko said, then she shook her head. "Don't distract me. I'm trying to help you. Mrs. Aitken told Gordon's wife that Mr. Byers wouldn't sell if he were offered a million pounds. Even if he closes the business, he'll hold on to the site. Just to be difficult."

"How does she know so much about it?" said Murray.

"Her new husband worked in the city council planning department before he retired, and he remembers Mr. Byers from another situation, which was never resolved. I think you'll be all right."

Murray shook his head. "Willie might have seen off a few planners, but he's no match for Jimmy McKendrick," he said. "What are the other two things?"

"What?" said Keiko, thinking about the planning department. She should have used it in one of the filler questions; people seemed to have very strong views about planning. "Oh, yes! Number two. You're in business, right? Perhaps you're eligible for grants or sponsorship, like Fancy." Murray shook his head again and stared at the carpet. "Maybe the Traders' Association could help ..."

Murray sat back and stared straight up at the ceiling. "You really haven't got a clue, have you?" he said.

"And the third idea is the best of all," she said. "One too hot, one too cold, and one juuuust right!" Murray frowned at her. "You need premises," she said. "You need an unused building, for a reasonable price?" She waited, then leapt to her feet and dragged him by both wrists out of the room and along the corridor to the kitchen, steering him through the darkness towards the window.

"What?" he said.

"Oh, you can't be serious!" she cried out. "It's really true we can't see what's right underneath our noses every day." She pointed out at the yard. "That building must be almost the same size as the motorcycle half of your workshop, and Malcolm says it's not used any more." She nudged him. "You would have to join a public gym, but something tells me the owners would offer a good deal for you." He said nothing and she turned towards him, squinting up into his face in the dark.

"Murray?" she said. And then she whispered it. "Murray?" She stepped back to the doorway and switched on the overhead light. For a split second the brightness dazzled her, the room whirled, and she couldn't make sense of what she saw: the snarl of a dog, the gleam of blades, eyes flashing half-hidden in leaves. She blinked.

But there was nothing there. Nothing but the knives in the rack on the wall, the herbs in their pots on the sill, and Murray's face, all reflected in the window.

"It's *not* used any more, is it?" she asked.

Murray turned round so slowly that he looked like an automaton. "I'll go and let you sleep it off," he said, brushing past her. "I shouldn't have come, only I wanted to make sure you were okay."

TWENTY-ONE

THE LAST WALKIES BEFORE bed were getting later and later; the poor old thing would need a puppy mat again if it got much worse. Shame a dog couldn't be trained to a box of litter the same as a cat, really. Still, it was pleasant enough on a clear night, out under the stars, when the rest of the town was asleep and there was always the chance, the later it got and later still, that one of these nights whoever it was would be surprised in the act, caught red-handed. A quick glance into the crook of the rowan tree at the top of the drive on leaving and again on their return. Almost always there was nothing, but then one night there it would be again: a flash of white against the dark bark of the tree, the envelope FOR YOU and inside: TRY AS HARD AS YOU LIKE TO COVER YOUR TRACKS. THERE'S NO WAY BACK FROM WHAT YOU DID. I WILL TELL THEM ALL.

And then the quick sprint down the back garden, hugging the side hedge, out of view, to where the burn passed along just behind the fence, and over it went. It hit the water with a sharp smack and floated away, spinning, as bright and white as the moon, until it was gone.

Monday, 11 November

At five a.m., with gritty eyes and a bitter taste in her mouth, Keiko blundered to the kitchen for a glass of water, gulping it straight down, tepid. She breathed in the warm, foul drain smell, then bent over the sink to let the water wash back up again, holding on to the taps, resting her forehead against the porcelain. Then she laid a cool pad of kitchen paper on the back of her neck while she rinsed the sink out and poured herself another glass to take back to bed and sip carefully, working up to swallowing two painkillers and two vitamins before lying down again.

The second time she opened her eyes, in the light of near dawn, a hot, sour feeling was pricking her high up in the stomach and her limbs were leaden. Perhaps if she just stayed there, lying still and cosy for a couple more hours? But she was not cosy, she was somehow hot and cold at the same time, her feet icy but her hair damp, so she threw back the bedclothes and fanned her nightie.

How much of that had happened? The line between the end of the day and the start of the short night was blurry. She wasn't sure if she had really asked Craig about his cousin, whether Nicole had got fat before she vanished, like Tash, or wasted away, like Dina. She couldn't remember his answer anyway; perhaps she'd been dreaming. The rabbit carcasses and the snarling dog face in the kitchen were dreams for sure. She hadn't rolled and rolled naked on the living room floor with Malcolm, mashed against the hairy flab of his chest, while Fancy and Craig watched and laughed and Mrs. Poole jabbed her with her mop. But had she really thrown herself at Murray, and what had she said to make him slam out again? She swung her legs to the floor and stood, trailed into the living room, and lifted the phone.

"Fancy?" she croaked. "Are you feeling all right?"

"Jeezy-peeps," Fancy cackled. "Maybe compared to *you*. Bloody Craig McKendrick and his bloody Pink Squirrels."

"I've been sick," said Keiko shuddering again at having to say the word. "And I've had the strangest … I really need to talk."

"Get round here right now," said Fancy, "and I'll cure you."

Keiko stood beside the bath and looked into it for a while, then tottered back to her bedroom and pulled jeans on over her nightie, tucking the bulk of it down into the waistband. She put underwear and socks into a bag and tossed her contact lenses and hairbrush in on top. Then she tied her hair back, shoved her feet into shoes, grabbed her coat, and let herself out.

Viola was eating breakfast in the upstairs kitchen, prim in her school uniform with her hair battened under grips and bands, ignoring Fancy slumped beside her in a dressing gown. Keiko sat carefully and, after one glance, looked away from Viola's spoon dipping in and out of her bowl, racing against the spreading slick of chocolate melting into the milk. But when she got to scraping the spoon along the bottom, slurping over the last dribbles, Keiko couldn't help a small moan escaping. Viola laid her spoon down very gently.

"I've got to go now," she said. "Me and Katie are walking backwards this morning."

"Oh yes," said Keiko, not really listening. Downstairs the doorbell gave a long peal, another even longer, then after a pause and a scuffling sound, a third short chirp.

"That's Katie's wee sister," said Viola. "She can't really reach it yet. Yeah, we're walking backwards this morning cos we fell out on the way home on Friday. So, you know, we're rewinding."

"What?" said Keiko.

"You should try it," Viola said. "You and Mum. Rewind and it never happened. That's what we do."

190

"If only," said Fancy. "Brush your teeth," she called in a half-hearted voice as Viola bounded out of the door.

"Look who's talking," Viola said, coming back and standing in the doorway with her hands on her skinny hips. "Your breath stinks like cheese this morning, Mum. That's why I'm not kissing you. I'll give you two kisses tonight." She threw a final pitying look at Keiko and left.

Keiko put her head down on the table with a groan.

"I can't stand having a hangover when Vi's here," said Fancy. Keiko giggled. "Right," said Fancy, louder and firmer, "what are we looking at? One puke, but you're up and walking and you're dressed—"

"Not really," said Keiko sitting up and leaning back in her chair, "I've still got my nightie on underneath."

"Well, near as damn it. So . . . I think hot shower, port and brandy, and some breakfast. Trust me." She glanced over her shoulder to check the position of the fridge and took a couple of backwards steps towards it, then stopped and put her hand out to steady herself. "Not good," she said, swallowing hard. "Don't try it."

Under the hot water, Keiko felt streaming off her not only the sweaty horrors of last night, but six weeks' film of bathtub; it lifted and washed away, globules of suet rising to her skin and thudding out of her pores. She squeezed another dollop of Fancy's gel onto the scratchier side of a washing mitt and scoured herself without mercy.

Back in the kitchen, Fancy handed her a glass. Keiko swirled the resinous mixture around, breathing through her mouth so that she couldn't smell it. She couldn't remember ever tasting port *or* brandy before.

"Honest," said Fancy. "Down in one, trust me." Keiko glanced at the sink; it was piled with dishes, so if this didn't work she would need to make the bathroom. She pulled her chair back from the table in readiness, swigged, gasped, then swallowed hard with her hand clamped over her mouth.

"Hold on, hold on," said Fancy and, as the fumes cleared and the good taste of toothpaste flooded back, Keiko felt a kind of calm settle over her insides like a thick blanket, like an x-ray blanket, and she breathed.

"Thank you," she said. "Everyone says to trust them, trust them, and I'm beginning to think it's not always such a good idea, but this time—thank you."

"Who's everyone?" said Fancy, putting a plate down on the table. It was, Keiko saw to her relief, just a sandwich. She began to fold back one corner of the top slice to peek inside but, since Fancy was watching her, she made herself lift the whole thing towards her mouth.

"That'll finish you off," Fancy said, "Careful though, the sausages are red hot and the egg's runny." She prodded a sausage out of a frying pan onto a fork, nipping the end with one precise bite, so that it flapped back on a hinge of skin and steamed. Keiko shut her eyes and bit.

"So who's everyone?" Fancy asked again a few minutes later. "Who says you should trust them? Apart from me and I'm right, because I've just cured you, haven't I?"

Keiko nodded. "The Pooles," she said, "Well, Murray. I don't know. I had nightmares and I'm confused." Fancy waited. Keiko thought back over the previous day and then shook her head. "Murray came round late yesterday and he was upset, but I have no idea why."

"Look," said Fancy. "Last night was stupid. I'm sure Murray *was* upset."

"Last *night*?" said Keiko. "It was lunch. What happened at nighttime?"

"Nothing," said Fancy. "Nothing at all. Nothing of any importance anyway."

"But why would Murray suddenly be angry with me? He was friendlier than ever—more than friendly—when he arrived."

"Good for you," said Fancy. "I'm glad to hear it. So…he was probably jealous. Don't knock it, Keeks. It beats the other thing."

"Jealous of *Malcolm*?"

"Who knows? Maybe he was jealous of Craig."

"But Craig was there for—"

Fancy quelled her with a stare. "God knows *what* Craig was there for," she said. "God knows what Murray was doing *not* being there. God knows what poor Malcolm thought *he* was doing. It was just an awkward situation and we all drank too much and nobody'll mention it again and no harm done. We won't see Craig again till the Christmas holidays now anyway," she said. "With any luck."

"I should forget about everything and concentrate on work," said Keiko.

"Get lost. I'm the one who should forget, since there's nothing to remember," said Fancy. "What you should do is get Murray out on a proper date—not in Painchton, with no home-cooking and absolutely no pink cocktails."

"He *said* he wanted to get away," said Keiko, this memory suddenly lurching forward in her.

"There you go then."

"No, he said he wanted to get away and he wanted me to get away and this was a bad place for both of us."

"Are you sure?" said Fancy.

"Not really," said Keiko. "That might have been in one of the nightmares. Did I ask Craig about his cousin's weight? Or is that another one?"

"Definitely a dream," said Fancy. "How did you even know Craig had a cousin?"

"She's one of the missing girls," Keiko said without thinking. It was only the silence that followed which made her, too late, wonder whether it was wise.

"What?" said Fancy finally. "What are you talking about?" She had finished the sausages in the pan and now she wiped her lips with a square of kitchen paper.

"It probably doesn't seem that way to you," said Keiko. "But I heard about them all one after the other. Dina from next door and Nicole from across the road and Tash from round the corner."

"What are you on about?" said Fancy. She held the sausage pan under the tap and let it fill with water. "What's leaving got to do with being fat or skinny? Are you sure you're not still drunk?"

"You gave me port and brandy," said Keiko, "so it's not my fault if I am." She wiped her mouth. "I think I must have talked to Murray about the missing girls. I know I said *some*thing ... and that would explain why he talked about getting away."

"I wish you'd stop saying 'missing girls' like that," Fancy said. "People move around. Look at you—you're thousands of miles from home."

"But Murray doesn't want to go somewhere," Keiko said. "He just wants to leave here."

Fancy was scrubbing at the sausage pan so hard that her whole body shook. Keiko waited, and eventually she banged the pan down and turned round again.

"*What?*" she said. "What do you want me to say?" Her voice was clear and much louder than it need to be, but she did not meet Keiko's eyes. Then she sighed. "Look," she said, more calmly, "there's any number of reasons Murray might want to leave, you know." Keiko waited. "His dad died."

"But parents die," Keiko said. "I know I sound harsh, but it's not like a child dying. It's sad but not a tragedy."

"And his mum made him give up doing what he loves and work in a bloody butcher's shop that he hates. Why would he *not* want to get away? Why would he not want to take you with him? Be flattered—I would be."

So Keiko went home, her brisk return matching Painchton's Monday-morning tempo, shop doors propped wide to let the floors dry, open vans parked with their lights flashing. Only the petrol station sat as bare and dusty as Sunday night, with its window stickers faded out to three shades of beige, and the stout padlock on Murray's workshop door the one flash of brightness about the place.

Keiko remembered Malcolm's story and wondered if Mr. Byers was in there now and could see her crossing the Green. She could have sworn that someone somewhere was watching her. She looked up the street and down it, into the shops, up at the flats above, and inside her a little weight settled back into its place. She shouldn't have let Fancy shout her down. The very fact that Fancy was so upset meant something.

Upstairs as she stood at the kitchen window waiting for the kettle to boil, she almost caught it. It was there somewhere, not spoken, not seen, not even as solid as a scent, not so much as a memory;

something as faint as the turn of a season and just as real. She saw movement in the yard—Mrs. Poole and her buckets, no doubt—and stepped back out of view.

Work, she told herself, going to her desk and sitting. Good mindless busy work, starting by clearing her desk.

It made her smile to see Mrs. Watson's questionnaire there on the top of the pile, her name printed out in full—Mabel Nadine Taylor Watson—below the sentence ensuring anonymity. Then her smile wavered as she remembered again Mrs. Watson's stricken face when she saw the letter in Keiko's hand that first day. She shook the thought away.

The next paper down was Mr. McKendrick's, without his name but signed just as clearly by the strokes of that fine blue fountain-pen ink. She fanned through the rest of them, down to Mrs. Campbell's sheet, the last one. She glanced at the sample sentence *There's no smoke without fire*. Mrs. Campbell had made her mark right up at one end, a definite yes, a thick confident line made of three strokes on top of each other. She touched the paper, feeling the dents where the pen had been pressed into the page, and remembered Mrs. Campbell's sudden chill as soon as she mentioned Murray, remembered Malcolm's explanation for it. Did that make any sense, really? And why should Malcolm remember it in so much detail? And now that she thought about it, had Keiko even said Mr. Byers's name?

She walked through to the hallway and stopped where she had stood to tie her shoes, trying to bring the words to mind. She had said to Mrs. Campbell not to worry, that Murray had machines in his ... *workhouse, workshop, backshop, outshop*? The English slid around inside her head, slick enough to be out of her conscious control, but still strange enough that she could never be sure exactly which word she had spoken. Surely, though, she had only said that Murray had a gym in his workshop. Would that be enough? Would even hearing someone mention the place where Byers worked flood Mrs. Campbell with shame?

TWENTY-TWO

WHATEVER MEMORIES MIGHT STILL prick at Janette Campbell, surely no thoughts of *her* troubled William Byers. Did he have an inner life at all?

Young Yvonne at Janette's salon liked to use the question as a mental workout. "Imagine him cooking!" she'd say. "Where do you think he does his shopping? Who cuts his hair? I wonder what he dreams about. Somebody had a little baby once and it was *him*!"

That's what Mr. McKendrick was thinking as he strode towards the Green on Monday afternoon. *He's somebody's son. He may not be anyone's husband or father or friend, but he must have been somebody's son once and there must be some way to get through to him.* Mr. McKendrick's step faltered for a second, as a different thought struck him: in the eyes of the world he himself, James McKendrick, was just the same—nobody's husband or father, just like Byers. But he didn't even to have to shrug to cast the notion away. He was entirely different, a man whose life had been spent growing into itself, whose stature was a comfort as well as an example to everyone around him, whose place in the world was secure. His wealth was solid and considerable and plain to see, his clothes were ever more correct and expensive, his every car was bigger and came quicker than the one before. Mr. Byers, though, Mr. Byers was a man of the same age who, if he hadn't been a mechanic, would not have had the wherewithal to keep even his ancient Volvo going. He wore tee-shirts and baseball caps, and Mr. McKendrick hated to see a baseball cap on grey hair. He wore the kind of canvas shoes you used to see hanging in bunches from shop doorways—an acceptance of failure, shoes like that, an admission for all to see that his life had unravelled like re-used string. So there was no doubt that Mr. McKendrick would get his way, but he would proceed with tact. He would be kind.

And he would keep in touch with Byers once the man was gone. He saw himself at a Traders' meeting in the future, announcing Byers's death in a sombre voice, talking about their "friend and colleague," pretending not to see the surprise on the faces around him, watching everyone being impressed with the kind of man he was, the span of his influence, the depth of his dignity.

Unless Byers outlived him. The easy leap of Jimmy McKendrick's imagination was not always a friend to him, and unbidden thoughts like that one came more and more frequently now. *What have you started, Duncan Poole?* he thought. *Weren't we all going to live forever? Well, God rest you, you bugger* (which was as close as he would ever get to a prayer), *you've opened the door and let the draft in now.*

Mr. McKendrick shook his head like a dog shedding water and, sticking his thumbs into his waistcoat pockets, he turned and walked across the Green.

"Willie!" he exclaimed as he neared the filling station and Mr. Byers wandered into view.

"Mr. Chairman," Byers said. Mr. McKendrick let out a sigh. They both knew (and knew they knew) that there was only one possible motive for the visit, but to have his friendly overture sneered at this way, to have the decision of how to broach the subject wrested out of his grip so neatly before he had even started ... Mr. McKendrick's moment of fellow-feeling, his generosity in acknowledging even to himself the echoes of Willie's life in his own, were snuffed out and left nothing behind them but annoyance and the desire to deal with the matter swiftly and get away from the source of the annoyance as soon as he could.

"Willie, my solicitor wrote to you and you haven't answered the letter," he began.

"And that's my answer," said Mr. Byers, pulling a bristling bunch of keys out of his overall pocket and picking over it. "If you don't understand, I'm sure 'your solicitor' could explain it." He found the key he was looking for and fitted it into the boot-lock of his car. Mr. McKendrick concentrated on breathing slowly but didn't trouble to keep the sneer from forming on his face. He was not about to let a man of sixty-odd who drove a car without power locking stand here in the middle of his town ... (He half-shied away from this thought, lifting one hand as if to scratch his nose; then he steeled himself and leaned his hand on the car roof instead.) ... stand here in his town, *his town*, and make a fool of him. Mr. Byers finally got the boot open and lifted out a couple of petrol cans, which he set down at the side of the car.

"We need to get this sorted," said Mr. McKendrick. Byers didn't answer but removed the petrol-tank cap and put it down on the roof of the car less than an inch from Mr. McKendrick's crisp white shirt cuff. Mr. McKendrick pressed his fingers against the dusty paint, fighting the urge to move his hand away.

"Willie," he said, calmly, then stopped as he finally digested what was happening. Mr. Byers was pouring petrol carefully from the first of the cans, standing here in the forecourt of a bloody filling station, a business that the good Mr. and Mrs. Swain had built up by the sweat of their honest brows, pouring petrol not even through a proper funnel but through an old coke bottle with the bottom cut off. Mr. McKendrick raised his arms in disbelief and looked around for witnesses, then slapped his hands down against his thighs and let his shoulders sag.

"Willie," he began again. "I have already offered you a handsome price for this"—he jerked his head, just catching a glimpse of pink out of the corner of his eye— "and I'm willing to offer more, to top it up out of my own personal funds. And"—he held up a hand as Mr. Byers looked about to speak—"*and* I'm willing to gift you alternative workshop space, should you feel, in your wisdom, that you require it."

"Where would this be, then?" said Mr. Byers.

"Far end of the caravan site. The old lock-ups."

Mr. Byers snorted. "Down the back of the camp-site toilets, you mean? In beside the septic tanks and bins?"

Where you belong, thought Mr. McKendrick, *where you belong.* He leaned in close to the man's face before he continued. "What are you getting out of it, Willie?" he said. "I don't understand. It's not even a business anymore."

"Aye, you'd know all there is to know about doing business, James," said Mr. Byers. "But minding your own's a good start."

"It *is* my own," said Mr. McKendrick. "I'm the chairman of the committee in the association working to regenerate this town, that I have lived in my whole life, and you've been here ten minutes—"

"Five years."

"—and just because you get some kick out of being awkward, you think—"

"So it's the regeneration of the town, is it?" said Byers, cutting in on the rising swell of Mr. McKendrick's tirade. "That's what's in your heart, eh, Jimmy? That's what this is all about? All the meetings and the quiet wee visits and the chequebook waving in my face?"

"What else?" said Mr. McKendrick. He never blushed. His cheeks were ruddy from the golf course—and from the clubhouse afterwards too—but they were no barometer of his feelings. Still his eyes slid to one side and then the other before he could stop them. "What have you— I mean, what are you on about?"

"What have I heard?" said Byers. "Ah now, Mr. Chairman, that would be telling."

"You're bluffing," said Mr. McKendrick. "You've heard nothing because there *is* nothing, and even if there was, who would be telling you?" Then, suddenly pushed beyond his patience at last, he shouted. "Christ, Willie, you ken fine we'll never get grant money with this dump sitting in the middle like a boil on the bum."

———

He edited slightly for Mrs. Poole.

"So I said to him, 'Willie,' I said, 'I'm not going to play games with you. Name your price for this eyesore and let's get on with it.'"

"And how high would you go?" asked Mrs. Poole.

"Well, I'm not a rich man, Grace," said Mr. McKendrick. Mrs. Poole's mouth twitched into a quick pucker and when it released again he saw a little curl left at one side where one muscle refused to come under control. He shifted in his seat, two instincts fighting. He hated to be laughed at or even taken lightly, but how he loved to see Grace with a smirk on her lips.

Grace's lips occupied Jimmy McKendrick's thoughts more than he cared to admit to himself. She always wore lipstick of a good clear pink (he disliked to see a woman of their age without a bit of lipstick almost as much as he loathed the overdone lips of girls, either too bright and sticky or too thickly coated, pale as wax). Gracie was just right; her lips coloured without being masked and above and below was the perfect downy skin of a handsome woman growing older with ease, fluffy enough to be soft but without either of Mr. McKendrick's two aversions: bristles, or what was worse, the naked, shining skin of a woman who is dealing with her bristles somehow, whom he always felt scared to look at too closely in case he caught her pathetically halfway between appointments. Mr. McKendrick, being a bachelor, had never grown out of looking at women, or rather, *seeing* them when he looked, unlike a married man who withdraws into memories of his wife's young face and looks at what is before him but sees none of it, so that coming upon his wife unexpectedly in the street can be unsettling in a way he'd rather not explain. And visiting her in hospital has him walking up and down the ward looking for the face he holds in his heart and passing by the reality over and over again until a nurse takes pity and steers him and his flowers to the bedside.

"Jim?" said Mrs. Poole. "You were miles away."

"Not so far as all that," said Mr. McKendrick. "But anyway, as I was saying, I'm far from rich, Grace, but I've been careful. I've been more than careful, I've been prudent, and besides that I've been lucky. So between you and me..." He glanced at Mrs. Poole, to reassure himself of what he knew already: Grace was no gossip. She nodded seriously, but still with a bit of a twinkle. "Between you and me I'm willing to match the bid. Double it. I'll sell one of the holiday cottages if I have to." Mrs. Poole looked startled. "I'm like you, Gracie, and like Duncan, God rest his soul."

Mr. McKendrick blinked. Unexpectedly, he had landed in just the spot he had been trying to reach for weeks, and so he plunged ahead with it. "Business is business, and taking care of business is the only thing that'll ever get you anywhere. I have no time for anybody who doesn't understand that. They're all swank and credit cards, anyway. You know what I'm saying? I support—no, I applaud—I applaud your decision to take rent for the flat, and anybody who says otherwise is just jealous of your good sense." Mr. McKendrick kept talking, couldn't stop now he had started, like a pram on a hill, but he could see Mrs. Poole's face lose the twinkle and the little puckered muscle and turn blank again. Mr. McKendrick, back out in the cold he knew not why, thought about reaching out and taking hold of her, forcing her to talk to him, shaking her if he had to. He came near enough to doing it to make his blood pump faster at the thought, but when he moved it was only to rise from his seat, tuck it back squarely under the table, and say goodbye.

"Jim," said Mrs. Poole before he could leave. Mr. McKendrick stopped like a dog on a choke chain and came back to her side. "What you were saying about renting the flat and good sense and all that?" She paused; he waited. "The thing is I'm having second thoughts about it. About her." She raised her eyes to the ceiling, and Mr. McKendrick followed her gaze. "I'm not sure it's such a good idea. I'm not sure I can go through with it after all."

"What's happened, Gracie?" said Mr. McKendrick. "What's wrong?"

"I shouldn't have agreed. It's too soon after Duncan."

"But it's what Duncan would have wanted," Mr. McKendrick said. "He loved Painchton just like we do."

"And she's ... not what I was expecting," Mrs. Poole continued. "I'm just not ... I'd be happier if ... Besides she's a right noticing wee sort too. Watches, sees everything. She says nothing, but it's all going in, you know."

"All what?" said Mr. McKendrick.

"And young Craig's been speaking to her too," said Mrs. Poole.

"Craig?" said Mr. McKendrick. "Speaking about what?"

But the words, too painful to forget, were too harsh to repeat, and she just shook her head.

"She can't have found out anything that she shouldn't from Craig. He doesn't know."

"I'm just not sure I can carry on," said Mrs. Poole. "And I wish you'd listen when I try to tell you."

Mr. McKendrick patted her shoulder softly and left, thinking hard. He let himself out onto the street and righted himself, plucking each shirt cuff firmly out from inside his jacket sleeves, twanging each cuff-link gently then grasping the points of his waistcoat and giving a sharp downward tug. He took great comfort in the feeling this produced, of layers of well-tailored and properly fitted clothes snapping into place on his frame. He stood for a moment or two until to stand any longer would look aimless and then, almost without conscious thought, he turned about on himself, went in the house door, and climbed the stairs.

She was working, the computer whirring and a desk lamp lighting up piles of papers, the rest of the flat beginning to sink into darkness.

"I think you just keep that thing on in case somebody comes to the door," he said as he settled himself into an armchair. "I bet if I go through into the bedroom, I'll find magazines and chocolates and the radio playing, eh?" Keiko laughed back at him. "Now you know I'm only joking, hen, don't you?"

"Oh, yes," said Keiko. "And anyway, I'm used to it. If my mother went out when I was supposed to be doing my schoolwork, she always put her hand on the television when she came back to see if it was warm. But it never was, because I was always working. I'm *always* working."

"Well, that's a good girl," said Mr. McKendrick. "So long as you don't work too hard." He waited for inspiration about how to begin. To fill the lengthening silence, he went on: "At least that's one worry I don't have with young Craig." He laughed. "He's full of nonsense, always was. I hope you'd take anything he says with a grain of salt."

"A grain of salt?" said Keiko. "Is that a proverb? I hear so many things and if I don't understand, I just ignore them."

It wasn't quite the assurance he was looking for, but it would have to do.

"So … how's it all going?" he said. He laced his fingers together across his stomach in a comfortable gesture and felt his cuffs begin their upward creep.

"The pilot study is complete."

"This was the smoke and fire questions?"

"It was."

"And the food will come up next time, you assured me. Because it was food you said you were studying, and it was that that convinced us you were right for Painchton. Someone interested in traditions and beliefs and willing to learn our ways."

"I'm not an anthropologist, Mr. McKendrick," she said. "But yes, the food will be there in the end. I'm working on it. The pilot study smooths out the wrinkles in the format and then the profiling questionnaire…smooths out the wrinkles in the subjects—or shows me where they are so I know to allow for them—and *then* the study itself can begin."

"You must have patience of a saint," said Mr. McKendrick. "Not that doesn't sound very—I mean to say, I'm sure it's—" He cleared his throat.

"When eating poison, lick the plate," Keiko said. "That's a proverb my mother often says. In for a penny, you would say. And also, each to their own," she said, echoing Malcolm.

"Exactly," Mr. McKendrick said. "And how's everything else? The house…et cetera." And then, his nerve failing him, he changed the subject, almost. "I hope everybody's treating you well. I drew up a schedule. I hope it's being adhered to."

"You mean for entertaining me?" said Keiko. "I can assure you, Mr. McKendrick—"

"It wasn't supposed to be just tea and a bun for entertainment now and then," said Mr. McKendrick, frowning. "We agreed we would help you out day to day."

"Oh!" said Keiko. "You mean the groceries. If it's the groceries, I don't know where to begin. I can't keep up with it all. I'm drowning. In soup."

Mr. McKendrick chuckled at her and sat back in his chair. "Drowning in soup!" he said. "What a turn of phrase you have on you."

"I'm not joking," Keiko said, gesturing towards the kitchen as though Mr. McKendrick could see what was in there; the tubs of soup she made as a last resort when all hope of finishing up the food was slipping away, tubs stacked three deep in the freezer and more than once already defrosted and poured away when new consignments of frozen foods arrived and there wasn't an inch to spare. Kilo bags of chip shop chips, thin French fries, Cajun skins, extra-thick wedges, crumbed croquettes, and Granny Sarah's roasties (oven or microwave). And towers of cinnamon bagels, blueberry waffles, croissants (cook from frozen), and brioche (defrost at room temperature for twenty-fours and check that product is thoroughly thawed throughout before serving). And Mrs. Watson's cauliflower cheese in Pyrex, Mrs. Dessing's shepherd's pie in Le Creuset, Mrs. McMaster's cottage pie in a tinfoil tray like the tinfoil trays from the Imperiolos with the cardboard lids and the sauce seeping out along the seal. And then the knock at the door and it was Mr. Glendinning straight from the cash and carry and he couldn't resist the Boston cream pies at two-for-one, and she could have a slice now and just put the rest in the freezer.

"Good," said Mr. McKendrick. "As long as you're not going hungry. I'd hate to send you home to your mammy like some wee waif and stray and have her thinking we didn't take care of you."

"There's no chance of that," Keiko said.

"Not that I'm assuming we'll be sending you home at all, mind," he added. "Maybe you'll stay."

"Maybe I will," said Keiko. "I have never met with such kindness before. Mrs. Watson and Mrs. McMaster and Fancy. Rosa and the McLuskies—well, Mr. McLuskie, since his wife is so busy with her political life."

"And Mrs. Poole," said Mr. McKendrick, resisting the temptation to pass comment on Etta McLuskie's *political* life. As if he couldn't have been the new provost if he hadn't thought it would be too hard on Grace to see him in Duncan's chain of office. In a roundabout way, annoyance at Etta helped him. He finally dived in and said what he had come for.

"Do you think Mrs. Poole is all right?"

Keiko could not help her eyebrows rising.

"I just thought," continued Mr. McKendrick, "with you trained up in it, you know."

"Trained up? In?"

"All of this," said Mr. McKendrick, waving his hand at the papers on her desk. "People's … How people cope with things like … like what Grace is going through."

"Ah," said Keiko.

"And what with you being right here."

"I'm sorry, Mr. McKendrick, but I would never use my training to encroach on my neighbour's privacy. And even if I couldn't help forming a view, I wouldn't share it with anyone. It wouldn't be ethical."

Mr. McKendrick drew himself up and back a little in his chair. "Very proper," he said. "Very commendable." Then he paused. This was the second time in one day he had found himself bested, but this wee lass was no Willie Byers, surely. "Up to a point, mind you," he said. "But you're only human—ethics or no—and seeing her every day you must have some—"

"I'm not trained in clinical psychology, Mr. McKendrick," she said. "I have no specialism in grief and mourning. And I don't see her every day, actually. I really can't help you."

"Grief and mourning," Mr. McKendrick said. "So you think that's all it is, then? Good. I'm glad to hear it. Good to know." He gave her a sharp look. "Are you all right? You've gone a wee bit peelie-wally all of a sudden."

Keiko nodded. "Just tired," she said, and he got to his feet.

She could barely hear his goodbyes as she saw him out, struggling to find her feet in a flood of ideas that had surged up too fast for her to get astride them. She had just lied to Mr. McKendrick. She *did* see Mrs. Poole every day. Because every day Mrs. Poole scrubbed the building in the back yard, even though Malcolm said no one ever used it. Why would anyone do that? Her own words came back to her. "I am not a clinical psychologist; I have no specialism in grief and mourning." *I don't need one though,* she thought. *You don't need training to know that a woman doesn't clean an unused room because her husband died. You only need to have seen a bit of Shakespeare to know why someone keeps on endlessly cleaning.*

There was something rotten here. Wrong play, but true nevertheless. Murray knew and wanted to escape. When he thought she was teasing him about moving his business in there, he had looked ready to kill her. And Janette Campbell knew too. What Keiko had said to Janette Campbell was that Murray had workout machines in the back of the shop, and Mrs. Campbell had thought she meant the little place in the Pooles' back yard.

The slaughterhouse. Never used but cleaned every day, disgusting to Murray, frightening to Mrs. Campbell.

And what about Tash and Dina and Nicole? Did they know too? Did what they knew make them leave Painchton forever?

She couldn't explain what Mrs. Watson's fear might have to do with it. Except that as soon as she had the thought, she realised she could. Mrs. Watson owned the upstairs flat next door; she used it for storage. If she looked out of one of the back windows, she would be able to...

Keiko raced along the hall to the genkan, felt under the pipe, and drew the envelope out. If Mrs. Watson had been looking, she would have SEEN YOU. And she would KNOW WHAT YOU DID. And certainly she would have been horrified to see Keiko clutching the letter that threatened to TELL THEM ALL.

TWENTY-THREE

WHICH WAS RIDICULOUS, OBVIOUSLY. Mrs. Watson, sending a threatening letter? Mabel Watson, greengrocer, fruitseller, and poison pen? It was ... there was only one word for it, that wonderful word, unpronounceable by any Japanese person without decades of immersion in English-speaking circles, but since there was no one to hear her mangling it she could say right out loud, kneeling here on the genkan ... it was *preposterous*.

But what about her niece Dina who used to be so happy here and then suddenly was not? Might she have witnessed IT and sent the note? Might Mrs. Watson have found out and sent her niece away?

And besides, what was she imagining IT was that was done in the old slaughterhouse? An assignation? An empty building was an obvious trysting place for lovers. Her thoughts flew to Murray, of course, but there was nothing for them to settle upon. Murray— and Malcolm, come to that—were young single men; no affair of theirs would cause a scandal. But what if the woman were married—or what if the "woman" was a man? Keiko could not imagine that any of the Painchtonites would care about *that*. Mr. Callan of Palmer and Callan (surveyors) was married to—in Mrs. Watson's own words—a lovely boy called Martin who was a good cook, one of her best customers, and had beautiful sensitive hands. "Not like these old trotters," she had said, turning her own hands over and back and shaking her head at them. "Only good for rummaging in the tattie sack, these are."

Anyway, it couldn't be Murray: he had been alone since the break-up with his beloved girlfriend—whose name she couldn't bring to mind, if she had ever heard it. And Malcolm? Keiko considered this for a moment and rejected it too.

That left Mrs. Poole. And then it wouldn't take Sherlock Holmes to puzzle out who the other party might be for her. Keiko smiled to herself, recalling him sitting on the edge of his seat, his bright black eyes fastened on her as he jabbed her with questions. And—this was all conjecture, but to let it run for a moment—if Mr. Poole had found out and if the shock had killed him, wouldn't that explain his widow's numb dismay and her hysterical scrubbing in the hated place which had seen, no doubt, the confrontation between all three points of the love triangle?

But would that make sense of Murray? Would his mother's affair, even if it had felled his father, trap Murray the way he seemed to be trapped here? Would it make him tell her to be careful and wish that he could get her—get both of them—safely away? Would it make him, despite all that, glad that she was here, someone who could help him solve mysteries?

It would not. Nor would it suddenly make three young women leave. Even if one of them tried her hand at blackmail, that still left the other two. And anyway, Mrs. Watson—Keiko was sure now that she thought about it calmly—would have handled Grace Poole's affair by coming over, laying one of those tattie-sack hands on her friend's arm, and talking to her.

So if IT wasn't an affair, what was it? What were the facts? *Were* there any facts when she stripped away all the conjecture?

Keiko was aware of a sick feeling settling not into her stomach but somewhere behind her jaw, like the insidious nausea of a journey in a vehicle with a dirty engine, where the fumes build up so gradually that you just gulped them down. There was only one fact, really, one thing was not *preposterous* but rather *incontrovertible*: Mr. Poole was dead. Murray's father had died, and no one seemed to know what had killed him. And—returning to conjecture again, but with a certainty which made the bend in her jaw flood with saliva and caused to her to swallow hard—she could only too easily combine a death, a certain kind of death, with a neighbour too scared to talk plainly.

Her thoughts were racing along now; Murray hated the shop, but Malcolm loved it. Duncan Poole's death had ended one son's ambitions, but it had handed the other all that he desired. And wasn't it strange that Malcolm alone of the three of them spoke of his father so easily, so soon? Didn't it hint at a lack of feeling, perhaps a *block* to proper feeling? How could Malcolm be so contented while his mother stumbled through her days numb with sorrow and his brother fretted and ached? And if it seemed outlandish to think a boy might value a butcher's shop above his own father, she could pull to mind more instances than she cared to of Malcolm stroking bloody steaks as though they were kittens, delving with glee into a wriggling mass of ground beef or a slithering vat of liver. She could hear Murray's voice: *Malcolm's a butcher. That more or less sums it up as far as Malcolm goes.* And Craig's voice: *That creep across the road.*

But even Murray stayed, despite everything. And Craig regretted saying even as much as that, which was nothing. *We've all been pals since we were wee.*

The problem was that everyone in Painchton was loyal to the town. Its ways, Mr. McKendrick had said. Its traditions. If only she could find the missing girls. They would have no loyalty; they would tell her the truth.

She opened the browser on her laptop and sat with her fingers on the keys. But she did not even know their full names. Nicole might be a McKendrick, and Dina might be a Watson, but unless Tash had taken Mrs. McMaster's name—which was not likely—she could be anyone. Keiko closed the laptop again.

If she couldn't find the people who had left and those who stayed were too bonded to the place like Fancy or too scared like Murray, then she might as well give up on this tenuous mystery.

Then she remembered Mrs. Poole turning pale at the thought of the questionnaire, forbidding her sons to take it. Keiko turned her head and looked along the passage towards the sideboard in the living room, to where Mrs. Watson's answer sheet lay. It would show up, wouldn't it? A sneak, a secret holder, a writer of that horrid little note—a person like that couldn't have answered all those questions on rumours and gossip and disbelief without *something* showing.

And so Keiko took the first small steps down a path she had never dreamed she would find herself on, one from which there was no returning. She made herself a cup of tea and, with a very soft pencil that she could rub away almost by breathing, she copied the names from her sign-up sheet onto the answer pages in the order of when people visited, opened her stats software, and began.

An hour later, she stared unblinking at the graph she had made until her eyes started to water. She went to the bathroom, took out her lenses, and came back again, threading the wires of her spectacles around her ears.

Maybe Mrs. Watson had seen something surprising behind Keiko in the street that first day. Or maybe she'd been trying not to sneeze. One thing was for sure: there was nothing in her profile—not in scruples, trust, discretion, anywhere—that marked her out as different from Pet McMaster, Pamela Shand, or Moira Glendinning. They were all as innocent as newborn babes.

They were, but it wasn't like that for everyone. Hidden in the crowd of forty was a very worried little band. Their names, when she put them together, rang a faint bell somewhere. Imperiolo, McLuskie, Dessing, and Ballantyne. Where had she come across them bunched together before? Murray, she remembered, had told her she'd be better off without the Imperiolos and McLuskies as friends. Except that it wasn't both Imperiolos that stood out on this graph she was staring at; it was Kenny Imperiolo, him alone. And it wasn't Andrew McLuskie, Master Baker, but his wife, Provost Etta. Likewise, Alec Dessing and Margaret Ballantyne ran with the herd, and it was only *his* wife and *her* husband who had made the anxiety indicators shoot off the top of the scale.

What did these four have in common? She was sure there was something. She could see them as clear as day, as if she was looking down on them from above.

That was it! Of course she *had* seen them, across the street. She had seen them going into the flat door beside the ironmongers, to

Mr. McKendrick's offices up there. They, along with Jimmy McKendrick himself, were the Painchton Traders committee.

Well, of course they were worried! Her shoulders fell and she let her held breath out with a hiss, almost laughing. They were steering a massive project, involving all kinds of decisions and initiatives—including having her here in the flat doing this project. She heard again Mr. McLuskie's voice telling her she must be wondering why they'd brought her there. And then she remembered his voice saying it was anyone's guess what was wrong with Etta. He had said she was *up to high doh.* And Mrs. Imperiolo had said her husband was *stressed to his oxters,* and Keiko had had to ask Fancy for translations.

But if they were merely anxious about Traders business, wouldn't their spouses understand that? Why would Andrew McLuskie and Rosa Imperiolo be puzzled if that was all that was going on?

So what *was* worrying them? Keiko glanced back at the graph again. She hadn't asked the right questions; she didn't know. And she *couldn't* ask the right questions—simply couldn't—because of conscience, ethics, morals … and the small fact that the questions she asked were supposed to help with her PhD and not with Painchton's secrets, whatever they were.

Unless … Keiko lay back in her chair and stared up at the ceiling. The target questions—food fads and health scares; her shitty kale, as Fancy called it—they were sacred and they were harmless. But the filler questions could be anything at all. And if she wrote on the front page that responses to the *study questions* were anonymous, then possibly, logically, technically, you could say that the *filler questions,* not actually a *part* of the study, were …

Well, if she never put a name to this, it would be that much easier to forget once it was done.

She was surprised to find herself wondering what her mother would tell her to do. *Let the stream flow past you*, was a favourite of her mother, who would not let the slightest trickle flow anywhere without her permission. But sometimes, and more honestly, she would say: *Cover your ears, Keko-chan, and steal the bell.*

It would be for a good cause—for Murray. No one should have to laugh to keep from screaming. No one should have to know things that were crushing them and be sure that no one else would understand. Another saying of her mother's popped into her head, the best one yet. She said it aloud to herself.

"The weak are meat. The strong eat." And she nodded, decided at last.

But would it work? Could she find out Painchton's secrets this way, through a questionnaire? She gave a dry laugh. Everybody else certainly thought so. As soon as Murray had heard about her work he had thought she could help him. And Mr. McKendrick reckoned she could analyse Mrs. Poole. All of them believed that Keiko's training, her expertise, her methods, would let her crack open their secrets like eggs against stone.

But that was the mark of a layman. Keiko sat up a little straighter in her chair. A professional always acknowledged the limits as well as the scope of her discipline. So, yes, she would design a study within a study to see where the secret lay. She would also, however, complete her investigation of the committee. If Sandra Dessing's husband and Iain Ballantyne's wife were as worried and puzzled about their spouses' stress as Rosa Imperiolo and Andrew McLuskie were, she would have discovered something.

She turned over a new page on her scribble pad.

Fillers, she wrote.

Snoop spouses

She stood at last, knuckling her back, looking out across the empty street to the dark buildings across the way. She stretched and made her way across the room towards bed. Then she wheeled back and added a third line to her list:

Find the girls.

TWENTY-FOUR

Tuesday, 12 November

THE PIANO DIDN'T QUITE stop playing as she walked into the bar of the Covenanters' Arms, but Margaret Ballantyne rushed towards her, came right out from behind the bar, and had her away to the empty dining room before any of the drinkers had gathered themselves to call a greeting.

"Different if you were meeting someone," she said. "Different if Fancy or Murray"—she winked at Keiko—"was coming, but you can't just sit there in the public bar on your lonesome."

"Can I sit alone in here?" asked Keiko looking around.

"Away, I'm not going to leave you," said Mrs. Ballantyne. She drew out two chairs opposite Keiko, sat in one and put her feet up on the other, kicking her shoes off. "The bar can manage without me for half an hour," she said. "Pulling pints is great for your arms, but it's murder on your ankles. Anyway, I'm pleased to get the chance to do my bit."

"Your bit?"

"Feeding you up," said Mrs. Ballantyne. "Getting a good dinner down you. Mind and tell Jimmy McKendrick too. He had plenty to say to Iain and me about us dodging the schedule, but what could we do about it? We're always busy in here and he was adamant that it was home-cooking he wanted for you. He said as bold as brass: 'I'm not wanting her stuffed full of all the additives and chemicals. They're just poison.'"

"He'd drop dead if he saw my freezer," said Keiko, thinking of the honey-dipped Southern-style boneless breaded buffalo bites (deep fry, shallow fry, microwave, or oven).

"I told him," said Mrs. Ballantyne, not listening to her. "I said: the Covenanters' *is* home-cooking, Jim. Local suppliers and all made from scratch in the kitchen. But there's no telling him. So, what are you in the mood for?"

"Whatever you recommend," said Keiko, choking back the impulse to suggest that they phone Mr. McKendrick and ask him.

What Margaret Ballantyne recommended was sausage and mash and onion gravy.

"Oh my goodness," said Keiko when she saw it.

"And seasonal vegetables," Margaret said, putting a dish of them down beside the plate.

"Gosh," said Keiko. And then: "Ah! Is it for me? Is that supposed to be Mount Fuji rising out of the ..." Her voice faded at the frown that met her words.

"Mount Fuji?" said Margaret. "It's just a wee drop of mashed potato."

The sausage was curled round the edge of the plate and swimming slightly, and the potato corralled by it *did*—she was not imagining things—rise up in vertiginous slopes and crags almost to her eye level. She turned to the vegetables, as you might turn from a sickroom to look at a garden.

"Roast Parmesan parsnips," said Margaret, "creamed greens, baby sweetcorn in tempura batter—you'll like them, eh?—and stuffed mushrooms."

"Do you get your vegetables from Mrs. Watson?" said Keiko, thinking to kill two birds with one stone.

"We go to the same wholesaler, dear," said Margaret. "What are the mushrooms stuffed with?" she called through to the kitchen.

"Mozzarella," came the reply. The moment for questions about Mrs. Watson's niece Dina had passed. And anyway, Keiko could not imagine how to get from vegetables to a missing niece. Certainly not in English. She turned back to the first bird: did Mrs. Ballantyne know why her husband was on edge?

"It's very good of you to take the time to sit with me," she said, digging her fork into the summit of the potato. "I know how busy you are."

"If only," said Mrs. Ballantyne.

"I mean the Traders as a whole," Keiko said, trying again. "Or the committee anyway. With the initiative. Including me, Mr. McKendrick tells me." She smiled.

"Oh, me too," said Margaret. "You're the centerpiece and no mistake, but Iain's the one that's neck deep in all of that." Mrs. Ballantyne smiled as she spoke. "I just make the sandwiches. Try a bit of sausage."

"I will," said Keiko. "It looks lovely."

"Aye, he's a fair sausage hand, that boy."

"Malcolm Poole," Keiko said, and it was not really a question.

222

"A fine butcher for a young one, so he is," said Mrs. Ballantyne. "And he understands what people come to a pub for—when they're hungry, I mean."

"And what's that?"

"A good plate of hot dinner," Mrs. Ballantyne said. "A right good feed, hot and rich and easy going down. Doesn't even matter what it is as long as it's piping hot, well seasoned, and there's plenty of it. A lining on your stomach, if you'll pardon the expression, but that's what my old mother used to say. She was a pub landlady too, you know, with the veins to prove it. You'd not have half the mess on the night buses if these youngsters kept to it. But there's no telling them: eatin's cheatin', they say."

Keiko sipped at her glass of spring water and hoped the subject would change.

"But what was I . . . Oh yes," Mrs. Ballantyne said. "Yes, Iain's the committee man." Keiko ventured on a mushroom. "And it's getting to him, it's true. He's that crabbit these days, you wouldn't know him."

"*Crabbit*?" said Keiko.

"Tripping over his own chin," said Mrs. Ballantyne. "Not to me, I have to say. He's always been a good husband. Flowers every Friday, tea in bed on a Sunday morning, and he's all that just as usual—more so, if anything. But he's nipping at folk like a wee ferret, and that's not like him. He's got some kind of stooshie going with the Dessings across the way, for one thing." Keiko pricked up her ears. "There's two pubs in Painchton; there's always been two pubs in Painchton. They serve Belhaven beer, we serve McEwan's. We both do lunches and suppers, but we make sure and not clash our quiz nights. But I don't know, since this new initiative got going, all of a sudden this town ain't big enough for the both of us. The four of us, I mean."

"Times are tough?" said Keiko.

"Not really," said Mrs. Ballantyne. "No worse than ever. The smoking ban hit the bar years back, but it actually helped the suppers. We're okay. And if it was business Iain was worried about, he'd not be spending money like it grew on trees, would he? No. And is he? Yes."

Keiko summed up, "So you know your husband's anxious and you don't know why."

"That I do not," Mrs. Ballantyne said. "I don't even know where he is tonight. He went out with the dog, and that's the last I've seen of him. Are you not a lover of spinach then?"

It took Keiko a moment to change gears, but she smiled quickly enough. "I like spinach very much," she said. "It's one of my favourite things."

"Aye? No wonder you're the wee scrap you are then," said Mrs. Ballantyne. "I'm only asking since you've not touched it." She nodded at the dish of vegetables, at the mound of pale, pale green glistening there.

"That's spinach?" Keiko said.

"And a wee tate of cream just to help it on its way."

———

Stressed to his oxters, up to high doh, and crabbit as a ferret, Keiko thought to herself later. Three out of four and one to go, but she was getting nowhere with the girls' names.

Wednesday, 13 November

She excused herself from her weights session the next evening and went to the Bridge Hotel. She had eaten nothing all day except two rice crackers and a tangerine, in preparation.

"Hallo, hallo," said Mr. Dessing as Keiko entered the bar. He was a large man, even to the eyes of someone who saw Malcolm Poole every day. An egg-shaped head with a fringe of hair around it like a ribbon. A spherical body, its equator marked by the meeting place of his shirt and trousers, which stayed up apparently by magic since they made no dent in his middle.

"I've come for a little bite to eat, Mr. Dessing," said Keiko. "I'm so busy now, I can hardly cook for myself at the end of the day."

"If God had meant people to live off home-cooking..." said Mr. Dessing. "And you're nice and early." Indeed, the place was deserted except for a couple Keiko didn't know sitting on the love seat under the window. "Once the rugby training finishes you'll not be able to move in here. Or breathe. Aftershave, you know."

"I went to the Covenanters' last night," said Keiko, hoping to get things moving.

"But you've seen the light!" said Mr. Dessing. "I don't mean it, of course. Margaret Ballantyne should have been a farmer's wife and not a publican's, if you ask me, but they're good people."

"It's lovely the way you all get along," Keiko said, wondering if she could really pull off such a sickening act of innocence. She had hopped up onto a bar stool and clasped her hands together on the polished surface.

He grunted absentmindedly while he searched through a muddled drawer of handsets and phone chargers. "Tell that to Sandra," he said when he had found what he was looking for. "And Iain."

"Professional rivalry," said Keiko, half to herself. Was that all it was?

"Aye, these things can turn nasty," Mr. Dessing said. "I've seen it before and I'm seeing it again. And if you ask me—" He broke off and rubbed his hand over his mouth, scrubbing the words away. "But you're not. Now what can I tempt you with?"

"Something very light," said Keiko.

Mr. Dessing gave a huge gulp of laughter that shook the shirt fabric over his middle. "I'll bet," he said. "After your 'good plate of hot dinner' yesterday." Keiko giggled. "See what I mean? A farmer's wife! Now over here at the Bridge, we do things differently. Presentation is key."

"I agree, Mr. Dessing," said Keiko. "We think so in Japan. Eat with the eye then with the lips."

"Pree-cisely. I'll bet you had a round plate over by." Keiko nodded and Mr. Dessing shook his head. "Round plates! Everything jammed on and spilling over. I don't know."

And when her supper came, the plate was no shape Keiko knew a name for: a kind of bulbous S or melted rectangle. She gazed at it. "I'm sorry, Mr. Dessing," she said, her voice rising in a question. "But I ordered tapas? From the light bite selection?"

"Mixed meat tapas," Mr. Dessing confirmed. "Light bite, aye. I'll just talk you through. Mini kilties—that's wee sausages with bacon kilts on; deep fried haggis balls—self-explanatory to an old hand like you, but we have a laugh with the tourists about them; steak and kidney puffs—the steak ones are the square and the kidney ones are the wee love-hearts there; then you've got your spare ribs; your belly lollies—pork belly, most like; and the specialty of the house, lamb and mince koftas—my own invention. Malcolm makes them up for me, mind."

"Lamb and mint?"

"Lamb and mince. Wee bit of minced beef and pork mixture with the lamb to help them stick together. He's always got plenty of his special mixture to spare. All served on a bed of—would you like some mint sauce, though?"

Keiko assured him that she had everything she could want and more. "About what you were saying," she began when she had eaten three of the so-called tapas. "What if I *did* ask you?"

"Ask me what, lovey?" Mr. Dessing was engrossed in the handset for his music system, the instruction booklet open on the bar in front of him. He pushed a button, cocked his head, listened to silence, then tutted and turned a page with a licked finger.

"About things turning nasty." Keiko bent her head as he raised his, to avoid his eye.

"I shouldn't have said that," he told her. "But if you *did* ask me . . ."

She had, Keiko thought, waiting.

"If somebody *did* ask me, I'd say there's no way a few new signs and picnic tables have put this wasp up Sandra's ar—uh, this bee in her bonnet. Or Jimmy McKendrick's either. Kenny. Any of them."

Keiko tried very hard not to look too interested. "I'm glad to hear it," she said. "I'm sorry there's *anything* wrong, of course. But I'm glad it's not the Traders initiative that's worrying everyone. I'd feel responsible."

"You?" said Mr. Dessing.

"Well, I'm part of it, aren't I? Their pet project. Mrs. Ballantyne called me the centrepiece. The international section of the . . . what's the word, like menu, but for financial things?"

"Search me. *Portfolio*? And anyway, you've been no trouble to anyone. We're glad to have you, and it's a pleasure to show you a bit of hospitality. I've been feeling it, I can tell you; seeing you traipsing round to everybody's houses for your tea and here we are at the end of the road, dead handy."

"Mr. McKendrick didn't want me frequenting bars," Keiko said.

"He did not," said Mr. Dessing. "He said the Japanese weren't good with strong drink. He said it would ruin your liver."

"Mr. McKendrick was worried about my liver?" said Keiko, blinking.

"As if you'd be getting plastered just because you'd come in for a supper!" said Mr. Dessing. "Anyway, never mind J McK. Never mind any of them and whatever's got them all birling."

"He was worried about my liver?" said Keiko again, unable quite to understand why that was so troubling.

TWENTY-FIVE

WHICH MADE THE FULL set: *oxters, high doh, crabbit, wasp up her.*
There were four people wound like springs with worry. Five if she
counted Jimmy McKendrick. Six if Mrs. Watson's dropping the
cauliflower that day was proof of anything. Seven including Murray. Eight in total, with Mrs. Poole. The only one *not* anxious at all
was Malcolm!

She opened a new document and set her fingers lightly against
the keys.

Death of Mr. Poole
Slaughterhouse
Letter FOR YOU
Mrs. Watson
Committee

Then she added another column.

Death of Mr. Poole	*Crime?*
Slaughterhouse	*Scene of Crime?*
Letter	*Report of Crime?*
Mrs. Watson	*Witness to Crime?*
Committee	

There was only one way to fill that last slot, as far as she could see. Another word she could type but would never try to pronounce: *Perpetrator*. But where did that leave Malcolm—innocent by-stander? And what about the missing girls—more witnesses? She leaned on the delete key until the two columns were gone.

There was definitely a secret in this town, but was it a secret crime in the past or a secret plan for the future? She was almost sure that all the worry was about something coming, something loom-ing, not leftover guilt about something over and gone. But if that was so, then what did Mr. Poole have to do with it?

Keiko sat back and stared across the room. Maybe he found out about it. Maybe he even threatened to stop them.

This theory had a gaping hole, of course: she had no *real* evi-dence that Mr. Poole's death was suspicious in any way.

Thursday, 14 November

"Murray's round at the bikes," Malcolm said as she entered the shop. He was staring at a large haunch of pale meat on his cutting block, perhaps deciding where to divide it.

"I'm not looking for Murray," said Keiko.

"Not a problem upstairs, is there?"

"None at all. I want to speak to you because you find it easy to talk about your father." She took a deep breath. "Is there any reason I shouldn't be asking about food and health? It occurred to me that it might be unfeeling. Because of … heart trouble … and your father."

"Oh, right!" said Malcolm, looking up again. "My father didn't die of heart trouble."

"I beg your pardon, then. I thought someone told me so."

"At least not in the way you mean," said Malcolm. He ran the flat of his hand back and forth over the haunch of meat, smiling at her. "I once heard a doctor say that heart failure is what kills everyone in the end." Keiko couldn't match his smile. Malcolm said nothing for a moment and then he nodded as though deciding.

"No, you're all right with food questions," he said. "But it shouldn't be cheese and chocolate and apples and kale."

"Oh?"

"You should stick to this," he said, slapping down with both his hands.

"Why?" said Keiko, glancing at his hands and then away again.

"If it's why people eat what they do, meat's best," said Malcolm. He was absentmindedly plucking bristles from the skin of whatever animal was on the cutting surface. "Because it's the only food that needs an explanation, isn't it? It doesn't make sense if you think about it too long. Animal lovers who eat meat. Cruelty-free meat. That's where the beliefs are strongest, because they have to be."

———

"Malcolm told me you were here," she said, in answer to Murray's look of surprise when he opened the door to her. She looked past him and saw that the covers were off all of the bikes.

"Do you know," she said, "you never did introduce me to the last one." It was true; they had fallen into a pattern of warm up, work out, cool down and, except when Murray saw her passing the shop and came out to speak to her, there was nothing more. He looked behind him and stepped aside to let her enter.

"Aerial Square Four," he said, squatting down beside it. "A Squariel it's called, because of how the crankshafts and cylinders are geared together. And a 1000cc engine—totally ridiculous when it was new. 1956. Beast of a bike, really, more trouble than it's worth."

"Like the Golden Flash?" said Keiko.

"No, no," said Murray. "Not that way—this is a great bike, smooth as silk. It can overheat a bit but no, I mean the insurance and everything. There's guys I would trust with the rest, but I wouldn't trust them not to slip in here and make off with the Squariel if they thought they could."

Keiko scrutinised the machine; it was certainly beautiful, with its red painted parts gleaming like pools of silk, but it was just another motorbike to her and, glad as she was that it had got her inside and got Murray talking today, she was even gladder she wouldn't have to try to remember the names and quirks of any more.

"So," he said, looking up at her from where he was crouched. "I'll see you tonight then."

"Of course," she said. "I'm sorry I interrupted your …" She looked around to see what it was she might have interrupted. "But now that I'm here, can I say something to you?"

"Okay."

"About what's wrong?"

He was silent, waiting.

"You said one time—more than once, actually—that you couldn't tell me anything because I wouldn't understand and maybe I wouldn't even believe you."

He nodded.

232

"But you also said you thought I could help. Well, I want you to know that I'm working on it. And I'm getting somewhere—maybe not to the bottom of it—but somewhere."

"How?" said Murray, staring up at her.

"The way I do," Keiko said. "By looking at the wiring, remember?"

His eyes shone as he nodded.

"Also, there's something I need to ask and you're the only one I can trust," she said.

"You trust me?" he said. "You've no idea how much it means to hear you say that."

"It's about Dina and Nicole and Tash," she said.

Murray blinked twice. "Who?"

"Mrs. Watson's niece and Craig's cousin and Mrs. McMaster's foster child."

"*Who?*" said Murray again.

"Do you know their full names? I want to speak to them but unless I can find out their names, I have no hope of tracking them down. Is Dina a Watson? Is Nicole a McKendrick? And what about Tash?"

He was shaking his head very slowly now and his eyes were wide and strained. "Don't," he said. "They got away safe and sound, Keiko. Don't do anything that would drag them back here. They got away."

Now it was her turn to stare at him. "Are you serious?" she said.

"Always," he replied.

"But … if the danger was real—*is* real—shouldn't we try to speak to them? Double-check they're okay?"

He thought about it for a while and then shook his head. "No can do," he said. "I don't know their second names. You know how it is; everyone's so friendly here—first names all the way."

"Who *would* know?" said Keiko.

"It's not a good idea to ask too many questions," said Murray. "Trust me."

———

She heard Murray lock the door behind her after she left and stood staring at it—was he really that scared?—until something moving caught the corner of her eye. Mr. Byers was standing on the forecourt, smiling broadly around his chewing gum.

"Better than the telly any day," he said and sauntered back through his open workshop door and into the shadows. Keiko watched him go and kept watching the spot where he had disappeared, straining her eyes to see if he had turned to face her.

"Mr. Byers," she called. She followed him into the darkness. "Mr. Byers? I just realised I haven't managed to rope you in to my questionnaire yet and you'd be a very interesting addition because you haven't been here that long. Mr. Byers?" Right at the back a light was on and she thought she could hear the sound of a tap running. "Mr. Byers?" She pushed the half-open door and saw him standing with his back to her, urinating into a filthy toilet.

"What do you want now?" he said over one shoulder, but Keiko was gone, racing back through the workshop towards the street, with the sound of his laughter ringing in her ears and a negative print of his straddled figure in the block of light etched on her eyes.

Monday, 18 November

"Okay then," said Fancy, looking straight up at Keiko's living room ceiling and breathing hard. "I worked all bleedin' weekend and finally got two scenarios each for conformity, conscientiousness, compliance, optimism, orthodoxy—but I still think that's a kind of toothpaste—lawfulness, discretion, compartmentalisation, and suggestibility. And I made sure and got theft, murder, rape, blackmail, incest, domestic violence, fraud, corruption—what's the difference?—and ehh … bigamy, yeah. And *you* haven't even added red meat to your shitty spinach, you lazy article." She sighed heavily. "I thought this would be a laugh when you asked me, you know."

"It does do your head in, doesn't it?" said Keiko. "You are an angel. Flop your arms over one way and your legs the other."

"Yeah, I'm the guardian angel of your English," Fancy said. "You can't say it does your head in." She moved her arms and legs to opposite sides. "Man, this feels good. Those are killer crunches."

"I know. And I only made you do ten and now we're having this lovely rest. Murray says fifty."

"Well, just say no. What would he do?"

"He said he would put me over his knee and spank me."

"Way-hey! Just say no, then!" said Fancy.

Keiko jabbed her bottom with a toe, making her wobble. Then she put her feet flat on the floor and laced her hands behind her head. "Scissors," she said.

"No," groaned Fancy, "not scissors. I'll never get up again if we do bloody scissors. I'll take my questions back and then you'll be sorry."

"I'm going to show the questionnaire to Dr. Bryant tomorrow," said Keiko, and something inside her fluttered at the thought of it; the questions about murder, rape, and incest—everything she could think of that the problem in Painchton could possibly be—seemed to pulse on the page as though they'd been printed out in some special fluorescent ink. More than half of her expected Bryant to throw the paper down, call the servitor, and have her removed from the building, removed to the airport, stripped of her funding, stripped of her first degree, her high school diploma…

"And if Biscuit-man says okay, you should get cracking," Fancy was telling her. "The very next day. Everybody's in a good mood on half-closing." She rolled over onto all fours, stood awkwardly, and stepped up onto the coffee table to look at herself in the mirror. "Still fat. I told you it wouldn't work." She pulled down the waistband of her leggings and pinched a roll of skin between two fingers trying to make it waggle.

Keiko rose to her feet with a thrill at how fluid the movement was now after all those evenings with Murray. She stretched and walked over. "Fat!" she said. Fancy's navel, currently at eye level, lay flat on the surface of her stomach, its neat banana-slice pattern not shaded by the slightest overhang of flesh. "There's not even enough there to pierce," she said, then immediately put up her arms to steady Fancy as she sank down and put her head between her knees. "I'm so sorry. I'm so sorry," she said.

Fancy lifted her head again and glared. "Body piercing! That's my worst thing. It's like the world's gone totally mad." Her face was patched with unnatural colours, her lips grey and the skin around her nose yellowish, but a blue flush still blooming high on her cheeks and round her eyes from being upside down.

Keiko clapped her hands. "No scissors," she said. "To make up for me being so thoughtless."

She started for the kitchen to begin cooking but Fancy, stopping in the bathroom doorway, beckoned her back. Perfumed steam was spilling out, casting Fancy into soft focus and beading her bright hair. Keiko put her head round the door and blinked through the vapour. Viola was lying almost completely submerged in a heavily scented, deep-tinted bath, just an island of face sticking up. Her eyes were shut and her hair, tame and lank under the water, was swished out in a waving fan behind her head, moving in the slight eddy made by her twirling hands. As they watched, one lock of hair slicked against her neck and she stopped the figure-of-eight dance of her hands, put her feet flat on the bottom of the bath so that her small knees rose steaming into the air, raised one hand to scoop the hair free again, then resumed her pose. She waited until the water had stilled and then began again to trace her hands through and back, through and back, just enough to make the surface plane of the water slide and keep her hair moving.

Keiko stepped back, uncomfortable, as Fancy bent over and knocked gently against the side of the bath, but when Viola opened her eyes she just smiled up at them and moved only to raise her head out of the water.

"Your bath's great, Keiko," she said. "Can I put some more salts in?"

"Yes, of course," said Keiko.

"No, you can't, you monkey," said Fancy. "We'll have to get a licence from the Environmental Health before we take the plug out anyway." She took the towel from where it was warming on the radiator and tucked the middle of one edge under her chin. Viola stood and turned her back and Fancy lifted the child towards her with one hand under each skinny armpit. Viola felt for the hanging corners of the towel and pulled it around herself. She kicked drops of water from her feet as Fancy stepped away from the side of the bath and swung her round onto the floor, then she scooted off along the passageway towards Keiko's spare bedroom, huddled in the towel and with her hair plastered in clumps to the sides of her face, already beginning to frizz again.

In Keiko's future memories, this evening was the last innocent time. The sight of the small girl in the perfumed water, perfect little body and perfect unconcern when she opened her eyes and saw them looking down at her. The choreography of mother and daughter getting her out of the water and back on her feet, and the three of them in a row on the sofa later watching a movie together to make Viola feel grown-up, making Fancy and Keiko feel like little girls again. This remembered evening—even though the sick feeling had already arrived and even though there were times to come when briefly it left her—this warm, glowing evening was the last real moment before what was coming began.

TWENTY-SIX

Tuesday, 19 November

DR. BRYANT READ SLOWLY, pulling on his nose. Keiko watched him, unsure whether she was tensed against discovery or tensed against a go-ahead, permission to do it, having to carry out her plan after all.

"These look competent," he said. "Where did you get them?"

"They're original," said Keiko. "A friend helped me."

"An English speaker?" he said, looking up, ready to find incompetence after all. Keiko nodded. He rolled his fingers together, dealing whatever had come of pulling his nose, and then started flicking the pages over again. "Strange fillers," he said. "Rather dramatic." Keiko waited for something more like a veto, but nothing came.

"I sometimes think," she said at last, "that filler questions are so bland and boring, it's too obvious what they are. These will be much better at distracting the subjects." She felt sure he would argue with such a definite opinion. He wouldn't be able not to.

"You could be right," he said.

Keiko felt her shoulders slump down a little. "You don't think the fillers are *too* offensive? Or anything," she asked.

"Good luck offending the first years," he said, pulling at his nose again.

"I'm not using the first years," said Keiko. "I'm using the members of the association who're sponsoring my accommodation." She paused. "I'm experimenting on the people who're funding me."

"Well, let me know how it goes," Bryant said. This time he wiped his fingers on the underside of his desk.

Keiko took the papers from him, holding them by the opposite corner from where he had leafed through them with his nose-pulling hand. She kept them clear of her body until she came to a litter bin, then dropped them in it and went to get Viola.

It had been a first dress-rehearsal for the end-of-term show, and Viola came out overexcited and still in lavish feline make-up, with her hair sprayed dark and sticky into a little cake on top of her head. On the bus, she tucked herself under Keiko's arm and was drowsing before they slowed at the next stop.

"Your wee one's knackered," said a woman opposite with a comfortable smile, when Viola's arm flopped out of her lap and swung loose as they rounded a corner. Keiko looked down at the elongated sweep of her closed eyelids, the black sheen of her sprayed hair, then smiled at the woman, tucked Vi's arm back into her lap, and held her a little more tightly.

———

Fancy lay on the waxing table in the back room of Janette's salon, waiting out the pain before young Yvonne applied the next strip to her leg.

"How about your bikini line, Fance?"

"Bog off and die," said Fancy. "Who gets their bikini line waxed in November?"

"Wouldn't you like to know?" said Yvonne. "Loads of people'll get it done next month for parties."

"Yeah, well I don't get invited to that kind of party," Fancy said. Craig McKendrick's face popped into her head, but a surge of pain saw him off again. She breathed in a gasp so sharp that the cold air hurt her teeth.

"You're so polite," said Yvonne, blowing onto the red area. "The first and last time I did Mrs. McLuskie—when she was off on that golf exchange with all the other old trollops—guess what she said?"

"'Dearie me, how painful'?"

"She said 'Ayabastard.' Dead loud. She's never been back since."

———

Etta McLuskie, sitting in her car in the darkest corner of the multi-storey, was using all the wiles that had deserted her on the waxing table that day.

"No one's going to put two and two together and build a scaffold," she said, speaking loud enough for her voice to carry through the open window of her car and into the open window of the car pulled up beside her. "Your … problem was years ago. I wasn't the Painchton provost, you weren't the minister. Everyone has remarried, moved house, retired, or all three. We have no connection and there's no paper trail."

"I hope you're right," the voice came back from the other car.

"We just need till the new year," said Etta.

"And you're sure it's not going to leak? Painchton's not what it was, I heard. Incomers, folk with no loyalty. Troublemakers."

"But none of them know," said Etta. "There's only five of us, Painchton-born and -bred, who know what's happening. Of course, there's newcomers in the town—there's a vegetarian numpty in the Cat's Whiskers, for one—but we keep them where we want them. Outside."

———

Pamela Shand was in the Cat's Whiskers with the shutters down, busy pricing stock. Marking down sale stock, actually. Putting half-price stickers on her rack of vegetarian cookbooks, to be more precise than she felt like being. She had got them in when the horse meat scandal took off (which was how she put it to herself, although she was careful to say *struck* to others). But the stream of neighbours seeking advice on mung beans had never started, and the Pooles were busier than ever. She heard the bell clank again and again every morning as she stood in the queue at the post office. Just once she had asked Mrs. Watson:

"How *can* you? You're surrounded by all that bounty and yet you eat the flesh of the dead?"

"The Flesh of The Dead?" said Mrs. Watson. "It sounds like a movie. Dina always loved a zombie, and she left her DVDs for me. Anyway, Malcolm gets all his meat from Malone's, what he doesn't prepare for himself."

"And where do *they* get it?" said Pamela.

"Och, who cares?" said Mrs. Watson. "That boy could season a scabby rat and you'd not say no. Rosa Imperiolo tells me some of his special mixture—it's a shame to put it in a curry."

In his little study under the stairs, Kenny Imperiolo cocked his head and listened to the sounds of Rosa moving about the house, so familiar after all these years; the creak of a board in the smallest spare bedroom, a faint hiss, the clunk of plastic on metal, and then the creak again. She was ironing. Kenny screwed up his face trying to remember what the level had been in the plastic basket on top of the dryer that morning when he'd gone to the freezer to get his good fresh coffee beans. Surely it was piled high? Didn't she always leave it until there was a mountain and then groan to herself as she carried it upstairs? She would be busy for hours, wouldn't come anywhere near him. All the same, he moved a heavy box against the door of his little hidey-hole before he turned his computer on. There were no locks anywhere in this house, never had been—not even on the bathrooms, since that time Michael shut himself in in a tantrum when he was four and Kenny had put his foot through the garage roof climbing to the rescue. He pulled the door hard and the box didn't budge. And anyway, Rosa never came checking up on him; it wasn't her way. She was a good, trusting, loving wife who'd never done anything except make him proud to stand beside her, and she deserved no less than the same back from him. Kenny imagined those warm brown eyes of hers narrowed and hard, staring at him, asking him why. Then he shook the picture out of his head and started working.

———

Sandra Dessing followed Carmen and Melisande into the wood and put the little black bag with the integrated scoop away in her anorak pocket. She always carried it out for everyone to see while she was on the street, but she was damned if she was going to use one on the bark paths at £3.99 for ten. Ahead of her she could hear faint tuneless whistling and she pinched her cheeks and tucked her hair behind he ears. Iain Ballantyne came around the corner with Tig on his lead.

"Hello, hello," he said. "I was just on my way home, but I'll maybe turn back and have another wee stroll."

"Why not?" said Mrs. Dessing. "Nice to see them having a good run and play together."

"If you're sure," said Mr. Ballantyne, and something in his voice made Sandra look away from the dogs and glance at his face instead, right into his eyes.

"Why?" she said. "What's wrong?"

"We need to talk," said Iain. "We really need to talk today." He bent to unhook Tig's lead from his collar and all three dogs, well used to one another by now, bounded into the trees with their owners following after.

———

As Keiko held Viola in the warmth of the swaying bus, as Fancy and Yvonne egged one another on in the fug of the salon, as Etta McLuskie stood her ground in the parked car, as Pamela Shand whacked the books with the pricing gun, as Kenny clicked and dragged and deleted, as Iain and Sandra's dogs raced on into the darkest part of the woods—no one thought of the letters.

Some, reduced to ash with the rest of the clearings from the grate, were tipped into carriers, tied in binbags, burned again in the council incinerator, tipped out of the back of the truck eighteen miles away and scraped flat by men with masks and heavy gloves against the dust and grit they were spreading.

Some, in shreds, had rotted to compost with clippings and peelings, until the narrow lines of ink were gone. And in the spring when the bin was emptied and barrowed over to the border, there would be no sign in the crumbling brown that any paper was ever there.

Some had been pressed between pages never to be parted again, not even when the executors put the house on the open market and the eaves were emptied after the place was sold. That whole year's worth of *Woman's Realm* would be bound up with brown string and taken away by the clearance companies, sold on to the recyclers, and entered in the bill under sundry other items as "non-confidential printed paper: three bales."

Some grew pulpy on their way downstream, heavy and sloughing apart, turning to grey paste in the water, one piece tangling itself in a length of plastic twine and floating for miles before the line snagged on a jutting rock and the balls of sodden paper were washed away.

Only a single letter remained, resting again where it had rested for years, behind the radiator, by the door, under the shelf, above the genkan now, as secret as ever—except that Keiko knew.

———

Murray knelt beside the Harley, waiting just the right amount of time for the WD-40 to loosen the nuts under the saddle but not long enough for it to drip down between the rear mudguard and the battery. Malcolm stood at his bench in the back room, boning and rolling, dividing his store of fat evenly amongst the joints, tying the skin snugly over the pink and white spirals and patting each one before he laid them into the tray for the morning. Mrs. Poole could hear the regular slap of his palm on the skin as he finished another one, but she barely registered such a familiar sound as she snapped her ledger shut and pulled the first bundle of banknotes towards her.

TWENTY-SEVEN

Wednesday, 20 November

Mrs. Poole was there again the next evening, listening, her hands spread flat on the empty desktop, when Keiko's phone rang. She cocked her head to catch footsteps or talking, but nothing much came down through these stone floors. She of all people should know that by now.

"I can't," Keiko was saying. "I've planned something with Murray."

"Oh, yeah?" Fancy said.

"I'm making him a meal. A proper Japanese meal. The works."

"Just Murray?"

"Just the two of us."

"After all Malcolm's done, feeding you up like a Christmas goose too."

She had made miso soup, stuffed fish, shaped dumplings. The first two batches, bland and heavy, she threw away but on the third attempt they came out as light as seed heads, as gold as sunshine.

That would surely be enough, with the noodles and all the pickles, to make up for no sushi.

She laid two settings at the coffee table before the fire, put an extra pair of slippers on the genkan and put on her kimono, shaking out two months of folds and breathing in the scent of home. Murray arrived right on time, with flowers for her.

"Oops," he said as she flung the door open and bowed. "Did I get you out the bath?" She smiled. "No really, you look great. And is it shoes off, then?" Keiko nodded and waited while he hopped around, unlacing his boots. "The total Tokyo experience, eh?"

"One night only," said Keiko. "Starting tomorrow I'm going to have time for nothing except the experiments until Christmas."

"Not even workouts?"

"I wouldn't give up the workouts. I can't tell you how grateful I am. And so tonight is like a thank-you. I want you to have a lovely evening." She hesitated. "You deserve one."

He held up his hand. "If we're going to have a lovely evening," he said, "could we agree not to talk about … things?" Keiko nodded. "Good. So, tell me what to do then. If you've gone to a lot of trouble, I want to get my end of it right."

"No, no, no," she said. "No etiquette, it's too … I wanted to cook for you—just enjoy the food."

Murray frowned, then smiled tightly. "Too complicated for me?"

"Well, if you're really interested," she said, backtracking. "Most foreigners think it's silly." She excused herself and went to the kitchen to set the noodle water on to boil. Murray had wriggled himself into a comfortable position on his cushion when she came back and folded herself down opposite him to pour sake.

"I was just thinking," he said, "for anyone else, there's not enough furniture in here," he said, "but I suppose it's fine for you, eh?"

Keiko looked around at the skinny sofa and chairs, the trolley with the television on it, the stretches of bare carpet.

"Was there much more furniture when you lived here?"

Murray folded his arms. "We weren't going to talk about things," he said.

"I didn't mean to," said Keiko. "I didn't know I was." She smiled at him. "It *is* fine for me. It's a shame it was empty so long." She wondered if this would count as talking again, but he only laughed.

"Hardly empty," he said. "There was never a minute's peace."

"Who was here?" said Keiko, trying not to sound too eager.

"The Traders," Murray told her. He had finished his sake and Keiko poured him some more. "When Dad was chairman, they used the flat as their gang hut." He laughed. "That's what Craig called it. Had the meetings up here and stored all the Christmas lights and Gala stuff and that."

"The Traders," said Keiko. "They used this place?"

"Not the whole squad of them. Just the committee."

Everything, Keiko thought, *leads back to the committee.*

There was a fizzing noise from the kitchen as the noodle water boiled over, and she hurried away through there again.

"*Itadakimasu,*" she said ten minutes later, as she knelt again. "You say it too." She repeated it until he could chant it smoothly after her, and then they said it once more to each other.

"Now, hold your chopsticks like something for eating and not for gardening," she said. Murray made a passable attempt and she nodded at him. "Easy, see?" she said. "And remember not to put the same end into the big dish as the end you put in your mouth. Don't stick them in straight up and down but always tilted to the side. Don't pick up a dish in the same hand as you hold your chopsticks. Don't wave them over the food, don't point them at me—either end—and, most important, never *never* pass any food from one person to another in your chopsticks. But you can't get that wrong because I wouldn't take it anyway."

"Makes sense," said Murray. "So basically, don't spit in the food and don't poke your eyes in."

He watched her as she made mosaics on the surface of her soup with tiny pieces of shredded spice, then took a piece of chicken from her bowl and bit into it. Next a tangle of noodles that she scooped up to her lips and sucked in with the proper sound. He drew back, his stare hardening, but she nodded and smiled. Then she lifted her bowl and took a slurping gulp of the broth. He looked away from her.

"This is how," she insisted. "Bite, suck, slurp. Especially a good noisy slurp. That's the polite way to eat soup. And you say *ro-ro-ro* when you're eating your noodles." Murray stared down into his bowl in disappointment. "I'll get the dumplings," she said.

"Dumplings?" His voice sounded cold.

"Gyoza. Special lighter-than-air Japanese dumplings. I'll show you how to eat them."

The dip, bite, dip, bite, dab of the gyoza seemed to please him more. He copied her movements, letting go of his chopsticks only once to shake a cramp out of his hand. When he had grasped a particularly neat piece and dipped it with two elegant swipes into the sauce, he held it out to her over the table, smiling, inviting her to take it. She pulled back, shaking her head but laughing.

"No, no, impossible," she said. "I can't." He kept his chopsticks out towards her, waving the steaming dumpling back and forth.

"Come on," he said. "There's nobody watching." She wanted to, and almost did, but she took too long and by the time she had steeled herself to raise her hand, he had begun to lower his and the smile had disappeared.

"Just enjoy the food," said Murray, in a high piping voice, with his mouth turned down into a pout like a carp. "Don't worry about the etiquette." Keiko flushed and had a sudden urge to upend the table into his lap. She could see the noodles sliding and spattering over his shirt, the soup, still hot enough to scald with any luck, spreading in a dark stain over his trousers. She blinked the image away.

"When a person dies," she said, "their body is cremated and their bones are laid to rest." Murray stared at her. "And during the ceremony," she went on, "the bones are handled with special chopsticks and they are passed from person to person, and that is the only thing that's ever passed that way."

"Christ," he said, flicking the piece of dumpling right off his plate and then staring at it where it lay on the tabletop. Keiko picked it up in her hand and took it out of the room. When she came back he was composed again, and they ate in silence until they were done. Keiko laid her chopsticks down.

"*Gochisousama*," she said. "*Goh chee soo sah mah.*"

"*Gochisousama*," said Murray, and they stood. In the kitchen, Keiko tidied the bowls into the dishwasher and tidied the leftover dumplings into herself. Then she blushed and went back to Murray. He was sitting on the sofa reading a blank questionnaire.

"Are you still hungry?" she said.

He looked up in surprise. "No. Is there more?"

"No, nothing. Only Japanese food—it can be fiddly."

"Some people aren't happy unless they're face down in the stew," he said. "Not me."

251

She joined him on the sofa, reading the last questions over his shoulder.

"Well?" she said when he had finished and was smoothing the pages flat again.

"What will you be able to tell from all that?"

"I'll plot the subjects' positions on various continua of attitudes, allowing me to judge their responses to later stimuli against a normative scale."

"Say no more," said Murray. Then: "Sorry about that chopsticks thing." She shrugged to show him it was nothing. "But how can you stand it?" he said. "Using the same things for food and dead bodies."

"Not dead bodies," she said. "Just bones, clean from the fire."

"Bones are bodies," he said. "How are bodies different from bones?"

"The same way that frames aren't bikes," said Keiko. "Otherwise how could there be a Vincent—a bike without a frame? They're two different things."

"Don't," said Murray, and when Keiko turned to him in surprise she thought he was pale suddenly. "Don't talk like that about the bikes."

"Like …?"

"Dead bodies," Murray said. "It's completely different. Bikes last forever if you keep them oiled. Bodies rot. Even if you clean the bones, they crumble to bits in the end. Bikes … if something goes wrong, you can take them apart, fix it, and put them back together, good as new. Bodies … if you take bodies apart, it's just … meat." He stood, gulping as though he were about to retch. "Sorry," he said. "I need to get out. It's this place. I need some fresh air. Sorry."

And then he was gone, picking up his boots as he passed, but fleeing downstairs in her spare slippers, leaving her gazing after him.

She breathed in deeply to steady herself and then groaned. That bloody smell! No wonder he needed fresh air. What was the point of trying to make everything pretty and dainty with that stink in the background? She gathered the last of the place settings—the napkins and placemats—and stamped into the kitchen. And another thing! Who knew what it would do to a load of results about eating if the subjects were halfway to nauseated because of her drains? What *was* that smell?

She threw down the napkins, opened her laptop, and when the browser started, she typed *why does my kitchen drain smell?*

She could dismiss all the answers saying it was dirty; she had poured a swimming pool's worth of bleach down there. And it wasn't tree roots outside because the bathroom drain was fine.

The cartoons on the plumbing DIY site made her shudder, little grey-green monsters hiding in the trap like trolls under a bridge.

"Bones or other solid objects may form a framework which collects debris," she read. Murray had said bones crumble eventually, even if you clean them. *Not fast enough*, she thought, going to the kitchen drawer and taking out the flower-patterned wrench the Traders had put there for her.

She followed the instructions like the scholar she was, placing a bowl under the pipe joint and turning the water off just in case (of what, the website didn't say), and truth be told she was pleased at how easy she found it and yet how competent it made her feel.

But when the U-shaped piece of pipe came free, as she unthreaded the coupling, she could not help starting back at the sudden rolling outward of that same foul familiar smell, stronger than ever. She let the pipe fall into the bowl and then stood up, lifting it into the light, giving a grunt of satisfaction as she peered in one end. There *was* something in there; something criss-crossing the space that should have been clear, something furred with old grease and shreds of vegetable peelings. She could even see a strand of tonight's soup noodles caught on it and wound around.

She seized a chopstick from the pile of dirty dishes and poked it into the end of the pipe, waggling it around trying to dislodge the object. It didn't budge, so she poked harder, felt something give way with a snap. It sounded like a bone, small and thin, and deep inside her a tiny shrill of fear began as she turned the pipe over and banged one end hard with the heel of her hand.

When the thing fell out, she let her breath go in a rush.

It was only a chicken bone. A broken wishbone, nothing more. But then, as she turned to rip off a piece of kitchen paper, she saw something glint and turned back, bending to look more closely. There was more than peelings and noodles caught in the vee of the bone. What had made it into a cat's cradle was a chain, fine and gold-coloured, tangled there. She picked at a loose loop of it and slowly it came clear. It was a necklace of small gold links, and hanging from it was a pendant shaped like a letter *N*.

"Nicole," she breathed. "Where are you?"

TWENTY-EIGHT

Thursday, 21 November

PAMELA SHAND ARRIVED ON time, declined coffee, and got straight to work while Keiko pretended to be reading. Should she show Pamela the necklace, saying she had found it out on the street? But if she said that she'd have to take it to the police as lost property, and she already knew she didn't want to give it away. It was in her pocket right now and she ran her fingers over it. *I will find you*, she promised.

What she *should* do, she knew, was show it to the Pooles since they owned the flat, but just thinking about that made her pulse thrum.

Then she tried to tell herself that Nicole might have visited and the necklace might have come undone while she was washing her hands. Except the clasp was closed, and visitors do not wash their hands in the kitchen.

Finally she told herself that *N* could stand for lots of things, but when she thought of all the women and girls she had met here—

Grace, Fancy, Pet, Etta, Mabel, Sandra, Margaret, Janice, Viola, Yvonne—she didn't believe it was true.

There was a polite cough. Pamela Shand was staring at her.

"If you're finished we can take a few moments to discuss anything," said Keiko. "But only if there's time before the next person."

"Why not come round tonight and have some supper with me?" said Pam. "You'll be drained after a day of appointments, and I would like very much to talk to you."

"Really?" said Keiko, looking up.

"I've been trying to get to you," Pam said, "but you're very well minded. I really wanted to say there's no need for you to feel you should put up with it. Even though it must be awkward for you, living above the Pooles."

"Awkward?" Keiko said. She was aware of her pulse again.

"Uncomfortable," said Pam. "Oh, why am I mincing my words? It must be hell and it's about to get worse."

Keiko's heart was banging now.

"Christmas is coming," said Pam. "I can't begin to tell you what's coming at Christmas." She leaned in closer across the table. "Imagine a turkey so fat it can barely stand, stuffed with minced pork and covered in bacon and butter, roasted for hours with the fat ladled up and over it again and again until it glistens, served up burnt skin and all, with thick gravy."

Although it was only an hour since breakfast, Keiko's stomach gave a slow, luxurious rumble that she tried to cover by rustling the pages of her book and clearing her throat.

"Ah yes," Keiko said, slumping in disappointment. This woman had some kind of fixation. All this outrage and drama and she was only talking about food again! "Yes. Yes, certainly, that's a lot more meat than a Japanese family would eat even when feasting." She gave a shrug. "But feasting is supposed to be out of the ordinary. And when the everyday custom is to eat so very much, then to make a feast seem like a feast they must need to …" She trailed into silence.

Pamela had those plump but narrow hands with dimples at the base of each pointed little finger, and she gripped the edge of the table with them now as she leaned even closer.

"I admire your fortitude," she said. "But that's not all. I'd love to warn you about the local delicacy for New Year's Day, but I can't bring myself to describe it. All I will say is that the time is coming for its preparation, and if it gets too much for you—here above the Pooles'—you are welcome to come round at any time to visit me."

"You are most kind," said Keiko.

"Not at all. Is there anything you don't eat?"

"Nothing you're likely to serve," said Keiko, hearing the rudeness too late as Pamela frowned.

"I am a great devotee of world cuisine," said Pam evenly, and they left it there.

———

Mrs. McMaster laid down her pen after less than five minutes and Keiko could see that she had stopped halfway through a page.

"Fancy helped you with these, did she?" Keiko nodded. "I see." She paused a moment and considered Keiko's face closely. Then she shifted her gaze slightly off to the side and spoke again. "Of course Fancy was around the shop quite a lot when she was just a wee girl and … it's a funny thing, you know, but a florist is right up there with a priest and a doctor for hearing things."

"That *is* rather surprising," said Keiko.

"Aye well, there it is," Pet said. "Christenings, weddings, and funerals loosen the tongue. People will put it down to the drink, but drink it cannot be, for it's just the same first thing in the morning across a florist's bench. Things people would never breathe a word of face to face, eye to eye, you know? But there's me not looking at them, busy with the flowers, and they're watching my hands so they're not looking at me, and they get to talking."

Keiko waited.

Mrs. McMaster took off her spectacles and hooked them by one of their earpieces through a ringed brooch pinned to her bosom. "Some of your wee scenarios here are pretty close to home," she said. "I'm surprised at Fancy."

"I don't think she meant to betray any confidences," Keiko said. Mrs. McMaster only raised her eyebrows. "Really. She said she just let it all bubble up out of her subconscious. I thought she meant her imagination. If I'd known she meant subconscious memory ..."

Mrs. McMaster looked less convinced than ever.

"Really, Mrs. McMaster," Keiko said. "You must believe me: Fancy is always discreet about anything that could hurt anyone."

"Oh?" said Pet. "Like what?"

Keiko flushed. "That girl—Tash—who left," she said. "Fancy could have spoken about that and she didn't. Ever." Keiko swallowed. "She didn't even tell me her last name."

"Turnbull," said Mrs. McMaster, her face clouding briefly, before the arch look returned. "Well, she'd hardly have dwelt on Tash to you now, would she?" she said.

"To me?"

"You're stepping out with Murray Poole. And Tash was Murray's first love. Broke his heart for him. No wonder Fancy didn't have much to say."

It took a few moments for Keiko understand. "Tash was Murray's girlfriend?" she said. Her thoughts were reeling. Tash who left was the same person as Murray's girlfriend who broke up with him? "He didn't tell me," she said. Then she remembered something even worse. "He said he didn't know her!" She could hear his words again in her head: *No can do. I don't know their names.*

"Sounds like he didn't want to talk to his new girl about his old one," said Mrs. McMaster. "It's hardly surprising."

Keiko didn't answer. She was gone, reliving every conversation with Murray. How many times had he lied to her?

"I don't think that's what it was," she said at last. "He said he didn't know Dina either. And she left too. Or Craig's—"

"Who?" said Mrs. McMaster. "Oh, you mean Dina Taylor. Mabel's girl?"

"Taylor," said Keiko.

"That's right," said Mrs. McMaster. "Nadine Taylor. Dina for short. Aye, she hung around him a while. But it didn't last. What's she got—"

"*Nadine?*" said Keiko, feeling her face changing colour.

"Now why would that surprise you?" said Mrs. McMaster. "What on earth are you up to together, the pair of you?"

They weren't up to anything together, Keiko thought. He had hidden so much from her, even while he dropped all those hints of trouble.

"What 'pair'?" she said with a dry laugh.

"You and Fancy," said Mrs. McMaster. "What's Nadine Taylor got to do with this?" She tapped the paper with her pen.

Fancy. Keiko felt a chill as if a door had been opened on a winter night. As many times as Murray had lied, Fancy had lied even more.

She had spoken of Tash and of Murray's girlfriend and never admitted that they were the same person. What was going on?

"Mrs. McMaster," Keiko said. "Do you think I should cancel the profiling? Scrap all of these questions and start again?"

Mrs. McMaster blinked in surprise. "What?" she said. "Och, no. There's nothing in there that wouldn't be just the same in any small town in the land. As long as the names are changed, there's no harm to anyone."

"So ... it's not something terrible? I'm not in danger if I carry on?"

"Danger of what?" said Mrs. McMaster.

"Oh, being sued" said Keiko. "For example."

Mrs. McMaster threw back her head and let out a merry peal of laughter. "What an imagination you've got," she said. "You and Fancy are as bad as each other. No, you're not in any danger. There might be one or two red faces here and there, but you've worked hard on this, so go ahead and don't worry."

She did go ahead. Full steam ahead now that she was able. She only wished she had remembered to ask Nicole's other name while Mrs. McMaster was laughing. All day long, she let her subjects take their time while she hunched over her laptop, Googling.

She got Tash Turnbull out of the way first, aware that her interest might only be because of Murray. *Tash Turnbull + foster + Painchton + McMaster*, she typed and then, in desperation, *missing girls*. Of course she didn't know how common a name Tash Turnbull might be, how odd it might be that she found nothing.

Then she turned to the real task at hand. She took the gold chain out of her pocket late in the day and held it tightly as she typed. *Nadine Taylor + Painchton + Dina*. She clutched the pendant so hard she could feel the points of the *N* digging into her palm. Again, there was nothing. Pages of businesswomen—realtors and attorneys—in Canada and Arkansas. Pages of Taylor genealogies.

She was alone by this time, the last of her subjects gone away. She opened her fist and spoke to the pendant.

"Where are you?" she said. "Who are you? Nadine or—"

She jumped at the sound of footsteps inside her flat and only just managed to get the chain back into her pocket as the living room door was opening

"Knock, knock," said Murray. "You're late. I've been waiting for you." He was wearing warm-up trousers and a sleeveless tee-shirt, even though the night was cold with a squally rain lashing against the window.

"Sorry," said Keiko.

"D'you always leave your door unlocked? That's a bit too trusting for this town."

"I wish *you* were a bit more trusting," she said, blurting it out before she could think better. And without giving him a chance to answer she went on: "You did know Tash's full name. Of course you did. And I bet you knew Dina's name was really Nadine. I bet you know Nicole's name too."

Murray had taken a step backwards as she started talking. Now, he pulled in one long deep breath and let it go, hissing. "Sneddon," he said. He came over and sat down at one of the other dining chairs set around the table. "It's Nicole Sneddon. And I'm sorry."

Nicole Sneddon, Keiko typed. *Painchton.*

Murray bumped his chair around to look over her shoulder.

'You could try Nikki too," he said "N-I-K-K-I. I'm sorry, Keiko."

"Good," Keiko said, watching the results scroll by. More realtors and executives, more genealogy.

"I should have just told you straight and asked you straight."

"Yes," said Keiko, still scrolling. "Asked me what straight?"

"To leave this alone," he said. "What did you Google for Tash?"

"Tash Turnbull," Keiko said. "Her name. The one you said you didn't know."

"I'm sorry," said Murray for the third time. He paused. "Did you find her?"

"I didn't find any of them," Keiko whispered. "Nothing at all. All three of them are just … gone."

Murray took her hand, lifted it from the mouse, and clasped it in both of his. "Please leave it to me," he said. "Promise me you won't put yourself in danger."

"If you would tell me what the danger is," began Keiko, but he was shaking his head. So she shut the laptop and went to change into her workout clothes. But she promised nothing.

TWENTY-NINE

Saturday, 23 November

IT WAS TWO DAYS before she could face Fancy. But at last she steeled herself and walked around the corner. Fancy was trotting back and forward with a delivery of dry-cleaning when Keiko came hurrying in out of the rain.

"I'll need to tape these up," she said, "keep them out the puddles." She heaped the clothes up on the counter in a slithering bale and folded the bottom halves up to the shoulders, leaning down on them to push out the air. She looked over her shoulder at Keiko. "You okay?"

"Not really," Keiko said. "Mrs. McMaster did my questionnaire."

"God, yeah, she told me," Fancy said, straightening up. "I nearly got put on the naughty step."

"I'm not talking about the gossip," Keiko said. "That's not the problem."

Fancy pulled a long strip of tape from the dispenser with a screeching sound. "Oh?" she said.

"She told me Tash was Murray's girlfriend," said Keiko. "Why did you lie to me?"

"I didn't—"

"By omission," Keiko said.

"Jesus," said Fancy. "It's like being back with the nuns." Instead of taping the bags, Fancy wound the strip round and round one of her hands until her fingertips turned purple, concentrating hard on it, saying nothing. Then she looked up. "When I came back," she said, "Pet was in bits. I thought she'd never stop crying. She used to sit with Viola, both of them bawling their eyes out." She gave Keiko a bleak kind of grin. "Brilliant ego boost."

Keiko said nothing, didn't even smile.

"So I suppose I was angry," Fancy said. As she spoke, she unwound the tape from her fingers and screwed it into a ball. "With Tash, I mean. For hurting Pet. And I just didn't want to think about her. Or talk about her."

Keiko weighed her words for a moment. "Understandable," she said. "I'm sorry."

"What for?" said Fancy. She threw the tape ball at the wastepaper basket. It missed.

"Doubting you. I thought you knew something about them."

"Who?" said Fancy, frowning.

"The missing girls," Keiko said. "Tash and Nadine Taylor and Nicole Sneddon."

"Not this again!" said Fancy. "They're not 'missing.'"

"But I've searched and searched online for Nicole and Dina," Keiko said. "Why can't I find them?"

Fancy rolled her eyes and opened her laptop. "What did you look under?" she said. "Cos the best place to find Dina Taylor is in St. Abbs, where she lives. Or under photography, which is her hobby."

She typed in silence. "And there she is. North Berwick High School, summer photography show. This summer, Keeks."

"High school?" said Keiko. "But Mrs. McMaster said she hung around Murray. How old is she?"

"She didn't hang around him that way," said Fancy. "She just liked the bikes. Likes black leather anyway."

"And what about Nicole Sneddon?"

"Horses," said Fancy, typing again. "She's a showjumper. Did you know that? If you don't add in something extra all you get is LinkedIn and family history. Nikki's a showjumper and anyway, she was here about two weeks before you arrived, visiting Jimmy and Craig."

"Well, what about Tash then?" said Keiko. "Can you find her? What were her interests before she got fat and unhappy and broke up with Murray and went away?"

Fancy pressed her lips very close together. As they stood in silence, the shop door opened, letting in a surge of damp air and the sound of cars swishing slowly past in the fog. From Fancy's face Keiko knew without turning that it was one of them, she just didn't know which until she looked over her shoulder.

Malcolm was just inside the doorway, wrestling with the neck fastening of his waterproof cape, trying to remove it before stepping from the doormat onto the carpet. The black rubber squeaked against the glass as he struggled, then he gave up and, planting one foot out away from the door to give himself room to manoeuvre, he reached one hand over the opposite shoulder as far as it would go and flung the cape across his back with a grunt, then scrabbled to catch it and pluck it away from him. Underneath, his white overall showed a faint whiter ghost where his apron had been. He had on the white rubber boots he wore in the shop too and as he turned and stretched up to hook his cape over the door hinge, Keiko could see that the boots had been cut down in the back to fit around his ankles. His socks had disappeared, wrinkled down during the slow walk around the corner, and there was a cold, pink vee of wet skin briefly visible before the hems of his sodden trousers came down again.

"I've come for my posters, Fancy," he said in his soft boom.

"They're ready," said Fancy. She took a roll of paper from under the counter, plucked the middle sheet free, and spread it on the counter. Malcolm paced over towards them and then stood reading carefully, his eyes pinched up in concentration.

"Good," he said at last. "You see what I've done?"

Fancy and Keiko bent to look. They were price lists for Christmas packs of meat, written in red with a suggestion of snow covering the bigger letters, and decorated at the corners with robins and spruce trees.

"Christmas preparations begin very early," Keiko said. "Pamela has already been discussing it with me."

"Can't come soon enough for me," said Malcolm. "I'm dying to see how these go. The Family Deluxe is actually the budget option, but I don't say that. The selling point is that the turkey comes all ready to go in the oven, and the ham's ready cooked. Now, I'll let you in on a secret." He rested the heels of his hands on the counter and relaxed slightly, treading his feet. "The Family Deluxe is going to be just as delicious as the Butcher's Finest. You know why?" Keiko shook her head. "Because," he went on, "nobody can cook a ham like me. So the cheap hams that I did are going to taste better than the expensive hams that Mrs. So-and-So tries to do herself. People are scared of the salt, see? They soak out all the flavour and then they're too scared of the sugar to do a proper glaze. And as for the turkeys. A turkey's a turkey's a turkey—it's what goes in it and on it that makes the difference. Fat, basically. You need fat to cook a good turkey and Mrs. So-and-So won't have the bottle. She's terrified of fat. She'd rather pay more for lean bacon and high-meat sausage and have a dry one. So that's what she's getting. But the Family Deluxe is stuffed front and back with fatty pork, and I put extra fat under the skin and cover the breast with good fat belly strips. It's going to be gorgeous. That's the one to go for. The fat one." He beamed at them, breathing rather hard after such a lot of speaking.

"Well," said Keiko. "That's ..." She looked at Fancy for help, but she was just staring, slack-jawed. Malcolm lowered his head.

"I'll walk back round with you, if you're going," said Keiko. "I must settle down to some work soon or today will be lost."

Despite her umbrella, raindrops—or maybe fog drops, she thought—were clinging to her eyelashes before they had reached the corner. She hugged the roll of posters closer and took an extra little step to keep up with Malcolm, surprised, since he had always seemed to move so slowly, to find that she had to hurry to walk beside him, her feet taking two steps to every one of his. They stopped at the kerb and as Keiko lifted her umbrella to check the traffic through the sheeting rain, Malcolm peered out from under his hood. They caught each other's eyes and smiled.

Keiko was suddenly overwhelmed with a wave of homesickness like a heavy blanket thrown over her. When she was small, rain like this was funny, never bothersome; it was something to raise her face to and dance in, and she could never understand why grown-up people hunched their shoulders and scowled, why they tried so hard to be angry with the rain. And she knew it was an effort because if the rain got the better of them—if her mother's umbrella blew out of her hand, or a passing truck soaked her father from head to toe—

they would give up the pretence and whoop just like she did. *Laugh or cry, it's the same life, Keko-chan,* her mother said.

And then, all of a sudden, as though he had read her thoughts, Malcolm said, "Oh, stuff it!" He stepped into the brimming gutter and splashed a few paces up the road and then down again, kicking up gouts of water with his feet like the man in the old musical. Keiko was about to close her umbrella and join him when she remembered she was holding his posters, so she stayed put but cheered. Then the little stream of traffic came to an end and they crossed the road, Malcolm raising one arm protectively behind her like the wing of a gigantic bird, the ear of some monstrous, dripping elephant.

Murray was perched on a stool behind the counter reading a magazine. She stepped boldly behind the counter, squeezed his hand, and pecked him on one cheek. He wiped his face where her damp hair had grazed against it, so she made a show of smoothing the frizzy tendrils back and holding them against her head with both hands before kissing his other cheek. He smiled and put his hand on her shoulder.

"Why are you so chirpy?" he said. "How can you stand this weather?"

Keiko wondered whether to try to explain about rain, but in the end just kissed his head and said nothing.

"Where's Mum?" asked Malcolm, when he got back from putting away his cape. Rainwater still rolled down his face in fat drops and he cranked a piece of paper towel out of the dispenser and wiped his head roughly.

"Gone to see Byers," said Murray.

Malcolm nodded, one upward jerk of his chin, making him look very like his mother, and then made his way towards the cold store.

"What's happening?" asked Keiko. "Is Mr. Byers going to sell his workshop to the Traders?"

"God knows," said Murray.

"Is that the secret?" Keiko asked, dropping her voice until she was only murmuring. "Is it something to do with the committee?"

"How many times—" Murray began.

"Oh!" said Keiko, interrupting him. "Dina and Nicole are both fine."

Murray let go of her and propelled her away from him, but just as she began to ask what was wrong the shop bell rang and the door swept wide open to admit Mr. McKendrick, who would not appreciate—what did Fancy call them?—public displays of affection.

He backed in, closing an enormous umbrella, which he shot deftly into the stand before righting his tweed jacket and turning to face them.

"What a day, what a day," he said comfortably. "Now don't you be booking yourself a seat on the plane home, mind." He twinkled at Keiko and then craned towards the passage to the office with an expectant look. "Is your mother busy, Murray? Will I just go through?"

"She's not here at the mo," Murray said.

"I'll catch her at home," said Mr. McKendrick. "Just as good."

Malcolm emerged from the cold store, swinging a chunk of dark meat from a hook in one hand. *What does he do in there, in the cold?* Keiko asked herself. *What could take him all of the time he spends in there with the door shut on him?*

"By, that's a good-looking rib," said Mr. McKendrick.

Malcolm swung the meat up and rested it against the back of his wrist twisting it this way and that to show it off like a waiter with a bottle of vintage wine.

"I've never seen a better colour on a piece of beef when your father himself was alive," Mr. McKendrick continued, admiring.

Malcolm looked up. "Mum," he said.

Keiko looked towards the door, where Mrs. Poole was standing, pushing her dripping hair back from her face, her white overall transparent with wet, showing the colours of her clothes underneath.

"Gracie, for God's sake," said Mr. McKendrick. "Where have you been? Where's your coat?" He shook out a large handkerchief and seemed about to dry Mrs. Poole's face with it but settled for passing it to her and shifting from foot to foot, pointing to where she needed it.

"Just round the corner," said Mrs. Poole. "I had my brolly, but I've left it behind." She tried a laugh, which came out oddly. Mr. McKendrick frowned at her then turned to look at the water coursing down the window pane and guddling away along the pavement. He caught Keiko's eye briefly. How could anyone step out into that and forget her umbrella?

"Round the corner where?" he asked.

"Post box."

"I never saw you."

"I came back along the lanes." Mrs. Poole gave a shiver, tiny but too much for Mr. McKendrick; with one movement he had swept off his jacket and settled it around her shoulders. She stiffened for a second, then drooped again.

"And now," Mr. McKendrick cried, "it's soup kitchen time." Being in his cardigan sleeves seemed to have released even more energy in him. "I say soup, Keiko, but ask Malcolm what he made last year. Eh? For the Christmas dinners for the homeless? Eh, Malcolm?"

"Venison casserole," said Malcolm, with a small smile at Keiko.

Mr. McKendrick reached up and clapped one hand against his shoulder. "Venison casserole for the homeless," he said, triumphant.

"It's meat from deer, isn't it?" said Keiko.

"Aye, Bambi's mum," said Murray softly behind her. "Kids love it."

Mr. McKendrick chortled. "Not at Christmas, Murray. Stewed Rudolph. Very seasonal." He laughed richly and rubbed his hands again. "So what's it to be this year, son? Ostrich steaks? Spit-roasted partridge?"

"Not this year, Jimmy," said Mrs. Poole. "Malcolm's not going to be doing it this year."

Mr. McKendrick sobered himself with a gruff cough. "No? No, no, I quite understand. You'll want them round you this year on Christmas morning, Grace. I quite see that. But you'll do the cooking on Christmas Eve?" He addressed the question to Malcolm, but Malcolm continued to look at his mother and she answered.

"No, I'm afraid not, Jim."

Mr. McKendrick was still smiling gently, although a worried look was beginning to form. "But I can count on you to donate the meat?" he said.

"I'm afraid not," said Mrs. Poole, very quietly. She threw one look in Keiko's direction and then walked with her head down towards the back shop.

Mr. McKendrick looked after her and spoke with every last wisp of a chuckle gone from his voice. "Can we borrow your big pans?"

Mrs. Poole wheeled round and rolled her eyes as if searching the ceiling for some attacking bird. Her voice was ragged. "Of course you can borrow—For God's sake, Jimmy. What do you think I am?"

"Well, that's something," said Mr. McKendrick into the silence she left behind. He mustered himself. "That's grand. We couldn't do it without the big pots. We couldn't do it without you." He retrieved his umbrella from the stand and nodded goodbye to the three of them, managing a medium-sized smile but not quite meeting their eyes.

"What's going on?" said Malcolm, staring after his mother.

Murray's eyes were narrowed and he spoke slowly, thinking it through. "Mum lied to Jimmy there," he said. "She was seeing Byers, not at the post box."

"Maybe she did both," said Malcolm.

"Yeah, but she kept the Byers bit quiet, didn't she? And if she thinks there's no cash to spare, that must mean they've struck a bargain about my workshop." He caught hold of Keiko, pulled her close and kissed her on both cheeks, her wet hair forgotten. She tried to smile at him, but she was thinking about him saying this was a bad place for him and that he had to get away.

"Great," Malcolm said. "Mum's rooked herself, the town plans are up the spout, and the homeless can forget their dinner on Christmas Day. Congratulations, Murray." Before Murray could answer, he lumbered away.

"Do you *want* the workshop?" Keiko said.

"I need it for just a wee while longer," said Murray. "Wait and see."

"Your mother seems very upset," said Keiko.

"She's defied Jimmy and the Traders," Murray said. "She's probably terrified. Who wouldn't be?"

THIRTY

Monday, 25 November

Mrs. Poole did not look terrified, Keiko thought, as she watched her. She had cracked open the kitchen window to clear the rice steam, and she looked out when she heard the scrape of the slaughterhouse door. She saw Mrs. Poole emerging. The woman looked the same as ever: head down, shoulders slumped, plodding listlessly up the yard with her buckets.

But something was different. It niggled at Keiko while she sat at her desk trying to concentrate, and it was only minutes before she was back again. There it was! Mrs. Poole hadn't closed the door this morning when she was finished. It was still was ajar and that wasn't all. Drifts of steam were curling out. Someone was in there.

She let herself out and trotted down the stairs. Murray and Malcolm were nowhere to be seen. Mrs. Poole stood behind the counter, unsmiling.

"What can I get you?" she asked Keiko. "Or if it's Murray you're after, he's at home today."

"A hundred grams of lean beef for frying," Keiko said. She couldn't quite admit that she had come to ask questions of this woman, with her stony face. "What is Malcolm doing in the slaughterhouse?" she added. "He told me it was never used."

"Only on special occasions," said Mrs. Poole. "The back shop does for most things, but this time of year Malcolm does things we don't need to see."

What could she mean? Keiko thought. Malcolm described cleaning tripe and brought kidneys to trim as though it were a side-show. He played the skin on roasted meat like a snare drum and wanted to tell everyone the different ways of adding fat to a turkey. What worse thing could there possibly be?

"On the other hand," said Mrs. Poole, handing her the bag of meat, "you're interested in food, aren't you? Why don't you go and watch? Save him coming up to the flat and trying to persuade you."

Keiko took the bag and left but paused outside her own door, then started off again. Up the street, right and right again at the top around the Bridge Hotel, until she was standing at the mouth of a narrow lane, bounded by the brick walls of the shop yards on one side and the stone walls of the big house gardens on the other. It was fringed with weeds at the edges but there was a well-trodden path down the middle that led in a straight line right to Poole's Butcher, and she could see one lurid pink corner of Mr. Byers's place at the end of the block. Still swinging the bag and with a fresh, out-for-a-morning-stroll look fixed on her face, she ventured off the pavement and into the shadows.

The pattern of window and gate, window and gate repeated itself and she looked with interest as each pair passed. The peeling paint and cobweb-choked glass of the Bridge was followed by a wrought-iron gate and a newly glazed window belonging to the Imperiolo's Chinese take-away, the Dragon Pearl, where a whirling fan blew steam from a funnel on the outbuilding roof, to be snatched away by the wind. She passed McLuskie's Bakery with the morning wash of hats and oven mitts just visible on a clothesline, and then Mrs. Watson's grocery, where the window was rubbed shiny even though the building was used only for storing boxes, and finally the back yard of the butcher shop. The spot in the wall where the little window should be was a square of newer bricks, looking faintly grotesque, like a blind eye sewn shut or a mouth taped over. The gate was closed, as she knew it would be—the padlock on the other side was visible from her windows—but she tried the handle anyway. It turned. She let go in surprise and watched as it continued to turn and the gate opened silently on oiled hinges.

"Keiko," said Malcolm. He neither advanced nor retreated but stayed planted on well spread feet, blocking the gateway completely. "Can I help you?"

"I'm being nosy," she said, thinking rapidly but stumbling over the words a little. "What are you doing? Your mother thinks I won't want to see."

"Making hough," said Malcolm.

Keiko blinked at the unfamiliar sound, like a choked-off sneer. "What is *hokko*?" she said, doing her best with the sound.

He didn't answer, just smiled and beckoned her into the slaughterhouse.

The little room had walls blindingly white, running with condensation, and the scrubbed painted floor was beaded with it too in the corners, slick and shining anywhere that Malcolm's feet had been. The whole place was filled with steam, a few shapes rising out of it. She breathed out hard and slow and the air shifted, clearing her view, showing her a hulk of a grey metal stove with two rings and a work table of the same scoured plastic as the cutting benches behind the shop counter. Two huge high-sided pots of the same dull grey, as big as barrels, were bubbling on the stove; it was these giving off the lazy vapour. Keiko sniffed and the cocktail of smells made her dizzy. The steam was peppery and sweet, but there was new paint here too and strong soap, chlorine bleach, disinfectant—they mixed into something choking and pungent, unlike anything she had ever smelled before. She opened her mouth and drew the heavy air in that way.

"Hough," said Malcolm, with a declamatory sweep of his arm over the stove. "It's a fair old guddle. Makes sense to use this place for it—keep the mess and heat out of the shop, eh?"

She stepped up beside him and peered over the rim of one of the pots. Under the curling steam, a thin grey liquor spat up small bubbles to burst on its surface. She looked at him inquiringly.

"It's a plain enough dish," he said. "Only it takes a good six hours, so it's only worth it if you're doing a load at once. Maybe that's why it's made at New Year's, when a lot of folk are gathering."

"What is it?" Keiko asked.

"Meat," said Malcolm. "Beef traditionally, but it doesn't have to be, boiled in water with a knap bone."

"Knap?" said Keiko.

"Knee," Malcolm told her. "The bone makes the jelly. You should have shreds of meat in a good clear jelly, set firm, but I've seen it made by folk who don't know what they're doing and it comes out cloudy, like a mousse." He was warming to his subject.

"This would be a very popular dish with the Japanese," said Keiko, although she could not imagine ever eating a morsel of anything that smelled this way. "We're not ... silly about 'eat this but don't eat that.' And texture's very important in our cooking. Many of our greatest delicacies have a jellied texture."

"Is that right?" said Malcolm, stopping stirring for a moment to take this point in. "Well, the secret of a good jelly is nothing more than standing over it and skimming off the scum." He swiped a flat, pierced ladle up in one fist and swirled it across the pan just under the bubbling surface. When he lifted it out again, it bore a mound of foam, streaked grey and brown and instantly forming a skin as it cooled. Malcolm tilted the ladle over a jug until the dollop of scum plopped in on top of what he had already gathered.

Keiko swallowed and returned her attention to the cooking pots.

"Yep," said Malcolm, "it doesn't matter what you make it with." He peered into first one pot and then the other with a rapt smile on his face. He was pressed hard against the stove, his stomach jutting out and filling the gap between the cooking pots and she could see the damp on his apron front where his chest bulged over their edges into the path of the steam. He turned slightly to include her in his grin. "It makes no odds at all what you make it with. As long as you're willing to spend the time and skim the scum."

"And it's a feast dish for the New Year?" she said. She was beginning to feel uneasy. Just the heat, probably. And the smell.

"That's right." Then he gave an unhappy laugh that ended as a sigh. "But people are starting to lose the old ways. Getting more—what did you call it?—silly about what they'll eat and what they won't. And here's another thing: sometimes I think they can't appreciate food unless it's expensive."

"Is hough cheap, then?" asked Keiko. "I would have thought it would be a great delicacy. If it has a whole knee bone in it."

Malcolm nodded again, very solemn as if weighing her words carefully, and gazed down into his pans, rivulets of what might have been either sweat or condensation running over the swell of his cheeks and dropping from his jaw.

"It should be, eh? But knap bones are dirt cheap even though there's only two to a carcass."

"Four," said Keiko, without thinking.

"No," said Malcolm, still looking into the pan. "Just two."

Hot as she was, Keiko now seemed to feel the cold of the floor in her feet, tiles over stone. "But you said beef," she said, the cold creeping up her legs, slowly.

"No," said Malcolm again. "I said meat. It *can* be beef."

"What—what is *that*?" The cold was rising farther through her body, washing the thought towards her head.

He struck one of the pot edges with a dull clank, the sound driving out more of Keiko's fading steamy stupor, forcing the knowledge up as far as her throat. "That's beef in there right enough. But this one is a speciality of mine." He plunged the ladle deep down into the other pot, dug it in under something, and started to lift it with both hands.

Keiko was at the end of the yard before she heard the splash of it dropping back into the pan. She tried the gate to the yard next door and was into the back of Mrs. Watson's shop, out through the front, up her own stairs, and crouched at the kitchen windowsill just in time to see Malcolm plod into the back lane. He stood for a minute or two with his hands on his thighs craning one way and then the other, wheezing, before he turned around and ambled back through the slaughterhouse door again.

THIRTY-ONE

KEIKO RUBBED AT HER eyes with bunched fists like a baby, trying to scrub out that picture of Malcolm heaving the weight up from the pot with both hands, barely aware through her sobs of a rhythmic cellophane crackle as she moved and a soft bumping against her chest from outside as well as in. Slowly though, as the stink and steam fell away and she came back to the cool kitchen floor and the quiet sweet air, it dawned on her that she still had the bag of meat she'd bought from Mrs. Poole clutched in her hand. She threw it away with a shriek and it skittered across the floor until it hit a table leg where it rested, letting out quiet rustles as the wet weight inside settled onto the lino with a serious of tiny relaxing shifts.

A curious thing was happening inside her. While her body sank unstoppably down towards that sickness that had been waiting for her just below the surface all this time, her mind rose up out of itself and began calmly to sort through the jumble. It made her dizzy, this pulling apart of body and mind, but it was refreshing too, like looking up from small print to glance out of a window at a distant view.

Malcolm had said it didn't matter what you made it with as long as you took the time to skim off the scum. People here didn't worry about horsemeat scandals, but they were losing the old ways. People like Pamela Shand were moving in, and Murray, who should have been one of their own, couldn't be trusted, had to be kept at home and in the shop where his mother could watch him. And he wouldn't tell Keiko what was wrong because she would never believe him.

She stood up on shuddering legs and stumbled to the front door to double lock it. Murray was trying to get to the bottom of things, solve the puzzle, and meantime he worked hard every day—and made her work hard too—to stay skinny and safe, while Malcolm fed her suet and Mrs. Ballantyne fed her sausage and it didn't matter what kind; it was the good big portions that mattered. And Mr. Dessing fed her haggis balls and puff pastry and it didn't matter what was under the pastry, it was the presentation that mattered. And it made no difference what was in Mr. McLuskie's bridies as well, since the pepper masked the taste of it. And Rosa Imperiolo knew that it was the batter that counted, no matter what you dipped in it to fry. And all of their wives and husbands on the committee, making the plans, were twisted up in knots with the knowing and waiting and couldn't hide it. Couldn't pretend they had no secrets eating away like rot inside them as she sat at their tables and they stuffed her, endlessly stuffed her, tamping the food into her gullet like grain into a goose for foie gras.

And Mr. Poole knew. And what he knew had killed him. And his body wasn't up there in the cemetery, in its grave, waiting for visitors. Because—oh God—bodies, once they were taken apart, were just bones and meat.

And this flat, this flat that no one wanted her to ask about, this flat had never been empty, never been used just for meetings. Who could say how many people had lived here, hardly believing their luck—all the gifts, the friendly faces, the feasting? And now they had an ambitious international project. Something more exotic than Tash for them all.

Tash. Murray kept her safe, but she left him and then she got fat and vanished. But Dina hung around him and got skinny and got away. And Nicole got away too, from the creep across the road. But Tash Turnbull got fat and was gone now, a foster child whom no one would search for.

How many children had Mrs. McMaster fostered until they were big boys and girls of sixteen? How many of them had disappeared? Was Fancy the only one who had really run away? And why did she come back? How could she bring her baby back, if she kn—

Keiko stopped pacing so abruptly that she swayed and had to take a steadying step. She was in the living room facing the fireplace, and she smiled at her grey face in the mirror. No. Fancy could not stand the thought that there was anything beneath her own skin, could not bear talk of a pierced navel, could not sit through an anatomy lecture even with her eyes shut. Fancy was no part of this.

She took the sharpest knife from the rack in the kitchen and put it up her coat sleeve, holding it in place with the tips of two fingers, then she crept downstairs, leaving the door to her flat ajar in case they heard it shutting, steeled herself to get out of the street door and away. Away, away, away. She was passing on the far side of the Green before she let out her breath.

Fancy's front shop was empty, but the door to the back was open and she sang out as Keiko approached the counter, "Come through!"

"It's only me," said Keiko.

Fancy was kneeling at the foot of a tailor's dummy pinning the hem of a red cloak. "Hiya," she said, sitting back on her heels and smiling. "What do you think of this? Toxic, eh? It's for Etta McLuskie to wear to help hand out presents at Christmas. I don't know who she's meant to be. Santa's sister? Santa's granny? Lady Provost of Lapland? There's about a million elf costumes but oh no—What's up?" she said suddenly. "What have I done now?"

Keiko talked for half an hour to get everything out, her eyes wide and fixed on the floor. Then she raised her gaze to Fancy's face, which was wooden and unreadable.

"Do you feel sick?" Keiko asked.

"Just a bit, yes," Fancy said, through clenched teeth. "Can't think why. Keiko, do you think I would have brought Viola back here if this wasn't a good place?"

Keiko knew her words were going to hurt, so she said them very quietly. "I see how much you need to think that, and I'm sorry to take it away from you, but you're not—after everything you've been through, you can't be—a good judge of this place, these people."

Fancy's jaw firmed again as she clenched her teeth back together. "Okay, I can't deny that. I'm just a dumb bint that don't know nothin'. I wondered when you'd realise you were too good for m—"

But Keiko sprang out of her chair and took hold of Fancy by the elbows, the knife clattering out of her sleeve and falling to the floor, making her jump. "No!" she said. "You are the best, kindest … and the best mother and the best friend …" Both of them were fighting tears, their noses turning red.

Fancy pushed Keiko back and addressed her again. "Listen to me," she said. "It's just not possible, Keeks. It couldn't happen that so many people could all be bad all at once. Even if it started from one person, like from Malcolm, how could he persuade all those people to do something so disgusting and crazy?"

"Little by little," said Keiko. "Like he did with me. He's easy to talk to and easy to listen to. It is as though he puts a spell on you until you find there's no disgust and it doesn't seem crazy anymore. It's easy and comfortable, and that's why he's so dangerous."

Fancy pressed her hands to her face and then pulled them out to the sides, stretching her skin. "You're dead wrong," she said. "He's easy because he's a nice guy. He's a bit weird about his job and he's freaky to look at, but basically he's a really nice person." She looked at the knife on the floor and then back at Keiko with a lighter kind of exasperation. "Just because Murray's the pretty one, it doesn't mean Malcolm has to be a monster."

Keiko's mind eddied back down to somewhere nearer her body where it belonged, but she shook her head, insisting. "Why would Malcolm say the carcass had two knees—I'm sorry!"

Fancy shuddered, even at the second hearing. "They do have two knees! There's only one animal in the world that has four knees."

"*What*?" said Keiko.

"Elephants."

"How do you know that?"

"From Vi. From homework. Ask me some dinosaur names. Ask me anything."

Keiko blinked. "But why did Murray say he didn't know what killed his father?"

"I don't know," said Fancy. "Why does anyone say anything?"

"Well, why did he say that his father's body wasn't in his grave?"

"He *didn't*!" said Fancy. "I was there, remember. He didn't say his dad's body wasn't in the grave—I can't believe I'm talking about this, I'm never going to sleep again—he said his dad wasn't in the graveyard, because he loved his dad and there's more to a person than what they leave behind to be buried. Keiko, I was here when Mr. Poole died, you weren't. He was laid out in the house for viewing. It was an open coffin."

"You saw him?"

Fancy almost laughed, almost. "Have we met? No, of course I didn't see him. I couldn't bring myself go near the place because the bloody coffin was open, and I felt terrible about it. But do you think I'll ever forget everyone else going on and on about how peaceful he looked?" Keiko wanted to interrupt, to protest that of course people would say the right thing, but Fancy held up her hand. "Mrs. Watson was there. Hm? Mabel?"

"Yes, but Mrs. Watson is involved somehow. I told you about her face when she saw the letter."

"Okay," said Fancy slowly, "but if she isn't one of them and she sent a letter threatening to expose them, why would she lie about Mr. Poole being in his coffin all ready to be buried?" Keiko twisted her mouth in grudging acknowledgement. "And anyway, Pet took Vi to the wake."

"Viola saw him?"

"Oh yes, and it gave her great satisfaction to come home and tell me all about it. She said he looked like Fred Flintstone—whatever that's supposed to mean—and that they had dressed him up like a baby and she thought it was a shame because everyone knew he always wore men's clothes."

Keiko nodded slowly. "Viola saw Mr. Poole in his coffin. Okay." She bent her head briefly. "But what about the rest of it? If it's not what I think it is, then what is it? What is *wrong* with them?"

"Who?"

"Mrs. McLuskie, Mrs. Dessing, Mr. Ballantyne, Mr. Imperiolo. You see what they've got in common?"

"It's the committee," said Fancy.

"Exactly. And they all did my dry run questionnaire and they're all in a . . . a *state* about something."

"Wait a minute, wait a minute," said Fancy. "What do you mean? You said that stuff you do was supposed to be confidential."

"It is," said Keiko. She couldn't meet Fancy's eyes. "Supposed to be. I was desperate, Fancy. I was trying to help Murray and he wouldn't tell me what was wrong."

"Well, I can tell you what Iain B and Vinegar Tits Dessing are in a state about," said Fancy. "They're having a fling. They walk their dogs at the glen. Pet can see them from her shop window, says they're in the woods for hours sometimes. And once she saw them in a bar in Dirleton."

Keiko shook her head. "That's only two of them," she said. "What do all *four* of them have in common to be so scared about? And the Pooles, of course. They wouldn't let themselves be tested. They refused."

"Maybe they didn't trust you," said Fancy, making Keiko flush.

"A butcher, a baker, two publicans, and a restaurateur," Keiko said.

"What about Mrs. Watson?" said Fancy. "Did you snoop at her answers too?"

"Mrs. Watson sells fruit and vegetables," said Keiko. "She doesn't get any supplies from Malcolm Poole."

Fancy rubbed her face again then stood and went to the cupboard to get her bottles of port and brandy. She poured two and pushed one across the table towards Keiko.

"You really have gone absolutely barking mad," she said, and she began counting off on her fingers. "Iain and Sandra are at it. Etta

McLuskie? Pet reckons Etta's pulling strings about the redevelopment. Kenny Imperiolo ... I don't know."

Some distant memory was stirring in Keiko. "I think he writes all his own reviews for restaurant websites," she said.

Fancy gave a shout of laughter. "Genius!" she said. "Of course he does! Man, I can't believe nobody rumbled him before now. He must be shitting hedgehogs. Jimmy McKendrick's got that hotshot web manager picking the Painchton site to bits trying to do that ... you know when you get it up the Google rankings?" She laughed. "No secrets from those guys. They're like hackers."

"Yes, all right," said Keiko. "I admit all of that, but are you telling me you never thought the committee was doing anything except plan the redevelopment?" Keiko said, watching Fancy closely.

"No way, Jos—" Fancy began. Then she stopped. "Actually yes, I did. I do. I don't know what it is they're up to, but please believe me: top of the list of what it's *not* is ... that thing you said."

Keiko bit her lip. "Why does Mrs. Poole hate me so mu—" She shook her head as Fancy tried to protest. "She *does* hate me. Why did Murray leave the butcher's shop in the first place, before his dad died? Why has she dragged him back?" She waited while Fancy chewed her lip in silence for a minute.

"Who knows why Murray left," she said. "Because he doesn't like it? Who knows why she wants him back. Because her husband's just died and she wants her sons near her? Why does she hate you? Maybe because her husband's just died and she doesn't want you to take her son away. Maybe she doesn't want you to make her big fat miserable son even more jealous of his brother. Maybe she's just a racist. It happens."

"Okay," said Keiko, "but listen to this. You admit that the committee is up to something, but you think it's a coincidence that they're all supplied by Malcolm and they all meet up at Mr. McKendrick's all the time and they're all *up to high doh* and *oxters* and *crabbit as wee ferrets,* but—"

"Jesus Christ," said Fancy.

Keiko raised her voice and kept going. "But what about the food? What about the schedule? They didn't even hide it—it was like a *campaign*. It was unstoppable, an obsession to get me into their houses and stuff me with four-course meals and give me great big tubs of leftovers and come and check to see that I'd eaten them. It was … it was madness."

"Yeah," said Fancy. "Death by drop scone. See I never got much of that—except from Pet—because they didn't approve of me, but you were always going to be for it: a good girl like you, all on your own and thousands of miles from home. You might as well have had a red cloak on and a basket of stuff for Grandma."

Keiko was nodding, but Fancy saw through it. "What?" she said. "What else is there?"

"Janette Campbell," said Keiko. "Why was she so cold when I talked about the slaughterhouse? I don't believe it was what Malcolm said."

"Neither do I," said Fancy. "I never did. Janette Campbell doesn't have much time for Murray. I reckon it was finding out you'd taken up with him that bugged her, not the mention of that back shed."

"But why didn't you *tell* me that?" said Keiko.

"Because Malcolm was there, remember?" Fancy said. "It was steak and kidney pudding day. And I didn't want to say that someone didn't think much of his brother in front of him. And then I forgot."

"But why?" said Keiko.

"Oh, for God's sake, Keiko!" said Fancy. She poured herself another drink and after a sip of it, she spoke very slowly and loudly. "Okay, I didn't forget. I just don't like talking about it, but okay, you win. I, Frances Mary Clarke, did not tell you that Janette Campbell bears a grudge to Murray Poole. Shoot me."

"I didn't mean why did you forget," Keiko said. "I mean why doesn't Janette—"

"For God's *sake!*" said Fancy and then started speaking very loud and slow again. "Because Natasha was her shampoo girl and she probably told Janette that Murray was a crap boyfriend. Or … I don't know."

Keiko frowned.

"What now?" said Fancy.

"Who's Natasha?"

Fancy blinked. "Tash," she said.

Keiko stood up and jammed her hand into her jeans pocket. She pulled out the necklace and let it swing in front of Fancy's face.

"I found this in my kitchen drain," she said. "This is what was clogging it."

Fancy reached out and grasped it. "That's Tash's," she whispered. "Pet's got a picture of her wearing it."

"It was fastened," Keiko said. "It didn't just fall off."

"Oh my God," said Fancy.

"Has anyone heard from Tash since she left?"

"Mother of God," said Fancy. She held the chain and put it to her lips. She looked up at Keiko with fresh tears in her eyes. "What have I done?" she said.

Keiko took her free hand. "Please," she whispered. "Tell me."

Fancy waved to the bottles, and Keiko refilled both glasses with even bigger measures than before.

"I lied to you," Fancy said when she had taken a big swallow from hers. "It was true about the state Pet was in when I came back, rocking with the baby, crying, all that. And the ego boost, that was true too. Except the more time went on, the more I got the idea that it was Tash she was mourning, and Vi and me were like a consolation prize." Keiko shook her head but Fancy ignored her. "And I sort of knew I should try and get in touch with Tash and tell her she was wrong about foster mums. We all get so cynical so young, you know? Toughen up so no one can hurt you? We all used to tell ourselves the carers were in it for the money. Only I must have known it wasn't true with Pet, or why did I come back, right? And I knew I should find Tash and tell her. But …" Fancy ducked her head down between her shoulders the way she had the first time they met. "I didn't want to share. I didn't want Pet's favourite coming back and shoving me out."

Keiko was shaking her head faster now. "Pet loves you," she said. "She adores you. And Viola. No one could shove you out!"

"Well," said Fancy. "That's what I did, anyway."

"You didn't do anything," Keiko said. "All your feelings are understandable and natural, even if they're wrong."

"Yeah, but I did lie though," said Fancy, in a tiny voice. "By omission."

Keiko groaned. "Please forget I said that."

"And the other thing too. I didn't look for her to try to get her home again." Fancy's voice had grown hoarse. "And then—Jesus, this is hard to say!—when Pet asked me to, cos she's useless with the Internet, I said I would, and then I said I had, and I said couldn't find her." She caught a sob before it could get free. "But I never checked at all because I was scared if she came back there'd be no place for me. And then, after you asked about her and Nikki and

Dina the other day, I did search and there's nothing. I left it too late and she's lost now. She's really gone."

Keiko put down her glass and took Fancy's out of her hand, then she wrapped her arms around Fancy's shoulders and hugged her close. Fancy buried her head into Keiko's middle and finally let go. Keiko bent and kissed the parting of her hair.

"I am so sorry," she said as Fancy wept. "I've dredged up your worst memories and made you feel badly. You did nothing wrong."

"I let her stay lost," said Fancy, her voice sodden and muffled.

"You were young," Keiko said. "Then you grew up into a good person and a good mother, and you are a wonderful daughter and friend. You did nothing wrong."

Fancy sniffed and pulled back, turning her face up to look at Keiko. "Well, neither did you then," she said with a watery smile.

Keiko went to get a cool cloth and took her seat again.

"You know what the real mystery is?" Fancy said after she had blown her nose and finished her drink. "Murray thinks he can tell you what to do and what to look like and drop mysterious hints until he's got you demented. And Craig McKendrick has been play-ing silly buggers with me since he first stuck his hand up my jumper on a school trip. Jesus, you jumping when Murray says jump must be making him as happy as a pig in shit, you know! And so the only real mystery is why I—after everything I learned the hard way from Viola's dad—and you—who spend your whole life studying human nature—give one single solitary sod about either of them."

Keiko finally felt her body and mind smash back together at last. "I've made such a fool of myself," she said. "I just want to crawl into a hole and hide. I don't know how I'm going to face anyone."

"Nobody knows what you were thinking, you bampot," said Fancy. "Or hey! You could always walk home backwards like Vi does. Rewind!"

"I must have gone mad. I really thought—"

"Look," said Fancy. "You're in a new country, a long way from home and it must seem like, 'Oh my god, what a crazy place, what's going on?' Like all kinds of things that could never happen at home might happen here. But it's not real. It's like if I went to Tokyo, I would be just the same. Total head wreck."

"Well, I'm over it now," Keiko said. "And you're right about Murray. But ..." She hesitated. "Don't be too hard on Craig. He did warn me. Except I thought it was Malcolm he was warning me about."

"Did he say he warned Tash?" said Fancy. Her voice was cold. "Or was he another one who reckoned she didn't matter?"

"He didn't mention Tash," Keiko said. "He felt bad even saying what he did. He was trying to be loyal to his friend."

"Yeah, well, his friend's not worth it and he's definitely not worth you. And poor Malcolm—he's done nothing!"

"Please promise me you will never tell anyone what I said, what I thought," Keiko said.

"Cross my heart and hope to die and be served at a barbecue to all my friends and neighbours," said Fancy with a smirk. "I won't tell a soul."

———

Keiko called in to say sorry to Mrs. Watson for dashing through the shop earlier. Mrs. Watson stroked her arm and made soothing noises through her giggles.

"Well now, you must just put it out of your mind in time for New Year's Day, so you can sit down to your hough dinner and enjoy it. I'm just the same with tongue, mind. I love a slice with a good sweet pickle, but I couldn't cook it for a king's ransom. Lying there in the pot looking just like a great big tongue." She shuddered and then squeezed Keiko's shoulder. "So I won't tell if you don't tell. And don't you worry about Malcolm; he's used to the rest of us being more squeamish than him."

Keiko stood still, staring at her, wondering if she could ask—just ask straight out—about the letter and why Mrs. Watson had looked that way. If Fancy was right, there would be some silly, innocent explanation for it.

"And speaking of the Pooles," said Mrs. Watson. "I was hearing in the post office first thing that Willie Byers has finally caved in and agreed to sell to the Traders. He went round and told Jimmy McKendrick last night."

"Really?" said Keiko. "That's excellent news. Well, not for Murray." What would he do? she wondered. Cut the ties, leave Painchton, and find a proper place of his own? For a split second, the feeling this thought produced—a flattening out, a downward swoop in her insides—might have been mistaken for disappointment, but in no time at all she had identified it: it was relief.

THIRTY-TWO

Wednesday, 27 November

AFTER TALKING WITH FANCY on Monday, Keiko did not put on her tracksuit and trot over to the workshop at the time set by Murray for their sessions. She sat in the flat listening for him and rewording her explanation until bedtime. The next night she waited again, thinking of all the times she had skipped downstairs to find him, of how he had watched for her passing and come out onto the street to talk to her, of how he only climbed the stairs—all that effort!—when he needed something.

So when the knock finally came at seven o'clock on the third day, as she was standing in the kitchen slicing vegetables for her dinner, she was almost tired enough of thinking about him to feel no triumph at all. She stood aside to let him in and he slouched towards the living room and threw himself down into a chair with a groan. Keiko settled herself on the sofa.

"Have you heard?" he said at last.

"I don't think so," said Keiko, almost sure what he meant but refusing to go along with his estimation of its enormity.

"Willie Byers said to McKendrick that the Traders can have his place. He's going to sell."

"I see." Was she trying to provoke him with this performance of calm?

"It must have been right after Mum went to see him. For sheer spite."

"He is not a kind man," Keiko said. "But does it matter? Since you want to leave anyway?"

"What?" said Murray. "Who said I want to leave? Why would I want to leave after the work I've put in on the place?"

Keiko was speechless for a moment. "*You* said it," she said, when she had got her voice back. "You said it over and over again. That Painchton wasn't right for you. Or for me. That it was dangerous and you wanted to get away."

"Oh," he said. "That. Yeah, well, it was just the shop really."

"But you said there was a secret. You said I was in danger."

"What secret?" he said. "Yeah, I said you were in danger—of ending up like Malcolm and the rest of them."

Keiko thought hard. Could that be right? Had Murray really never mentioned a secret? Was that her own imagining? "You said there was a puzzle," she told him. "You definitely said that to me."

"Yeah: how to keep my workshop when the Traders were trying to get it," he said.

Keiko felt the last twist of tension leave her. Fancy had driven most of it away, but there had been wisps left behind. Small questions, small worries. Now she felt nothing. Absolutely nothing at all.

"It might be for the best that Byers is selling," she said to Murray. "This way you can look for better premises, perhaps in a busier place where you'll have customers. Start taking on repairs. Get a bank loan, draw up a business plan." Like Fancy had done when she was only seventeen. "Or," she softened her tone, "if it's to be just a hobby, then make it a hobby. Build a shed in your garden." *Get a garden,* she thought. *Get a house.*

Murray shook his head, as if she didn't understand. "There's no reason for him to sell to the Traders," he said. "He doesn't give a stuff about the town. And he should compensate me. We had an agreement." His eyes darted to and fro across the pattern on the carpet as though the answer was hidden there in the brown and orange swirls and he could catch it if he was quick enough. "Someone must have nobbled him. He wouldn't have done this. I know him. I know how he works."

"Clearly you don't," she said. "Unless he's only toying with the Traders. Has he signed anything?"

"I don't think so."

"So talk to him." She did not quite manage to hide the exasperation. "If you really think you want the whole redevelopment stalled so that you can have your bikes and your gym where it suits you to have them ..."

"Mum won't—" he began.

"Oh Murray, it doesn't matter if your mother won't do it for you. Do it for yourself. At least enforce the contract yourself. Try to *get* compensation."

"But he's made up his mind," said Murray. "I'm no good with things like that."

"At least try!" Keiko said, even louder. "Don't just say you can't. Change his mind. Unmake his mind." He was staring into the fire again and his breathing was getting quicker. "People are *not* lumps of meat, Murray. Take it from me. You can change them and fix them, just like motorbikes. What do you think I spend my time doing?" He was almost panting now listening to her. "Byers is playing you and the Traders off against each other, and you shouldn't let him." She was getting to him. She tried to sound like Fancy, who made all things seem so clear. "He's ..." She groped for the phrase. "He's as happy as a pig in shit, making all this trouble," she said. Murray turned his whole body towards her and gave her a stare that was both hard and vacant at the same time. "And," she went on, "you shouldn't let a shitty old pig decide your life for you."

"You're right," said Murray. "I knew that. I just needed to hear someone else tell me." He sprang out the chair so suddenly that she flinched. And then he moved, faster than walking, smoother than running, out of the room. She heard the front door bang behind him.

"It doesn't have to be this minute, you ... plank," she said to the empty air, then shook her head at her reflection in the mantelpiece mirror. Not a word. Not a single word about her, about them. Just total concentration on his own little problem. Like a child. She laughed out loud and went back to the kitchen.

The red onion, green pepper, and white radish were sliced into thin lengths with pointed ends like quills, and she sprinkled them into a smoking skillet smeared with a drop of oil. She took an egg from the fridge. She would make it into a thin omelette to wrap around her vegetables, slice the tube into rounds and then sit at the table and nibble away until she was tired. Except that she was tired already. She watched the vegetable strips beginning to crisp at the edges and, moving with sudden speed, she got another two eggs, broke all three into the pan and stirred the mess until it was mixed. While the underside browned, she grated cheese on top, holding the grater over the pan, ignoring the sound and smell of stray shards hitting the stove. She roasted it under the grill until it was bubbling and then, holding it between two slices of toast, she carried it, plate-less and licking the melting butter from her wrists, over to the table and ate the lot.

She was in her bedroom about to start undressing when the next knock came.

"Hello?" she said through the door, striking just the right note of caution to let him know that she didn't assume it was him. And if it was him, he could forget it; he was not getting back in tonight.

"Keiko?" came the answer, just as soft. Malcolm.

He was as uneasy as she had ever seen him, swaying in the famil-iar side-to-side shuffle, looking down. She had always thought of him as looking at his feet, but she realised now that when he looked down he must be looking at his chest or maybe his stomach; he couldn't see his feet from there.

"Keiko, I'm sorry to trouble you so late." It was almost midnight. "But I really need to speak to Murray."

"Murray's not here," she said more sharply than she intended, and Malcolm looked up.

"But he's been here?" he said. She nodded. "Have you had a row?"
"No."
"Do you know where he is?"
"The workshop, probably," said Keiko. "Have you tried there?"
"There was no answer," said Malcolm. Then he just stood there, waiting.
"Do you want to come in?"

He nodded and she led him to the kitchen, turning to fill the kettle while he rearranged the table slightly out from the wall and squeezed himself into the sturdiest chair. He looked tired, his lips pale and less clearly outlined than usual against the smooth expanse of his face, grey smudges like thumbprints in the inner corners of his eyes. She put sugar into his tea without asking and sat down opposite.

"Did you hear about Willie Byers?" he asked. She nodded. "And you knew my mother was hoping to buy the place for Murray?" She nodded again and felt the look of incredulity, possibly picked up from Murray himself, pucker her eyebrows. How solemn could everyone be about this? Malcolm blew across his tea, drew in a loud mouthful, and went on. "Murray's very disappointed." He looked at her through the oily locks of his fringe and chewed his lip, then seemed to come to some decision. "He was at the house earlier and he was very … upset, and I thought I should ask you to be careful with him."

"Careful?" said Keiko. Was he warning her or threatening her?

"Gentle, I mean. I know you don't understand and it's hard to explain. Impossible to explain, really. So just be kind. And if he needs to talk, just listen. Would you do that for us?"

"It's too late," said Keiko. "I've already told him what I think and I'm afraid I wasn't 'kind and gentle and careful.' I was straightforward. I actually dared to speak my mind. I know that's wrong."

Malcolm smiled at her tone and acknowledged the point with a bow. "Not the Painchton way of doing things?" he said. "Is that what you mean? Or not the Poole way at least?"

"But I think I helped him come to some decision."

"What did you say to him?"

"I said he should take control of the situation. I simply suggested that he could make it happen if he really wanted to and if Mr. Byers had made up his mind, then Murray should change it. I hope he doesn't. I hope he fails. The Traders' plans are more important than Murray's whim."

"You told him to change Byers's mind?"

"I was talking in the most general terms, but Murray seemed to think I'd given him an idea."

Malcolm put his cup down with a smack, slopping his tea. His eyes were an echo of Murray's from hours before, piercing but blind. "What *exactly* did you say to him?" he asked her.

Keiko could remember her words clearly. She had been proud of them, inelegant as they were.

"I said—why does this matter, Malcolm?—I said Mr. Byers was causing trouble and enjoying it, and that Murray was pathetic to say he could only deal with bikes and not people and he should take charge, unmake Mr. Byers's made-up mind and I said—excuse me, but what I said *exactly*—was that Mr. Byers was like a pig in shit and that Murray shouldn't let his life be decided by a stupid, shitty pig."

Malcolm rose straight up like a whale breaking water and with no backward movement, so that the flimsy table was shoved towards Keiko and pinned her to the wall. He loomed over her, swaying, for just two or three of her racing heartbeats, then he turned and thundered to the door, gathering speed as he went, making the stone floor under Keiko's feet shudder. She scrambled out from her chair and followed him along the passage, watching the hanks of hair flap, the clods of flesh wallop and shiver with every thumping footfall.

Down the stairs he went, two at a time, the hallway booming back at him. When he turned on the landing, Keiko could see that his whole face was putty grey, his blue lips working grotesquely as he tried to summon his voice. She could feel each of his steps through her own feet and up to her teeth as he pounded along the passageway to the yard, and she was right behind him as he slammed in through the back door of the shop. The moan in his throat got clearer and louder until it burst out of his mouth.

"Mm. Mm! Mum!"

Mrs. Poole was in place in the puddle of light at her desk, with her ledgers spread open before her. She moved only her eyes as Malcolm lurched into the doorway and stopped dead, making Keiko smack into his back.

"Keiko?" she said, her voice defeated and odd-sounding after Malcolm's panic. "Where is she?" Malcolm reached behind him and dragged Keiko to the front, clamping her to him tightly, her waist in the fold of his elbow. She rocked back and forward against his heaving belly as he laboured to catch his breath and did not even try to struggle as Mrs. Poole rose to her feet, crossed towards them, reached out, and put her hands on either side of Keiko's face.

"Thank God," she said. For the first time, in the dim light of the lamp, Keiko could see colour, a bloom of warm brown, in the dark eyes. Mrs. Poole looked up at her son. "What then?" she whispered. "What's happened?"

"Byers," was all Malcolm managed to say. He released his grip on Keiko and turned away, letting the cold air sweeping in from the yard door move around her body again. He went back along the passageway at a stumbling trot, barely lifting his feet from the flagstones. Mrs. Poole hesitated until he was halfway down the yard, almost out of sight, then went after him. Keiko followed her. They heard Malcolm fumble for the padlock on the slaughterhouse door and yank it down hard against the hasp, testing it, finding it locked. Then he started to move again at a shuffle; as their eyes grew accustomed to the darkness, they could see him pause in the yard gateway before turning and heading down towards the green.

Malcolm shouldered open a back door into Byers's part of the building, splintering the lock, and they hurried inside, he first and Mrs. Poole and Keiko in his wake like two tugboats following a liner. They passed the filthy toilet Keiko had once glimpsed and burst into Murray's room. The darkness was so deep it was like stepping into ink. They could see nothing and it sounded still and empty. Only the smell was wrong. Rising up through the mix of wax, oil, and paint was something else—sourness and sweetness combined, metal and animal, perfume and stink.

Mrs. Poole clicked on one of the lights just long enough for Keiko to see but not to comprehend. There was something spreading across the floor and splattered out, something smeared thin, something clotted. Heaps jagged and piled, smooth white and rags, and Murray's face as the light snapped off again.

Then came Malcolm's calm voice. "Come on," he said. "We can phone from the shop."

"Not yet," Mrs. Poole whispered. And before Keiko had time to catch a deep breath against the sight that was coming, the lights were on again.

Murray was sitting propped up by the Bantam with his feet braced on the floor and his hands cradled in his lap, head down, eyes half-open. He was dead. Keiko had never seen a dead person before and could not have said how she knew, but there was no urgency in the steps she took towards him, inching close enough to see the cuts running from the base of his palms to his elbows, thick-edged and gaping, the veins inside ripped, the tendons stretched, and all bleached out to the colour of dirty string. She turned away from him to the spread tarpaulin behind her.

Skin, bones, and flesh were more or less separate, although the seeping blood had carried some of the smaller pieces with it and merged them. The skin was folded in a square-edged pile, topped by something like a nubbly deflated beach-ball that Keiko couldn't identify. She took a step closer. It was a scalp, the hair kinked into crests with blood. She stared at it and took another step, but a movement caught her eye. Mrs. Poole, standing at the opposite edge of the tarpaulin, had raised her hand, telling her not to go any closer. When Keiko looked down, she saw that her feet were less than another pace away from the edge of the spreading.

"Come on, Mum," said Malcolm again.

Mrs. Poole shook her head. "We don't even know who it is," she said. "At least let's make sure."

Keiko looked back at the heaps on the floor, searching for something to tell her that these bundles had been Mr. Byers, and for the first time her stomach threatened to give way in a slow roll forward like a child tumbling over in water.

Mrs. Poole crossed to the bench, to another neat stack, this one only a bundle of clothes, and picked up a wallet from the top of the pile. She opened it gingerly, fingering the contents with great tenderness, as if a small display of respect could make up for the degradation behind her. Keiko felt the urge to laugh but caught herself. Hysteria had no place here.

Mrs. Poole put down the wallet and turned to them with a nod. Then she cast her eyes around the room with a speculative gaze, so unfitting to the moment that if Malcolm had not been there, Keiko would have felt fear at being near her.

"There's tape over the doors," she said. Keiko looked at her in puzzlement for a moment before turning to the big double doors to the street. They were sealed around their edges and over the keyhole with broad grey tape. She glanced at the small window. It was covered with a square of cardboard cut from a crisp box and taped around the edges.

"Nobody can see that the light's on," Mrs. Poole said. She nodded and cast her eyes around again with the same calm, thoughtful look.

"It's over, Mum," said Malcolm. "Come on. It's over now."

"Wait," said Mrs. Poole. "Just a minute. We need to decide what to do."

"What are you talking about?" Malcolm said. He ran one massive hand, dark-looking against his candle-white face, over his mouth.

Mrs. Poole's voice was lighter than Keiko had ever heard it as she answered. "Everything's changed now. Let me think. Stop rushing me." She looked away from his set face and towards Keiko.

"Are you talking about trying to cover this up?" said Malcolm.

"Trust me," said his mother. "No good would come of letting it out."

"Mum, you can't be serious," said Malcolm, plaintive and wheedling now. "We could never clean this up, never mind explaining where Byers and—" He choked on the name and pressed his hand against his mouth again.

"I think Malcolm's right, Mrs. Poole," said Keiko. Malcolm held out his arm towards her, displaying her to his mother like evidence. Mrs. Poole watched him for a moment, then Keiko saw a spark of light in her eyes and a suggestion of a smile twitch at her lips.

"What?" Keiko asked her.

"No, *we* couldn't manage it," she said, "but I can think of someone who'll help us." She was almost laughing. "Who can you think of who knows how to do everything, or thinks he does, and would do anything in the world for me without turning a hair, would do anything for this town?"

Keiko smiled back at her.

"Jimmy McKendrick?" said Malcolm. "You're going to ask Jimmy McKendrick to cover up murder? Mum, please. You've lost your mind." His voice was rising.

Keiko looked between one and the other. If Malcolm was beginning to panic, then it was up to her. What she had to do was get Mrs. Poole away from here so her senses would return to her.

"Let's at least ask Mr. McKendrick what to do," Keiko said. "And whatever he says, we'll be guided by him. We can phone him from my flat."

Mrs. Poole picked her way around the edge of the tarpaulin, moving towards Murray. Keiko watched her bend over, smooth his hair up away from his face. Briefly, she saw the peak on his forehead and the hook of his brows before it fell forward again. Mrs. Poole pushed down his eyelids with the tips of her fingers.

"My bonny baby," she said. The toe of one shoe was in the blood and Keiko hoped she would notice and not need to be told to wipe it clean before walking out into the lane. "My baby boy."

As she let go of Murray's face, Mrs. Poole rocked her foot back onto the heel and looked at the blotch. She didn't wipe it, but took her shoe off and cradled it in the crook of her elbow before turning and limping away.

THIRTY-THREE

Somewhere between the workshop and the lighted warmth of her kitchen, Keiko's calm deserted her and she started to shake, unable to stop her teeth from chattering behind her cold lips, unable to make her feet move in anything but a clockwork totter that would have pitched her down the stairs had it not been for Mrs. Poole's strong arm across her back.

Malcolm sat opposite her again, as he had less than ten minutes ago, in that other world where she had lived before here. Mrs. Poole pressed a mug into her hands and cupped them around it, got another for Malcolm, then went into the living room to the telephone.

His face was white now, not grey, only the absence of stubble showing where his lips began, and the thumbprint smudges between his eyes were darker, as though some brutal giant had pinched him there. And when he looked at Keiko, his expression told her that her own face must be just as stricken, just as strange. He slid one arm across the table towards her, and she unlaced her hands from the mug and put a fist into his upturned palm.

Mrs. Poole must have stayed in the living room for some time after she put down the phone, because she had been back with them for only a minute—chafing Keiko's hands, smoothing Malcolm's hair back in a gesture that made all three of them shrink at the memory—when they heard the purposeful clack of Mr. McKendrick's brogues climbing the stairs. He let himself in and came to join them. Despite the late hour, he was dressed in his usual array of coat, waistcoat and tie, pressed trousers, and polished shoes. His hair was neatly combed across his head, but his eyes were wide open without a trace of a wink or twinkle and his mouth hung open too, making his face a foolish egg-shape. He plopped down onto a chair with none of his customary bustle.

"Tea, Jim?" said Mrs. Poole.

He turned to her and stared. "Not just now, Gracie, you're all right," he said. He wet his lips by pushing the bottom up over the top then the top out over the bottom, before he spoke again. "So. Murray has killed Byers and himself and they are both in the petrol station. You've all seen them." He put out a hand to Mrs. Poole. "Grace, I'm sorry for your loss." Keiko was sure that this phrase, from the way he said it, was a stock condolence. There was the answer: Mr. McKendrick would do what was right and proper. "Terrible thing," he went on. "Feelings running very high about the development. A laddie who's just lost his father and an old trouble-maker like Byers stirring everything up. I blame myself for this, Gracie, I do."

"The thing is," said Mrs. Poole, "he didn't just knock him over in a brawl, and as soon as the police come they'll know it's more than that." Mr. McKendrick pursed his mouth and waited. "I had to look at Byers's wallet to be sure who it was." Her voice had lost its calm and sounded harsh. "He's in pieces. Dismembered. *Butchered*." She swallowed, squeezing her eyes to help her clear her throat with a dry click.

Malcolm shifted in his seat as though to prepare himself to speak, but Mrs. Poole continued, her voice ragged now. "And the thing is, Jim, the trouble is … it's happened before. Or I think it's happened before. I can't be sure. And it's going to come out now, unless you can help us stop it. It'll all come out and no good of it to anyone."

Malcolm had squeezed Keiko's hand in a single, tight spasm, but he was not looking at her. He stared at his mother and tried to say something, but what came out was no more than a croak.

"I'm sorry, Malcolm," said Mrs. Poole. "We should have told you."

Mr. McKendrick narrowed his eyes in an effort to understand. Squinting at Mrs. Poole with distaste clenching his jaw, he looked at last more like his capable self again, the egg-faced idiot gone.

"You can't be sure?" he echoed. He waited for Mrs. Poole to speak, no inkling in his face of the idea that was forming in Keiko's mind.

"He got rid of the body."

"How?" said Mr. McKendrick. "Where?"

"Don't make me say it," said Mrs. Poole. She fixed her eyes on a spot above Mr. McKendrick's head. "It was back when Duncan still did all the work out in the old slaughterhouse."

Malcolm relaxed his grip on Keiko as though to allow her to snatch her hand away from him, but she opened her fingers and wrapped them around his thumb, squeezing until he closed his hand on hers again. She could hear Mr. McKendrick's breath coming faster.

"When was this?" he said.

"Just over five years ago," said Mrs. Poole. "We weren't just thinking of ourselves, James, you've got to believe that. You know Duncan would never have tried to save his own name if it hurt somebody else. We didn't find out until long after. We never found out for sure, to tell the truth."

"Who was it?" said Mr. McKendrick.

Mrs. Poole bit her lip and said nothing.

"Tash," Keiko said.

"Who?" said Mr. McKendrick.

"Natasha," said Mrs. Poole, nodding. "Tash that Pet McMaster had after Fancy went. I found her clothes. That's all. I found her clothes and her watch and the leather bracelets she always wore. And we never found anything else. But there had been other … things before, so we were pretty sure what he'd done." Mr. McKendrick was gulping repeatedly, but Mrs. Poole went on. "Tell me I was wrong, Jim, if you think I was wrong. Tell me I should have told everyone that had been in our shop, months later when it was too late to do anything but have nightmares for the rest of their lives. Tell me I should have told Pet McMaster, when she was beside herself with the girl taking off and I was round there every night with … with … so she wouldn't need to cook." Mrs. Poole started to weep silently, holding her bottom lip in her teeth and letting the tears spill and fall.

Mr. McKendrick sat for a long time without speaking, staring unblinking at the tablecloth, until the rise and fall of his chest had begun to slow, then he squeezed his eyes shut. When he opened them again he looked up and took in all three of them with one gleaming sweep.

"You did the right thing. No question. And we're going to do the right thing now. I love this town." He paused and struggled for a way to express his next thought. Finding a suitable phrase, he cleared his throat and began again. "Everything I love is in this town, and I will not," his voice rose, "stand by and let what I love become a freak show. Jesus God, I nearly—But never mind that now. So." His voice gentled again and he leaned forward to take Mrs. Poole's hands into his. "I used to be a volunteer fireman, Gracie, as you know, and in my capacity as Chairman of the Traders I had occasion to speak to Mr. Byers more than once about his safety provisions. Basically, he doesn't have any. If someone put a match to that place," said Mr. McKendrick, beginning to pat his pockets with useless busyness, "it would go up like straw. So, I have two things I need to ask you, Grace, and neither one of them is easy. First, could you live with it if Murray went in a fire?" He clasped Mrs. Poole's hands again, waiting until she nodded. "And second—I'm sorry to have ask to ask you to dwell on this—about Willie. Is he—" He turned to Malcolm, out of some chivalrous impulse, and dropped his voice as though letting Keiko and Mrs. Poole not hear him. "Is he somewhere you'd expect him to be?"

The image of the tarpaulin with its leaking bundles blared at Keiko for a moment and she saw a shudder pass through Malcolm, felt another squeeze, on and off again, in his fingers.

"Far from it," he said, slowly.

"But will I be able to rearrange the—" began Mr. McKendrick.

Malcolm shook his head and looked towards Keiko in desperate appeal.

"It's very thorough," Keiko said, and even this sounded like a monstrosity.

"We've got a problem then," said Mr. McKendrick. "It doesn't matter how complete the burning is, there's still going to be remains, identifiable remains. If the petrol station was still on the go, if it was an explosion we were looking at, that would be different. But they'll be able tell if the body wasn't—as it should have been— before it burned." He clipped this last word off short with a look at Mrs. Poole, but she only closed her eyes and waited.

"Son," went on Mr. McKendrick, "I don't suppose you would be able to deal with it? No of course not, why should you? I was just thinking with you being a butcher..." Mr. McKendrick's voice died again. He blew out hard and cleared his throat preparing, Keiko assumed, to begin talking them into giving up a bad job. She blurted out what was in her head before she had time to rethink it.

"Fancy!" All three turned to stare at her. "Fancy Clarke. She's done an anatomy course. She would know what to do with the body. How it should...be."

Mr. McKendrick started wetting his lips again, over and up, over and up. "Fancy Clarke is not a Painchton girl," he said.

"Yes, she is," said Keiko. "Whether you like it or not. Everything she loves is here, Mr. McKendrick, just like you."

"Could she do it?" he said.

Keiko tried not to think of Fancy putting her head between her knees to stop herself from fainting at the thought of her lessons, tried to see Fancy walking into the workshop. She would surely do it if she could.

"She could do it if she had to," Keiko said, which was not the same thing at all.

———

Fancy's voice on the phone was groggy, and she whimpered at Keiko's urgent tone.

"What is it now? It's one o'clock in the morning, Keeks. Tell me tomorrow."

"Get Viola up and go downstairs to the back lane," said Keiko. "Mr. McKendrick is coming to get you."

"Mr. McKen—"

Keiko put down the phone and nodded to Mr. McKendrick, hovering at her elbow.

He was gone and back, with Fancy tiptoeing behind him, wide-eyed over the bundle of blankets, before Keiko had finished closing the bedroom curtains and getting the bed ready. Fancy laid the little girl down, kept her hand on her shoulder until she was back in deep sleep, and then crept out to join the others.

Perhaps it helped that she hadn't been in Painchton at the time, but Fancy stood up to it better than Keiko could ever have hoped. Only her constant glances over her shoulder to the back corner of the house, towards the lane, the pink workshop, and what lay inside it, told them that she was anything but calm. Keiko did not spare any details, simply laid out the facts in a clear voice, like a teacher.

"So," she said, finally, "we need your help. Because you under-stand how the bones and muscles fit together and you'll be able to sort out and rearrange the parts of Mr. Byers's body." She looked straight into Fancy's face as she spoke, thinking that perhaps if Fancy was going to faint, they could make it happen now and get it over with.

"What about fingerprints?" said Fancy in a whisper.

"There's going to be a fire," Keiko reminded her.

"Oh yeah."

Mr. Kendrick pulled his watch out of his pocket and looked at it, tapping the back softly with his fingernails, thinking hard. Then he dropped it back and put his arm along the back of Fancy's chair.

"We should aim to get it started by three, get a good couple of hours' burn in the dead of night before anyone raises the alarm if we're lucky." Fancy didn't move, so Mr. McKendrick cleared his throat and tried again. "We better get started, lovey." This time she shot to her feet before he had finished speaking.

Mrs. Poole also rose. "I'll get you some things from downstairs," she said, and when Fancy frowned her misunderstanding, she went on: "Boots and an overall, dear. Gloves."

Mr. McKendrick guided both of them out of the kitchen with a hand at their elbows, and Keiko and Malcolm sat in silence until they heard the front door open and close, then he took his hand away and rubbed his face slowly, the scrape of stubble against his palms sounding as though he was grinding sand into his skin. When Keiko couldn't stand it any longer, she reached across and pulled his hands away.

"You said you didn't know about Tash," she said. "But you don't seem shocked."

"I think I'm just ... I'm trying ... I thought I understood him." He paused, scanning the air above her head as though watching a slide show passing there.

"Tell me what you thought you understood," Keiko said.

"I don't know anything about it, not really," said Malcolm, "but I don't think anyone starts out bad."

"Of course they don't. Tell me."

Malcolm heaved a great, shuddering sigh, deep enough almost to sound like a moan in the back of his throat.

"He's younger than me," he said. "Three years. And that's a lot. Should have been a lot, anyway, except Murray was so quick, such a bright spark, I think they forgot he was just a baby. And when I was eight and he was five, something happened. It can't explain tonight—no way it could even begin to—but it's just what you said about the pig, you see."

"What *I* said?" said Keiko.

"It used to be that a family butcher would do all their own pig-killing. That's why there's a slaughterhouse. Somebody would bring in a pig, and we'd see to it for them. Or if a farmer wanted beef for the family, we'd go out to the farm and kill the beast ourselves, bring it back here to dress it. That was before my time, really though. By the time Mum and Dad had us, it was all beginning to stop, but Dad decided we should see a pig-killing, just once before it was too late."

"What happened?" said Keiko.

"Well, this old boy had a baconer he wanted done. It didn't bother me too much. I mean, I wouldn't get it out on video, you know. But it was interesting. Also me being me, I stood where Dad told me to stand, and Murray being Murray, he was right in there darting about getting in everybody's way, so he was round at the front, in close, when Dad cut its throat."

Malcolm remembered—had never been able to forget—the pig squealing and twisting and then the sudden silence and the still, hanging weight after the first cut, the split second before the blood gouted out of the neck wound.

"The old guy—Marsh, that was his name! Pete Marsh—he was at the other side, cutting out the gut. You cut round and grab it before it drops into the belly and then you keep a hold of it till you've opened the underside and strip the whole gut out at once. That's the trickiest bit, to stop the guts spilling into the meat and spoiling it, but there's no need for it all to be done so quickly. That's the thing. There was no need for him to be at it already before Dad was finished at the throat. But I think it must be some kind of a... you know? To get the guts out, get the dirt away from the carcass before it's hardly dead?"

He closed his eyes and saw again Murray shrieking, backing away from his father and the fountain of blood.

"And he got under Marsh's feet and Marsh let go of the gut end, so then Murray tried to get out of the way of that and put his foot in the blood bucket. By this time he was squealing his head off, and it sounded exactly like the pig when they were lifting it." Malcolm stopped for a couple of breaths, remembering, and then went on in a harder tone.

"All I could think about was getting Murray out of there and getting him cleaned up, and maybe if my father had left Marsh and the pig and taken Murray away in to Mum for a cuddle, he might have been okay. But Dad got angry. Mr. Marsh too. I think Dad was mad with himself for not having the sense to know that Murray was too young, but it was Murray he shouted at. Shaking him and shouting at him. And Marsh must have been angry with my father for letting his kids muck everything up—the carcass was completely ruined—and he was shouting too.

"So they're both really giving it some and Murray's screaming and skidding about, covered in blood and pig dirt and bile—it maybe sounds like nothing now, but—"

"It sounds horrific," said Keiko. "Poor little boys, both of you."

"I was all right," said Malcolm. "I was eight, not five. I could have done something."

"You mustn't say that. You mustn't think that way. It was up to your father to—"

"Well, anyway, Dad took him by the scruff and yanked him upstairs here, and then he starts shouting at Mum saying how she's turned him into a sissy, and she starts yelling back about the mess traipsed up into the flat. It was the worst row they ever had, and I'm sure Mum must have been against letting us see the slaughter in the first place. That's why she was so angry and how come Dad was shouting his head off at her. For being right, you know?"

Keiko nodded.

"They still weren't speaking by the time we went to bed that night. We could hear my dad scrubbing away at the slaughterhouse and my mum trying to get the footprints off the hall carpet, so when Murray had a nightmare there was no way I was going to get either of them. I took care of him myself. Tried to anyway."

"Just that first night?" said Keiko.

Malcolm shook his head. "That was my big mistake," he said. "My parents never mentioned it again, not a word, as if it never happened. And so I never told them how bad it was at nighttime."

"They never said sorry to Murray?" Keiko asked him.

"They never said anything. And anytime they had a wee row about something, Murray would run away and hide, shaking. And I never told them about that either. I just tried to take care of it. Every night, I tried. When he had the bad dreams I used to get into his bed and tell him stories. No animals, no fighting or shouting, or shooting or swords, nothing to do with eating or dying. Nothing with smells." Malcolm gave a short laugh. "It doesn't leave much," he said.

"I used to tell him stories about Robotland. One about a robot who lived at a junk heap and used to fix up all the old beds and fridges and sell them to the other robots to save up his money and build a space rocket and fly away to the moon."

"Ah," Keiko said.

315

"And I know you're going to tell me he must have been headed the wrong way all along," Malcolm said. "You're going to say one day couldn't cause ..."

"Of course it could," Keiko said. "That one day and all the silence afterwards."

"I know," said Malcolm. "I should have told them."

"I didn't mean *your* silence," Keiko said. "You were eight, Malcolm. You were a child."

"I should have told them," Malcolm said again. "But eventually, the nightmares tailed off. Probably he got used to telling himself his own stories, and when he got his first motorbike and started learning how to fix it up, they stopped altogether. He was too young to get a licence to ride it, and he used to get laughed at, but that didn't bother him. He had the slaughterhouse and the bikes, and he seemed fine.

"Anyway, Dad was still determined he would come into the shop and start his apprenticeship, go to college one day a week—meat processing, hygiene, health and safety—same as I had done when I was sixteen. And as far as Mum and Dad were concerned there was no reason why not. I don't suppose they had thought about that pig for years. And, funnily enough, Murray seemed okay about it too. I tried to bring it up with him one night in the summer when he'd just finished school. I thought if we both went to Mum and Dad together we'd persuade them that Murray could go his own way. But he said he had no problems with it. He had worked it out and he wanted to show me. He invited me in to see.

"There were birds, rats, one or two rabbits, all mixed in with the bike parts. Separated, you know, like ... like Mr. Byers. He was bleaching the bones, putting them together with hinges and screws.

He told me it didn't have to be like it was with the pig. His exact words were that people didn't have to be like pigs, they could be like him and the bikes, that he could always fix it no matter what was wrong. And as soon as he got a free hand with something bigger than rabbits, he would prove it." Malcolm's eyes filled with bright crescents that balanced, trembling, on his lower lids before two drops detached themselves, ran to the points of his lashes and splashed onto his cheeks.

"The mobiles," Keiko said. "I thought they were models. I thought he had carved them out of wood."

"What mobiles?" said Malcolm.

"In the workshop. Birds. Skeletons, I suppose. I admired them and he took them away." She blinked. "Sorry, Malcolm, go on."

"It feels good to be telling someone," Malcolm said. "Can you believe, I *still* didn't tell Mum and Dad when I went to them. Can you believe that?"

Keiko tried to put herself in Malcolm's place, imagining coming at all at this from the other end and how long she herself might have tried to hold things together. She nodded firmly.

"Of course," she said. "You do what you think is best. Tonight we're doing what we think is best, and we'll only find out whether it's crazy or not depending on what we don't know yet." They both sat for a moment, letting in the realisation of what must be happening out there right now with their consent and collusion, then they each retreated to Malcolm's story again.

"I told them Murray didn't want to be a butcher. I tried to make them see that we didn't need another person, but Dad was full of the notion to expand, open another branch, maybe one each. So then I tried to say that I didn't want Murray there, it was too much working with him all day long when we had never been that close. They just laughed. What did I mean not all that close? Being Murray's big brother was like my idea of what I was put on this earth for. If anything, they said, I should back off a bit and let him go. I nearly told them then. Nearly told them why I spent my whole damn life being Murray's big brother and it still wasn't enough." He smiled and slapped his hands against his chest. "You don't often hear me saying I'm not big enough, eh?"

Keiko smiled awkwardly. She had never heard Malcolm mention his size before.

"So he started in the shop, started at college, and just for a while I thought maybe I had been wrong. Then out of nowhere Dad came to me and said Murray was giving up his apprenticeship and they were setting him up with the workshop at Byers's place instead. Dad was trying to be discreet, but I told him I knew, had known longer than him. And it turned out, you see, that Murray had been caught in the meat preparation suite at the college after hours. It was a lamb this time, and I don't know what he said to whoever it was that caught him, about what he had worked out or what he was trying to do, but it was enough to put the willies up them."

He paused. There were footsteps coming up the stairs, and then the front door opened and shut softly. Malcolm tried for a smile as the kitchen door opened.

"Mum," he said. "Fancy all right?"

"God love her," said Mrs. Poole.

Keiko dragged herself to her feet, meaning to lead Mrs. Poole to a chair and get her something to drink, but she was shocked by the ache in her calves and knees, the sourness in her stomach, and the shivering that started again as soon as she moved. Two kinds of shivering—one on the surface of her skin like insects scuttling around under her clothes and another deep juddering as though she had just clanged the whole length of her body into a wall and was still reverberating from the blow. Mrs. Poole scraped her chair nearer to Keiko's and put an arm around her shoulder trying to stop the shaking, but she had no comfort to give. Her hands were cold, her body rigid, and it made Keiko want to pull away; instead both sat still, clashed together at the shoulders in a semblance of an embrace, waiting for some shared warmth to stop one of them from shuddering.

THIRTY-FOUR

"How far have you got?" said Mrs. Poole after long minutes of silence.

"As far as I can take it nearly," said Malcolm. He kneaded one hand across his brow, snarling the hairs of his eyebrows out of line. He started to speak again, but the first words were sucked out of his mouth in a sob.

Keiko stretched towards him with her free hand, so the three of them were joined together.

"I was surprised when Murray took up with Natasha," Mrs. Poole said, picking up the story. "He'd never had any time for girls before that, but all of a sudden there she was, round at the workshop every night in her leotard and every time the doorbell went, it was her looking for Murray. And then she stopped doing the workouts. She still came round to the house asking if Murray was in, but as often as not he would get us to say he wasn't.

"I knew what was up, of course. She started walking different. She always wore a ponytail high up on one side of her head and it used to bob up and down like a pom-pom whenever she moved. She washed her hair every day like all you youngsters. Well, around about the time Murray seemed to go off her, that ponytail wasn't bouncing any more. It was swaying from side to side instead. And I knew exactly what that meant—when you start rocking sideways as you walk and even your nose and fingers are looking bloated. She was pregnant, and it was Murray's and he was having nothing to do with it. So I got his father to talk to him. Duncan went to him and told him that if it was too late to fix it, then Murray would have to face up to his responsibilities and make the best of things."

"*Fix* it?" Malcolm echoed.

"I know," said Mrs. Poole. "We've gone over and over it until we were ready to scream. Your father trying to remember exactly what he said and if it could have been taken the wrong way."

"But that's crazy. Dad couldn't have blamed himself. It's mad."

Mrs. Poole choked him off. "Don't you think I tried to tell him that? I *know* only a madman would think he was telling his son to do away with the girl. And your father's answer to that was that he should have faced the fact that it was a madman he was talking to, and he should have had the sense to watch what he was saying."

"But," said Keiko, trying to bring them back to the story and lay out another fold of it for her, "why did Mrs. McMaster not do something? She must have known Tash was pregnant too."

"Pet McMaster broke her heart when Fancy took off," said Mrs. Poole. "And she blamed herself for being heavy-handed. She had tried to get Fancy to stay on at school, stay on with Pet even once her birthday was past. Then it was only months after Fancy left that Tash came. She was fifteen, and I think Pet would have walked on eggshells for the rest of her life to keep her. She would never have confronted her. She was waiting for Tash to turn to *her*. Didn't think she could bear it if another one ran away. Well, she was right. She couldn't. When Tash disappeared, I thought Pet was going to fall to pieces. She had tablets in the morning to wake her up and tablets at night to put her to sleep again. I don't know what would have happened if Fancy hadn't landed back here with her wee one, looking like a dog that was overdue for a kick. Of course, Fancy was that taken up with her own problems I don't think she even noticed how things were with Pet. And anyway as soon as Pet had got the pair of them installed, she started to pick up again too. She eventually gave up the idea of looking for Tash and, my God it shames us all to say it, but I don't think any one of us would have given the wee soul another thought.

"Except that I found her things, stuffed in a bag in the bottom of his cupboard." Mrs. Poole pointed out of the kitchen door, towards Keiko's bedroom.

"Here?" Keiko said. "Murray lived here?"

"Not for very long," said Mrs. Poole. "Just for a while, not even a year. After he gave up in the shop, you know, when we were trying to . . . he lived in the flat and he had the bikes. Then I found everything. Bra and pants, wee twists of leather she used to wear on her wrists. That's what made me sure it was Tash. I couldn't understand why he had kept them, but we saw the same tonight. The clothes separate from the rest. I suppose it made some kind of sense to Murray.

"I was looking for stuff for a jumble sale; having a good clearout just like you do when you really believe you've turned a corner." Her voice was rising. "Tash was out of sight out of mind, and Murray was more like himself than he'd been for a long time. He had been doing a bit more for us in the shop, you know." Mrs. Poole withdrew from Keiko and hugged her arms around her own chest and shoulders, clawing at herself. "He had offered to do the rendering, for once. It's a horrible job, rendering bones. I thought it was a good sign. He made batches of sausages, which wasn't like him. Queer-tasting things they were, too much spice, but we encouraged him. He made the gravy for a load of Malcolm's pies and they—they—they—they went down very well." She retched and pressed her hands against her mouth until it had passed.

"And then I found her things, and we agreed together, the pair of us, that we would keep the secret. Duncan spoke to Murray, warned him, put the fear of God into him from what I could make out: no more girlfriends and he was barred from the shop. One of us was to inspect his workshop every week. Ridiculous now, to think how we had it all planned out, but we really thought we could handle it. We really thought we were doing the right thing."

She stopped and fought for a deep breath, gasping again and again until finally her chest filled and she sighed it out again.

"The first letter came about a month after we found out, about six months after Tash disappeared. Somebody knew."

"The letter!" said Keiko. "I found it."

"What?" said Mrs. Poole. "You can't have. I burned it."

"What letter?" said Malcolm. "Who from?"

"It wasn't signed," said his mother. "They just said they knew what had happened because they'd seen it and they threatened to tell everyone. And then there was another one and another, and the fourth one asked for money."

"Ah, I see," said Keiko. "There were a lot of them? Well, you missed one. I found it here. In the flat. I KNOW WHAT YOU DID. I SAW YOU. I WILL—" She bit off the words at the cry they had torn from Mrs. Poole. "Sorry!"

"A blackmail letter?" said Malcolm.

"They wanted five thousand pounds sent to a post office box number."

"Why didn't you tell me?"

"I know what you would have done," his mother said. "Same as tonight. You would have said to call the police. Tell the world, let it all out."

"But I would have told the police that you knew nothing," said Malcolm. "I would have been more than willing to take my share of it."

"But you were all we had left that wasn't ruined, Malcolm. We wanted to keep you out of it, so that one thing in our lives would still be right."

Malcolm stared at his mother, slowly beginning to nod.

"We were stripping ourselves bare," said Mrs. Poole. "Every penny we had and more, and the letters kept coming. I knew it was somebody local—had to be. Someone who'd seen something the night Tash went. On and on, everything we had worked for all our married life, any hope we had of getting Murray into a clinic if he'd ever agree, all our hopes of setting you up in a place of your own far away from here. Oh, yes—that's what we wanted. We wanted you at the other end of the country, independent, then we were going to put Murray into treatment. But the letters just kept on coming. I watched your father winding himself up like a spring, and I knew it couldn't go on."

Keiko looked from one to the other of their faces. Normally so unlike each other, but now with identical dark blooms under their eyes and identical deep lines etched from the sides of their noses to their grim mouths, they looked like mother and son at last.

"We had stopped paying your father's life insurance," she said, "and mine. The business was in debt, we were nearly a year behind with the mortgage on the house, the tax wasn't paid—every blessed penny we had and more went to that post office box number. And everyone talks about weight and blood pressure and hypertension and genes, and on and on, but every time you press them—the doctors—if you press them, every leaflet you read, somewhere in the small print it's there. 'Stress is a factor.' 'Stress could be a factor.'

"And he died. I knew then we would go under, and I should have given up. But all of a sudden I wasn't scared any more; I was angry. I wanted to keep going just long enough to find out who it was and face them with it, and then I would take whatever was coming.

"So Murray had to come back into the shop, because there was no money to pay anybody else. He would have had to give up the workshop too if Byers had pressed us, because there was no money for the rent. At any rate, there was no chance of buying it for him. Buying a property! I can't even afford to do the Christmas cooking for the homeless. Keiko moving into this place was just about all that let me keep going this last few months. Your father had offered it for the student way back when it was just an idea, and I pretended to Jimmy that we had always meant the Traders to pay us rent.

"Meanwhile, I started marking the notes."

Her voice grew hard as she described it to them: the hours spent every day after closing time, hunched over the desk in the back office, making marks on bundles of grubby fivers and tenners, then spreading out the day's takings before her and looking for her old marks coming back. She put up with people's kind and not so kind remarks about the length of time it took her to do her books, shrugged off all offers of help. She had a plan. She kept a mental note of who was in the shop every day, and when she found a marked note she was going to narrow it down, start taking the money out of the till after every customer. She would think of something to say to the boys, she would make up some story. But it never came to that, because not one of her notes ever came back. In six months of her poring over them every night, she found not a single one. She looked at them through a magnifier, wondering if perhaps whoever it was was cleaning them or painting them out, but there was nothing. Every day she thought, *just one more day. If I can keep going just one more day.*

"I'm sorry," she said, turning to Keiko. "But when you arrived it seemed like the last straw. I thought God was laughing at me. I thought I was going mad. Because, it might sound daft, but it never occurred to me that you would be a girl. Even when we heard your name, we had no idea. I told myself you would be some wee bloke in specs coming to do an engineering degree, and when Jimmy told me it was a Miss Nishisato and showed me your picture and told us you were a psychology student, interested in *food* . . . Before I had time to call a halt to it, here you were. Beautiful wee thing, and as soon as Murray clapped eyes on you, I knew where it would go." She smiled at Keiko, a calm, tired smile and then a small breath of laughter.

"I tried my best to keep you away from him, you can't say I didn't. I could hardly have been less welcoming, and I don't blame you for taking against me. Which you did!" she insisted as Keiko began to protest. "Which you did. All the same, I was terrified. Every night you were in that place doing your exercises together, I was outside the back door listening to you. Every time Murray came round here, I was downstairs. I felt sure you must know there was someone watching you.

"Still, you must think I'm wicked. How could I stand by and let you get close to him? I'll never forgive myself. But Tash was years ago and Murray was fine, seemed fine, ever since. And I knew, I thought—"

Tears were spilling from Malcolm's eyes again, faster and faster, the dark spots where they fell on his chest joining up into splotches. Now he sobbed.

"Son?" said Mrs. Poole.

"What were you thinking?" he said. "I don't mean about Keiko. I mean tonight."

His mother only shook her head.

"What about tonight, Malcolm?" said Keiko.

"Don't you see?" he said. "If someone knows—the black-mailer—then Jimmy and Fancy are down there for nothing."

Keiko stared at him, feeling her blood drain away.

"It's got to stop now," he went on. "I'll go and get them back before it's too late and then we are going to call it a day. Maybe the police will keep things quiet as much they can. And maybe they'll be able to find the blackmailer for you, eh?" He was almost crooning, like a parent trying to coax a sulking child into smiles.

Mrs. Poole did smile, and again there was that air of calm, almost serenity, that made Keiko briefly wonder if she really had lost her mind.

"I sent two hundred pounds off at the weekend," she said. "And I put a note in saying that it was the last. There would be no more. Tonight when I looked in Byers's wallet, there was a hundred and sixty left."

They were silent then and so they all flinched at the sudden sound of the door. Fancy stood in the doorway, her hair plastered with sweat to the sides of her grey-white face. She raised one arm straight out from the shoulder holding a black plastic sack in her fist. She was trembling so much that it seemed she was shaking the bag in their faces like a cheerleader's pom-pom. Both Keiko and Mrs. Poole rose to draw her towards them.

"I'm not coming any closer," said Fancy. "I stink. I'm sorry but I was sick quite a lot and it's on your stuff, Mrs. Poole."

"I'm going to come home with you," said Keiko, but Fancy shook her head.

"Can you keep Vi till tomorrow and I'll come and get her?" she said.

"Well, at least I'll walk home with you, sweetheart," said Mrs. Poole, reaching out again.

Fancy retreated a step. "No, you've got to wait for Mr. McKendrick. He said I was to call him Uncle Jimmy and he'll be here very soon to take you home."

She walked backwards along the passageway to the front door, like a ceremonial page-boy, keeping eye contact with Keiko as she fumbled behind her for the handle and then stepped backwards onto the landing as the door closed on her.

"What's she doing?" asked Malcolm. "Is she all right?"

Keiko nodded. "I think she's trying to be."

THIRTY-FIVE

Mr. McKendrick arrived just after 3 a.m. and joined Keiko and Malcolm in the unlit living room, dropping into a chair and resting his head against the back of it. He smelled of oil and faintly of smoke, causing a jolt like an extra stair in the dark, reminding them of what was going to happen—what was already happening, while they sat here in the stillness. Keiko spoke first.

"Fancy's gone home and Mrs. Poole is downstairs with the washing. Did everything—"

"I'm not going to tell you," he said. "The less you know the better, in case you're questioned."

"And did you really not know any of this, Mr. McKendrick?" said Keiko. "I was so sure that you had a secret."

"Me?" said Mr. McKendrick.

"The committee," Keiko said. "I was convinced that something was going on and that everyone on the committee knew."

"Aye well, you were right enough there," Mr. McKendrick said. "But I can't blame the committee. It was me pushing it all the way. Hand-in-hand with the redevelopment, you know."

"What was it?" said Malcolm.

Mr. McKendrick shifted about a little before he spoke. "A grand idea," he said. "Etta tipped us off. She got wind of it from a pal of hers at Holyrood and she let us get ahead of the pack here in Painchton, so we'd win the bidding."

"Win the bidding for what?" said Keiko.

Mr. McKendrick laughed, but it was a dry and ugly sound. "Oh, a high honour," he said. "Lots of publicity, lots of press, good for business. We were going to be Scotland's Food Town."

"Jesus Christ," said Malcolm.

"Ah," said Keiko. "*That's* why I was so important then. A scholar of food."

"Studying our traditions and writing about them," said Mr. McKendrick.

"Jesus," said Malcolm again.

Mr. McKendrick's jaw worked for a while, then he sniffed deeply, clapped his hands onto his knees and pulled himself forward until he was sitting up straight. "Now, I don't think anyone saw us, but still we'd all better get gone. Malcolm?"

"I'm going to stay here," said Malcolm. "I don't want Keiko to be on her own with Viola when the sirens start."

"Keiko can manage," said Mr. McKendrick. "Your mother shouldn't be alone."

"You stay with Mum," said Malcolm. "My place is here."

And that was the start of it; Malcolm saying straight out what he wanted to do. Typical though, that what he wanted to do was take care of someone.

And perhaps that was all there was to it, but she didn't think so. She lay in bed beside Viola listening to her breathing and remembered. Malcolm, saying if aliens came he would talk to them. Malcolm, making suet pudding and yakitori, making sure people on the budget option didn't feel their poverty. Malcolm, dancing in the streaming gutters when it rained. She slid out of bed and went to stand outside the spare bedroom door, talking herself in and out of it twice before knocking. There was no reply and she wondered if he was sleeping, but when she went in he was standing in the middle of the floor as close as he could get to the window without his shadow cutting into the block of moonlight. He had wrapped himself in a blanket and his silhouette was mountainous. When she walked up and leaned against him, letting her whole tired weight fade into his, it was as if he had taken root there; it was like resting against an oak tree.

She put one arm across the middle of his back and clutched the blanket in a fist to hold it there, remembering their collision and struggle, Craig McKendrick's hoots of laughter rising behind them, their swift embrace cluttered with wineglasses, how she had backed away.

In a moment, she heard or felt him shift to look down at her, taking his gaze away at last from the window. One side of his face was in deep shadow, and where the moonlight hit the other it made pale, lava-lamp shapes of his features. His breathing was laboured, his mouth hanging slightly open as usual, and the breaths warming her face were sweet, as clear and clean as Viola's breath when she was sleeping.

He turned to look out of the window again, forcing a draft of cool air between them with his movement, making Keiko shiver.

"Cold?" he asked. She nodded and he opened his arms, making a space for her in the roll of blanket, releasing a trace of that rosemary-scented warmth. Keiko stepped in and his arms engulfed her, spreading so that she felt swaddled from her neck to her waist and she let him take her full weight. She couldn't make her arms reach around him, so instead she threaded them under his armpits and hooked them over his shoulders, squeezing as hard as she could, trying to make something big and strong out of her small body to comfort him. She rested her face against the middle of his chest where his shirt was open. And it didn't feel clammy after all, but fur-covered, solid and warm, with the thump of his heart in her ear like a club beating on bark. He cupped the back of her head in one hand and she looked up at him, put her hands to the sides of his face and found that his hair was not oily as she had always imagined, but so soft and fine that she could draw her fingers through it from the roots to the tips and let it fall back like hanks of silk. He bent and kissed her head before pulling her against him again and, although her heart was racing, his remained slow and steady against her cheek until the first shout came from outside.

———

By the time the crowd had gathered, standing outside with coats over their nightclothes, the fire was burning as high as the two-storey buildings framing it at either edge of the Green, making a giant yellow-red cradle of flame wisping off into the black of the winter's morning, occasionally split by a gust of wind that revealed a skeleton of rafters with the roof peeling back from them.

The heat kept the crowd swept back in a perfect arc, unable to take another step towards the oven blast that would tighten the skin on their faces like baking apples. They peered over the shoulders of the police patrolling the line and watched the firemen, distant stick figures against the glare.

Mr. McKendrick, persuaded to give up on his relay of buckets and stay out of the firemen's way, stood on one side of Mrs. Poole with his arm around her shoulders. Malcolm held her other hand and although the crowd kept back from them as much as from the fire, Mrs. Poole could hear the whispers swoop and ripple.

"Murray Poole."

"Nobody knows for sure."

"All she said was he wasn't at home."

"But nobody knows."

"Dear God."

"God in heaven, no."

The firemen retreated, hacking and steaming, lighting incongruous cigarettes and muttering to each other. A group standing close together bent respectfully and listened to a police sergeant, who looked like a doll beside them. She stretched out her radio hand again and again as she spoke, pointing into the crowd, and each time the firemen's heads lifted and followed the gesture. Then two of them made their way over to Mrs. Poole and asked her where they could talk.

Just inside the street door, they peeled off their stinking armour and followed Mrs. Poole, Mr. McKendrick, and Malcolm upstairs, with the little policewoman behind them.

Fancy was sitting with Keiko in the kitchen. She had left her house at just the moment she might have if she had been woken by the sirens, and had come straight to the flat to check on Viola, clenching Keiko into a hug, enveloping her into the smell of washed hair and bathed skin.

"I just saw the fire," she had said. "Is she awake? Is she sleeping through it? Listen, I've just been having the most disgusting nightmares I've ever had in my life. I must be psychic, eh? Do you hear me? I had a really bad dream. But I don't ever want to talk about it, right?"

The firemen insisted, with practised rhetoric, that they should stay on washable surfaces, away from fabric, so they all huddled into the kitchen, Malcolm squeezing himself into the window casement to make more room for the others. Keiko and Fancy started making tea.

"And what makes you fear your son might be in there, madam?" asked what Keiko and Mr. McKendrick decided must be a pre-arranged spokesman, perhaps a trained communicator, whose job it was to liaise with the public in these soothing and confident tones.

As the sky lightened, dimming the fire ahead of its death, the talk in the kitchen circled and thrashed. Keiko put pans of extra water on the cooker to boil and rummaged out spare cups, Malcolm made toast, Fancy ferried trays of tea up and down to the parched throats of the rest of the crew, busy now. Once the fire had had its glory, there were small victories to be won.

Upstairs, the two firemen's early hunch—that no discarded cigarette butt could do that much, that fast—was strengthening. The building was changing hands? There was some dispute over who was going to buy? So the missing young man might be angry? Mrs. Poole, clouded by lack of sleep, was not pretending as she reached out for what was being suggested here. She grasped at the fantasy that Murray was on the run from a terrible crime, sickened for real at the other story the fireman skirted round: that he had choked in the smoke while the rest of them were sleeping.

"Nobody seems to know what Mr. Byers's home address might be," said the policewoman.

"We'll just wait for him to turn up for work," said Mr. McKendrick. "See what he has to say."

"And Forensics will start as soon as they can, Mrs. Poole," said the fireman. "If your son was in there, and God forbid that he was, we'll find something, but it's not going to be much. You should prepare yourself for that, if you can." He shook his head in practised sorrow, although he'd always found that a loved one gone with only zips and buttons curled into petals behind them wasn't as hard to face, after months and cards and flowers had gone by, as a good-sized box of remains. He couldn't say that right now, of course. Right now, the story of an absconding arsonist was still on the table, but he had been in this game too long not to know the feel of a site where souls had got away. He pulled a sigh up from his stockinged feet. "Whoever set that fire knew what he was doing," he said. "And I'll bet my pension that somebody set it."

Fancy, pushing the door open, coming back with a tray of empty cups, caught Malcolm's eye, and Sergeant Ballam, seeing the flash that passed between them, drooped into her tiredness just a little more. They cared about this biker boy, then, and she had a feeling there were no happy surprises to come; these good people had only pain ahead. She had seen them before, these shifts between despair and relief that were crossing Mrs. Poole's face, the exhaustion of worry and that strange euphoria that every fire brings with it, and she knew that when you start your grieving bone-tired already from hope, it was a hard haul to the other side.

She and the firemen did not have to speak as they parted out on the street in the grey light. The men headed back to the trucks in the hero swagger of their heat-proof boots. The sergeant spent another while in desultory interviews with witnesses, each one confirming what she already knew, some of them even joking.

"Bloody good thing the fire was tonight and not yesterday, eh? Or Jimmy McKendrick would be cuffed and cautioned for sure."

She chuckled. Laughing at their jokes was a big part of community policing.

"Aye, if they knew where to look for him," said someone else. "I heard it wasn't his own place he came from this morning."

"Is that a fact?"

"And Malcolm Poole was on the scene pretty quick too."

"Oh?"

"Oh yes."

Behind her smile, the sergeant wondered—and not for the first time—how in God's name anyone could live in a place like this. They'd eat you alive.

POSTSCRIPT

KEIKO STOOD AT THE kitchen window, staring down into the yard. If she shut her eyes tight she could still just get the sequence to play: the grim-faced woman with her buckets, kicking the door shut behind her and plodding to the centre of the concrete to tip out the water into the drain. But the features were beginning to blur and no amount of effort could map them on to Grace's face in her imagination, just as no amount of trellis and clematis could disguise the three hulking bins down there and make it look less like a yard and more like a garden, even with the extra space where the slaughterhouse used to be.

She would be sorry to leave. More than that if she were honest; she was scared to leave. The memories were ever a little paler, a little smaller, against the changed reality of the place where she had lived through them, but they might begin to grow again once their only home was in her mind.

The printer was still whirring on the big table in the living room, and she padded through to check on its progress. Seventy pages done and the same to go. It was going to cost her a fortune to post it to Dr. Bryant, but she knew if she took it to him by hand he would make a point of pretending it was nothing very special and, although she didn't believe he could take away her swell of pride and relief, she wasn't sure she could resist crumpling up the pages and hurling them at him one by one, or just whacking him in the kidneys with the ring-binder. She squared up the cover sheet on top of the first seventy. *Forty-three Cooks and a Pot of Broth: decision-making by committee.* The title had been Malcolm's idea and she knew Dr. Bryant would veto it, but it had made the Traders laugh when she'd presented her final report at the last meeting, and any respect Dr. Bryant might have started out with had been killed off by her swerve into a completely different topic halfway through her first year, despite all the profiling work she'd done.

Keiko heard a car slowing down and glanced out of the window. Surely they weren't here. If she was working when they arrived, the visit would be off to a very frosty beginning. The car carried on up the street and away.

Of course it was too soon for them to be here. There was a speed-bump at the top of the memorial gardens, where the petrol station used to stand. It marked the beginning of the twenty zone, and she still thought every car was stopping.

No one had minded giving up the roasting pit and picnic tables; everyone agreed three trees to honour the dead were much more fitting. A maple for Mr. Byers, a willow for Murray Poole and a magnolia that most thought a strange choice for Duncan Poole, but a few knew was perfect for Natasha Turnbull.

Forty pages still to go. Keiko took another bundle out of the printer tray and added them to the bottom of the pile. She knew her parents wouldn't mind that she hadn't gone to collect them at the airport. It was better for her to be here to welcome them into her home. If she had turned up in the terminal, swinging car keys, it would have shocked them. *The nail that sticks out gets hammered,* her mother would say. Much more fitting for Malcolm to greet them and bring them home and for her to be waiting. They liked Malcolm. They had cowered at first when she took him to Tokyo, despite her warnings that he was "large, mother, very large indeed," and even Keiko—who was used to him—had been astonished at how enormous he seemed there, someone to break all the furniture and knock down buildings. But they liked him. They knew he lived here with her, because he answered the phone, but he would stay with Grace and Jimmy during the visit, and they would like that too.

"Don't you mind?" she had asked him.

"We've got the rest of our lives, Keko-chan," he said. "I don't mind anything."

Twenty pages left. She had plenty to do after this, after her visit to the post office to send it on its way. Eight people for dinner tonight, and she was cooking, thinking perhaps her parents would need a little time to recover from their flight before sitting down to one of Malcolm's dinners. He liked her cooking almost as much as his own now and, although she knew Mrs. Watson was joking when she pretended to scold Keiko for letting him fade away, it was true that he no longer needed extra tape sewn to the strings of his work aprons.

Eight for dinner; she must be mad. She had invited Craig McKendrick as Jimmy's nearest relation and good company in any gathering, and of course Fancy was going to be there. Keiko smiled to herself. Fancy had taken Mr. McKendrick up on his invitation to call him Uncle Jimmy, and it didn't seem so odd after a while, when she was installed at his right hand in the long months of meetings and when she walked beside him with a hard-hat and clipboard just like his as the work on the memorial garden finally got underway. Craig McKendrick said nothing. He said nothing either when he saw Fancy and her first fireman out for a drink in the Covenanters' Arms, and he only mentioned to Keiko in passing that Fancy seemed to have found a good supply when he saw her with her second fireman in the Bridge. Keiko told him gently that she was sure there was nothing serious going on, but Craig wouldn't admit to the worry she was trying to soothe, and Fancy threatened to warm her arse for her if she scuppered Fancy's chance to get her own back on bloody Craig McKendrick for all the fannying around she'd had from him. Keiko couldn't argue.

However, the firemen were in the past now and Craig was home from his travels, and so something Keiko must remember to do in this busy day was write out place cards for the dinner party and make sure they were sitting together.

Fancy would be angry with her.

"He didn't say a word to Tash," she reminded Keiko last time the subject of Craig came up. "A foster kid, like me."

"And like Craig," Keiko said gently.

"Living with your uncle, who's king of the hill, is *nothing* like getting farmed out to whoever'll take you," said Fancy.

"He didn't harm Tash," said Keiko.

"What? Not like me, you mean?"

"You didn't harm her either. But you'll never find peace in anger."

"He's not right for Vi and me," Fancy said. "We don't all get a fairy tale ending."

Ten pages. Keiko hoped she'd have time to cross to the river and stand at the railings, look down into the water and clear her eyes.

Perhaps she'd even have time to walk up the bark path through the woods to the little look-out platform above the waterfall. Maybe someone she knew would happen by, and she would tell them that she was finished and they would hold out a hand and say well done. *Or more likely,* she said to herself, *they would say what a good thing to get it over and done with just in time.*

The town was very excited about the wedding. The town. If she tried she could still just about think of it that way: the town that had been shocked numb and silent after the fire; the town that hated its notoriety and wouldn't want to be famous for anything.

"I thought the committee would have my guts for garters," said Mr. McKendrick. "Me changing my mind after all the work I'd done to persuade them about Food Town. Going on about a big splash in the national press, Painchton in the spotlight. But they didn't mind. They seemed … relieved."

"Really?" said Keiko. "I wonder why."

But she didn't wonder; she knew. Because she had asked them. Sandra and Iain with their affair. Kenny and his sock puppet reviews. Etta McLuskie and her backroom deals to start the Food Town bid early. All of them thinking their secrets were bound to come out, and a big splash would only make the stories worth more to whoever was selling.

She had asked Mrs. Watson too, one quiet evening, about the envelope FOR YOU. And Mrs. Watson had told her about those dreadful days—years ago—when the nasty things started up, one after the other and the last one asking for money.

"Of course, I knew it was just nonsense," she said. "I've done nothing to make someone blackmail me. But when I saw you with one in your hand that day and thought it was starting again …"

"Why didn't you tell the police, Mabel?" said Keiko.

"I didn't know who it was who'd sent it, poor soul," Mrs. Watson replied. "Some friend, some neighbour, not in her right self."

"*Her*?"

Mrs. Watson flushed. "Grace was going through a right bad spell just then," she said. "Very low. I couldn't have lived with myself if I'd made it worse for her." She sniffed. "And anyway, they stopped after the one that asked for money, didn't they?"

They stopped for anyone who didn't pay, Keiko thought. *Anyone innocent. But there were plenty of others.*

"Willie bloody Byers just picked a town and set up shop," Fancy said.

"No trouble with planners and zoning in the blackmail business," said Keiko.

"And paying him killed my father," said Malcolm. "Even though Byers knew nothing."

They all agreed that Grace should never hear the truth—that they'd paid for no good reason, after all. Grace was looking forward to the wedding. And Keiko had offered herself up to all the rituals she must follow, from the borrowed veil to the hen night to the first waltz, which Mr. McKendrick had taught them. But she would be glad when it was over.

There had been such a regular drumbeat of occasions, all different enough to other people, she assumed, but all so much the same to her, with their flowers and toasts, hats and handbags. The opening of the memorial gardens, James and Grace's wedding, even Mrs. McMaster's adoption of Fancy in the registrar's office, where Viola pirouetted with excitement. All the gatherings took Keiko back to Murray's funeral—the empty coffin lowered into the grave beside his father's, and Mrs. Poole, after the guests had left, sliding down the wall to the floor, rucking her skirt up to her waist, spewing out the ugliest, most wretched noises Keiko had ever heard, draining the blood from Mr. McKendrick's face and drying Malcolm's tears.

The printer came to rest with its fan purring. She took out the last warm bundle and lifted the rest of the pages onto the top of it, making the finished pile as tidy as she could get it, knowing it would never be the same smooth sculpted block of cool blank paper as when she'd begun.

FACTS AND FICTIONS

The Psychology Department at the University of Edinburgh is no longer in the venerable old building in George Square where Keiko found it, but has moved to splendid new quarters in the Dugald Stewart Building. This intentional mistake might make it even clearer that Keiko's experience is entirely fictional. The unhelpful secretary, the charmless roommates, and, of course, Dr. Bryant are not based on any real people at my beloved alma mater.

Painchton is imagined to be in East Lothian, but it and its inhabitants were born in my head. Scotland's real Food Town is Castle Douglas. The incomparable Grierson Brothers Family Butchers as well as Henderson Butchers and Ballards Butchers are to be found there. The Pooles are not based on any of them.

Photo © Neil McRoberts

ABOUT THE AUTHOR

Catriona McPherson was born in Scotland, where she lived until moving to California in 2010. She is the author of the award-winning Dandy Gilver historical mystery series. Catriona is a member of Mystery Writers of America and the 2014–2015 president of Sisters in Crime. *As She Left It* was her first modern standalone, earning her an Anthony Award for best paperback original. Her second standalone, *The Day She Died*, was released in 2014. You can visit Catriona online at www.catrionamcpherson.com.